Everythin[...] and a John[...] You" on the stereo.

A little shiver ran through Angel just before she opened the door. But no fantasy could have prepared for the powerfully charged reality of Jim Rhodes. Droplets of rain glistened like diamonds in his dark hair and beard. Her breath caught when she saw the glow of his smile.

He leaned down and kissed her—softly, sweetly—then pressed his gifts into her outstretched arms. He'd brought a loaf of bread, a jug of wine, and a note that read simply, "And thou."

"The flower in your hair," he murmured.... He caressed the velvety petals, then let his fingers slide through her long, bright-as-flame hair. As he slipped his arms around her, gathering her gown close to her body, he whispered, "Are those naked toes I see peeking out?"

Angel blushed. Were the bare feet ... a bit too much?

"You know what they say about barefoot angels, don't you?" he said softly.

"No. Tell me."

"Later." His whisper was uttered so close to her parted lips that the word flowed into her mouth—a rush of sweet hot air.

* * *

"It's betwixt and between the beautiful romance and the luminescent and enchanting fantasy, Becky Lee Weyrich comes up with another winner!"

—*Affaire de Coeur*

Zebra Books by Becky Lee Weyrich:

ALMOST HEAVEN
SPELLBOUND KISSES

Pinnacle Books by Becky Lee Weyrich:

ONCE UPON FOREVER
WHISPERS IN TIME
SWEET FOREVER

ALMOST HEAVEN

BECKY LEE WEYRICH

ZEBRA BOOKS
KENSINGTON PUBLISHING CORP.

ZEBRA BOOKS are published by

Kensington Publishing Corp.
850 Third Avenue
New York, NY 10022

Copyright © 1995 by Becky Lee Weyrich

All rights reserved. No part of this book may be reproduced in any form or by any means without the prior written consent of the Publisher, excepting brief quotes used in reviews.

If you purchased this book without a cover you should be aware that this book is stolen property. It was reported as "unsold and destroyed" to the Publisher and neither the Author nor the Publisher has received any payment for this "stripped book."

Zebra and the Z logo Reg. U.S. Pat. & TM Off.

First Printing: May, 1995

Printed in the United States of America

*For my special friends, Ellen and Roger Breen (the
redhead and the professor)
and
to Bernard Wurger of the Brunswick Music Theater,
many thanks for hours of entertainment and years of
friendship,
also
worlds of gratitude to "Wonderful, Wonderful" Johnny
Mathis for "Open Fire, Two Guitars" and a lifetime of
special love songs.*

*Last, but by no means least, this book is for my
husband, Hank, who has shared all the love songs in my
life.*

Angels can fly because they take themselves lightly.
                    —*Scottish saying*

Prologue

The flash blinded her. She couldn't see, but she heard his voice clearly—a deep, rumbling peal of thunder that turned her heart into an echo chamber.

"Focus on the light."

"I can't. It hurts my eyes."

"You must. It's time now."

"Time? Time for what?"

"Time to cross over the bridge into the light. Come!"

"You have the wrong person. I'm not ready to cross over."

"You *are* Angela Gentry Rhodes, aren't you?"

"Yes, but you can call me Angel."

"Only when you've earned it, Angela."

"Whatever you choose to call me, I'm telling you, there's been some mistake."

"We never make mistakes."

"*We?* Who do you mean? Who are *you?*"

"I am your companion. You are to follow me. Come now. Everyone's waiting for you. This way."

Angel opened her eyes. She looked about to see

where she was. Vaguely she remembered hospital corridors, hushed voices, pain. But maybe she'd dreamed those things. Within the range of her vision now was a vast nothingness, stretching on forever. She seemed poised in a dark void, weightless as a feather. Only the light and the softer glow of her companion relieved the warm, velvet blackness.

"This way please," he repeated.

"Where am I? Is this Heaven?"

"Not quite. Follow me."

Angela stayed put. If this wasn't quite Heaven, then where the hell was she? she wondered.

"I can't go anywhere until I find Jim and Hope. Where are they?"

"They're where they belong. Their names won't come up on the list for many years. But yours is right here. See for yourself."

Angela turned in the direction the shimmering, faceless apparition pointed—away from the light—and watched a page of fancy, old-fashioned script float down out of the nothingness. It glowed like a giant movie screen. She read her name at the top, and next to it, "Angel Candidate—Rainbow Class." Then followed a brief summary, stating the reasons for her summons to Heaven, along with the faults that gave her only a probationary status. According to the "Power-That-Be," who had signed the official-looking document, Angela's fiery temper was a definite strike against her. However, she had loved her husband and baby unselfishly, with all her heart. She had made her parents proud of her. She had followed all life's rules and only occasionally questioned authority. On all counts she had been a caring person. She had taken in

ALMOST HEAVEN

stray animals, visited shut-ins, donated to flood, earthquake, and hurricane victims. Furthermore, and much in her favor currently, she had given up smoking and she never wore furs. A postscript at the bottom added, "Would have been a wonderful mother, if only she'd been a better driver."

"Hey, I'm a *good* driver! The accident wasn't my fault. The snowstorm came on so fast. The ruts were so deep that . . ."

She stopped in midsentence, wondering what she was talking about. *What accident?* She couldn't remember. Her thoughts seemed distorted, as hazy and indistinct as the man she was talking to.

"You were saying?" he prompted.

"Yes, well, I was about to say that, as for my temper, I never *asked* to be born a redhead. You people did that, didn't you? So don't blame me if I have the temperament to go with the hair."

A rumble like thunder shook the skies. "You're not the first redhead to test that argument. Even Nero tried it, with disappointing results. Take my advice, don't mention this again. The Power-That-Be is rather touchy on the subject Herself. Hair like a sunset before a storm!"

"None of this matters anyway since I can't stay. It's been nice talking to you—whoever you are—but I'd better be going now. If you'll just show me the way back home."

"That won't be possible. There's no turning back from here. The light, remember? It's late. Come along now, Angela."

"You just don't get it, do you, mister? I've got a little baby down there who needs me. A husband who

12 *Becky Lee Weyrich*

can't even boil water and will wear one blue sock and one argyle if I'm not there to sort them for him. And who'll walk The Monster?"

"The monster? Oh, yes, that puppy you rescued from the pound."

"He's not a puppy any longer. Monster's *big*. He needs a romp on the Mall twice a day. And we just put all new carpeting in the house."

"That bad, is it? I hadn't realized. Tell me more about your family. Tell me about yourself. Begin at the beginning."

"I don't have time to tell you my whole life story. Besides, I can't seem to remember the details."

"Certainly you can, Angela. And you have all the time in the world. Think! How was it the day you were born?"

"I was too busy to notice." A sudden icy blast of cosmic memory made her hug herself and shiver. "My mother told me it was cold that day. Cold and snowy."

"Ah, then you arrived just as you left. And after your birth?"

"The best I recall, I was an average kid, raised in an average family, who got average grades in school."

"Can't you be more specific? If you want my help, I'll have to have more details. You must remember *everything.*"

Angel glanced about thoughtfully as another scrap of memory flitted through her mind—a warm one this time. "One day does stand out."

"Yes? Tell me about it."

She shrugged. "There's not much to tell. Colors. I remember colors—my yellow-and-green sundress, my

ALMOST HEAVEN

pink birthday cake with five blue candles, a red balloon, and a carousel painted like a rainbow."

"Ah, your fifth birthday."

"No, my fourth. We always added one extra candle to grow on."

"As I recall, birthdays are always nice. But what made this one so special?"

"It was November, of course, but warm like summer. We celebrated at Disney World in Florida. And everything was perfect until I got separated from Mom and Dad. I was so scared. I couldn't stop crying."

"That sounds dreadful!"

"Oh, but it wasn't! This guy named Al—real tall with long blond hair—took care of me. He bought me the red balloon. He stayed with me and kept me safe until he found my parents. And all the while we were searching—hours it seemed—he told me funny stories and kept me laughing so I didn't remember to be scared."

"Your mother and father must have rewarded him well for bringing you back safe and sound."

"No. It was the oddest thing. They claimed they never saw him. They said I wandered back all alone— that Al was just someone I made up so I wouldn't feel alone. But they were wrong. He was there with me the whole time, and he held my hand and stopped my crying. After that day, whenever I was sad, I'd think about him. I never saw him again, but it seemed like he was always with me after that. I never forgot that birthday or Al."

"That's quite a tale."

"You don't believe he was real either, do you?"

"I believe whatever you tell me. We all have others

14 *Becky Lee Weyrich*

who watch over us. Is there more you'd like to share?"

"Lots more! But if you really want to know about the day I was born, I should tell you about the day I met Jim and the night he proposed and the day we got married. Jim was really the beginning of everything that matters. Until he happened into my life, I was just biding my time waiting for him to come along."

"You must have cared for him very much."

"Don't use the past tense. I *care* for him very much. Right now! This minute! And I care for our daughter and I want to be with them."

"I realize that, Angela, but I'm afraid I can't help you unless you tell me the whole story. How did you meet Jim? When did you fall in love?"

"I met him in my English Lit class at the University of Maryland. He was my instructor. We fell in love between Byron and Yeats. No, before that. I think we fell in love the minute we first met."

"Yes? Go on, please. Let's look at it together, from every angle."

Angel caught a movement out of the corner of her eye. The huge document that was still floating in space turned suddenly into a real screen. As she watched, a picture materialized—a man's bearded face.

"Jim!" she cried, her heart hurting to touch him when she saw him larger than life before her. He looked exactly as he had that very first day of class— tall, lanky, clad in jeans and a faded blue oxford-cloth shirt open at the neck.

She whispered his name again, looking into his silvery gray eyes, framed by the dark, horn-rims of his glasses that gave him a boyish appearance. She longed to run her fingers through his thick, black hair, as she

ALMOST HEAVEN 15

had done so often over the years, and to caress his softly curling, salt-and-pepper beard. The feel of its silky texture was imprinted forever on her memory, along with the woodsy evergreen scent of his after-shave and the sweet, delicious heat of his hard body pressed to hers.

He turned and looked directly at her. "Miss Gentry? I'm afraid you'll have to redo this form. I can't read your handwriting. Neatly this time, please." A slight smile touched his lips as he continued staring at her. "Did anyone ever tell you your eyes are the most in-credible blue—like the sky over the Aegean Sea at moonrise?" Jim Rhodes said the words in a voice so soft and rich it was like a caress. And Angela's heart melted all over again, just as it had that first time he spoke to her.

"Right there!" she told her ethereal companion. "Freeze that frame. That's the very moment when I first knew I loved him. Six months later, he asked me to marry him."

"And you accepted, of course."

"Oh, yes! There was never any doubt in my mind that Dr. James Randolph Rhodes was the only man in the world for me."

"One can never be quite sure of that."

Angel simmered, ready to do pitched battle as she glared at her companion. But before she could re-spond, Jim's image on the screen flashed and ran as if someone had just pressed the fast forward button on her life.

"Wait!" she cried.

"There's no time for that. We must move forward. The light, remember? Others are waiting behind you."

16   *Becky Lee Weyrich*

"Why don't I just step aside and let them go ahead of me?"

"Not possible. Each in his own turn. And it's your turn now, Angela Gentry Rhodes."

"No, wait! There's more to tell—our wedding day, our honeymoon, New York, Maine, our daughter, her first Christmas . . ."

A weary sigh. "Very well. Get on with it, then. We don't have all Eternity!"

Chapter One

"Where should I begin?"

"It's always been my opinion, Angela, that the beginning is a good place."

"You don't need to be sarcastic."

"Sorry. I didn't mean to be. But when you've had this job as long as I have, you've seen and heard it all. Surprise me, if you can."

"Okay! You want surprises? I'll begin with the night that looked like the end."

"But it wasn't?"

"Pay attention and you'll find out."

Colored lights flickered and swirled on the heavenly screen as it warmed up to tell Angel's tale.

It was a hot, stormy June night—rain coming down in silver sheets and lightning doing a sultry tango across the sky. Perfect! Like a scene out of one of those romantic old black-and-white movies from the forties. Bogie might have played Jim's part, with Rita Hayworth eagerly anticipating his proposal. But if this had

18 *Becky Lee Weyrich*

really been a movie, instead of the garage apartment just off the college campus in Maryland, Jim and Angel would have found themselves in a hotel room in Paris or London, or maybe in a thatch-roofed hut on some exotic island in the South Pacific. The night itself had the feel of the tropic of Cancer—humid, languid, and crackling with emotional tension.

Spring quarter and graduation were over. Summer school had yet to begin. Angel planned to start work on her master's in art history come September, but her summer plans called for her to leave the next day. She was supposed to drive to Boothbay Harbor, Maine, where she'd accepted a position as arts and crafts instructor and lifeguard to the adolescent summer campers at Lake Tangawanda. The job had seemed ideal when she'd been accepted back in January—part work, part play. But that was before her advanced English Lit class . . . before Jim . . . before love.

And love was the main thing on her mind these days. For the first time in her life, Angela Gentry was totally, rapturously, marvelously in love.

The bedside phone rang just as she slipped into a filmy white Indonesian cotton caftan. Blindly, she fought her way out through the armholes and snatched up the receiver, her heart pounding. What if it was Jim with some last-minute meeting that would cancel their date? Their *last* date for at least three months.

"Hello?"

"Angel? It's your mother. I just wanted to touch base with you before you leave for Maine."

"Hi, Mom! I was going to call you later."

"Is everything all right? You sound out of breath."

ALMOST HEAVEN

"Everything's fine, Mom. I was just getting dressed."

"Another date with Dr. Rhodes?"

"Could be my *last* with him," Angel bemoaned.

"He still hasn't proposed? What can the man be thinking?"

"Maybe he's thinking that he doesn't want to get married."

"That's absurd, dear. Every man wants a wife, whether he realizes it or not."

"No, Mom. I don't think it works that way nowadays. I think some men just want a *friend.* Could be Jim's one of those."

"Well, your time in Maine should make him realize how much he needs you. Absence makes the heart grow fonder, you know."

"Oh, Mom, I'm so tempted to phone in sick tomorrow—sick for the whole summer. I don't want to leave. Not like this."

"Maybe he's only waiting for the perfect moment, the perfect mood."

"Well, if that's what he wants, I've sure set the stage for him tonight. I've cleaned this apartment to within an inch of its life. If he doesn't open a closet or look under the bed, he'll probably award me the good housekeeper's badge for the month. I have candles all over, I got that old Johnny Mathis album he loves, and I've made a perfect dinner."

"My crab cakes?"

"Your crab cakes, Mom."

"Then he won't be able to resist."

"Hey, I don't want him to propose to the crab cakes. I want him to ask *me* to marry him!"

20 *Becky Lee Weyrich*

"Have you slept with him yet?"

"Moth-er! What kind of a question is that to ask your own daughter?"

"A meaningful question on a meaningful topic. Your father and I never realized how perfect we were together until after—"

"I don't want to hear this. Okay?"

"You young people today complicate things so. Why, back in the sixties we learned to go with the flow, let it all hang out."

Small groan. "I know, Mom. 'Make love not war.' "

"Exactly, darling. So why complicate love? Put flowers in your hair, beads around your neck, and dance barefoot for him. It works every time."

Angel smiled in spite of herself. The thought of her pillar-of-the-community parents as flower children of the sixties, living in a commune, staging sit-ins, and marching for peace, simply did not compute.

"Barefoot, eh? At least you didn't suggest I dance for him naked."

"Only as a last resort, dear. But I wouldn't dismiss that entirely as a possibility, if all else fails."

"Mother, I am shocked!" She wasn't really. Little her mother ever said or did shocked Angel anymore. Oh, yes, there was one thing. Shirley Gentry, comfortably entrenched in her middle years, had actually mentioned to her daughter a few weeks ago that she was toying with the idea of getting a tattoo. Now *that* had been shocking!

"Chin up, Angel! If he's still holding back tonight, why don't you just ask him? Some men need a little help out of the starting gate."

"He loves me, Mom—he's told me so."

ALMOST HEAVEN

"Of course he does! I never thought for a moment that he didn't. So the two of you *should* be married. It's time."

"I think he may be gun shy."

"What do you mean, dear?"

"There's been some scuttlebutt around campus that Jim has a tragic love affair in his past. A woman he was going to marry several years ago left him standing at the altar, and he almost went nuts afterward."

"That's nonsense. Why, I don't believe a word of it, and you shouldn't either. Any woman who had a shot at Jim Rhodes would have to be deranged to let him slip from her clutches."

"How *poetically* put, Mom. But I think it's true. He's mentioned something about her on a couple of occasions. No details. Just remarks in passing. I heard the reason she left him was a psychic told her they were all wrong for each other and they'd be miserable together and, if she married Jim, she would miss out on marrying the man who was the real love of her life."

"What drivel! How could anyone believe such utter nonsense? We'd be in a sad state of affairs if we all had only one mate who could make us happy. What if you're born and raised in the States while your 'love' is a Russian or something? Now just explain to me how that is supposed to work out."

"I don't know." Angel sighed. "I just know that I love Jim and I want to marry him and spend the rest of my life with him."

"*Finally!* You've said ever since you were a little girl that you never planned to get married. That you were going to be either an exotic dancer with many men or a recluse with no men."

"Hey, I was just a kid when I used to make those cracks. I can't believe you even remember that silly stuff."

"When you have a child, Angel, you'll understand. A mother doesn't soon forget a statement like that coming out of her daughter's mouth—especially when it comes out at the Thanksgiving dinner table with the whole family in attendance. Why, Great-aunt Carrie nearly choked on her breast meat!"

Angela giggled. "I was just making a play for attention. That was the year Cousin Tory was born and everyone was making over her so. 'Oh, what a dear little baby! So sweet and pretty. Sure to grow up a beauty!' And me with a front tooth gone, skinny legs, and frizzy hair. I was jealous. Besides, I was only five years old. Kids that age are liable to say anything. I never meant it."

"*Now* you tell me, after I've worried so all these years." Shirley Gentry uttered a long, martyred sigh into the phone, then quickly recovered. "So, what about Jim? Do you think you can *make* him pop the question tonight?"

"Mom, please! These are the eighties, remember? Women don't play those sorts of games any longer. We're upfront and straight with guys. We're equals. Modern women don't connive and manipulate. If we have something to say, we just say it."

"Fine, dear! Just say it, then. 'Jim, you're in love with me and I'm in love with you, so I think the only sensible thing for us to do is get married. We have my parents' blessing. When should we set the date?' "

"Oh, right!" Angel rolled her eyes. She could just see herself delivering that little speech to Dr. James

ALMOST HEAVEN
23

Randolph Rhodes. "Listen, Mom, I've really got to go. Jim will be here any minute. Love to Dad. I'll call when I get to Maine. Promise!"

"You'd better call me after Jim proposes tonight. I'm going to wait up."

Angel smiled. "You bet I'll call if that happens! Hey, I love you, Mom."

"Of course you do, darling. I'm your mother; you're supposed to."

"But I would anyway. You're a peach!"

"Oh, Angel, don't get mushy. I'm all dressed to go to the club for the golf banquet. You'll get me teary-eyed and have my makeup running."

"You two have fun."

"And you'll call me later?"

"If I have news. 'Bye now."

In spite of the need for haste, Angel sat staring at the phone for a few moments, mulling over the conversation with her mother. A mischievous grin stole over her face. She reached into her jewelry box on the dresser and rummaged around for an old string of glass beads she'd had since she was a kid. She draped the glittery strand around her neck.

"Just for fun," she murmured.

She lifted the hem of her gold-threaded caftan and glanced at her bare feet, deciding to leave them that way. Next she reached over to the vase on her bedside table and broke a daisy from its stem. She pinned it in her hair and smiled at her image in the mirror.

The doorbell rang just then.

"Here goes, Mom. Wish me luck!"

One final glance around told Angel that everything was ready. Candles flickering, table set, spicy supper

24 *Becky Lee Weyrich*

perfuming the air, and an old album from the fifties, Johnny Mathis's *Open Fire, Two Guitars,* lending romantic atmosphere as the sad-sweet strains of "I'll Be Seeing You" wafted softly through the apartment.

A little shiver ran through Angel just before she opened the door. "This is it, kid," she told herself. "Better make it good."

No fantasy Angel had ever dreamed up could have prepared her for the look, the essence, the powerfully charged reality of Jim Rhodes when she opened the door. Droplets of rain glistened like diamonds in his dark hair and beard. Behind him, in the distance, lightning flashed through bruised clouds, silhouetting his tall form against the turbulent night sky. His raincoat was open, and his white shirt, unbuttoned at the neck, gleamed liked blue neon in the darkness. Her breath caught when she saw the glow of his smile.

He leaned down and kissed her—softly, sweetly—then pressed gifts into her outstretched arms. He'd brought a loaf of bread, a jug of wine, along with a note that read simply, "And thou."

Best of all, he brought love. Angel could feel it, a tangible force between them as his eyes moved over her—touching, caressing—his warm gaze lingering an instant here, another there. After a moment frozen in time, he reached up and stroked her cheek.

"You look wonderful, sweetheart."

Angel was still fighting to find her voice when Jim slid his hand from her cheek, under her rampant red curls, and around to cup the soft nape of her neck. Kneading her warm flesh gently, he drew her closer, closer still, so close she could feel his breath on her face. Her lips parted. Then his mouth covered hers. It

ALMOST HEAVEN

was a beautiful kiss, so light and sweet that it radiated his warmth all through her body, then settled with a bright glow in her heart.

Angel came away breathless, trembling.

"You taste even better than you look." His words were a husky whisper. Smoothing the tip of his tongue over his lips, he considered, then said, "Honey, a hint of lime, and, of course, ambrosia."

Fighting to control her rampaging heart, Angel took Jim's arm and urged him into the house. For a time, all she could do was cling to him, staring up at his smile and at the dancing lights in his silvery-gray eyes. As perfect as this moment was, she couldn't keep from thinking about tomorrow night. Twenty-four hours from now many miles would separate them. Her heart twisted at the thought.

With some determination, Angel forced all gloom from her mind. Right now, they were as close as two people in love could be, both physically and emotionally. She meant to keep it that way for the next few hours.

Angel set the bread and wine on the table, then turned back to Jim. He stared at her, his eyes reflecting the candlelight glowing behind her. Then he puckered his lips and let out a long, low whistle.

"What is it?" Angel asked.

"You!" Jim tilted his head and rubbed a hand back and forth over his forehead, a familiar gesture that meant he was amazed, puzzled, or thinking things through. "It's you, darling. I've never seen you this way before."

"What way?" Angel warmed through and through, anticipating some extravagant compliment. Jim was a man who wore his feelings on his sleeve, but he rarely put them into words. She had only to look at his face to know when she had pleased him. But since he voiced his private pleasures and emotions so seldom, vocal praise always came as a special delight. A gift from on high.

He didn't disappoint her. "That white gown and the shimmer of light from the candles on the gold threads . . ." He traced one finger down the bodice of her caftan. Angel caught her breath. "Your pretty beads . . ." He lifted the strand from her breast and rolled the glassy baubles between his fingers, tugging her gently toward him. Angel quivered. "The flower in your hair . . ." He caressed the velvety petals, then let his fingers slide through her long, bright-as-flame hair. Angel stood very still, feeling an exotic heat course through her blood. She closed her eyes and let her tongue glide out to moisten her recently kissed lips.

Jim slipped his arms around her, gathering her voluminous gown close to her body. He held her against him and whispered, "Are those naked toes I see peeking out?"

Angel blushed. Maybe the bare feet were a bit too much.

"You know what they say about barefoot angels, don't you?"

"No. Tell me."

"Later." His whisper was uttered so close to her parted lips that the word flowed into her mouth—a rush of sweet, hot air. Jim's tongue followed, fanning a new and urgent heat. Angel sizzled through and through.

Lightning flashed, shooting eerie blue light through

ALMOST HEAVEN

the room. Thunder shook the house. But Angel never noticed the storm outside; her own inner whirlwind was too strong, whipped by Jim's touch, his kiss, his embrace. Some kind of magic was building in the night—a bubbling, boiling cauldron of emotions that threatened to burn them both alive. In the midst of such passionate turmoil, Angel forgot about proposals and marriage and happy-ever-afters. All she could think of was love. She wanted it this night, this moment, with this man.

And she might have had it if a buzzer in the kitchen hadn't broken the spell with its gratingly raucous alarm. Jim's hands slipped from Angel's breasts. His arms dropped to his sides. He stepped away.

"Crab cakes," Angel muttered, her voice quivering like the rest of her, as if that single word explained and excused everything.

"I don't suppose they'll keep?" There was a note of pleading in Jim's voice.

"They get mushy," Angel whispered back apologetically.

"Lord, save us from mushy crab cakes." He offered his arm to escort his barefoot chef into her tiny kitchen.

Jim poured wine while Angel padded back and forth, carrying food from the oven to the small pine table beneath the front windows. He murmured sounds of hunger and awe as each delicious aroma assailed him. Angel beamed at his praise. She might not be much of a housekeeper on a day-to-day basis, but she could cook, and she loved to. She had outdone herself on this meal, and she knew it. Shrimp cocktails on cracked ice followed by spicy, crispy crab cakes, spinach salad, and perfectly chilled white wine. And for dessert, crystal bowls of golden, caramel-drenched flan with a dusting of nutmeg.

Conversation was sparse during dinner, consisting mostly of sighs and murmurs of pleasure. They ate quickly, as if they both knew that as wonderful as the food was something even more delicious awaited them afterward.

Filled to capacity and then some, they lingered over coffee and brandy. All the intimacy and the dread returned in full force—just the two of them with their cups and snifters, holding hands and thinking about tomorrow.

Jim played with her fingers. "Angel?" he said in a hushed voice.

Her heart gave an extra beat. If one of her mother's favorite clichés was accurate, and the way to a man's heart was really through his stomach, then this could be it.

"Yes, Jim?"

He hesitated for so long that she was sure this must be the moment she'd been waiting for. He was staring at her, searching her face, looking deeply into her blue eyes.

"What is it, Jim?" she prompted gently.

He smiled at her, but a sad look came into his eyes. "You'll love Maine. It's so green and cool in the summertime. I wish I were going, too. I'd enjoy showing you some of my old haunts. I think I told you, my parents used to take me there on vacation with them every year." He glanced down at their joined hands for a moment, then looked up at her. "I guess you're all

ALMOST HEAVEN 29

packed. I'll carry your bags out to the car before I leave tonight."

Angel shook her head and bit her lip, hard. She didn't want him to leave that night, and she didn't want to leave tomorrow.

"I don't want to go," she whispered.

He was still toying with her fingers, sending shivers of pleasure and pain up her arm and straight to her heart.

"Of course you do, sweetheart. It'll be a wonderful experience for you."

"The only wonderful experience I want is being with you, Jim." She had to fight the tears swimming in her eyes. "These last few months—"

"Hey, I know. It's been great." He shook his head and frowned. *"Great* is inadequate. You make ordinary things special, and bad things not so bad. Being with you, Angel, has made my life exciting, wonderful, perfect."

"For me, too, Jim. I don't want it to end."

Another long silence stretched between them. Angel thought she could hear her every heartbeat in the quiet room. Jim was working up to saying something else. But what? The suspense was maddening.

He gripped both her hands in his and looked directly into her eyes. "It doesn't have to end, Angel."

"It doesn't? Not ever?" She held her breath, waiting for him to go on.

But that was it! That was all he said.

Without another word, he stood, drew Angel up from her chair and into his arms. For a moment he held her. She trembled, thinking that any minute he would kiss her, and for some reason she felt this kiss would be different from all the others. More meaningful somehow. She never got used to the impact of Jim's nearness. Each caress seemed new and unique. Sweeter and sweeter and *sweeter!*

He didn't kiss her. Instead, he drew her closer, until she was nestled against him, the soft curves of her body proving an exact fit to the hard planes of his. Then, satisfied that they were pressed as tight as could be, and humming softly, Jim swayed into an old-fashioned slow dance to the sweet strains of "When I Fall in Love."

As Angel had blushingly confessed to her mother earlier, they had yet to make love, circumstances being what they were. She had shared her apartment this final quarter with two roommates who were always underfoot. And Jim had felt uneasy about seeing one of his students, even on a casual basis. So their relationship had yet to progress to that ultimate high. But things were different tonight. Angel had finished college, received her sheepskin. Her roommates had gone home for the summer. There was no longer any reason for them to hold back.

As Jim held Angel close and moved with her in perfect, sensual rhythm, she could imagine what it would be like once their time came.

God, let it come tonight! she begged silently.

His voice broke into her thoughts. "Angel? I have something to ask you."

She held her breath, nodding silently.

"Are you dead set on staying here for graduate school?"

She uttered a quick, disappointed gasp. "I don't

ALMOST HEAVEN 31

know." Her answer was honest, if noncommittal. "Why, Jim?"

"I've been thinking . . ."

"Yes?"

"Well, I've applied for a position at New York University. I think I have a good shot at it. What do you think about it?"

Angel's heart sank. If Jim took the job at NYU, by the time she returned from Maine, he'd be gone. It would be over between them. Her mother might claim that absence makes the heart grow fonder, but Angel knew better. By the end of her freshman year, she'd been unofficially engaged to a senior and sure that the pattern of her life was set. He'd graduated, gone to Alaska to work, and after a few months of decreasingly passionate letters, he'd broken things off to marry some bush pilot's daughter he'd met in the frozen North.

In a guarded voice, she answered, "I'm sure that would be good for your career. And I know it must be exciting to live in New York City."

He chuckled softly, sounding relieved. "That's sure a load off my mind. You'll never know how I've sweated over telling you about this. I didn't mention it when I first applied because we barely knew each other then, and besides, I figured I didn't have a prayer of getting the job. But yesterday I got a call to come up for an interview next week. So it looks like I have a good shot at it after all."

She went stiff in his arms, as stiff as her reply. "I'm very pleased for you, Jim."

He held her away from him and stared down at her face. "Hey, you don't sound it. What's wrong?"

For several moments, she didn't—*couldn't*—say anything. Breathing deeply, she tried to hold back her tears. Everything that had passed between them since they'd first met flashed through her mind. Little bits and pieces of tenderness and laughter and love. *Togetherness!* All of that would be over after tonight.

"Angel, what's wrong? Tell me! Why are you crying?"

"Because I love you," she managed at length.

They'd been dancing all the while—slowly, barely moving with the music. Now Jim stopped and gripped her in a fierce embrace. "Oh, God, I love you, too, sweetheart! You'll never know how much."

"Then why do you want to leave me?" Angel was practically choking on her tears with every word.

"*Leave* you?" Jim stepped away, but kept a tight grip on her arms. "Hey, girl, that's not part of the deal. I'm asking if you'd be willing to move to New York after we're married so I'll know whether or not to accept this job if it's offered. I thought you'd be excited about starting your art career in New York, but if you hate the idea and want to continue school in Maryland, then we'll stay right here."

For a few seconds, Angel couldn't respond. She seemed to be locked in an echo chamber with Jim's words bounding off the walls all around her, flashing rainbow-colored sparks and rockets in their wake. . . . *After we're married . . . after we're married . . . after we're married . . .*

"Angel? Did you hear me? Say something, darling. You're scaring me."

Slowly, she tilted her head up and smiled into his

ALMOST HEAVEN

troubled face. "You devil! Why did you put me through all this?"

"I don't know what you mean."

"If you wanted to marry me, why didn't you just come right out and ask me? I've been going crazy, waiting for you to propose."

"But I did propose." Jim, absent-minded to the nth degree, truly believed his words. "Don't you remember?"

"My dear love, that's not something likely to slip my mind, but just refresh my memory, tell me when, exactly, you asked me to marry you."

"Why, at midterm. Remember? The night I got tickets for us to see the college production of *My Fair Lady*."

Angel laughed softly. "Yes, you got tickets, but you couldn't go with me. You got called to a last-minute faculty meeting, so one of my roommates used your ticket. I saw you only briefly after the show, and you certainly never mentioned anything about getting married."

Jim frowned, perplexed. "That's right. I forgot. And after I'd practiced every word I meant to say to you." Then he grinned, looking utterly boyish even with his beard. "But I *meant* to propose that night; I had it all planned. When I couldn't go, I had to wait till later. I'm *sure* I asked you later."

"*When,* later?"

Jim mumbled through a list of other occasions when he'd meant to propose, still certain that somewhere along the way he'd actually popped the question. Finally, he gazed at her sheepishly and whispered, "Will you marry me, Angel?" He fumbled in his pockets until he located a small white velvet box. "Hey, look! I even remembered to bring the ring this time."

Angel threw her arms around his neck and hugged him soundly. "Yes, I will! Oh, yes, Jim! Yes!"

When he could disentangle himself, he led Angel over to the sofa. They sat down and he lifted her left hand and kissed her fingers. Then with infinite tenderness and trembling hands, he slipped on the solitaire diamond set in yellow gold—slowly, carefully, as if he meant to secure it for a lifetime, to bind them together for the rest of eternity.

"I love you, Angel. I never knew I could feel this way about anyone."

When Jim kissed her this time, there was no turning back. Their moment had arrived. They both knew it, both longed for it, both welcomed it. Angel tasted his invitation. No, it was more than that. It was a plea, a sweet command. She clung to him as he rose and moved determinedly toward her bedroom. Her heart was racing, and her whole body flamed with desire.

"Stop!" The heavenly companion had taken on an odd, fiery glow. His command caused the screen to go dark.

"Why did you do that?" Angel demanded. "We were just getting to the best part."

"I've seen enough."

"I thought you wanted the *whole* story."

"I don't indulge in voyeurism."

"Your light's turning pink. Why, you're blushing, aren't you?"

ALMOST HEAVEN   35

"Don't be ridiculous! I'm simply allowing you privacy for your intimacies."

"Suit yourself. But it would have been a fine scene to watch. It was almost a religious experience—that first time. Have you ever . . . ?"

"Enough! This is your life we're contemplating, not mine. What came next? *After* that night."

"We got married, of course."

"And then?"

"Our honeymoon." She glanced at her glowing companion. His color had toned down to a more normal bluish gold. "I don't suppose you'll want to see our wedding night either."

He blushed again, making Angela smile. He cleared his throat. "We'll deal with that when the time comes. The wedding—tell me about it."

"Whatever!" Angel shrugged nonchalantly, but inside she could still feel a wonderful warmth from the memory of that first sweet night with Jim.

Chapter Two

"Our wedding portrait was perfectly elegant, like something out of *The Great Gatsby*. Everyone looked so wonderfully formal and proper. It might have been a gathering of the carefree and idle rich who lived only for the next wedding, the next yacht race, the next opportunity to celebrate for any reason." Angel paused to laugh. "Actually, my mom and dad were never idle and were hardly rich."

She sighed. "I remember my whole wedding like one of those hazy, soft-edged pictures shot through a filtered lens."

"But isn't that what weddings are all about? Real life filtered through a film of fantasy to purify it of anything unpleasant so that it will be remembered forever as a fairy-tale moment?"

"You sound pretty cynical for an angel. Why shouldn't Jim and I have our moment of heaven on earth to hold on to for the rest of our lives?"

"No reason at all. Goodness knows, there's little enough of Heaven down there these days."

ALMOST HEAVEN

37

"Well, it was like a fairy tale. Love is always that way."

"At least at the moment when the 'I do's' are said and the glowing groom kisses his beaming bride."

"There you go, being sarcastic again."

"I'm only being realistic."

"Why don't you just let me tell my tale and stop interrupting?"

"I'm all ears."

Angel gave him a sidelong glance. "And wings," she pointed out.

Through her veil of lace and the mist of happy tears in her eyes, the solid gold wedding band on Angel's finger looked like a halo. And there in the quaint old church at the edge of Chesapeake Bay, with white roses perfuming the cool evening air and the man she loved with all her heart standing beside her, the new Mrs. James Randolph Rhodes realized that she could be no happier if she *were* in Heaven this very moment, strumming a gleaming harp and watching the breathtaking September sunset from a cloud high above.

Jim said, "Until death do us part."

Angel said, "I do."

The robed minister said, "You may kiss the bride."

The sunset sky took on a brilliant sheen of gold-tinged vermilion, and the first evening star blinked on—a silver pinprick in the rainbow heavens. Perhaps signaling its approval of their marriage?

Angel held her breath. Jim lifted her filmy veil. And then he kissed her. But this was not *just* a kiss.

When he leaned down to touch his bride's lips, she

felt it all—the whole universe falling into place. Her new husband promised her hope, protection, joy, completion, sharing. He promised her unqualified love for the rest of her life. Her beautiful, bearded, silver-eyed professor—usually terminally distracted—let Angel know with that one kiss of affirmation that she was now his whole world, that nothing else mattered except that they were together, now and forevermore.

If Angel had fallen in love with Jim the first moment she saw him, she loved him all the more now that they were husband and wife. He was all hers at last.

Every female in Jim's class had lost her heart to the wonderfully soft-spoken, handsome-as-sin prof, whose silver eyes glowed with a certain passionate fire when he recited poetry, and whose voice caressed each phrase of a love sonnet as if he were stroking a woman's warm flesh. He exuded a lazy charm, radiated latent sexual energy, and stole hearts coming and going without ever recognizing his powers.

The man seemed to breathe rarified air, to wander in a world all his own. Certainly he'd been oblivious to the adoration of the young women who rushed to sit at his feet five times a week, then had erotic dreams of him each night and while awake counted the hours until his next poetry session.

But Angel hadn't seen Jim simply as a hunk, a sex object to be worshipped and lusted after. She had indulged in loftier dreams. She'd spent her time wondering what their wedding would be like and whether their children would inherit his dark hair or copy their mother and be redheads whose locks tended to frizz in wet weather, doomed to suffer a lot of bad-hair days and fits of temper. For sure their kids would have nice

ALMOST HEAVEN

39

eyes, sort of silvery blue, if they borrowed equally from both parents.

Now all the rest was behind her—all the classes, all the pot roasts and crab cakes she had cooked for Jim in the tiny kitchenette of her off-campus apartment, all the anxiety of wondering if they would ever make it to this day of days. Now the love and the magic and the wonder of their life together was about to unfold and would, Angel was certain, grow with each moment of their marriage. And by the time they turned gray and took to their rocking chairs, they would be so close they could think each other's thoughts, finish each other's sentences, and look into each other's souls to share every twinge of pain or joy.

All these thoughts tripped through Angel's mind as Jim kissed her, then drew away and smiled down into her heaven blue eyes. His gaze promised her everything she had ever dreamed of and some things she had never dared hope for. She would be his Cinderella, his Beauty, his Maid Marian, his Pretty Woman, and his own special Angel from this day forward. And he would be her prince, her lover, her best friend, her husband.

The magical aura enveloping the bride and groom lasted only moments before Angel's excited parents rushed forward to shower hugs and kisses on the couple.

Ignoring the tears of happiness streaking her mascara, Shirley Gentry said, "Pete, did you ever see such a beautiful bride, such a handsome groom?"

Angel's dad, looking misty-eyed, but far more controlled than his wife, stood back for a moment and gazed at his only child, love and pride glowing on his narrow, golf-tanned face. "The last time I saw such a beauty was thirty-two years ago, the day I married your mother, Angel." Then he hugged her and whispered, "Be happy, sweetheart!"

"I'll see to that, Mr. Gentry."

The bride's father raised a snowy eyebrow at his new son-in-law. "You call me Pete, young man, or I'll start addressing you as Dr. Rhodes."

"Yes, sir, Pete."

"Oh, Jim, I wish you'd call us Mom and Dad like Angel does."

When Shirley issued that request, Angel felt uncomfortable for Jim. She knew his parents had died in a skiing accident in the Swiss Alps when he was in his teens. He had adored them, especially his father. For her mother to press him to call them Mom and Dad seemed almost cruel to Angel, even though she knew her mother meant well.

The uncomfortable moment passed. The sudden tension Angel had sensed in Jim vanished as the wedding guests crowded around to offer their congratulations and good wishes. Moments later, they all piled into cars outside the church to drive the short distance to the Gentrys' bayside home for a twilight reception in the garden.

Angel kept a smile on her face all the while. Actually, she couldn't help smiling. As guests filed by in the receiving line, names, faces, and relationships escaped her. She shook hands and accepted hugs, but her thoughts remained on her new husband and on the small plane waiting for them at a nearby airport, to whisk them away to Orr's Island, Maine, where she

ALMOST HEAVEN 41

and Jim would honeymoon at Land's End Lodge on Casco Bay.

Although Angel knew she should imprint every moment of this happy occasion on her memory, she was too busy dreaming of the future to take in the moment-to-moment details of her wedding day. So when her young cousin, a shy, awkward girl of fifteen, hung back, too embarrassed by her braces and flat chest to approach the princesslike bride and her regal groom, it took a nudge and a whisper from Jim to make Angel notice little Tory Cason standing a short distance away.

"Tory?" Angel called, holding out her left hand to the bashful girl. "I'm so glad you came with your folks. Come over here. I want you to meet Jim."

Angel couldn't help noticing the deep blush that crept into Tory's freckled cheeks when she glanced toward Jim. For a moment it seemed the girl might turn and bolt, but slowly she inched toward them.

"It was a beautiful wedding, Angela," Tory said breathlessly, not quite meeting her cousin's eyes, focusing instead on the antique cameo at Angel's throat—*something old,* the brooch Great-great-grandmother Rachel and all the family's brides since had worn for luck at their weddings. "The brooch looks so pretty."

Angel smiled. "You'll get to wear it one of these days, Tory. Why, you may even be the next bride in the family."

"Not *me,*" Tory murmured, pleased but embarrassed.

"Jim, I'd like you to meet Victoria Cason, my second cousin once removed or something like that."

42 *Becky Lee Weyrich*

Angel laughed. "I can never keep all these family connections straight."

"Me either." Tory blushed again and tried to cover her braces with one hand when she smiled.

Jim offered his hand. "Hello, Victoria. I guess that makes me your new second cousin once removed, by marriage."

A deeper flush bruised Tory's cheeks, making her freckles blend with the rest of her face. Forgetting the loathsome braces, she beamed at Jim. "No one ever calls me by my real name. It's just Tory."

"I'm sorry. I didn't know, Tory."

"Oh, no, Jim! Please call me Victoria. I like the way it sounds when you say it."

Angel smiled at her husband. He could charm the birds out of the trees. She'd never seen her shy little cousin light up that way. Obviously, Jim had made another conquest.

Tory went up on tiptoe and gave Jim a quick kiss on the beard, then darted off into the crowd like a startled rabbit.

Angel laughed. "You've done it again, love. Poor little Cousin *Victoria* will probably sleep with a piece of our wedding cake under her pillow tonight, dreaming wickedly sweet dreams of *my* husband."

He tightened his arm around Angel's waist and whispered, "The only sweet dreams I'm interested in right now are the ones I'm dreaming of Maine—and *you*. Let's get this reception behind us and fly off to heaven together, Mrs. Rhodes."

Angel gave Jim a long, lazy look and pressed close to the warmth of his body. She needed no words to tell

ALMOST HEAVEN 43

him her thoughts on that subject. She'd been waiting all her life for this night.

Then she remembered something she'd meant to do. "Hold my arm, Jim, while I take off my shoe."

"What in the world are you doing, sweetheart?"

"I owe the old wishing well a reward."

Jim's gaze followed Angel's to the roofed, stone-rimmed well that stood at the back edge of the Gentry property.

"When I was a kid," she explained, "I used to think that well was magic. All my pennies went in it to buy wishes."

Jim laughed. "What were you wishing for, darling?"

"*You!* I wished all my life for you, Jim, and now you're mine."

"And you think that wishing well had something to do with it?"

"Could be."

Angel bent down and lifted her white satin pump to show him the silver dime inside. " 'Something old, something new, and a shiny sixpence for my shoe,' " she quoted. "I figure the well's earned this."

Arms around each other, they walked across the lawn. They stood beside the well and stared down.

"Looks deep," Jim said.

"It is—deep, dark, and magical."

Holding the coin up, Angel closed her eyes. Her lips moved soundlessly as she made one last wish. Then she kissed the dime and dropped it into the well. They both stared down in silence until they heard a faint splash.

"What did you wish for this time?" Jim asked. "You have me already."

44 *Becky Lee Weyrich*

Angel turned and put her arms around his neck. She stared up into his eyes, her own half-closed.

"It won't come true if I tell," she whispered.

Going up on tiptoe, she kissed him. A soft, lazy, tender kiss. A special kiss she'd been saving all her life for a special man.

Jim responded with a new husband's eagerness. He drew her close, almost crushing her in his arms. Angel felt the heat of love and longing spread through her. Her heart fluttered crazily. Her breasts ached and quivered. How could he make it better every time?

When their kiss finally ended, they both came away breathless and silent with awe.

After a time, Angel whispered, "I think my dime was well spent. Yes, very well spent!"

It was almost midnight by the time Jim banked their light plane and began his approach to the tiny airstrip at Brunswick, Maine. Angel, who had been drowsing in the right seat, sat up and peered out. Above them, the night sky was blue velvet studded with diamonds. Below, Maine was spread out like a giant Christmas tree with lights of all colors winking in the darkness and their reflections shimmering in Casco Bay and Merrymeeting Sound resembling angel hair draped over evergreen boughs.

"All we need is a good snow and we could start singing carols," she murmured.

"What's that, honey?" Jim was only half listening, concentrating on the pattern of bright runway lights below.

"Nothing really," she answered with a sigh. "I was

ALMOST HEAVEN

just thinking it looks and feels like Christmas. Christmas when we were little kids. You know that moment when you wake up early and realize all the waiting is finally over and the time has come to get everything you've been wishing for. The excitement is so sweet you can hardly bear it." She linked her hand through his arm and squeezed. "You're my own personal Santa Claus, darling."

Jim managed a quick kiss on her cheek. "Ho! Ho! Ho! You've got that right, little girl. I figure on climbing down your chimney about an hour from now."

"Bringing goodies?"

"You bet!" He gave her a quick, smoldering glance. "More goodies than you ever dreamed of, sweetheart."

They both fell silent as the plane skimmed the edge of the runway and the wheels touched down. The sensation of landing gave Angel an odd feeling, as if she and Jim had been sailing along in their own private realm for the past few hours and now they were again connected to the rest of the world. She experienced a moment of regret, but the feeling changed almost instantly to keen anticipation. She had been Jim's bride for several hours. In only a short time she would truly become his wife, his mate for life.

Jim let out a deep sigh as the plane rolled to a stop. He turned and stared at Angel for a moment as if he couldn't quite believe that she was there, that she was real, that she was his. Then he leaned over and kissed her. It wasn't a hard, hot, passionate kiss. It was more like an affirmation, a point of tender contact to assure her that even though they were no longer soaring through the heavens together, they were still linked, still bound together by a love that was stronger than any other force in either of their lives.

Angel was trembling by the time he finished with her. She reached up and cupped her palms around Jim's bearded jaw, her eyes glistening with unshed tears of happiness as she gazed into his.

"How much longer?" she whispered.

"Half an hour, darling. Maybe less."

"Less, I hope."

"Seemed like a long flight, didn't it?"

Angel nodded. "I had to share you with the plane."

"How does a dark back seat and just the two of us sound to you?"

"Marvelous, thanks."

"Thank your folks. They've hired a limousine and chauffeur to drive us out to the islands."

Jim climbed out of the plane, then reached up to help Angel. As she paused a moment at the door, she gazed around her and took a deep breath.

"It's just like an old movie, Jim. Dead of night, a mist of rain, fog coming in, lights reflecting from the wet runway."

He closed his hands gently around her waist to help her down. "You've left out the best part. Two people in love and all alone, together."

Angel felt a moment of weightlessness when Jim lowered her gently to the ground. Their bodies brushed. Their eyes met and lingered. Angel studied the planes and angles of his face, noticed the moisture gleaming in his hair and beard—*like tiny jewels,* she mused. He bent to kiss her again, when out of the sea smoke and shadows a dark figure materialized to break the spell.

ALMOST HEAVEN

"Dr. Rhodes?" The man touched the bill of his uniform cap. "Ma'am. I'm George. I'll drive you out to Land's End. The car's over there, sir."

George, a burly Down Easter with the accent of a lobster fisherman, led the way. He helped Angel into the back seat, then got their bags from the plane and stowed them in the limo's gaping trunk. Moments later, he loomed beside the back window, a sweating silver bucket in his hands.

"Champagne!" he announced, then deftly popped the cork. "A glass for good luck never hurt."

Angel watched, fascinated, as if she were gazing upon a magician at work, while Jim produced two crystal flutes from the recesses of the back-seat bar. With a flourish, he held them out to George.

"We'll take you up on that. We need all the luck we can get."

For no reason she could think of, Angel felt a sting in Jim's casual remark. He'd meant to be witty, of course, but she wasn't amused. To Angel's way of thinking, they didn't need luck when they had love. She started to tell him just that, but instead accepted the brimming, bubbling glass in silence. This was certainly no time for cross words. She was simply tired from all the excitement of the day and their long flight from Maryland. Champagne was exactly what she needed.

And another of Jim's kisses. She got that before she had a chance to sample her sparkling wine. Holding his glass carefully, Jim slid across the seat, slipped his arm around her waist, and drew her close to him. With sure aim, he found her lips in the darkness. Just before she closed her eyes, she glanced toward George. Obliv-

48   *Becky Lee Weyrich*

ious to the amorous couple in the backseat, he kept his gaze fixed on the dark road ahead. Angel relaxed in Jim's warm embrace, her tension of moments before turning to a new kind of heat.

By the time George swung the big car into a right turn at Cook's Corner, the main intersection on the old Brunswick to Bath road, Angel and Jim were sitting close, holding hands, and talking softly while they sipped their champagne. The rest of the world seemed fast asleep as they sped through the night. At last it began to dawn on Angel that she and Jim were really married, together forevermore.

"It's about to begin," she whispered, almost in awe.

Jim touched her cheek with his cool crystal flute, squeezed her hand, and kissed her.

He was about to say something when George turned into the drive and came to a smooth stop at the porch steps of the old stone lodge at the edge of Casco Bay.

"I think we can stop right there."

Angel turned on her heavenly companion. "Are you crazy? This part is important."

"I don't see that my intruding on your honeymoon could have any bearing on your life story. If you merely want me to see how much in love you were—"

"*Are!* How much in love we *are!* And that's not the point at all. We said things that night. We promised things to each other that have tremendous bearing on the situation now. You can't possibly understand my life without seeing and hearing what happened that night. I demand that you let me continue."

A heavy sigh. "This is going to get graphic, isn't it?"

ALMOST HEAVEN   49

Angel noted that his blush glow was back. "Listen, if you're a virgin or something and you're too embarrassed to watch, close your eyes till it's over. Hey, I'm not into strangers peeking into my bedroom, but what was said was important—special. You need to hear it."

She gave her companion a sidelong glance. To her utter astonishment, he was no longer simply a bright glow beside her. Features were beginning to emerge. He was staring at her with real eyes—eyes that seemed to hold all the pain and compassion of the ages. Eyes that looked not simply at her, but through her, straight into her soul. She had always thought that any angel, by reason of profession, would be ethereally beautiful, without blemish. Her companion disproved that theory. He had a wide mouth, a prominent nose, and a high forehead. He had a man's face, not an angel's. His former brilliance still surrounded him like a shining, hooded robe. She squinted at him, trying to get a better overall picture, but his aura was too bright for that.

"Do I know you?" she asked.

Instead of answering, he waved an arm toward the dark screen. Instantly, Angel saw the front entrance of Land's End again.

"Dr. and Mrs. Rhodes, ayah?" A hefty woman in her fifties hailed them from the front door. She had mannishly cropped, steel-colored hair and wore jeans, work boots, and a red plaid wool shirt. "Come right in out of the damp air. This September chill can sink clear down into your bones. I been waiting up for you. I'm Hilda Benoit. Welcome to Land's End."

The lodge was pine paneled throughout. The main room glowed with warmth from the huge fireplace and the rustic, wrought-iron chandelier. A moose head glared down from over the mantel, and other glassy-eyed hunting trophies stared at the newlyweds from around the room. The furniture was large, overstuffed, and well used. The place looked and felt as comfy as home, if you could avoid direct eye contact with the dead animals.

Hefting all their bags, Hilda nodded toward a stairway to the right of the registration desk. "Sign your name in the book, Dr. Rhodes, then follow me on up. It's late. Time I was locking up for the night."

Both Angel and Jim tried to apologize for their middle-of-the-night arrival, but Hilda shook her head. "I been to bed earlier than this, but I been up later, too. Won't kill a body to lose a few winks." She grinned over her shoulder at them. "Besides, it's not every night we get honeymooners up to the lodge. Me and my Burt—God rest him—spent our first night in the same room I'm giving you. Hope tonight goes as well for you folks." She ended with a wink, a chuckle, and a nostalgic sigh.

Moments later, Angel and Jim were upstairs in their pine-paneled room with its brass bed, cottage furniture, and window view of the moon over Casco Bay. They stood, arms around each other, staring out. Off in the distance, a loon called to its mate. It was the sweetest, saddest sound Angel had ever heard. A tear slipped down her cheek.

ALMOST HEAVEN
51

Jim leaned down and kissed her damp face. "They'll find each other," he whispered. "We did, didn't we?"

Angel turned into Jim's arms and clung to him, her heart beating furiously. How did he know she was crying for the loon? How did he know exactly what to say and what to do? She'd heard that husbands and wives who had been married a long, long time could read each other's thoughts and sense each other's emotions. But they were newlyweds. Still, Jim understood.

"You know me so well, darling," she murmured against his shoulder.

"You are as easy to understand as lyric verse, but as complicated as the most intricate sonnet, darling. I hope someday I'll understand you—everything about you from your most casual smile to your deepest thoughts."

She smiled for him, but not casually. "All my deepest thoughts are of you. I've hardly been able to think of anyone or anything else since the day we met, Jim. You've mesmerized me. You've made me dream dreams I'd never thought possible. You've made me want things I never considered important before."

"Like what, sweetheart?"

"My whole life I've thought I wanted to live fast and die young. But not now. Now, I want a home—with you. I want a baby—with you. I want to live a long, long time so I'll have all those years to love you. And I want to grow old and silver-haired and mellow—with you. I want it all, Jim, and I want to share it all with you."

"Oh, Angel!" Jim gripped her suddenly, fiercely. When he kissed her, his whole heart went into it. She felt his love for her, his passion for her, his need for her. She felt it and she shared it.

Somehow—Angel never remembered exactly how it happened and she doubted that Jim did either—that kiss wound up with the two of them together, naked, on the same feather mattress where Hilda Benoit had surrendered her long-guarded virginity to her Burt years before. The old brass bed swayed like an erotic cradle with the motion of their loving. This was not their first time, but it was certainly the time that counted—counted for everything. From this night on, they would be together; they would be the two perfect halves of a single unit, a single soul.

As Jim held Angel close after they had made love, she felt more alive than she ever had in her life, and protected and needed and loved. Jim was a wonder—a man of powerful emotions and infinite tenderness. He had made Angel feel that she was the only woman in the world who could ever make him happy, ever satisfy him, ever love him as he needed to be loved.

"I still can't believe you're mine," he whispered, leaning down to kiss her breast.

"I am," she answered, fighting tears called up by some emotion so deep she couldn't put a name to it. "I am now and I always will be. Oh, Jim, it's almost scary."

"What, darling?"

"The way I feel about you. Less than a year ago, we hadn't even met. Now, it seems like my whole happiness, my whole life depends on you. I don't think I could live without you. I know I wouldn't want to."

"You'll never have to, darling. Why would you say such a thing?"

ALMOST HEAVEN 53

The tears won. "I don't know. Things happen. But if anything happened to you, I know I'd never marry again. I'd never be able to love anyone else this way."

When Jim didn't reply, Angel hugged him closer to her. "Do you know what I mean, darling? Do you feel what I'm feeling?"

"Need you ask?" He kissed her deeply, feverishly. "Oh, Angel, I never figured I'd marry. Now, I can't imagine life without you. As for even considering anyone else, that's impossible. I'm a one-woman guy. I never really loved anyone until I met you. Without you, love would be impossible."

A long silence stretched between them. Finally, Angel sighed and said, "Then this is it for us. We'd best make it last because it will never be any better."

"Amen to that, sweetheart! I mean to make every day of your life from now on the best day you've ever lived."

"And what about you?"

"As long as you're happy, darling, I will be. You just tell me if something's making you unhappy. I'll fix it."

Jim slid his hand from her breast down over her hip and then to the tops of her thighs. Goose bumps covered her warm flesh.

"Jim," Angel whispered with a quiver in her voice.

"Yes, sweetheart?"

"Keep doing that. It's making me *very* happy."

"And how about this?" he whispered warmly into her ear.

"Um-m-m!" she sighed. "Even better."

* * *

"There! You see. That wasn't so bad, was it? We had that big coverlet over us the whole time."

"Thank God for chilly Maine nights!"

"What are you, some kind of prude?"

"No, as a matter of fact. If you want to know the truth, I'm a *man*—one who hasn't had the pleasure of sharing a feather bed with a woman in nearly a hundred of your Earth-years."

"Oh, how sad! I'm sorry," Angel said, really feeling for him, but at the same time secretly amused at the thought of a horny heavenly being. "You should have told me before. But you do see why it was important for you to hear what we talked about that night, don't you?"

"Most brides and grooms swear eternal devotion on their first night together. And half of them end up with other partners—through divorce or infidelity—before a year's gone by."

"Not Jim and me! We really, truly love each other. Why, we were the happiest couple in the universe. There was never a more perfect union. Jim won't even consider marrying again. And that will leave Hope to grow up without a mother. I must go back to him!"

"Happiest couple in the universe, eh? You wouldn't fib to me, would you, Angela?"

"I don't know what you're talking about." She turned away, but his glow grew so intense it almost seemed accusing. "Stop that!" she commanded.

"You stop coloring the truth. You and Jim had your problems. Admit it!"

"Never! We were perfectly happy."

"What about New York?"

ALMOST HEAVEN 55

She turned and narrowed her eyes at him. "What *about* New York?"

"I'm not certain, so why don't we have a look?"

"Wait!"

"No time to wait, Angela. The light, remember?"

Chapter Three

The only thing hotter than the sidewalks of New York that simmering July afternoon was Angel's temper. She smoldered inside the same tiny apartment she and Jim had rented for all the years of their marriage.

"Five years!" Angel muttered to herself. How could so much time have passed? So little have changed while so many dreams slipped away? The closest Angel had gotten to the art world was the collection of bad paintings on the walls of the funky little gallery in the Village where she worked five days a week, year in, year out, selling mostly posters and pop art to latter-day Bohemians. But jobs were scarce and living expenses in the city were sky-high. Since Jim was still low on the food chain at NYU, with no major promotion imminent, Angel had to take whatever she could get to help make ends meet so they wouldn't have to dip into their savings.

She glanced at the clock on the wall of her miniscule kitchen. "Seven-twenty. Jim's late *again*. I wonder what excuse he'll have this time."

Angel grabbed the orange juice out of the wheezing

ALMOST HEAVEN

fridge, stood in front of the open door to take advantage of the cool air, then, not bothering to wash a glass—they were all in the sink, dirty—took a swig straight out of the carton.

Her dress, stockings, and underclothes seemed fused to her skin by the heat. More than anything right now she wanted a shower. But a note taped by the elevator had announced to all tenants that the water in the building would be turned off until eight o'clock for repairs to the pipelines.

Angel sauntered into the living room, shoved yesterday's *Times* out of the way, and flopped down on the sagging sofa. She scowled at the ancient piece of furniture, which matched nothing else in the room, or in the entire apartment for that matter.

"I always wanted Early American," she grumbled, "but I meant to buy reproductions. This damn piece is the real thing."

She kicked off her heels, then peeled the stockings from her sticky legs. She could almost feel her skin take a deep breath. Her sweat-soaked blouse was half-off when she heard Jim's key in the lock. Her anger at his tardiness quickly changed to relief that he was home. But by the time he undid the three locks and walked into the living room, she was annoyed again.

"Don't tell me!" she said, holding one hand up to demand his silence. "Let me guess. Your watch exploded in the heat? Your subway train was hijacked to Queens? You were kidnapped by pirates on the Hudson River?"

"None of the above. I stayed to help one of my students." Jim tried a smile on her, but knew immediately that it hadn't taken. "Look, Angel, I'm sorry. Okay?"

58 *Becky Lee Weyrich*

He came over to the sofa and bent down to kiss her, but she turned away. Jim sighed, shrugged, and backed off.

"You're *always* sorry!"

She got up and went to the window, where she nervously fingered the dead plant on the sill—a housewarming gift from her mother. The brown, crumbling philodendron had put up a valiant struggle to survive, but had lost the battle in the end. In a moment of painful frustration, Angel identified totally with that withered, dried-out plant. Dammit, she had struggled, too!

Turning, she gazed toward the end of the block where she could just catch a shimmer of Central Park's summer green. The color blurred like a runny watercolor through the tears in her eyes. She didn't want to fight with Jim. So why was she doing this? Maybe it was the heat. Maybe it was five years of watching her dreams grow long, white whiskers. Hell, maybe it was nothing more than PMS! But whatever the cause, at this minute she felt everything in the world was wrong and it was Jim's fault. He'd probably even killed the philodendron.

"I really am sorry, Angel. But this kid, Luther, is struggling. He needs a break. He's had a rough life."

"Haven't we all!" Angel muttered under her breath, feeling immeasurably sorry for herself at that moment.

Jim prudently ignored her sarcasm and went on in a quiet voice. "I should have called, but I didn't know we'd be so long."

"I told you I wanted to go to that concert in the park tonight. I've been counting on it for weeks."

"We can still go, sweetheart." Jim touched Angel's

ALMOST HEAVEN 59

shoulders, but she shrugged away. "Grab your shorts and we're out of here. We haven't missed much."

"Oh, right! We'll be able to see Pavarotti great with only a couple of hundred thousand people between us and the stage."

"We'll still be able to hear him, honey. Come on. Let's go."

"If you're so eager now, you go. Don't mind me!"

"But you're the one who wanted to hear this concert. I don't really care anything about it."

She turned on him, her face streaked with makeup-muddied tears. "You don't care about anything I want to do, do you? You don't even care about me anymore."

"Of course I care about you, Angel. I love you!"

"Oh, yeah, right! Then why don't you ever tell me that?"

He moved toward her, trying again to touch her, to hold her. "I just did, sweetheart. *I love you!* There . . . I said it again."

She whirled away. "Only because you know I'm mad and you're trying to soothe me and make me be nice to you. Well, I don't feel like being nice just now." Her voice rose with every word. She was working herself into full-fledged hysteria. "Why don't you just go away and leave me the hell alone!"

For a moment, Jim stood stunned and silent, staring down at the paper-littered floor. His shoulders sagged and he rubbed a hand over his forehead. He looked like a hurt little kid. Then, without a word, he turned and left, closing the door softly behind him.

"Jim?" Angel whispered, a fresh rush of tears coming. "Jim, come back. I'm sorry. I didn't mean it."

60　　*Becky Lee Weyrich*

Her apology came too late. He was gone, leaving her miserable with self-loathing in the stuffy, cluttered apartment that had once seemed like heaven, but was now her private hell.

"What's wrong with me?" Angel whimpered. "What am I doing to us?"

She fell into a crumpled heap on the old sofa and let it all out. She was still sobbing ten minutes later when the phone rang. She meant to ignore it, but it wouldn't stop ringing. When she finally answered, her voice was husky with tears.

"Angel? What's wrong?"

It was Tory. Her cousin had moved to New York—Brooklyn, actually—eight months ago to make her mark on Broadway. The awkward girl with braces and freckles had grown into an attractive, vibrant young woman whose dreams had yet to be tarnished, who still gloried in the excitement and hustle-bustle of the Big Apple. Angel marveled at Tory's ability to cope. While sharing a house with five other aspiring actors and dashing about from one disappointing audition to the next, she always managed to lift Angel's spirits when they were sagging.

"Tory! I'm so glad to hear from you."

"You aren't sick, are you? You sound strange."

"I'm not sick, but I feel sick. Jim just walked out on me."

"Oh, Angel! Not for good, surely!"

"No, just to cool off—to get away from me."

"You two had another fight?"

"Not the two of us. I fight. Jim takes as much as he can stand; then he leaves. I don't know what I'm going to do, Tory. I'm turning into a rotten, mean-tempered

ALMOST HEAVEN 61

bitch. I hate myself, and I hate what I'm doing to him."

"He's very intense, Angel. You know that. You argue to clear the air. But Jim takes every word to heart. He's easily wounded. You've told me that yourself."

"I know! I know! I don't understand why I let myself get so worked up. It's just so hot and my job's a miserable bore and we're still in this sleazy little apartment and it seems like we're going nowhere. Jim and I had such dreams when we got married. We were going to have such a perfect life."

Tory chuckled. "Hey, looking in from outside, you *do* have the perfect life. For starters, you've got Jim, no matter what. So you fight occasionally. Who doesn't? But after the smoke clears you make up and go on. Jim'll be back; you know he will. I envy you, Angel. It's got to be great to have someone to share things with—the bad things as well as the good. Marriage doesn't sound like a bad deal to me right now."

"You? Married? Tory, you change boyfriends as often as you change jeans. Your life is fun, glamorous!"

"Glamorous? Dream on, girl! Want to swap lives for a few days? I'm willing anytime you say. You come to Brooklyn and move in with my five housemates and endure their weird habits and strange hours and piles of dirty laundry and petty squabbles. You try finding a decent, straight guy these days in those meat markets they call singles bars. I'd gladly take the Upper West Side and your cute little place and Jim Rhodes to fix dinner for and have quiet conversations with when he's in the mood to talk. If he's not, silent companion-

62 *Becky Lee Weyrich*

ship has its merits, too. Think about it, Angel. Is life with Jim so bad?"

"I never said it was. I love him, Tory. It's life with me that's horrible. I tell you, I'm turning into a harpy. I get into these blue funks, and there doesn't seem to be anything I can do to keep a leash on my tongue. Poor Jim! I'm making his life a living hell."

"Gee, I didn't know it was that bad, Angel. I'm sorry. Have you thought about therapy?"

"Can't afford a shrink. But I do have an appointment with my doctor tomorrow. I'm going to see if he'll give me something for depression. I hear Prozac works wonders on ogres like me."

"Hey, you be careful with that stuff. I've heard some bad tales about it."

"Well, I have to do something. For the past three months I've hardly been able to live with myself. Lord only knows how Jim has managed."

"How's his play coming—the one he was writing when you got married."

Angel sighed. "It's been shelved. He probably won't finish it as long as we're living in New York. There's just never enough time. If he's not teaching, he's giving students extra help after hours or attending *endless* faculty meetings and fund raisers."

"No word yet on your move?"

"What move?" Angel paused, rummaging through her frazzled mind, trying to think what Tory could be talking about. "Oh, you mean that application Jim filled out for the position up in Maine. That was ages ago. I'd all but forgotten about it. Another dream gone down the tubes. Jim hasn't heard a word from

ALMOST HEAVEN

Bowdoin College. In fact, he hasn't even mentioned it in months. I suppose they've filled the spot by now."

"But you don't know that for sure, do you? Maybe there's still a chance."

"I'm not counting on it. It would be wonderful, though. A house of our own—with a garden—neighbors who drop in for coffee, green pines and wide open spaces." Angel sighed at the picture she painted.

"Sounds like heaven!" Tory agreed.

"You know it! If Jim got that job, I'd be packed and out of here with an hour's notice. I think the city's part of our problem. Too many people, too much noise, too much rushing around all the time. I never feel like I'm really alone with Jim. At least not the way we were back in Maryland. I know we could work things out in Maine, Tory. I just know it. And Jim could finish his play and renew his pilot's license. We could relax and enjoy again."

"I'd hate to see you leave, but I'll keep my fingers crossed for you."

"Don't bother. I'm afraid Bowdoin was just another pipe dream."

"Poor Jim! That's too bad. He really wanted that job."

A long silence followed on Angel's end of the line. Finally, she said, "Yes, he did. And that's exactly what I've been talking about. Here I sit, feeling sorry for myself because Jim didn't get that job. I should be helping him over the disappointment instead of brooding and bitching. I mean, what's a wife for?"

" 'Atta girl, Angel!"

"Hey, what about you, Tory? Did you land that part you auditioned for last week?"

"Don't ask!" Tory groaned. "I went on that starvation diet because they said they wanted an actress who looked almost anorexic. I weighed in at a few ounces over a hundred pounds when I went in. They'd changed their minds, decided the part called for a slightly overweight sort. Go figure! Now my jeans are hanging on me and my guy's complaining that I've got no boobs."

"Geeze! And I thought *I* had it rough. Tory, you know if you need anything that Jim and I—"

"Hey, cut it out! I didn't come up here so you'd take me under your wing to raise. Besides, I landed a cat-food commercial that's paying the grocery bill."

"It must be fun working with a cat," Angel said with a wistful sigh, thinking how much she'd love to have a pet.

"Working with a cat? I *am* the cat! At least there wasn't much of a script to memorize. I just had to learn to meow and purr."

Tory did her cat routine into the phone for Angel, and they both wound up giggling like schoolgirls.

Angel felt better after talking to Tory, but not much.

By midnight she had stopped giggling, stopped laughing, stopped smiling. The nighttime city noises screamed up through the open bedroom window from the street five stories below. Two motorists had a honking contest; then she heard car doors slam, followed immediately by a shouting, cursing bout. After a time, neighbors joined in the fray, yelling down for those guys to shut up and let a person sleep. The street

ALMOST HEAVEN 65

fight was annoying, but the sound that chilled Angel's blood was the mournful wail of sirens as some vehicle careened through the night, answering a police call or bearing a victim to a hospital.

Jim?

She lay in bed, too nervous and upset to sleep. Her ragged nerves produced one gory scenario after another. *A mugging in Central Park.* How often had she begged Jim to stay out of the park after the sun went down? *Trouble on the subway.* Angel refused to use that means of transportation at this time of night, but according to Jim, when your time came it came, whether you were in your own bed or riding a subway at midnight. *An incautious step against the light at a street corner.* When Jim was upset—and Angel knew she had upset him badly earlier—he tended to lose himself in thought and ignore traffic signals.

"Oh," she moaned, trying to block out those grim imaginings. "Come home, honey. Just come home to me."

It must have been after one o'clock when Angel heard Jim's key in the lock, then his footsteps in the hallway. Tears of relief sprang to her eyes. Suddenly, their tiny apartment, which had seemed so empty all evening long, was filled with his presence. Her fears vanished instantly, allowing her earlier annoyance to rear its ugly head. How dare he put her through this? How could he do this to her if he really loved her?

She turned her back to his side of the bed, pretending to be asleep, but she heard him enter the room, pull off his shirt, drop his shoes to the floor. The bed sagged when he sat down.

"Angel?" he said softly. "Are you awake?"

She didn't answer. She wanted to, but she couldn't make herself. During the night, she had passed through so many emotional stages—anger, fear, remorse, loneliness, self-loathing, jealousy. Even as she'd thought of Jim with another woman, she knew she was being ridiculous. But still . . .

Now, she was drained. She wanted to tell Jim she was glad he was home, that she had missed him. She wanted more than anything to say she was sorry, wanted him to hold her and let her cry it all out. She wanted things to be right and sweet and good between them again. But as hard as she tried to get out the words, they refused to be spoken. She lay there, inches away from the man she loved with all her heart, feeling his heat, breathing in his scent, longing for his touch, pretending to be asleep.

For what seemed an eternity, Angel lay very still, hoping Jim would speak to her again, ask her a question, give her an opening. He wasn't asleep; she could tell by his breathing and by the tension in his body. So, why didn't he say something? Why didn't he reach over and touch her—kiss her good night? Why didn't he make some move to bring them as close emotionally as they were physically?

And then it happened. Angel was about to break the painful silence herself, about to turn into his arms and give up and give in and beg him to love her. But her moment was lost. As she turned, she heard the small, telltale snore that signaled Jim's first level of sleep. Disappointment washed over her, making her whole body ache. She turned back on her side and let tears wet her pillow until, emotionally and physically

ALMOST HEAVEN

drained, she slipped off into the lonely darkness of slumber.

"Stop it! How can you do this to me? That was such a painful night. I thought Heaven was supposed to be all sweetness and light—all happiness."

"You're not in Heaven yet, Angela. And life isn't—wasn't—all a bed of roses. You say you loved Jim, but it wasn't all good times, was it? You can't hide the bad from me and hope I don't notice. The bad times are only an extension of the good. It takes both to paint the whole picture—to create a whole lifetime."

"All right! You've made your point. But I still want to go back. I'll gladly take the bad with the good to be with Jim and Hope again. Don't you see? That night and other times like it are all the more reason for me to return. I have so much to make up for, so many wrongs to put right."

"You had your chance, Angela." His voice turned gentle, sympathetic. "If only we were allowed to understand—while we're down there—that every moment counts, that never a second should be wasted in anger or meanness. Life is too short!"

"That's what Jim always said." Angel sniffed back a tear.

"You should have listened to him."

"You're quite a Monday-morning quarterback, aren't you?" she snapped.

Ignoring her flare of temper, he asked, "Do you want to see the rest?"

Angel was too upset to think past that awful moment when she realized Jim had fallen asleep. She hesi-

68   *Becky Lee Weyrich*

tated, trying to remember the next morning. Then it came to her in a flash. She smiled at her companion. "Oh, yes! *Please!*"

Coffee and roses. Those unrelated scents were Angel's first grips on consciousness when she woke the morning after her fight with Jim. The next thing she became aware of, even before she opened her eyes, was that Jim was gone again. There was no sag to the bed, no warmth from the other side, and she sensed the emptiness that always came when he left.

She sat up like a shot and glanced about. Had he taken a suitcase? Had he left her for good? It would be no less than she deserved for her childish behavior last night.

Her panic vanished when she looked around. No drawers left open from hasty packing. No signs of suitcases. Only a mug of freshly brewed coffee, a single pink Queen Elizabeth rose, pinched, she knew, from their neighbor Mrs. Corelli's tiny, but much-prized garden plot by the building's entrance, and a note from Jim.

Sweetheart,
    I hate to leave while you're still sleeping, but I can't bring myself to wake you. You had a rough night. We both did. Why do we do this to each other? I'm sorry, sorry, sorry! If I had time, I'd write that a hundred times for you. No, a thousand! And after I finished doing that, I'd write, I love you , Angel! at least a million times. I'll be home

ALMOST HEAVEN 69

early tonight. I promise! Let's make it a special occasion. We're due one of those—overdue.

He signed it: "Your loving, remorseful, and stealthy, Jim." Then he added, "P.S.—We're home free. I got up early to swipe Mrs. Corelli's rose for you. She'll never know who did it. Enjoy, my darling!"

Angel couldn't help but laugh at the thought of Jim, probably still in his bathrobe, sneaking downstairs to kidnap one of the old busybody's prize blooms. "Good thing we don't have a doorman." She chuckled.

She sat for a long time, sipping her coffee, sniffing her rose, and rereading Jim's note while she planned her day. On the way home from the doctor's office, she'd stop by Zabar's and pick up the fixings for a small feast. She'd make this night a truly festive occasion. For the five years she and Jim had been married, their wedding china, crystal, and silver had been packed away in the closet, waiting to be used "when we move to our own place." Well, maybe that was part of the problem. Angel was just coming to realize that "her own place" was anywhere Jim was. She didn't need a bigger apartment or a sales contract to make the place she shared with her husband a real home. All she needed was will and determination.

"Yes!" she whispered, smiling and twirling the rose. "Candlelight, china, Mom's damask tablecloth. And the old Johnny Mathis record, I'll dig that out. I'll make it the perfect evening."

A glance at the clock snapped Angel out of her happy reverie. She'd have to hustle to make her eleven o'clock doctor's appointment on time. A quick

70 *Becky Lee Weyrich*

shower, no breakfast—she hadn't felt like eating in the morning for weeks—and she'd be off. She'd get some "happy pills" and then life would be beautiful.

"I'll make Jim happy, by damn, or know the reason why!"

An hour and a half later when Angel left the doctor's office, she was grinning, but not because he'd prescribed "happy pills." She moved along the crowded sidewalk, feeling as if she were floating a foot or two above it.

"Depression is not unusual for one in your condition," Dr. Alessandro had told her. "And now that you know the cause, I'm sure the problem will correct itself. If not, call my office and make an appointment. If there are no further problems, I'll expect to see you next month, Mrs. Rhodes. And congratulations."

As Angel walked along Broadway toward Zabar's, she had the sudden urge to stop strangers in the street and tell them her good news so they could congratulate her, too. It seemed like the whole city should be celebrating—the whole world. What a surprise she had for Jim! She thought about calling him at work, but decided she'd rather tell him face to face so he could hug her and kiss her and they could share their excitement.

Zabar's was packed as usual, the shoppers shouldering each other to get to cheeses, spices, salads, fresh meats, and anything else that was edible or was used in the preparation of edibles. At the fresh fish counter, faced by a display of tiny squids on ice and gutted salmon with staring eyes, Angel felt her stomach turn.

ALMOST HEAVEN 71

She moved quickly away. No breakfast, the heat, the jostling crowd, and the mingled aromas of the foodstuffs were doing a number on her. Quickly, she filled her basket with the fixings for meatless spaghetti sauce, angel hair pasta, and a large loaf of crusty bread, still warm from the oven. On her way to the cash register, she grabbed a jar of mango-lime chutney, Jim's favorite, and cream cheese to go with it. The long line moved at a blessedly rapid pace, and soon she was back out in the fresh air—as fresh as air on a hot day in New York gets. She headed home, her bag heavy, but her spirits light.

When Jim arrived at five-thirty, bringing wine, Godiva chocolates, and roses that he had paid for this time, Angel was ready for him. Her spaghetti sauce with fresh basil was simmering aromatically on the stove, the apartment was spotless, and the table was gleaming with white damask, Wallace sterling, and Lenox china and crystal.

As for Angel herself, she'd decided to surprise Jim by wearing the outrageously sexy Christmas gift he'd bought her at Frederick's of Hollywood. The micro miniskirt and halter top of silver-pink metal mesh barely covered her thighs and breasts, and left her midriff enticingly bare. She had never worn the outfit before, nor would she dare show herself this way outside the privacy of her own apartment. But it felt sort of fun tonight—her last hurrah at playing vamp for her husband before she donned the loose shifts of motherhood. She decided against the clear plastic spike heels that went with the ensemble, opting instead for bare feet.

"You know what they say about barefoot angels."

72 *Becky Lee Weyrich*

She smiled as she kicked off her shoes, then added silently, *Especially barefoot, pregnant angels.*

Jim gave her a wolf whistle, his eyes sparkling almost as brightly as her metal dress. "That's *some* outfit!"

Angel shot him a come-hither glance and said in a passionate whisper, "Hey, sailor! Wanna have some fun?"

She was her old self again. Teasing Jim, tempting him, turning him on as only she could. It felt wonderful!

Jim stood in the hallway, smiling at her, with a look in his eyes to warm the coldest heart. And her heart was anything but cold this evening. She'd been tempted all afternoon to call and tell someone. Her parents, retired in Florida now, would be wild with joy. Closer by, Tory would shower her with congratulations, then rush out to buy baby things. That girl was a sucker for kids. Now, as she waited for Jim to speak, she was so glad she had held off. She wanted him to be the first to know. She had guarded her secret all afternoon until she was absolutely aglow with it, and at last she could give him this gift they'd both waited and prayed for all these years.

Jim moved silently toward his beaming wife. His arms still filled with presents, he leaned down and kissed her—a soft, sweet, tentative brush of her lips.

"You didn't bite me," he said with a grin. "Does that mean we're friends again?"

Angel blushed and looked away, nervous suddenly. "We're far more than friends, I hope. Thank you for your note with my morning coffee. And Mrs. Corelli's rose. You're sure she didn't see you take it?"

ALMOST HEAVEN 73

"There were no cops waiting downstairs when I got home, so I guess I'm safe."

Instead of laughing at his little joke, Angel turned serious. "I'm sorry, Jim. I've been a pain and I know it. Forgive me, darling?"

Swiftly, Jim deposited wine, roses, and candy on a nearby table and drew Angel into his arms, cuddling her gently, stroking her bare back with warm, eager hands. "Angel, you don't have to apologize, and I don't have to forgive you. There's nothing to forgive. I love you. That's all either of us has to say. Forgiveness comes automatically."

"And I love you, Jim!" Suddenly, she felt she would burst with her secret if she couldn't tell him that very moment.

"I have a surprise!" They spoke the exact words at the same time.

"*You* have a surprise for *me?*" Angel's gaze moved from Jim's smiling face to the presents he'd brought home.

"Not those," he told her. "Something else. Something I think will make you very happy, sweetheart."

Glowing, bursting, Angel said, "But I'm already so happy I can hardly stand it. I've been dying to tell you. I could hardly wait for you to get home. Jim, we're going to have a baby!"

He touched her cheek with his fingertips, touched it as if she were made of the most fragile spun glass. "A baby?" he breathed out.

"A baby! *Our* baby! Yours and mine, Jim!" Angel hugged him, then stepped back and hugged herself, staring down at her flat belly. "I can hardly wait to start showing. I want the whole world to know. Oh, Jim! Isn't it wonderful?"

She hadn't really expected her news to make him cry. But when he embraced her and kissed her, she felt his tears, wet against her cheeks.

"Angel, my Angel," he kept saying over and over again. Then he added, "This makes my surprise all the better."

She'd nearly forgotten in the excitement of the moment. "Tell me, Jim. What's your news?"

He held her at arm's length, staring down at her belly and the precious little life he knew it contained. His words were addressed, not to Angel, but to their child. "How would you like to have your own sled? Until you're old enough, I'll pull you around the Mall. Then I'll teach you to skate on the pond. And we'll picnic on the rocks along Casco Bay and look for starfish. We can toss bread crusts to sea gulls. And at Christmastime we'll go out and cut our own tree—the biggest one we can find—then we'll put an angel on top that looks just like your mommy. How would you like to be born and brought up in Maine? In the very shade of the Bowdoin Pines?"

All of a sudden, the questions Jim put to their unborn child sank in. Angel gave a sharp, joyous cry and propelled herself back into his arms. "Oh, Jim! You got the job at Bowdoin! When do we leave? I can be packed in a day—well, a week."

He was laughing, crying, hugging his pregnant, jubilant wife and whirling her around the tiny living room. "Then you want to go, sweetheart?"

Angel's bare feet touched the floor, and she steadied them both. She stared into his wonderful face, trying

ALMOST HEAVEN 75

to tell him without words how happy he'd made her because she wasn't sure she could find words for so much joy.

"Jim," she whispered finally, "I could be happy anywhere with you. I love you, so wherever you are is my home. But to share my life and our baby's new life with you in Maine . . . well, it's almost too wonderful. I hope I'm not going to wake up in a minute and discover I've dreamed all this."

"No way, sweetheart!" He held her close and nuzzled her fragrant, shining hair. "It's real, all right! We're about to start a whole new life—the *three* of us."

"Can we make that four?"

Jim took a step back, stunned. "You mean, *twins?*"

"No, silly! I want a dog. Every kid should have a dog to grow up with."

"A dog it is, then. We're going to buy a big house, with lots of room for dogs and cats and kids and love. More love than you ever imagined."

The rest of their special evening passed in a happy haze. For the next few hours they were always touching, always kissing, always clinging to each other and to their glorious new dream.

As Jim poured wine and Angel served their spaghetti, he asked, "Can you take next weekend off to drive to Maine and house hunt, darling?"

"I have a better idea." She beamed at him and touched his hand. "Why don't I just quit that rotten job? Dr. Alessandro says that's probably the reason I've been such a grouch lately—too many hours on my feet. But can we afford my quitting?"

Jim frowned. "Listen, if the doctor thinks you

should stop working, you stop. I don't want you doing anything to jeopardize your health or the baby's. We'll get by. Besides, we don't have that long to go here anyway. I have to be in Maine by the end of August. That's just a little over a month from now."

While Jim was still talking, Angel reached for the phone and dialed the gallery number.

"Who are you calling? Tory?"

She grinned at him. "No, I'll do that later. I'm calling work, to quit. As of this moment, I'm a full-time wife and mother-to-be. No latch-key kids in this family."

Jim beamed at her. "You'll even bake cookies for us?"

"You've got it!"

"Gee, I think I'm going to like this Mom and Dad thing."

Over china, crystal, silver, and spaghetti, they made plans. Big plans! Wonderful plans!

"We can get the station wagon out of storage and drive up Friday after I get off work. I'll call ahead and make arrangements with a real-estate agent to show us around on Saturday. I'm going to say we want a big, old place—one of those typical New England houses."

"I want a garden, Jim."

He glanced toward the dead plant in the window and raised one eyebrow.

"Forget that puny thing," Angel ordered. "That's no indication of my talents. I really do have a green thumb. That poor bastard just succumbed to exhaust fumes and foul street language. I can grow a lot of our vegetables, make fresh baby food for the kid."

ALMOST HEAVEN

Jim shook his head slightly. "Sounds like a lot of work, honey."

"It is work. Work I love. And maybe we could turn one of the extra bedrooms—one with good light—into a studio where I could paint."

He grinned and nodded. "I'd already thought of that."

"First thing, though, we have to get the nursery ready." Angel closed her eyes, imagining the whole thing.

"Nope!" Jim answered. "First thing, we have to find our dream house."

"Well, yes. That, too," Angel agreed, grinning, then chuckling, then laughing out loud with pure glee.

Later, after the dishes were cleared, washed, and put away, and all the plans for their house-hunting trip to Maine were made, Angel put the old Johnny Mathis record on the turntable and they danced slowly in each other's arms. All talk ceased. Now the only sounds in the room besides the sweet, old love songs were sighs of contentment and murmurs of happiness.

When they made love late that night, Jim touched his wife with infinite tenderness. They seemed to bask in a special light, as if someone in Heaven had looked down on them and decided they needed some help to know the purest form of love.

And they did know it that night and the time they had after.

"You!" Angel's voice was gently accusing. "You were watching us that night, weren't you? You made sure things were especially good between Jim and me."

"I haven't a notion what you could be talking about, Angela."

Her companion might deny it, but Angel was certain she was right.

"I felt another presence that night. It was like . . . like—"

"Yes? Like what?"

"It was like when Al found me and guided me back to my parents. Everything was so terrible, but then he came and made it all right again. That's exactly the way things were between Jim and me that night. Like we'd been lost to each other and someone had shown us the way home."

"You have quite an imagination. We should have added that to your heavenly résumé."

"Never mind! I know what I believe. You're my guardian angel, aren't you? *You're Al!*"

"Alexander, if it's all the same to you."

"I knew it! Just look at you. I can see your face now. You've materialized. You look older, but I'd know you anywhere. Gosh, I'm glad to see you, Al!"

"Please, Angela. It's *Alexander* up here."

"Okay, Alexander. When can I go back? You know as well as I do that this is all a mistake. I belong with Jim and Hope."

"Finish the story, please. Then we'll talk about it."

Angel sighed. "What else do you want to know? We moved to Maine. Hope was born. And then I died—*by mistake!*"

"Little that happens in the universe is by mistake, Angela. Please continue. Tell me about Maine."

Chapter Four

That July Friday of the big house-hunting trip dawned hot, hazy, and brassy in New York City. Angel was up early, packing for their exciting weekend excursion.

Jim watched his wife, smiling as he dressed for work. "Better pack a sweater, sweetheart."

She turned and wiped the perspiration from her brow. "You're kidding, right?"

"Not at all. Don't you remember how cool it got at night from that month you spent in Maine the summer before we got married?"

"But that was early June."

"Pack a sweater, darling," Jim insisted.

Angel did, then closed their weekend bag. "Ready!" she announced with a grin.

Jim laughed and kissed her. "You should have slept in. What are you going to do with yourself all day while I'm at work?"

She glanced about their tidy bedroom. She sighed and shrugged. She'd spent all week working at home—sorting things, throwing away junk, reducing their ac-

80 *Becky Lee Weyrich*

cumulation of belongings to the basic necessities. If the movers came on Monday, she'd be ready for them; she was that eager to relocate and begin their new life.

"I don't know what I'll do," she admitted. "I could read, I guess, or work crossword puzzles."

"I have an idea. Why don't you go shopping?"

"Shopping?" It was one of her favorite sports, but given their austere financial circumstances, Jim seldom encouraged her in it.

"There's that baby shop a couple of blocks down on Amsterdam. And I think I noticed a wallpaper store in the same area. I've passed them both on my way to the subway. It wouldn't hurt to browse."

Angel beamed at the thought, but then lost some of her enthusiasm. "Buy baby things and wallpaper *now?* We don't even have a house to put them in yet."

"I know. You'd enjoy looking, though, wouldn't you? It could save us some time later. And I'm sure you'll find a wider selection in New York than you will in Maine. Then, too, if you've checked out some wallpaper patterns before we look at houses, it might help. You'll be better able to visualize what they're going to look like after they're redecorated."

Angel was half-dressed before Jim finished talking. They shared a quick breakfast of coffee, juice, and bagels, then she walked him the few blocks to the subway station. After he disappeared down the dark stairs into the ground, she spent her next hour window-shopping and dreaming until the stores opened. She had expected the day to drag by while she waited for Jim, but the time flew as she debated various styles of infant furniture, then scanned hundreds of wallpaper samples. She had a *wonderful* time!

ALMOST HEAVEN

81

Less than an hour after Jim arrived home in midafternoon, they left for Maine. Angel was brimming with ideas, bubbling with plans. While he concentrated on the pre-rush hour traffic out of the city, Angel talked excitedly about her finds.

"I saw this darling pine cradle, perfect for the baby at first. But I don't know. It would be outgrown so quickly. I guess we'd better go with a crib from the start. There was a beautiful white one—all frilly, with a canopy and ruffles. But what if it's a boy? That would never do. Maybe we should go with a unisex model in light wood. What do you think, Jim?" She paused for breath, but not long enough for Jim to answer before she rushed on. "Boy or girl, I've found the perfect wallpaper. Oh, you'll love it, darling!"

Although Jim was concentrating on traffic, Angel could tell by his smile that he heard every word she said and was sharing her every dream. He nodded, his eyes still straight ahead. "Tell me," he urged.

"It's all covered with little angels dressed in rainbow-colored robes. They have tiny halos, golden wings; and each one is playing a different musical instrument. The pattern is called 'Heavenly Lullaby.' Isn't that sweet? There are boy angels and girl angels, angels with blond hair, brown hair, even red hair. So, it won't matter whether our baby is a boy or a girl. This paper will be perfect for either."

Jim spoke, almost to himself. "It's going to be a girl."

"How could you know that, darling?"

"I dreamed about her last night." He glanced at Angel. "I saw her just as plainly as I'm seeing you right now. I even know her name."

82 *Becky Lee Weyrich*

"Really?" Angel felt a bit put out with Jim. He *could* have discussed it with her. She'd come up with the perfect name for a baby girl just this morning. "We haven't even talked about names yet, Jim."

"We don't have to. Her name's Hope."

Angel had been primed to argue, no matter what name he suggested. But "Hope" stopped her cold and brought tears to her eyes. Hope was the name she had zeroed in on while shopping for a crib. She turned to stare at Jim. How could he possibly have guessed that?

"I love that name," she said softly. "It's perfect!"

"It's all going to be perfect," he answered. "Just you wait and see, darling."

Angel didn't have to do that. She believed what he said; their child would be a daughter named Hope.

It was long after dark before they drove into Brunswick, Maine, and found 63 Federal Street, the site of the 1807 Stowe House Motor Lodge—the former home of Harriet Beecher Stowe. She had lived there from 1850 to 1852, writing *Uncle Tom's Cabin* by candlelight in the kitchen of the rambling, Federal-style house while her husband Calvin taught Natural and Revealed Religions at Bowdoin College.

The inn with its pristine white paint and stark black shutters loomed up suddenly on a slight rise, the moonlight turning it ghostly silver.

"Here we are," Jim announced, pulling up the drive and into the parking lot.

Moments later, they were out of the car. As Jim had predicted, the night air had a fall-like nip to it. Angel was glad she'd heeded his words and packed a sweater.

ALMOST HEAVEN

83

"I hope our reservations will suit you, sweetheart. The new section was all filled this weekend, so we'll be staying in one of the rooms in the main part of the old house."

"That's great! I always thought it would be interesting to sleep in a museum. Sort of like time travel or something."

Angel wasn't disappointed with her accommodations. Their room was furnished in period antiques, not the cottage furniture of their honeymoon suite at Land's End but massive pieces of rosewood and mahogany carved by expert craftsmen over a century before. Marble-topped tables, a fireplace with mantel lusters of cranberry glass, and electrified whale-oil lamps added to Angel's feeling of being transported back in time. Portraits of Stowe family members stared out from ornate, gilt frames that hung on the wine-colored walls. The window was open slightly, allowing a cool, pine-scented breeze to drift in through the ivory lace curtains.

"Oh, Jim," Angel said with a happy sigh, "why can't we just live here? It's so cozy, so homey."

He laughed and gathered her into his arms, nibbling her tender earlobe as he hugged her tight.

"Want to fool around?" The question was a husky whisper, spoken directly into her ear.

As tired as she was, Angel responded to his invitation. "Can I grab a shower first?"

"Can I watch?" Jim made no move to release her.

She reached up and gave him a long, hair-raising, toe-curling kiss. "Sure!" she purred. "You can even scrub my back."

84   *Becky Lee Weyrich*

"And your front?" He was unbuttoning her blouse, untucking it from her skirt, unzipping her zipper.

"You can even undress me, if you like." (As if he needed permission.)

They drifted toward the bathroom, still kissing, touching, casting off articles of clothing. By the time they reached the shower stall, the path from the bedroom was littered with shoes, shirts, and assorted rumpled garments.

Angel was tingling all over before the first jet of spray hit her bare flesh. Lovemaking had become too routine over the past couple of years. Somewhere along the way, they'd lost their spontaneity. But tonight it was back in all its delicious glory. They wedged themselves into the tiny stall, still clinging as they took turns soaping each other all over. The slide of Jim's slick hands over Angel's breasts and belly made her tremble against him. She leaned into him, shuddering, and nipped at his shoulders.

"You taste soapy," she murmured.

Jim dipped his head to her peaked nipple. "You taste wonderful, darling."

Angel could only moan at this point.

"Damn shower's too small!" Jim complained. He'd twisted this way and that trying to gain purchase, but there was no way to do anything in such limited space. "Time to rinse off," he announced.

Once again, his hands caressed her, wiping away soap and leaving goose bumps instead.

A quick toweling, then they both dived for the bed.

"Ah, that's better!" Jim said, drawing Angel close, their damp bodies clinging.

ALMOST HEAVEN

"You'd better not fool around," Angel warned, feeling herself on the very brink of perfect pleasure.

"Just a little?" he begged, drawing his hand up between her legs.

When Angel shuddered and moaned, he gathered her into his damp arms, kissing her deeply as he entered her.

It didn't last long, but it was . . . oh, so good! Better than ever. *Thank God we haven't lost it!* Angel thought through her hazy euphoria.

"You know what?" Jim whispered.

Angel shook her head, not ready to trust her voice yet.

"I love you more now than I ever have. I never knew it worked that way. I thought love just stayed on an even plane. But I was wrong. It just keeps growing and expanding and filling me up with this feeling . . . this kind of wonder every time we make love. Do you know what I mean, sweetheart?"

In answer, Angel turned back into his arms and kissed him. Then in a soft little voice, she said, "I know, Jim. Isn't it incredible?"

They lay there in each other's arms, silent for a time, both thinking about love and the baby and the future.

Then he glanced at his watch. "Hmmm. It's nearly eleven. I should have called Mrs. Chamberlain, our real-estate agent. Do you think it's too late now?"

Before Angel could reply, the anachronistic touch-tone phone on the bedside table rang. Jim answered it.

"Hello?"

He smiled at Angel and nodded.

"Mrs. Chamberlain! I was just debating whether or not I should call you at this hour. No. We weren't sleeping. We just checked in a short while ago. Tomorrow at nine? Great! We'll meet you out front at nine on the dot. Yes, we're eager to see what's available."

A long pause on Jim's end followed. Angel watched as his face broke into a grin and then a broad smile. Finally, he said, "That sounds like exactly what we're looking for. Good price, too. Is the backyard large enough for a garden?" His eyes met Angel's. He winked. Again he nodded at something Mrs. Chamberlain said. "We'll see you in the morning, then. Thank you for calling."

Before Jim could hang up, Angel cried, "Tell me!"

He chuckled evilly. "I should make you wait. If I tell you, it will spoil the surprise."

"Jim, you'd *better* tell me. Right this minute!"

"All right! All right! I wouldn't sleep if I kept it to myself anyway. Mrs. Chamberlain says an old house on Park Row just came on the market today." He spread out a map of Brunswick on the bed, searched with his finger for a moment, then made a stab at the spot. "Right there. Park Row is on the other side of the Mall from Maine Street, right off campus. I'll be able to walk to the college in less than five minutes."

"And there's space for a garden?"

"You bet! And room for dogs and cats and lots of kids. The place was built back in the mid-nineteenth century. Mrs. Chamberlain said it's in good condition, but needs some cosmetic work. The present owner, a lady in her eighties named Emmy Joshua, lived there for over sixty years. She's a widow and moved to Boston a few months ago to be close to her son. The place has always been in the Joshua family. Mrs. Joshua had hoped that it would stay in the family, but her only son

ALMOST HEAVEN

and his wife are both lawyers, practicing in Boston. They have no children and no desire to live in the big house up here. They're her only relations, and they've finally persuaded old Mrs. Joshua to sell."

"Oh, Jim!" Angel hugged him. "It's like a guardian angel is watching over us. I won't sleep at all tonight. I'm too excited."

He kissed her long and tenderly. "You'd better get your rest, darling. We have a long day ahead of us tomorrow. Even if we adore the old Joshua house, I want to look at as many places as possible. We're taking a big step. I want to make sure we're getting the best buy for our money."

They held each other as they drifted off to sleep, both dreaming of tomorrow—of *all* their tomorrows.

Angel would be perfectly content to allow Jim to browse on the housing market as long as he liked, but in her dreams that night she was already redecorating the old Joshua house, sight unseen. She started with the nursery—a sunny room overlooking the garden, she imagined. By the time she finished her dream work, angels floated on the walls around a white crib that had a canopy and ruffles. And from beneath those frills, a tiny, beautiful face smiled back at her. Her little, doll-like daughter, Hope.

Mrs. Chamberlain arrived right on time the next morning. Jim and Angel had been up since six. After breakfast in the Stowe House restaurant, they'd taken a walk about the grounds to admire the colorful summer flowers in full bloom. They'd arrived back at the entrance just as a dark blue Ford pulled into the drive.

88   *Becky Lee Weyrich*

An inconspicuous sign on the door read "Down East Realtors." The woman behind the wheel was younger than Angel had expected, perhaps in her late thirties, and quite attractive in a motherly sort of way.

"You must be Dr. and Mrs. Rhodes," she called through her open window.

Angel and Jim waved and started toward the car.

"Hop in and we're off," the realtor invited. "I'm Sue Chamberlain. Welcome to Maine."

Before they reached Park Row, they were on a first-name basis with Sue. She was a warm, bright person with a winning smile and an infectious laugh, a born and bred Mainer, who obviously loved the place, no matter the season. To a question from Angel about the long, hard months of cold and snow, Sue replied, "If you can't take the winters, you don't deserve the summers. That's the way we Maine folks figure it."

Then she went into a thumbnail sketch of Brunswick's history for her clients. "The first settlement was founded back in 1714 by a group from Boston," she explained. "They didn't fare so well with the Pejepscot Purchase, though. The Indians—the Pejepscot—figured the land still belonged to them. In 1722, they managed to run the settlers back to Boston in Lovewell's War. But five years later, the white man was back and here to stay. The town was incorporated in 1739. The Pejepscot never really had a chance; the location was too good. With the Androscoggin River giving easy access to the Atlantic, industry and prosperity were assured from the start. The river was dammed in 1753. The falls provided power, and the river was full of salmon. The cotton mill went up in

ALMOST HEAVEN

1809, and besides that, the locals could depend on lumbering, shipping, fishing, and shipbuilding."

"What year did the college open?" Angel asked, impressed with Sue's vast store of dates and events.

Jim jumped in with the answer. "That was in 1802, but it was actually chartered in 1794. It's Maine's oldest college." He chuckled. "Back then, the entire faculty and student body consisted of the president, one teacher, and eight bright young men."

"Gee, it's grown some," Angel said as they passed the lush green campus with its old brick and stone buildings."

"Keeps growing every year," Sue agreed.

"Hey, Sue. I've been wondering about something."

"What, Jim?"

"When you drove up to the Stowe House," he said, "how did you pick us out? There were several other couples standing around outside."

Sue glanced in the rearview mirror and flashed Angel a smile with her dancing brown eyes. "Easy, Jim! I could claim to be a mind reader, but it was your wife who tipped me off."

"Really?" Angel said. "How?"

"Your black dress. It's supposed to hit eighty today. Only a New Yorker would wear black in this heat."

They all laughed. "I guess I'm going to have to learn to dress for summers in Maine, if I'm going to live here," Angel quipped, marveling at the pleasant coolness of the air after having endured the heat in New York for the past five summers.

Sue nodded. "Get yourself some jeans and a big cotton shirt. A straw hat, too, if you mean to plant that garden Jim mentioned."

90   *Becky Lee Weyrich*

Just then, they swung into Park Row and Angel caught her breath. If Jim had dreamed their daughter's name, Angel had seen this house in her own dreams, not just once, but many times. She knew it. She loved it. She wanted it!

She took in the whole scene in a glance. The green park called the Mall and across its lush expanse, Maine Street with its small stores and lazy traffic. No honking horns, no racing taxis, no screaming sirens, no hustling, tight-faced urbanites. Just small-town downtown. Slow-paced, clean, pretty, with spotless sidewalks and red geraniums in pots on the old-fashioned lamp posts. People nodded, spoke, and stopped to chat when they met on the street. A group of men—kibitzers at a checker game—stood around outside the barber shop with its candy-striped pole. A lady wearing a blue-flowered hat walked up the First Parish Church steps, carrying a large arrangement of flowers. Some boys on the Mall were playing kickball. Little girls were jumping rope. The whole scene looked like a Norman Rockwell painting.

"Here we are," Sue announced, parking the car beside a black wrought-iron spear fence.

Angel gazed out the window while Jim came around to open her door. The Joshua house was big and solid and permanent-looking. It needed a fresh coat of white paint and one of the black shutters hung down for want of a nail. But Angel refused to see these things. She saw instead a gleaming white home trimmed in pine green with laughter and music and love abounding in the rooms. She could smell bread baking—her bread—and see flowers blooming—her

ALMOST HEAVEN 91

flowers—and she could hear a child chattering brightly—her child.

Jim offered his hand to help her out of the car. When he did, he squeezed her fingers warmly. "You've already decided, haven't you? You're in love with this place without even seeing the inside."

Angel smiled up at him. "I'm afraid so. But we can look all you like, darling."

Before Sue led them inside, she took them on a guided tour of the fenced yard. Climbing pink roses, much in need of trimming, trailed along the fence. Several lilac bushes on the right side of the house—the side toward the Bowdoin campus—sheltered a white gazebo. Across the wide backyard was the garden, long fallen into disuse, but offering promise in spite of its tangle of zinnias, hollyhocks, and daisies. Blueberry bushes formed a hedge at the back of the lot, and the side of the house, shaded by tall pines, would provide the perfect play area for Hope as she grew. Angel could imagine happy sounds coming from this grassy patch as her daughter played there with friends.

"A swing set," Angel said suddenly, interrupting Jim's question to Sue about the water and electric meters.

He and the agent both turned to stare at Angel, then laughed in unison.

"I was just thinking out loud," Angel explained with a blush. "This will be a perfect place for a swing set—later on."

Jim put an arm around Angel's shoulders and gave her a gentle squeeze. "We're expecting in December," he explained to Sue. "Our first."

"Well, congratulations!" Sue beamed at the two of

them. "Then you *are* looking for a special place to buy. I don't want to pressure you, but this could be it. It's a wonderful house for bringing up children. Actually, it's much like the house I grew up in. I can remember to this day the feel of that dear old place and its warm smells, how the sun slanting through the windows looked when it lit up the waxed oak floors, how the starlight seemed magnified through the bubbled glass windows." She hugged herself, paused, then looked at them and laughed. "How I do go on! But I had a happy childhood, lots of wonderful memories. And the house *was* very much like this one."

"What about this one?" Jim asked. "Do you know its history?"

Sue nodded enthusiastically. "Oh, yes! Everyone around here knows about the Joshua house. D'Angelo Joshua built it for his bride back before the Civil War on the site of the log cabin where he was raised. You can still see the foundations down in the cellar. Lexie Mallette was the belle of Wiscasset, the youngest daughter of a timber tycoon who really would have preferred she remain at home, a spinster, to care for him in his old age. But she was a headstrong girl, and when she met Mr. Joshua, one of her father's business clients, she fell in love immediately, so the story goes. He was older than she was by several years, but a handsome, dashing character who had broken many a heart from Boston to Bangor before he set eyes on Lexie. Still, they had to wait several years before they could marry. Old Mr. Mallette, Lexie's father, refused to allow Joshua to have her until he could provide a perfectly furnished home larger and finer than the Mallette place in Wiscasset. He also required that

ALMOST HEAVEN 93

Joshua have a certain amount put away in the bank before the wedding. So, Joshua went to sea for several years to make his fortune in the slave trade. For two years, Lexie didn't see or hear from her betrothed. He was presumed lost. Then, suddenly, one day he walked up to the Mallette house and demanded that Lexie's father give him his true love's hand at last. He'd built her this house, furnished it with the finest things he could buy, and he had a sizable bank account left. Lexie by this time was an old maid of twenty-two. But they say she made a beautiful bride when she married her love. She and D'Angelo married here in the garden. They planted those lilac bushes to mark the spot."

"What a beautiful story!" Angel exclaimed.

"That's not the end," Sue added. "The Civil War soon separated the lovers again. Lexie lost their child while D'Angelo was away. But soon after he returned she had a son. Too soon. Joshua knew it, even though he'd came home more dead than alive, so the story goes."

"Oh, that's so sad!" Angel cried, clinging to Jim's arm.

Sue looked at Angel, a strange, solemn expression on her face. "Not sad, really. Just the way of things. As it turned out, he outlived his wife by many years. She drowned in the river in a freak accident, leaving General Joshua to raise the lad alone. But the pair had good times together. You can tell by the happy vibes in this house. Come on. I'll show you. Let's go inside."

Although the climbing sun outside had already pushed the temperature up, the moment Sue opened the front door, Angel felt a rush of cool, musty air. It smelled of history and home, inviting them in.

Angel had known she would like the place before she ever saw it, but she was unprepared for the impact of the house once she stepped inside. The heavy, moss green, twill and velvet drapes were drawn, throwing the interior into deep shadow. However, the hallway and the twin parlors at the front of the house were drenched in sunshine and warmth. Through the windows on the right, she could see lavender lilacs in bloom, a spring breeze ruffling their clusters of fragrant blossoms. From somewhere at the back of the house, Angel heard a woman singing softly, "Amazing Grace." She heard children laughing and a dog barking.

Hearing a step above on the stair, she glanced up. A man stood there on the second-floor landing. He was tall and rather handsome in an old-fashioned sort of way. Long coat, long hair, long beard. The coat had an empty sleeve. When his penetrating blue eyes met Angel's, he looked startled for an instant. He seemed about to speak to her. Then he vanished.

The sunshine went with him. It seemed he drew all the light and music and beauty away with him, leaving the old house as it really was—gloomy and musty, the drapes drawn tightly against the bright summer sun. Angel realized with a start that she was standing in the dark hallway of a silent, empty house.

No, not empty. Jim and Sue Chamberlain stood nearby. Sue was apologizing for something.

"I'm sorry, but the power's been cut off. I'll have to open some of the drapes so you can get a good look at the place."

ALMOST HEAVEN 95

Jim touched Angel's arm. "Is anything wrong, sweetheart?"

"What?" Angel started at the sound of his voice.

"You're trembling. You look so pale."

"Like I've seen a ghost?" she asked in a faltering voice. She was pretty sure that was exactly what had happened. The funny thing was, the apparition hadn't frightened her. Not in the least. He'd seemed familiar somehow, almost as if she knew the one-armed man. Of course that was impossible. Still, a sort of intimacy had existed between them for the few seconds of her vision.

"Sue, do you happen to know what General Joshua looked like?" Angel asked.

"Why, yes, I do. His portrait hangs in the museum over at the college. He was one of Bowdoin's early graduates. But the painting was done in later years, after he gained prominence in the community, after he'd lost an arm in the war. If memory serves, he was tall, rather thin, and he had long hair and an even longer beard."

Angel laughed nervously.

"Funny, I can't remember whether his hair's light or dark, but I sure remember those blue eyes," Sue went on. "You know the kind—they seem to follow you around the room, looking right into you."

A shiver ran through Angel. That's him, she thought. That's the very man I saw at the head of the stairs. She glanced back up, but the spot where General Joshua had appeared was now only a deep, empty cluster of shadows.

Sue's voice interrupted Angel's thoughts again. "The two front parlors would be perfect for your liv-

96 *Becky Lee Weyrich*

ing room and dining room, don't you think? Now, follow me, please. The back of this house is my favorite part."

Jim took Angel's arm and led her along the wide hallway. "Are you sure you're okay, honey?"

"I'm fine," she answered. And she was, but she had such an odd feeling. She could still see the man's bright blue eyes and sense his intense gaze upon her. Why had the sight of her seemed to startle him so? What was going on here? Were they about to move into a *haunted* house?

"As I warned you earlier, and you can certainly see for yourselves," Sue said, "the place needs a decorator's hand. But can't you just imagine this big kitchen painted bright yellow with the breakfast nook papered in a wildflower pattern?"

"Oh!" Angel cried. "A bay window overlooking my garden. Jim, won't it be beautiful? I'll cook us a huge breakfast every single morning, just so we can sit here and gaze outside. We'll need a birdfeeder, too, right there"—she pointed—"between the house and the edge of the garden."

Sue beamed at them, confident of a quick and easy sale. Then she motioned them back toward the central hallway. "Come this way. I have a surprise for you, Dr. Rhodes."

She led them into the library across from the homey kitchen. Angel heard Jim let out a low whistle when they entered the oak-paneled room. Tall windows at the end filled this space with mellow light. One wall was covered with floor-to-ceiling bookcases. A sliding library ladder provided access to the upper shelves. The corresponding wall on the other side had a cen-

ALMOST HEAVEN

tered fireplace with a marble mantel and more shelves to either side.

As Jim moved silently about the empty room, Angel knew he was mentally arranging furniture—his father's desk, stored for all these years, the leather sofa and matching wing chair that her parents had earmarked for their new son-in-law when they sold their large home in Maryland shortly after the wedding to move to a retirement condo on Florida's west coast. From Pete Gentry's home office Jim had also inherited a fine antique library table, several lamps, and a hand-tooled Moroccan leather ottoman.

Jim turned to Angel, grinning like a kid. "We'll finally have a space large enough to hang our wedding portrait, honey. Right over this mantel."

"And what a perfect place to work on your play, darling."

Jim was flushed with excitement.

After checking the pantry, the mud room, and the bathroom downstairs, they followed Sue to the second floor. "There's an attic above that has always been used as the children's playroom in winter. And, of course, there's a full basement and a root cellar."

"Plenty of space," Jim commented.

"Yes, plenty," Sue assured him.

Angel hurried ahead of them. She found the nursery. A sunny room overlooking the garden, at the south corner of the house. Ignoring the age-stained cabbage roses on the old wallpaper, she imagined tiny pastel angels flying about, singing a "Heavenly Lullaby."

"Jim, come look!" she cried. "Isn't it perfect?"

It seemed to Angel that *everything* was perfect. For

98 *Becky Lee Weyrich*

the next two hours, as they looked at other places Jim wanted to see, Angel just bided her time. She didn't want the new, efficient doctor's home on Thompson Street or the older place they looked at on narrow Cumberland Street. The place on Orr's Island was quaint and charming, but that would mean a long and treacherous drive for Jim in the wintertime. Besides, Angel had found her home. If she had to share it with a ghost, that was okay. He seemed harmless enough.

The three of them were sitting at a table by the front window of the Bowdoin Cafe, having a late lunch of cold lobster salad—Sue's treat.

"Would you like to go back and look at any of the places a second time?" the agent asked politely, already certain of what their answer would be. She'd been in the real-estate business long enough to recognize that gleam in a client's eye. And Angel Rhodes certainly had that look.

Neither Angel nor Jim spoke. Jim cut his eyes toward his wife. Her head was down as if her concentration was centered on a large clump of lobster meat she was chasing around her plate. She knew Jim had really liked the place on Thompson Street. What if he asked to see it again? She'd burst into tears, she just knew she would. She wanted the Joshua house on Park Row. *That* was their home! It was meant to be!

After a long pause, Jim said, "I don't think there's any need to look anymore, Sue. But you might run us back to the Joshua house so we can take some measurements. Then, if there's a wallpaper store in town, I think Angel would like to do some browsing."

Angel dropped her fork, flipping the piece of lobster

ALMOST HEAVEN

halfway across the room as she threw herself into Jim's arms. She was sobbing.

"Jim, oh, Jim! You won't be sorry. It's a wonderful place. And we'll make it into a real home."

"I know, sweetheart. I love it as much as you do. Now, let's go measure the nursery, then see if we can track down your 'Heavenly Lullaby.' "

"Did Jim and Sue see your ghost?"

Angel gazed at Alexander's glowing eyes to see if he was making fun of her. Or making fun of her ghost. But, thinking about it, when you got right down to it, wasn't he a ghost, too? What right had he to poke fun?

She said in a slightly accusing voice, "That's what you were when I was only four and you found me and my folks couldn't see you. So, no, I don't suppose Jim or Sue saw General Joshua's ghost."

"I was different."

"Different how?"

"I was a spirit guide, not a ghost."

Angel shrugged. "Dead's dead! I don't see any difference."

"That's because you're new at this. When you saw me at Disney World, can you remember what kind of shoes I was wearing?"

"Shoes?"

He gave her a quick, curt nod. "Shoes! You heard me correctly."

Angel stared off into space—dark space only moments ago that was now glowing with shifting, rainbow colors. After a moment of thought, she grinned. "Yeah! I do. You were wearing old run-down basket-

100 *Becky Lee Weyrich*

ball sneakers with the sides out and no laces. They were awful!"

"No, they were stylish at the time, at least in some teenage circles. My point is, you'll never see a ghost wearing Reboks, spike heels, wingtips, or run-over basketball sneakers."

"What kind of shoes do they wear?"

"None. They've got no feet."

Angel gave her companion a suspicious smirk. "You're putting me on."

"Cross my heart!" And he did. "We can't lie up here."

Angel closed her eyes and concentrated. In her mind she recreated every detail of General Joshua's person. But for the life of her, she couldn't picture his feet. Finally, she admitted as much to Alexander.

"So you bought a haunted house."

"I never thought of it that way. That's scary. General Joshua was never frightening. I sort of thought of him as my guardian angel."

A dramatic change took place in the color of Alexander's glow. His whole form pulsed green—a seriously jealous shade of sickly yellow-green. "You have only *one* guardian angel, Angela." His voice rumbled like thunder, causing her to step away.

"You?" she ventured rather timidly.

He nodded, then reached out and enveloped her in his glow. "And don't forget it," he said more gently. "We go a long way back, you and I."

"Really?" The idea fascinated her. "Tell me about us."

"That will have to wait until later. Right now the

ALMOST HEAVEN 101

topic is you, Angela. You and the life you've just left down there. Tell me what happened in Maine."

He was still holding her in his glow, but his light had changed back to a normal shade—a warm, protective, loving golden blue. She found it difficult to sort out her thoughts with Alexander this close, actually touching her, surrounding her.

"You'll have to give me space if you want me to go on."

He obliged, then said quietly, "You've always wanted your own space, haven't you? That hasn't changed through all eternity."

"I suppose. Yes! I need my own space. That's why New York was not for me. That's why I loved Maine. That's why I have to go back."

"I won't crowd you," Alexander promised. "I should have known better after all the lives we've shared."

Angel stared hard at her spirit guide, trying to summon some memory of their lives together. But it was no use. Whatever lay between them, that was Alexander's secret. And he wasn't about to give her any clues until he was good and ready. For now, she would concentrate all her will on getting back to Jim.

She closed her eyes and tried to conjure up those happy months in Maine. It seemed, though, that a shadow lay over the memories, tarnishing the bright autumn sunlight, dirtying the pure white snow, sending a warning chill through her soul.

Chapter Five

"I'm afraid to go on."

"Why? I thought your time in Maine was the happiest in your life."

"You're right. It was the best time of all—our move and Hope's birth. Our first Christmas as a family."

"Then what's bothering you?"

"At the end of the best time comes the worst time."

"What's the worst time? Do you mean coming up here? But everyone knows that this is the best part of all."

"Not without Jim and Hope."

"You still have both of them, Angela. They'll be a part of you forevermore. They live in your heart just as you live on in theirs. You can look down and see them anytime you want to."

"I can?" she cried excitedly. Then she lowered her gaze, smile fading. "It wouldn't be the same."

"Nothing stays the same, Angela. 'Time marches on,' as the old newsreels used to say." He waited. She made no reply. Gently, he said, "You have to tell it,

ALMOST HEAVEN 103

Angela. Never start what you aren't prepared to finish."

She glared at him. "That's a fine thing for you to say! I wanted to finish what I started. I wanted to take care of my husband and raise our daughter. But you people brought me up here before I had a chance to finish."

"You begged to come."

"I never!"

He offered a gentle reminder. "Don't you recall, Angela? When you lost control of the car, you prayed for this."

"No! I loved life! I'd never have prayed to die."

"Believe me. You may not remember now, but it will come back to you. It was the most fervent prayer of your life. In the spin, that split second when you knew you were going to crash. What went through your mind then?"

Tears pooled in Angel's blue eyes. "I remember thinking, Dear God, save my baby!"

"That was only part of it. You made a deal, a trade—your life for Hope's."

Her temper flared. "That's outrageous! Everyone knows you can't make deals with God."

"No, you can't. But it was an especially busy time up here. I happened to be on the receiving end of that prayer since all the direct circuits were tied up. You made your deal with me. You see, Hope was too young; she hadn't chosen her own spirit guide yet. So I had my hands full at the moment, looking out for the two of you. I couldn't save you both, and there wasn't much time. You took the decision out of my hands.

104 *Becky Lee Weyrich*

You begged God to take you instead of your baby. It was a noble request. I honored it."

"So you're saying this is all *my* fault?"

"No, not *your fault,* but a star in your heavenly crown."

Angel reached up and felt her head. "I don't feel any crown."

"You haven't received it yet."

"When?"

"When you're ready to accept it and wear it with pride, without regret."

"You mean, when you can talk me into going into that light."

"It's not just any light, you know. It's THE LIGHT."

"I'm not ready."

"I'm aware of that. So, get on with your story."

A pleading look.

A nod. "Yes, you must, Angela. Tell me about Maine."

"Maine," she repeated wistfully.

"Start wherever you like."

A lengthy pause followed before Angel finally spoke. "You say we moved into a haunted house. But I say our lives were touched by magic from the day we first saw the old place on Park Row."

"Describe this magic for me."

She looked up at the tall spirit guide through dewy eyes, remembering. "How do you describe love? Does it have a color? Or a special scent? A specific shape? I think not. And love was the magic."

"Then show me that love," begged Alexander, his voice sounding far off and hushed with wonder.

"I'll do my best. That's all I can promise."

ALMOST HEAVEN

* * *

Although modest about her organizational talents, Angel proved to be a miracle worker when it came to handling details of their move. Jim was excited, but not much help—distracted by all the imminent changes and lost most of the time in his own thoughts. As soon as they'd signed papers on the house and before they'd left Maine, Angel had lined up carpenters, painters, plumbers, and electricians so that by the time the movers came to pick up their meager belongings from the tiny apartment in New York, the house on Park Row glistened with new paint, hummed with state-of-the-art wiring, and smelled inside of crisp wallpaper and plush carpeting. Clean surfaces were everywhere. All the locals had watched for weeks in pleasure and awe as the old Joshua place was reborn.

It was a Friday, and the Brunswick Farmers' Market was in full swing on the Mall that cool, bright August morning when Jim and Angel moved in. The eyes of the whole town cut curious glances their way.

"Ayah! It's a dandy," remarked one of the checker players outside the barbershop on Maine Street. "Them Rhodeses have sure made the old Joshua place shine."

"City folk!" grumped his opponent, scowling as his king got jumped.

"May be," conceded the other player, "but like as not they'll stay a spell. Hear tell, his folks was from Rockport or thereabouts."

"Go on with you!"

"It's a fact! His mother, anyhow. Born and raised up there, so they say—ayah."

106 *Becky Lee Weyrich*

Both men fell silent and keened their sights on the big moving van that drew up just then to park outside the old Joshua place. A green station wagon pulled up behind it. A minute later, they watched the handsome redheaded woman and her bearded professor husband climb out. When the pair caught them staring and waved across the Mall, the two men looked, quickly, back down at their checkerboard.

"The checker game is still in progress," Angel pointed out to Jim. She was grinning like a kid, so excited she could hardly keep from bouncing up and down.

Jim laughed. "I doubt if they've been at it the whole time since we left last month. They do have to sleep."

"I don't know," she answered. "My guess would be that same game has been going on, shine or snow, for a century or more. They just switch players from time to time, when somebody needs to stretch his legs, change his long johns, or wring out his socks."

"Mrs. Rhodes, where do you want the piano?" one of the movers called.

Angel sprinted through the gate, across the yard, and up the steps. "Follow me, guys."

All day long, the hefty movers trekked back and forth, hauling furniture into the house. And all day long, the crowd around the checkerboard watched, their numbers growing and shifting with every hour.

"How you reckon they crammed all that stuff in one of those little, tiny places in the city?"

"You been to New York?"

"Never been, never going!"

"Then how'd you know the people there live in small places?"

ALMOST HEAVEN 107

"Stands to reason. Things is built up, not out there. I seen pictures."

The checker player was right. All that big, heavy furniture that had them wondering all day had been in a warehouse in Maryland for several years. It belonged to Angel's parents, but when they'd moved to Florida, they had stored it for their daughter's future use. Most of it was antique, heavily carved and solidly built. It was perfect for the Joshua house, what the curator down the street at the Pejepscot Historical Society would have called "period pieces."

Angel made her first new friend that day. It was lunchtime. The movers were taking a break and Jim was in his library, unpacking treasured books he hadn't had room to display since they married. She wandered out into the front yard, wiping the perspiration from her brow. The day had gone from cool to hot, at least for those who were pregnant and working hard.

Gazing out over the Mall, Angel shaded her eyes and smiled. The lush green park swarmed with colors and activity. Picnickers had spread their blankets under trees to consume their purchases on the spot. Children jumped rope or played ball. In addition to the twenty or so vendors, selling everything from vegetables to hand-knit woolens to spiced vinegars, the townspeople were out in force on this lovely day.

Angel sniffed the fragrant breeze. The scents of fresh vegetables, spicy peppers, and lamb roasting on an open grill made her realize how hungry she was. There wasn't a morsel of food in the house. She was about to

108 *Becky Lee Weyrich*

head across the Mall to the grocery store for sandwich fixings when a tall, wiry woman in baggy overalls and a floppy straw hat approached the gate, a basket over her arm and a potted jade plant in her hand.

"Morning!" the woman called. "Moving in, ayah?"

Angel smiled, then glanced about at the furniture littering the yard and the massive moving truck blocking Park Row. "How could you tell?"

Ignoring Angel's remark, the stranger said, "And you in a family way! You must come of stout stock to be working so. On an empty stomach, I vow."

Angel nodded and touched her grumbling belly. "You're right about that. My cupboards are bare. I was just about to walk over to the store and stock up on a few things."

"No need," the woman said, holding out the basket toward Angel. "We figured as how you and your man might need something that would stick to your ribs about now. It's from all of us over on the Mall." Then she handed Angel the plant. "Don't eat this. It's for your kitchen window. You folks look to be the sort that like some green things growing about you."

Angel accepted the gifts with a smile of gratitude.

The woman stuck out her hand like a man. "I'm Cora Shute from Peaks Island. Welcome!"

"I'm happy to meet you, Mrs. Shute. I'm Angela Rhodes." Just then, Angel caught a whiff of the food in the basket. "Hmmm! It smells wonderful. Thank you so much."

"Call me Cora. Everybody does. And think nothing of it. It's just a bit of this and that to get you through the day. Well, I best be getting back now. Got lobsters to sell and a line of folks waiting."

ALMOST HEAVEN 109

Angel was disappointed. She liked the gaunt-faced, straight-backed woman. She admired her directness and the firm grip of her handclasp. Most of all, she liked the youthful gleam in the steel gray eyes—eyes that matched the color of her braided hair.

"Won't you come in for a visit?" Angel asked.

"Some other time, thank you. Business to tend to just now. Don't you work too hard and strain that baby now, you hear?"

Angel flashed another grateful smile. "I'll be careful, Cora. I promise."

"You see you do that."

Once Cora left, Angel took the basket inside. She removed the red-and-white checkered napkin to find cold lobster salad, grilled lamb, baked beans, blueberry corn bread, and an assortment of pies, cakes, and cookies. There was also a quart jug of cider from one of the apple farmers in Bowdoinham.

"Jim!" she called from the kitchen. "Come see what we have for lunch."

He ambled in from his study across the hall, grinning like a kid on Christmas morning. "Wait till you see my books, Angel. There's room for everything and some to spare. No more stacks on the floor and all over the desk." He stopped and sniffed the air. "What's that I smell?"

"Lunch, darling." She spread their feast on the kitchen table. "Come have some. A woman named Cora Shute brought us all this from the farmers over on the Mall."

They sat in their sunny yellow kitchen with papered wildflowers climbing the walls around the bay window and shared their first meal in their new home. Food had never tasted so wonderful. Life had never been so sweet. Love had never glowed more brightly for Jim and Angel Rhodes.

From that day on, Cora became a fixture in their lives. They soon learned that her heart was as soft as her features were hard. Her tough, weathered look came not by accident. Widowed for the past five years, she had manned her husband's lobster boat after his death, "to keep body and soul together," as she said. But now "some yuppie city folks" were interested in buying her old saltbox house over on the island. She was thinking it might be wise at her age—she'd never say exactly what that was—to sell out and move to the mainland. She did just that in late September, renting an apartment on nearby Potter Street in Brunswick. But as time went by and Angel grew heavier with child, Cora could be found more often at the old Joshua place helping out than in her own tidy quarters.

She arrived one morning early, looking disgruntled and upset.

"Come in, Cora," Angel invited. "What's wrong? You aren't sick, are you?"

"Sick at heart." The older woman sighed and shook her head. "I should have stayed on Peaks Island. I just don't think like a mainlander."

"What is it?" Angel set a cup of coffee in front of Cora and sat down across the table from her.

"Well, back on the island, you see, we thought nothing of taking in a stray dog if it wandered up. As for cats, nobody owned any. They just lived about, going from house to house to catch our mice and beg hand-

ALMOST HEAVEN
111

outs at suppertime." She smiled, remembering. "They were all the long-haired, six-toed variety that captains in the olden days always carried on their ships for luck. People nowadays call them Maine coon cats, but there's no coon to 'em." She rubbed a hand over her eyes and sighed again. "Lordy, how I do ramble when I'm out of sorts!"

"There's no hurry, Cora. Take your time. Tell me what's bothering you."

She looked at Angel, her eyes blazing. "That's just it! There ain't no time! They'll be doing away with that black pup 'fore the day's out, and it's all my fault."

"A puppy?"

Cora nodded. "The day I moved in, I found this big friendly pup roaming around the neighborhood like he was looking for his mama. Like as not, somebody just dropped him off to get rid of him. Well, as I said, I was never one to refuse a stray. I took him home, fed him, made him a nice bed in a basket, and he seemed happy as a clam. Then my landlord hears him whimpering and tells me no dogs allowed. He claims that puppy's going to grow into a monster, way too big for my apartment."

Angel's eyes were shining. A dog—a big, black dog. Just like the retrievers she'd had as a child. "What did you do with him, Cora?"

"I put him outside in an old dog pen back of the house on Potter Street, just till I could find him a good home. But this morning he was gone—dug right under the fence. I asked around on my way over here. Some boys told me they saw the dogcatcher put him in the back of his truck." Cora shook her head and gave a shudder. "Today's the day they put them to sleep."

Angel was out of her chair in a flash. She grabbed her purse, then grabbed Cora's arm. "Come on! We don't have a minute to lose."

"What's going on?" Cora protested.

"I want that dog! You have to come with me. Show me where the pound is and which one's The Monster."

"Well, land sakes! I didn't know you wanted a dog. I would have brought him to you."

Angel drove like crazy. Ten minutes later they arrived at the pound. It was a sad place, but clean enough, and the attendants seemed eager to find homes for the strays. The unhappy fact was that there were just too many dogs and not enough homes.

As Angel and Cora filed past the rows of cages, puppies and grown dogs alike bounded at them barking, whining, begging to be set free and loved. Tears came to Angel's eyes as she passed by each beagle, basset, and Heinz 57, searching for Cora's black pup.

"There he is!" Cora cried. "Down in the very last cage. Thank the Lord!"

The two women hurried toward the bouncing, whimpering animal.

"Why, he's a Labrador!" Angel exclaimed. "And he's going to be a big fellow, if those paws are any indication."

One of the attendants hurried over, eager to finalize an adoption. "Is this the one you're looking for, ladies?"

"The very one," Cora said, beaming and muttering baby talk to the dog.

Seconds later, "The Monster," as they agreed to call him, was out of the cage and in Angel's arms. He licked her all over, yipping and squirming with joy.

ALMOST HEAVEN   113

"Well, if that don't beat all!" Cora said with a chuckle. "I never saw a dog take to anybody so fast. He was right standoffish with me at first."

As if to make up for ignoring his savior, Monster reached over and gave Cora a good lick in the face.

Angel held the puppy up and looked him right in those big, brown eyes. "Now, let's get you home and give you a good bath before you meet Jim. He's going to be thrilled."

And Jim was . . . once they broke The Monster of chewing up his newspapers, his bedroom slippers, and his favorite pipes. The big black pup soon became a member of the family—always underfoot, always well fed, always loved by his people.

By October, The Monster was housebroken, Angel was looking seriously pregnant, and Jim was busy writing his play in his every spare minute.

Cora's business dealings were settled by then, too. She sold her husband's lobster boat along with the house. "I hope Cap'n Shute won't be spinning in his grave the first time them young folks take the old tub out for a pleasure cruise," she told Jim and Angel, laughing, but wiping at a few sentimental tears. "That boat's like me, though. Ayah! It's worked hard all its life, and I reckon it needs a little relaxation before its time comes for drydock."

Angel wouldn't have called any facet of Cora's life relaxing. With no more lobsters to sell, she went a couple of weeks without setting up a stand at the Farmers' Market on Tuesdays and Fridays, but then said she missed her friends and the plain-out fun of those May

114 *Becky Lee Weyrich*

through November days on the Mall. So Cora set to baking. Pies, cakes, cookies, bear claws, Indian pudding. Her new stall was an immediate and unqualified success, so much so that she invited Angel to help her out on market days. Angel agreed, bubbling with enthusiasm. They moved the whole baking operation to her larger kitchen on Park Row, and soon their stand expanded to include Angel's homemade Christmas decorations—pine-cone wreaths, velvet-covered balls, patchwork stockings, and crocheted angels. From October through Thanksgiving, the two women were always together and always busy. Laughingly, the women called their enterprise "Fertile Minds and Nimble Fingers." Jim surprised them with a hand-lettered sign to display at their stand.

The day the market closed for the season, the November day of the first heavy snow, Angel turned to Cora with a wistful sigh as they drank hot chocolate at the kitchen table. "I don't know when I've ever worked so hard or had so much fun. I hate to see it end."

"Well, to my way of thinking, it's high time," Cora said. "Why, just look at you! That baby's right ripe. Could come any day. Time you were resting up for the birthing."

That evening, Angel stood alone at the kitchen window, watching the heavy snow swirl, turning twilight into early darkness. She turned on one of the outside lights and watched the delicate flakes dance like fairies in the shining beam.

She loved this time of day. She would make a pot of tea and sit at the kitchen window, watching for Jim to walk through the pines of the campus, cross Bath

ALMOST HEAVEN 115

Road, then take the shortcut up to their own back door. When he'd shucked off coat, scarf, and boots in the mud room, he'd step into the kitchen and into his wife's arms. Then, as dinner simmered on the stove, filling the air with enticing aromas, they'd sip their cups of hot tea with honey and lemon while they shared their day's experiences.

Tonight when Jim came through the kitchen door, he gave Angel an especially warm hug. "How're my girls?" he whispered after he'd kissed her long and thoroughly.

"Warm and cozy," she answered, "and perfectly happy now that you're home. We missed you, darling."

He grinned, always pleased to hear that he'd been missed. "You'll get your fill of me next week. I'll be underfoot all the time."

"Oh!" Angel cried. "Thanksgiving holidays! I'd completely forgotten." She snuggled close, as close as she could in her condition, and hugged him again. "That'll be wonderful, Jim, having you here at home for a whole week."

"You say that *now*," he teased.

"You know I mean it, darling."

The phone on the wall by the stove rang just then. "Oh, no," Angel moaned. "Don't tell me. Someone at the college is calling to remind you of a meeting you forgot."

Jim frowned, thinking. "No. I don't think so."

On the fourth ring, Angel reluctantly lifted the receiver, holding it with two fingers as if it were a snake that might bite. "Hello?" she said cautiously. Then she broke into a broad grin.

116 *Becky Lee Weyrich*

"Hi! How's my girl?"

"Daddy! Where are you?"

"We're here in Florida."

"Oh!" Her voice registered her disappointment. "You sound so much closer."

"Well, we may be soon, honey. We got your letter— the one inviting us to come up for Thanksgiving."

Her mother's voice broke in on an extension phone. "Are you sure you're ready for company, dear?"

"Of course we are. Besides, you and Dad aren't company. Jim has the whole week off. Your room is all ready. We'll have a wonderful time. Wait till you see our snow. It's gorgeous!"

"I guess that means I should leave my golf clubs at home."

"Unless you want to play with a black ball, Dad."

Jim motioned that he wanted to talk and Angel handed him the phone.

"Hello, Pete. Shirley. How are you?"

"Fat, tan, and lazy," Shirley answered with a laugh. "I figured it would be good for Pete to get up there and burn off some calories shoveling snow."

"How long can you stay?" Jim asked.

"How long can you put up with your in-laws?" Pete replied.

"As long as it takes for this baby of ours to put in her appearance."

Jim looked at Angel. She was beaming and brushing at happy tears. Quickly, she reclaimed the phone.

"Mom, Dad, can you really stay till the baby comes?" Angel was almost too excited to talk.

"Well, of course!" Shirley answered. "Don't you think I want to be there to see my first grandchild?"

ALMOST HEAVEN 117

"When can you come?"

"How would next Tuesday suit you? We've booked a flight into Portland already."

"This is so wonderful!"

"Don't cry about it, sweetheart," Pete soothed.

"I'm just so excited. I can't wait for you to see the house and the college and the town. Oh, you'll love everything up here. And it all looks like a fairyland now with the snow. In fact, I wish you could stay for Christmas."

Shirley laughed into the phone. "I think you'll change your mind after the baby comes. You'll have your hands full without having houseguests. Besides, we've booked a cruise over Christmas. Do you know if they have Christmas trees in Jamaica, dear?"

"If not, we'll just curl up under a palm tree and sing carols," Pete put in.

"Time to wind this up, Pete," Shirley told her husband. " 'Wheel of Fortune' is about to come on."

"Can't miss that!" Pete answered with a chuckle. "We'll see you next Tuesday. We're on flight 715, arriving at the Portland airport at three in the afternoon. Can you pick us up, honey?"

"You bet! Jim and I will be there waiting. Have a good trip."

"We love you," her parents chorused.

"Love you, too. We'll see you Tuesday."

Angel stood for a moment, staring at the phone. Then she whirled around and hugged Jim. "Oh, it's so wonderful, darling! Our first Thanksgiving in our new home and Mom and Dad with us. And to have them here when the baby comes. I just can't tell you how happy that makes me."

118　　　　　　　　*Becky Lee Weyrich*

Jim held Angel tenderly and kissed her forehead, her eyelids, her nose, her mouth. "I can't tell you how good it makes me feel to see you so happy, sweetheart. I'd say this is the best time of our lives, but I expect it to get better and better as the years go by."

"Oh, yes!" Angel whispered. "Better and better and better."

Just as Jim bent down to kiss her again, Angel glimpsed General Joshua standing in the hallway. He didn't seem to share their joy. His pale face looked solemn and his blue eyes plainly held tears.

"What's wrong?" Angel whispered, alarmed more by the ghost's sad expression than by his sudden appearance.

"Nothing," Jim answered. "Not a thing in the whole world, sweetheart."

He held her and kissed her for a long, long time. Faced with such an overwhelming display of love and sweet emotion, General Joshua dissolved into the shadows. By the time Jim was done with Angel, she'd all but forgotten that the shade of the Civil War hero had paid them a second visit.

Pete and Shirley Gentry arrived right on time the following Tuesday. They came bearing soft, stuffed kittens and bunnies, a lace-trimmed flannel gown for Angel to wear in the hospital, and a diaper-changing apron for Jim that read "World's Greatest Dad."

Angel had hoped her parents would like their new home, but she was unprepared for the praise heaped on her by Shirley and Pete. They loved seeing their cherished, old furniture in such elegant surroundings.

ALMOST HEAVEN 119

Their guest bedroom was a special surprise. Angel had furnished it with the bedroom suite Pete had bought for Shirley as a wedding gift. Although this furniture, which had been termed "modern" in the 1960s, hardly matched the rest of the house, it suited the Gentrys perfectly.

"They called that light finish 'Hollywood Blonde,' " Shirley explained. "It was all the rage when we got married, and I was the first bride in my group to have it. I was so proud!" She turned to Pete with tears glistening in her eyes. "You couldn't have made me any happier if you'd given me diamonds and emeralds, dear."

Pete chuckled. "I *hope* you appreciated it! I was paying on that furniture for the first three years of our marriage."

Angel had coordinated the room beautifully. Pale gold carpeting complemented the modern wallpaper with its burgundy and hunter green diamonds on an antique ivory background. Wine-colored drapes matched the quilted satin bedspread, and the room glowed with warmth.

The day of Shirley and Pete's arrival was clear, as bright as an Austrian crystal. Wednesday it snowed, heavily, all day long. The four of them sat in the kitchen, drinking mulled cider and eating fresh pumpkin bread from Cora Shute's kitchen. They watched through the window as the winter fairy dressed the pines in shining white lace. The ground below became an unblemished counterpane covering the earth. Late in the afternoon, the swirl of heavy flakes diminished, and they moved to the front parlor, where Jim had laid a crackling fire of birch logs. They sipped sherry and

120 *Becky Lee Weyrich*

watched the Mall come alive. Children swarmed out from the neighboring houses to build snowmen, play hockey, and pelt each other with snowballs. Tiny bundles of padded clothing flitted over the pond on miniature ice skates.

Angel's eyes were drawn to one little girl, dressed all in pink, as she turned and pirouetted. She couldn't have been more than three or four.

"Look at her, Jim." Angel pointed. "That could be Hope a few years from now." Then a sad note crept into her voice. "But how will I teach her? I've never skated."

Jim slipped an arm around Angel's shoulder and gave her a hug. "Don't fret, darling. I'll teach you both."

She turned to stare at him. "I didn't know you could skate, Jim."

"You're in for a lot of surprises, honey. There are quite a few things you don't know about me. Back in the city, we never seemed to have enough time to get to know each other. I was a fair hockey player in high school."

Angel stared at him, trying to picture her sweet, mild-mannered poet, ferocious in pads and mask, slugging it out in the thick of a duel on ice. She grinned. "You're kidding me."

Jim smiled back. "Cross my heart. I made All-State my senior year."

"A man of many talents, your husband," Pete said.

"You've got that right, Dad!"

They all moved closer together before the front window and fell silent, watching the skaters.

The Gentrys were so entranced by the magic of their

ALMOST HEAVEN

daughter's new home that they completely forgot about "Wheel of Fortune" and "Jeopardy" that evening. At supper they caught up on all the latest news of friends and family. Shirley was amazed to hear that "little Tory" was fending so well for herself in the big city. In turn, she gave Angel a blow-by-blow of all the bridge and golf action in Florida. But first, last, and most of all, the two couples talked about the baby, the precious little girl who would soon become a part of the family. As dusk faded into darkness, calls went out from various houses around the Mall. One by one, the little snow people drifted home for supper. Street lights blinked on up and down Maine Street. The whole town looked clean and sparkling with its cover of new fallen snow.

After dinner they all turned in early. Jim built a fire in the bedroom grate while Angel dug an extra quilt out of the blanket chest. Any chill in the air soon vanished. They climbed into bed and lay in each other's arms, talking softly of the days to come—of the baby and of their first Christmas and of the New Year that would be like a new life for them both. They talked of Hope's first birthday party, her first day of school, her first date, her first love. Everything seemed perfect, with the golden glow of firelight dancing on the walls and the silver glow of lovelight dancing in their hearts.

Finally, happy beyond any happiness she had ever known, Angel drifted off to sleep. Jim was still holding her. He held her close all through the long winter night.

*   *   *

122 *Becky Lee Weyrich*

Thanksgiving Day dawned clear, blue, cold, and glistening. Cora arrived in time to attend church with the family at the little chapel on the Bowdoin campus. The snow crunched beneath their boots as they trooped through the tall, silent pines. Most of the town was still sleeping. Only a few early risers were up and about, most of them headed for the chapel.

Angel felt a special glow of love in her heart. Inside the snug church, with ribbons of tinted sunlight streaming through the stained-glass windows, she stood between her husband and her father, holding the hymnal as they lifted their voices in praise for the day. "Come Ye Thankful" soared to the rafters of the chapel and out over the campus and the Mall. By the time the service was over, Angel's spirits were soaring with those voices.

After the service, as they walked back across the silent, snowbound campus, she squeezed Jim's gloved hand and whispered, "Was there ever such a perfect day, darling, such a perfect life?"

He smiled down at her and blew her a phantom kiss.

Back at the house, the women launched themselves into a flurry of kitchen activities. Jim and Pete offered to help, but were quickly banished to the library. Cora ran the kitchen like a captain commanding a ship. "First, we need to get that bird on. Then we'll do vegetables. I already fixed the pumpkin and minced meat pies last night. We'll pop them into the oven when everything else is done cooking, so's they'll still be piping hot come time for dessert."

Once everything was roasting, boiling, or baking, a sudden lull descended over the kitchen. The three women, all smiling with the feeling of accomplish-

ALMOST HEAVEN

ment, settled at the table for tea. Pete stuck his head in the door.

"Is it safe to come in now?"

"Sure," Angel answered. "Tell Jim to join us, too. Would you like some tea? Or there's coffee on the stove."

Jim and Pete settled at the round oak table over steaming cups of black coffee, sniffing the air and feigning starvation.

"Well, you can't eat yet," Angel told them.

Cora sneaked a plate of oatmeal-raisin cookies out of her ever-present basket of goodies. "A couple of these won't hurt. They'll hold you till the bird's done. Help yourselves."

Over Angel's good-natured objections, the men dug in.

"Would you look at that!" Shirley said suddenly, staring out the window. "Are those Christmas trees already?"

"Ayah!" Cora answered. "Lots of folks around here put their trees up the day after Thanksgiving. So there's usually a stand or two that sets up their balsams and Scotch pines before the turkey's finished cooking."

Angel's blue eyes lit up. In New York they'd always gone out and bought a small tree, then brought it home in a taxi on Christmas Eve to decorate that night. But no one ever said they couldn't change that tradition. And what fun it would be to bring out all of the old ornaments and decorate the tree with the whole family there.

"Jim?" Angel reached across the table and touched his hand.

124 *Becky Lee Weyrich*

"Ah, she wants something," Pete said with a chuckle. "I'd know that look anywhere."

"Dad's right," she admitted. "I do want something. Why don't the two of you go out and get us a Christmas tree? We can put it up tomorrow, and Mom and Dad and Cora can help. Besides, I'm likely to be too busy to enjoy decorating once the baby comes."

The two men exchanged looks, then grins.

"I'll just tell you, Jim," said Pete, serious now, "I've been trying to get that angel that goes on top of the tree to light up for years. Never could make the dang thing work. But I'll bet between the two of us we can light her up. What do you say?"

Jim smiled at his wife and squeezed her hand. "I'm all for shining angels, Pete."

"Fine! Let's hitch up the team and go cut us a tree."

All the women were laughing and chattering with excitement. "Forget it, Pete," Shirley said. "I think you'd better just take Jim's station wagon and *buy* a tree."

The men were already donning coats, hats, and gloves, ready to dash out into the cold.

"Jim," Angel called as he was going out the door. "Get a *big* one!"

"Big and beautiful!" he promised. "Just like my wife." Then he ducked out quickly, and they were off.

The turkey was browned to perfection. The dressing, with chestnuts, was moist and crunchy. The sweet potatoes were dripping with butter, and were spiced with cinnamon, nutmeg, and ginger. The cranberries were plump, red, and tart, and the vegetables, home

ALMOST HEAVEN 125

grown, were as fresh as if they'd been picked the day before. Cora's yeast rolls were so light they had to have a napkin over them to keep from floating right off the plate, and her pies recalled happy memories of other Thanksgivings to everyone at the damask-covered dining table over which candlelight flickered, shining on the display of Angel's wedding china, crystal, and silver.

The only thing more wonderful than that first Thanksgiving at the old house on Park Row was the anticipation of putting up the Christmas tree the following day—a beautifully shaped, twelve-foot balsam that Jim and Pete had selected. Along with the Gentrys' furniture, antique ornaments passed down in the family for generations had been stored for the past few years. Decorating this tree with those lovely baubles would be like greeting old friends after a long, long time.

"I just can't wait," Angel said as they were finishing their pie and coffee. "I've been saving the box of ornaments for opening when it's time to decorate. But I think I'll have to tear into them as soon as we finish dinner." She turned to her mother. "Remember that old glass Santa Claus I always loved?"

"I certainly do, dear. Why, that was my favorite when I was a child. He dates back to the time before Santa started wearing a red suit. He was made in Germany, bought when your grandmother was a baby."

"I always liked the silver airplane," Pete put in. "You know, the one with the paper Santa in the cockpit and the wired tinsel wings and prop."

"That came from my grandfather's family," Shirley

said. "One of my great-uncles was a pilot in the First World War."

"I can't wait to see them all again," Angel enthused. "The ruby slipper, the snow-covered church, the tiny manger scene from Italy."

Jim cleared his throat. They all glanced his way. He was smiling like a man with a secret.

"I have a surprise for you, Angel. I was going to put it under the tree on Christmas morning. But I've changed my mind. If you'll excuse me a minute."

He rose and left the table. His footsteps echoed down the hallway. He went to the library, but returned within moments, carrying a small white box tied with a pink satin ribbon.

"Here, darling." He handed the gift to Angel. "I want to be the first to wish you a very merry Christmas."

Carefully, Angel untied the bow, then opened the box, only to find a profusion of white tissue paper. She dug out the round, wrapped surprise, then lifted it gently for all to see.

"Oh, Jim! A new Christmas ornament. It's so sweet. I love it!"

Inside the clear, iridescent ball lay a tiny baby in its pink and white cradle. Atop the glass bauble, a smiling angel spread her golden wings protectively over the sleeping child.

A hush fell over the room. They all stared at the ornament.

This was Hope. This was Christmas. This was love.

* * *

ALMOST HEAVEN

The tree Jim and Pete had brought home was a perfectly shaped evergreen of monumental proportions.

"If we put together all the trees we decorated over the five years we were in New York, they would be half the size of this one," Angel declared. "Oh, Jim, Dad, it's a beauty!"

The balsam's size was no problem since the front parlor had a fifteen-foot ceiling, and the gracefully boughed fir filled the front windows of the parlor. It would shed its glow over the Mall and all up and down Maine Street.

The decorating took all of the next day. Jim and Pete set the tree in its stand, then placed it upright and began to string the colored lights. Among the many strands were old-fashioned bubble lights, bulbs shaped like icicles, and others that resembled glowing candles. The women strung popcorn and cranberries while the men did the lights. Finally, the last strand was in place and the last bulb tightened in its socket. Jim walked over to the wall plug. He turned and grinned at the others.

"Countdown!" he announced.

"Ten, nine, eight, seven . . ." They all joined in. When they reached "Blastoff," Jim shoved in the extension cord plug and the tree came alive with twinkling lights. Everyone gave a cheer.

Angel would always remember that day as one of the happiest of her entire life. With a fire crackling on the parlor hearth, Christmas carols playing on the tape deck, and snow falling silently outside the windows, the people she loved most in the world helped her transform a noble evergreen into something wonderful and magical. Most of the day, Cora busied herself in

128 *Becky Lee Weyrich*

the kitchen, supplying a never-ending stream of food to the tree trimmers—turkey sandwiches, cranberry salad, pumpkin tarts, and silver mugs of eggnog frosted with nutmeg. By the time darkness settled over the town, the first Christmas tree in Brunswick, Maine, glowed with the promise of the season to come. All that remained was to place the antique satin angel on the very tiptop.

With great reverence and ceremony, Angel opened the age-stained box that held this precious memento. A hush fell over the room. Only the crackle of tissue paper intruded on the silence as the angel was unwrapped.

"She's still perfect," Angel whispered, holding up the prize for everyone to see. "Just look at her. Isn't she beautiful?"

"My grandmother made that angel," Shirley said.

Angel smiled. She had heard this tale all her life. It was as much a tradition as putting the angel on top of the tree.

"It was during the depression. There weren't going to be many presents under the tree that year. In fact, there was no money to buy a tree. Grandpa went out in the woods and cut a pitiful little pine. But Granny was determined not to disappoint my mother and Aunt Janet. For years, Granny had been a seamstress, making clothes for all the rich women in town. She had a scrap bag filled with satins, laces, and fancy brocades. Instead of buying gifts that year, she labored far into the night for weeks before Christmas, after Mama and Aunt Janet were asleep. She made beautiful doll clothes and this special angel to put atop the little pine tree. My mother always remembered that as the best

ALMOST HEAVEN   129

Christmas ever. She said their dolls had the finest wardrobes on the street—fancy ball gowns, feathered hats, even tiny lace gloves, and velvet purses. But the satin angel at the top of the tree was the most wonderful surprise of all. This one is the original. My mother and Aunt Janet drew straws to see who would get it. Granny made a second angel for Aunt Janet after Christmas. But this angel has always been the special one. She has blessed every Christmas tree and delighted every child in our family for the past sixty years."

Jim took the angel and with all due reverence placed her in the position of honor. All eyes followed his every move.

A moment of silence followed, the close group staring at the top of the tree, at the red satin angel with her gold lace wings and beautiful, smiling face.

"Soon," Angel said in a soft, quiet voice, "she'll have a new child to enchant."

Jim moved close to his wife and took her hand in his. "Our Hope," he whispered. "She'll be here *very* soon."

Jim's words proved prophetic. Hope arrived a week earlier than anyone had anticipated, a week to the day after the tree went up.

That Friday was a bitter cold morning. It had snowed heavily the night before—a wet snow that clung to branches and bent the slender birches to touch the ground. Angel woke to a virtual fairyland of white ice. The bright sun made everything glitter with a blinding brilliance.

130 *Becky Lee Weyrich*

She had slept deeply all night and she woke up late. When she finally opened her eyes, she heard voices downstairs. Her parents and Jim were already in the kitchen having breakfast. Her heavy body made her feel like an overfed cow whose feed had been drugged. She hauled herself out of bed and slipped on her warm blue robe and slippers, then groaned at the dull ache in her lower back.

"What do you expect?" she chided herself. "Carrying all this weight around is bound to make your back hurt."

But this morning's ache was different from the other twinges she'd suffered in recent weeks. This was more pronounced, more insistent. She took the stairs carefully, holding onto the railing with both hands and inching her way down. She stopped midway to catch her breath. The ache was now real pain.

"Do you suppose?" Her eyes lit up and she grinned. Then she shook her head. "Couldn't be. It's too soon."

Just then, Jim came into the hallway. "Angel? So you're finally up, sleepy head."

She was still on the stairs, hanging on for dear life as a wave of dizziness rushed over her and more pain wrenched her body. She held out one hand to Jim. She tried to smile down at him, but her lips were trembling, her whole body was shaking.

"Jim," she said breathlessly, "I think I need your help."

He was by her side instantly, his arm around her, supporting her weight.

"Take it easy, honey. Slowly, now. Just hang onto me."

ALMOST HEAVEN 131

By the time they reached the hallway, Angel was having a full-blown contraction. She let out a yip of surprise as much as pain.

"What is it? What's the matter, honey?" Jim didn't realize he was practically yelling in his panic.

"It's okay!" Deep breath. "It's okay, Jim! It's passing."

"What is?" he demanded.

Pete and Shirley were in the hall by now, roused from their waffles by Angel's cry and Jim's shout.

Shirley, dressed in a pink quilted satin robe with curlers in her hair, stood in front of Jim with her hands on her hips. "My word, son, don't you know what's going on? Angel's in labor! Here, let me help." She hurried to her daughter. "I'll get her to a chair in the kitchen. You go call her doctor, Jim, and the hospital."

Jim stood, dumbstruck, staring vacantly at his wife and mother-in-law. "She can't be. It's not time."

"Babies don't punch time clocks, my boy," Pete put in. "Why, Angel came two whole weeks early. I was out fishing. Shirley had to send up a flare to get me in. We barely made it to the hospital in time. The women in this family don't fool around. When they get ready, there's no time to waste."

"Really?" Jim said blankly. "It can happen that fast?"

Angel gave another groan.

"For heaven's sake, will you stop talking about it and *do* something?" Shirley shrilled at them.

The drive to the hospital was nerve-wracking on the icy roads. Angel sat in the front seat clutching the dashboard, white-knuckled with pain. Shirley and

132 *Becky Lee Weyrich*

Pete sat in the back, recounting other family birth tales, trying to distract their moaning daughter. Luckily, the hospital was only a few blocks away.

Within an hour of Angel's first pain, she was in the labor room. By late afternoon, she was in her private room with a warm, pink-and-gold bundle in her arms.

Jim had suffered through nearly an hour in the labor room with Angel, but he was no good at it. Finally, Shirley had taken over and ordered him to the waiting room to sit with Pete. Months before, Jim and Angel had talked excitedly about Jim's video taping the birth. It had seemed a grand idea at the time. But both of them were glad when the time came that the video camera had been left on the kitchen table in their hurry to get to the hospital. When the moment had come for Jim to join Angel in the delivery room, he'd gone weak in the knees and as pale as General Joshua's ghost. Both Angel and the doctor had decided he'd be better off staying with Pete.

So when Jim tiptoed in to see Angel a few minutes after she left recovery, he got his first glimpse of their baby daughter. From the look on his face, Angel knew that he had been through hell.

"Darling, we're both fine," she said to him in a tired voice. "Come here. Come look at her. She's perfect. She's beautiful."

Jim hurried to the side of the bed, leaned down, and kissed Angel's forehead. "I'm sorry I wasn't there."

"You're here now. That's all that matters, honey. Look! Isn't she wonderful?"

Jim's eyes strayed from his wife's face to their daughter's tiny form. His worried look vanished, replaced by a smile. He leaned down and touched his lips

ALMOST HEAVEN 133

to Hope's forehead, just below the red-gold fuzz that capped her head.

"She smells nice—all warm and sweet."

He touched his daughter's tiny fist with one finger. It uncurled and she wrapped her fingers around his. Tears sprang to his eyes.

"Oh, Angel," he murmured, "you've created a miracle."

Angel closed her hand over her husband's and daughter's. "We did it together, darling. We made magic, you and I."

He looked into Angel's eyes. "I love you," he said simply.

She smiled, kissed their baby, and then kissed him. "And we love you right back."

Hope uttered a faint whimper as if to let them know that she agreed.

Chapter Six

"Well? What happened next?" Angel's heavenly companion leaned closer, his face aglow with expectation.

"Mom and Dad came in with flowers and balloons, and Cora arrived with a cherry cobbler and everybody laughed and cried and oohed and aahed over Hope. Then a couple of days later we took her home—and it was Christmas." She said it all in one breath, no pauses, no details. She added, "And that about covers it."

"You mean that's it? That's all you're going to tell me?"

Angel gave a firm nod. "That's it! There's no more to tell."

"Angela, there *is* more! You can't just lop off your life story like that."

She refused to meet his direct gaze. "I don't remember the rest."

"I think you do," he said gently. "I think you'd like not to remember it. But once you begin, you have to tell the whole truth up here. You asked that I hear

ALMOST HEAVEN   135

your tale, and I granted you this time. A special dispensation, you might say. Now you have an obligation to tell everything. That's the way things work. The rest of the story, please."

Her blue eyes looked huge, magnified by pools of tears. "I can't. It's too painful. Let me stop here. I don't want to remember the rest. I just want to go back to Jim and Hope."

"You won't go anywhere, if you can't finish. You'll have to spend the rest of your time in limbo."

"Would that be so terrible?" she asked defiantly.

"No, not if you don't mind drifting around out of body for the rest of eternity. Having no form, no consciousness, being unable to see what's going on down below."

She whipped around to confront him. "You mean I wouldn't be able to see Jim? I couldn't watch Hope grow up?"

He nodded, his handsome face long with sadness. "Limbo is nothing, nowhere. It's a star that's gone out, an angel who's lost his wings, a life totally without meaning—one that's never recorded in Heaven's journal of time."

"You mean I'd just cease to exist? Poof! And I'm gone?"

"I'm afraid so," he answered, lowering his brows over troubled eyes. "But more than that, it would mean that you *never* existed."

Angel mulled over these words for a moment. "Then Hope—"

"There'd be no Hope. She'd never have been born if you hadn't existed."

"Jim?"

136   *Becky Lee Weyrich*

"A lonely bachelor, wearing mismatched socks."

"And my parents?"

"Childless and unhappy for it."

"That's not fair! You can't make other people suffer just because I can't remember what happened to me."

He shrugged. "We don't want anyone to suffer. It's your choice, Angela. What will it be? The whole truth or limbo?"

"You don't give a person much choice, do you?" she lashed out. She felt cornered, angry.

"Life is all about choices. As you'll recall, you're here now because of the final choice you made down there. And I have to tell you, I'm not sure that choice was wise. Hope would have been a much more cooperative angel candidate than you."

"No!" Angel yelled and thunder echoed in the distance. "Don't even mention such a thing! Hope has her whole life ahead of her."

"Maybe. It's up to you, Angela."

She glared at him, but softened when she saw the pleading and sympathy shining in his eyes.

"Is it all right if I tell you about Christmas first? I need to sort of work up to the other."

"I'm here to listen to whatever you want to tell me. Christmas would be nice."

"Christmas was more than just nice. It was perfectly wonderful!"

He nodded and smiled. "As Christmas was meant to be."

Until Christmas Eve, Angel hadn't been out since she'd brought Hope home from the hospital. They'd

ALMOST HEAVEN 137

had two weeks of foul weather—bitter cold and heavy snows. In fact, Jim told her, they'd had so much snow the piles pushed up by the snow plows down the center of Maine Street were now so high that driving along in your car you couldn't see over them to the other lane of traffic. Angel couldn't imagine such a thing.

On the morning of December the twenty-fourth, Angel woke with a start. Buttery sunlight was streaming in the bedroom windows, warming the red-and-white quilt on the bed. Jim was up already. She lay still for a minute, listening. By the muffled sounds drifting up from below, drawers and cupboards opening and closing, she could tell he was searching for something. Smiling, she wondered what he'd misplaced this time. She was about to call down and ask him when she heard Hope's soft cooing from the nursery across the hall.

At the sound of her daughter's tiny voice, a rush of overwhelming love filled Angel. She still could not believe it. Her own baby! Her own precious little Christmas child!

"Coming, darling," she called, pulling on her robe as she hurried across the hall.

The pastel wallpaper angels glowed on the sunny walls when she entered the nursery. The room was warm and cozy, decorated with love. Often when Angel entered the nursery, she'd find General Joshua standing guard over her child. But his shadowy presence never alarmed her. Somehow, she knew that he loved Hope as much as she did. He was there now, sitting in the rocker. Their eyes met for an instant, then he faded away, relinquishing the care of his precious charge to her mother. Angel wondered why no one else ever saw him. He was so often in evidence these days.

But she quickly forgot about her friendly, sad-eyed ghost in her eagerness to see her daughter. It seemed that Hope grew and changed each night while she slept. This morning, her cheeks were rosy, her blue eyes wide; and her cap of red-gold hair appeared to have thickened during the night.

"How's Mommy's little darling?" Angel cooed.

She reached down into the white crib and caressed the infant's cheek. Hope trilled the happy greeting she always reserved for her mother. She seemed to be trying to smile. Angel knew it was probably just gas, but the expression was sweet nonetheless. While she changed Hope's diaper, the baby pounded the air with her tiny fists, battling a wavering beam of sunlight.

"What're you doing, precious? Trying to catch that sunbeam?"

Hope's large blue eyes met her mother's. Already it seemed to Angel that she and her daughter were communicating. She could almost sense Hope's thoughts—*What am I doing here? Do I get to stay? Will you stay with me? Will you love me? I love you, Angel lady.*

"Yes, I love you, Hope. More than anything. Now, how about some breakfast?"

Angel lifted her warm, sweet-smelling infant in her arms and cuddled her, kissing her forehead. Then she settled in the antique rocking chair next to the crib and put Hope to her breast. She sang softly—an old tune her own mother had sung to her—as the baby nursed hungrily.

The warm sun, the intimate contact with her child,

ALMOST HEAVEN 139

and the quiet creak of the rocker all worked together to lull Angel into a kind of trance. Jim had been standing in the doorway, video camera in hand, filming his wife and daughter for some time before Angel realized he was there. She raised her drowsy eyes to his and smiled for him.

"Good morning," she whispered.

"It is a good morning, isn't it?" he answered. "The best morning ever. Turn your head just a little to the right, darling, so Hope's face isn't in shadow."

"If I do, do I get a kiss?" she asked.

"You bet! In a minute. I just want to get a little more of this on film. The two of you make such a pretty picture." He paused and stared at them as if he were seeing them both for the first time. He seemed almost surprised to find them under his roof.

"What is it, Jim?"

He shook his head and grinned, seeming embarrassed. "Nothing really. It's just, I never knew"—he stammered—"I never understood before that I could feel so much . . ."

His voice cracked. He lowered the camera and came toward Angel. Kneeling beside her, he put his arms around her and Hope, then reached up and kissed Angel before kissing Hope. His daughter cooed with delight and gripped his beard in her tiny fingers. Already, it was clear that she was Daddy's girl.

Sensing that the rest of the family was together and that he was being left out, Monster ambled into the room and circled several times before he sank heavily onto the rug at Angel's feet. He closed his eyes with a satisfied sigh.

"Good dog," Jim said, patting the Labrador's shiny

140 *Becky Lee Weyrich*

black head. "You're going to get a special piece of Christmas turkey tomorrow."

"Christmas?" Angel cried. "Oh, Jim! I haven't finished my shopping yet."

"Hey, don't worry about it. You've given me the best Christmas present I could ever hope for." Again, he kissed their daughter.

"If you think I'm going to let you and Hope come downstairs Christmas morning and find nothing from me under the tree, you've got another think coming. Why, that would ruin my whole day!"

"Do you feel up to shopping, darling?" Jim asked with a worried frown.

Angel laughed. "Of course I do! The weather's the only thing that's kept me housebound this long. But just look at that morning out there. It's glorious! Cora said she was coming by later today. She can stay here with you and Hope while I dash over to Senter's and finish my shopping. It won't take me long. I know what I'm going to get."

Jim looked hurt. "I could take care of Hope."

"I know that, darling." Angel caressed his cheek. "But won't you feel better with Cora here?" She almost added, "I certainly will." Then she caught herself and bit off the words before they escaped. Jim was a dear, and he meant well. But . . .

All discussion ended moments later when the doorbell rang. It was Cora, of course, burdened down with brightly wrapped packages, a pine-cone wreath she'd made herself, and jars and tins of wonderful goodies for the Christmas feast. While Angel dressed, Cora set to work in the kitchen—a magician in the culinary arts.

ALMOST HEAVEN 141

In the few minutes it took Angel to don slacks and a red sweater with a sequin Santa on it, Cora had breakfast on. The smell of coffee perking filled the house, mingling with the aromas of Canadian bacon and of butter melting in warm maple syrup to be poured over fluffy pancakes.

"What can I do?" Angel offered as she entered the kitchen.

Cora flashed her a holiday smile. "Keep that dog out from underfoot, would be a help. Ayah! The Monster's trying to steal my bacon."

Angel grinned. She knew if The Monster was trying to steal food, it was Cora who had inspired him by giving him a tempting handout. Those two adored each other. They were partners in crime.

"I'll set the table," Angel said, reaching into a cupboard for her fancy Christmas dishes with poinsettias on them.

Jim sat in a corner by the bay window, holding Hope on his lap. "I'd get the silverware for you, honey, but Cora already assigned me my job and I'm doing it."

"Didn't want no man underfoot either," Cora affirmed. "But he's real good at entertaining Hope."

Once Angel had the table set, she reached for the video camera and shot several minutes' footage of Jim and Hope, then turned the lens on Cora.

"Here, now! Don't you shoot me with that thing! I look a fright this morning."

Jim laughed. "Cora, you look beautiful—sexy as all get-out in that flowered apron."

"Go on with you!" But she half smiled, pleased by Jim's teasing compliment.

142 *Becky Lee Weyrich*

Once breakfast was finished and the Christmas dishes washed and put away, the two women whisked Hope upstairs with them on "secret business." Happily stuffed with Cora's pancakes, Jim ambled off to his library where he settled in the leather wing chair with his favorite first edition copy of *Moby Dick.* But his concentration on Ahab's trials with the mighty white whale was interrupted intermittently by muffled voices and laughter from the floor above.

Upstairs, after bathing and dressing Hope, Angel and Cora got out the Christmas wrapping and ribbons. Angel had been buying Jim funny little gifts for months—"stocking stuffers," she called them, although some were far too large to fit in even a giant-sized sock.

"I think I like this nose cozy best," Cora said, holding up a bright pink, knitted stockinglike thing with ties to go around the head. "It looks the perfect size to fit over Jim's nose and keep it from freezing of a cold morning."

"I knitted it myself," Angel announced proudly.

Then there were toys for Hope and frilly little dresses. They cut and wrapped and taped and tied, giggling like girls all the while.

Finally, they sat back, surveying their colorful collection of packages.

"I think we did a fine job of it," Cora said.

"I just need two more things," Angel answered. "Can you stay with Hope while I run over to Senter's? There's a sweater I want for Jim and a pink lace dress for Hope."

"Why sure!" Cora beamed at Angel. "Truth be told, I was hoping you'd ask me to hang around all day. I

ALMOST HEAVEN 143

like being with you folks. It's as good as spending the holiday with family."

A sudden bright idea struck Angel. "Cora, why don't you sleep here tonight? That way you'll be here when we wake up and go down to the tree first thing in the morning to see what Santa's brought."

Cora gripped Angel's hand and squeezed. "You're a dear one to offer, and don't think I don't appreciate it. But, no. You and your husband and that baby need to spend this first Christmas morning together—just the three of you. I wouldn't butt in for the world."

"Cora, you could never butt in. You're like family."

She shook her head. "*Like* family is a whole lot different from *being* family. I'll be over about noontime tomorrow like we planned." Cora put up a hand to stop further argument. "It's the way I want it," she explained. "The way it should be. Now you go get your boots on and see to that shopping before it starts snowing again."

Angel glanced out the bedroom window at the unblemished blue sky. "It's not going to snow today."

"Of course it is. Always snows on Christmas Eve, ayah."

Cora was right. Before Angel finished her shopping at Senter's, clouds had gathered and the first glittering flakes had begun the fall. The roads and walkways became especially treacherous, with the new powder of snow hiding patches of ice underneath. Angel walked home, slowly, carefully, enjoying every moment and cataloguing every sight and sound and feeling in her mind. Her heart filled with Christmas spirit and her arms filled with packages, she crossed the Mall, staring at her own Christmas tree blinking its welcome in the

144   *Becky Lee Weyrich*

frosty parlor window. The gentle swirl of sparkling snow kissed her cheeks and frosted her shining red hair. She felt like a fairy princess or a Christmas angel.

Along the way, friends and neighbors spoke, wishing her a merry Christmas and asking after Jim and Hope. The kids skating on the Mall called to her, wanting to know if The Monster could come out and play. He excelled at retrieving wayward hockey pucks. He was also good at tag and sled-pulling.

Angel waved goodbye to the kids and was about to step off the curb into Park Row when a little girl cried out in pain. She whirled around and spied the child, lying face down in the snow. Dropping her bundles, Angel rushed to help.

"My goodness, you took quite a tumble!" Angel said. "Are you all right, dear?"

Putting a comforting arm around the child, Angel brushed snow off her. Then she fished a tissue out of her pocket to wipe away her tears.

"You're sure you aren't hurt?"

Just then, Angel heard other sounds from the street—the squeal of brakes, then the horrible crash of metal against metal. She jerked her head in time to see a delivery truck out of control on the ice, careening crazily down Park Row. A cold hand gripped her heart. The truck's skid marks had obliterated her own bootprints at the edge of the street. If the child hadn't called to her . . .

"I'm fine now. Thank you, Mrs. Rhodes."

"Good! You be careful now." Even as she spoke, Angel turned back to look at the wreckage along Park Row and to utter a prayer of thanks that she was safe.

Then, fearing for the little girl's safety with the snow

ALMOST HEAVEN

coming down heavier every minute and the streets so icy, she said, "You'd better run home now. Your folks will be looking for you."

But when she turned to give the child a hug, the girl was gone. Angel searched the Mall with her gaze, but there was no sign of a red snowsuit.

"That's odd," she mused. She thought about searching for the child, then changed her mind and decided it was time to head home. "Where it's warm and safe," she murmured, glancing again at her mangled bootprints on the curb.

She gathered up the packages she'd dropped and made her way very carefully across Park Row. Already a tow truck was on the scene, hauling away the delivery van and the three parked cars that had become its victims. Again, Angel could only sigh and shake her head, thinking of the close call she'd had. She decided not to mention the incident to Jim. It would only upset him.

As she climbed the steps to her house, tears sprang to Angel's eyes. The little girl in the red snowsuit had appeared to be five or six. She'd had Hope's red-gold curls and her sparkling blue eyes. Would Hope look like that cherub when she was older? Angel wished suddenly that she could make the years speed ahead so she could see her daughter as a pretty little girl playing on the Mall, a Girl Scout in her uniform, a teenager going to her first prom, even a bride on her wedding day. But in that same instant, she knew she didn't want the time to pass so quickly. She wanted to experience and treasure every moment of her baby's life. Every hour, every minute seemed as precious as gold.

Moved by a sudden urge, Angel ran up the icy steps,

146 *Becky Lee Weyrich*

flung the door open, and called, "Jim? Hope? I'm home!" She had never been more eager to be with them.

Hearing Angel's loud call, which sounded almost like an urgent cry, Jim flew down the stairs with Hope in his arms. "What is it, darling? What's happened?"

She hugged him and their daughter fiercely. "I just couldn't wait to see you both. What a Christmas!" she cried. "What a life! It's all so wonderful, Jim!"

She shuddered slightly in Jim's arms—not from the cold but from a feeling that everything was almost *too* wonderful. *Too good to last!*

After supper, and after Hope was in bed asleep, her stocking "hung by the chimney with care," Jim said he wanted to go outside and film their house while the tree lights were reflected from the new-fallen snow.

"I'll come too," Angel insisted. She didn't really want to go out in the cold. She was exhausted and still shaken from her close call that afternoon. But for some reason, she couldn't bear to let Jim out of her sight.

"What about Hope?" he asked.

"I'll only stay a minute. She's fast asleep." She almost added that General Joshua was at his post in the rocking chair the last time she'd peeked into the nursery, but thought better of it. The only time she had mentioned the ghost watching over Hope, Jim had been upset by such a notion. So the trusty old general would remain a secret—known only to Angel, Hope, and The Monster.

Angel could hardly believe the magic of that Christmas Eve in Maine. The virgin snow was perfect, as if every flake had been placed carefully to form a

ALMOST HEAVEN 147

smooth, shining quilt of white, which the tree lights colored in a patchwork of reds, blues, greens, and golds. The frosted windows glowed softly. Overhead, the heavens twinkled with millions of diamond chips as the wind blew through ice-encased tree branches, making tinkling noises—"winter's wind chimes," Cora called the sounds.

"Oh, Jim, isn't it beautiful?" Angel hugged herself and whirled round and round.

He focused the camera on her beaming face. "Once more around, darling."

She obliged, then fell backward into the soft cushion of unmarred snow. Moving her arms and legs rapidly, she made a snow angel. Jim shot that, too.

"Now you, darling!" Angel insisted, taking the camera from him. "We'll have side-by-side angels—his and hers."

Jim obviously felt awkward performing such a childish act. In fact, he didn't seem to know how to go about it.

Angel peered around the camera and grinned at him. "Just fall back. It won't hurt. The snow's soft. Then move your arms and legs."

"What if people walk by? What would they think?"

Angel laughed and aimed the camera. "Why, darling, they'll think you like to play in the snow and you aren't such an old fuddy-duddy after all."

"Who are you calling a fuddy-duddy?" Jim fell backward with a thud, then made swimming motions with his arms and legs. His jerky butterfly strokes made for a strange-looking angel, but Jim was obviously pleased with his accomplishment.

Back inside, they warmed up by the fire with mugs

of mulled cider. Johnny Mathis sang softly in the background about chestnuts roasting and sleigh rides, then begged in romantic tones for someone to give him her love for Christmas.

Angel felt Jim's eyes on her. She reached over and took his hand.

"I wish I could," she whispered.

"Could what, darling?"

"Give you my love for Christmas."

Silence fell between them and they listened to the song. They had been counting the days until they could make love again, but it was still too soon after Hope's birth. "Six weeks," Angel's doctor had told her.

Jim slipped his arm around Angel and drew her close. "There's no law against a good cuddle, is there?"

"Hmmm!" Angel sighed with pleasure. "None that I know of."

Angel turned until she was facing Jim on the sofa, her back to the fire, her arms around his neck. He slipped his hands up inside her fuzzy sweater.

"That's more like it," he said with a deep sigh.

The fire crackled, the Christmas-tree lights cast a soft glow over the room, and the snow continued its silent passage down from Heaven. But Angel and Jim, wrapped in the warmth of each other's arms, were oblivious. They kissed and touched and showered more love on each other than either of them had ever imagined possible. After a long, lovely, snowy Christmas Eve, they climbed the stairs, hand-in-hand, and settled in bed for "a long winter's night."

But it didn't seem long at all to Angel. Before she

ALMOST HEAVEN 149

knew it, the cold, peach-colored sun was peeking in their window, promising a glorious Christmas Day.

Jim and Hope were still sleeping. Spurred by more excitement than she had felt even as a child, Angel slipped out of bed and downstairs to the kitchen. She put on a pot of coffee, popped a pan of sticky buns into the oven to warm, then hurried back upstairs to nurse Hope. The baby cooed and trilled with an extraordinary amount of excitement. It almost seemed that she knew Santa Claus had come.

Once Hope was fed and dressed, Angel took her to the bedroom across the hall.

"Daddy's an old sleepyhead," Angel said. "Let's wake him. I'll hold you close and you give him a kiss, precious."

Hope's soft, warm cheek against Jim's only made him stir. It was Angel's long, deep kiss that brought him wide awake. He blinked, then rubbed his eyes, then grinned up at his two girls.

"Get up, lazybones!" Angel teased. "Santa's been here. Hope and I want to see what he brought."

If Jim was still half-asleep, he came fully awake when The Monster charged the bed and bounded in a mighty leap, squarely onto his master's chest.

"I give up! I give up!" Jim said, pushing the excited dog away and throwing an arm around Angel and Hope. "But how about one more of those Christmas kisses first?"

He got several—from Angel, Hope, and The Monster. Finally, he crawled out from under the covers and pulled on his plaid robe and slipper socks.

"Get the video camera," Angel reminded him. "We'll want to have Hope's first Christmas on film."

And they shot that first Christmas. Angel unstuffing Hope's fuzzy red stocking for her, pulling out a tiny doll with a soft body, a family of plush piglets, alphabet blocks, a fabric picture book, and finally a delicate gold locket in the shape of a heart.

"What's Santa thinking?" Jim ask teasingly. "Hope's too little for jewelry."

"Lots of baby girls have gold lockets or even rings to wear when they're dressed up." Angel tried the thin chain on for size, then smiled at her pretty daughter. "Just be thankful Santa didn't take my mother's suggestion. She wanted me to get Hope's ears pierced and put in tiny gold peace symbols."

Jim chuckled and rolled his eyes. "That mother of yours is something, sweetheart! I don't know how she ever managed to raise such a normal daughter."

"*Normal?* Well, I like that! And here all this time, I assumed you thought I was extraordinary."

Jim zoomed the camera in on Angel's pouting face, then put it aside and kissed her. Afterward, he licked his lips and seemed to be considering. "Yes. You're right. You definitely taste extraordinary, darling. How could I have missed that before?" He took up his camera again. "I think I'll make you a star."

"Mom-Shirley and Papa-Pete," as the Gentrys had decided they wanted Hope to call them when she started to talk, had sent dozens of gifts, including a sugary, aromatic rum nutcake from Jamaica. Hope's favorite seemed to be a white quilted satin rocking swan, trimmed with lace. While Angel and Jim opened presents, Hope lay in her cozy new crib and cooed with delight at everything around her.

"Open this one now," Angel insisted, handing Jim

ALMOST HEAVEN 151

the package from Senter's that she'd bought the day before.

He took the large box, wrapped in gold foil, with a huge gold bow. "Looks too pretty to open."

Angel smiled, pleased by the compliment. "Open it anyway. I want you to wear it today."

He gave her a mischievous grin. "Oh, darling! You got me the tiger-striped jockstrap! How sweet! I'm sure to be a hit at Christmas dinner."

"Sure, I did! The day I buy you a tiger-striped jockstrap, you'll wear it for me and no one else to see. Quit joking around and open it."

Jim made short work of the fancy gold wrapping, then opened the box. He gave a low whistle. "Hey, this is *nice!*" He looked at Angel, gratitude and love shining in his eyes. "Thank you, honey."

She got a kiss before he threw off his robe and pulled on the pine green cashmere sweater over his pajamas. He fingered the tiny gold Bowdoin College crest, still smiling. You'd have thought he was ten years old and she'd just given him a shiny red fire engine.

"You really like it?"

"You know I do! And it's a perfect fit."

Angel gave him a smoldering look. "By now, I should know the size and shape of your body pretty well. Don't you think?"

Hope gurgled with pleasure and rocked her swan as her parents exchanged more than a casual embrace.

"Now, you open yours from me," Jim insisted. He handed Angel a tiny silver box, obviously wrapped at the jewelry store on Maine Street.

"Hmmm, looks interesting," she mused.

"Well then, open it! The suspense is killing me."

152 *Becky Lee Weyrich*

"Oh, I think it will fit," Angel teased.

"But will you like it? That's what I want to know."

Angel ripped off the paper then popped up the lid of the pink velvet box. She gave a delighted cry and turned a beaming smile on her husband. "What's not to like, darling? And diamonds always fit."

"Here, let me do that for you, sweetheart."

She turned and lifted her hair so that Jim could fasten the gold chain for her. All done, he kissed the back of her neck.

Angel touched the tiny heart-shaped diamond at her throat. Tears flooded her eyes. "Jim, it's so beautiful. I love it! I love *you!*"

He was filming again, recording her reaction to his gift.

A short while later, the doorbell chimed. "That'll be Cora," Angel said. "Oh, and just look at this mess! I meant to clean up before she got here."

She glanced about. The room was strewn with glittering paper, shiny ribbons, and presents, half-in, half-out of their boxes. The Monster, with a red ribbon draped over one ear, had flopped down right in the middle of everything to gnaw his new rawhide bone.

Jim, on his way to the door already, called back over his shoulder, "It's a wonderful mess, honey. Cora will love it."

"I'll love what?" Cora asked, the minute she was in the door.

"The mess under our Christmas tree. Angel said she should have cleaned up before you got here."

Cora came out of her coat, scarf, and gloves before she hurried into the living room. Her cheeks were rosy with cold, her eyes twinkling with delight. "Lord have

ALMOST HEAVEN

153

mercy, I never saw such damage! And ain't it a pretty sight, ayah? Reminds me of when my brood was young."

"Cora!" Angel cried, rushing to embrace her friend. "Look what Jim gave me. It's a real diamond!"

Cora chuckled. "Not as real as those gleaming in your eyes this morning, Angel."

"It's been a wonderful Christmas, Cora."

"And it's only just begun," Jim added, camera whirring again, taking in the homey chaos before Angel and Cora could destroy the happy mess.

"Land, yes! It's just starting," Cora agreed. "We've dinner to fix and eat, callers to entertain, all manner of fun yet to come."

"First, open your gift," Angel insisted, pressing a shiny red package into Cora's hands.

"My gracious! What did you go and buy me?"

"Santa left it," Angel assured her.

For once in her life, Cora Shute was speechless. She unwrapped the large box, carefully folding the paper before she looked inside. "My word!" she gasped. "A new dress? Why, I haven't had a pretty frock like this in I don't know when!" She hugged Angel, then turned to embrace Jim, but he was too busy filming. "I thank you both. You'll pass on my thanks to Santa, won't you?"

Cora held up the sky blue dress with its dainty lace collar, smiling at her reflection in the mirror.

"Well, I guess everything's unwrapped now," Angel said, glancing around.

"Not quite! I have a surprise for both of you," Jim announced.

"What?" Angel and Cora asked together.

"You missed one present, darling." He pointed. "There in the branches of the tree."

Angel hurried to pluck the white envelope from its perch. She ripped it open, then read the card aloud. " 'Good for one Christmas sleigh ride from Park Row over the river and through the woods. Merry Christmas and "God Bless Us Every One"! Love, Jim.' "

"A sleigh ride!" Cora cried. "Why, I haven't been in a sleigh since I was knee-high to a lobster trap. What fun!"

"I've *never* been on a sleigh ride," Angel said. Then she picked up the baby and whirled her around. "And it'll be Hope's first time, too."

"Here! Give me that child before you have her all dizzy and faint." Cora took Hope and cuddled her close. "Well, if you don't look cunning this fine Christmas morning!" she said to the baby, "I do believe you're going to be even more beautiful than your mother. And that's going some."

Soon, Angel and Cora had dinner preparations underway. A plump turkey, stuffed with oyster dressing sizzled in the oven, mingling its mouth-watering aroma with all the other spicy-warm scents of the holiday. Hope was upstairs napping after her exciting morning. Jim, bundled to the ears, was outside shoveling the new snow from the front walk while Monster had a romp on the Mall.

Caught up with their work in the kitchen, Angel and Cora sat down at the table for a brief rest and a cup of coffee.

"Well, this has been one grand holiday," Cora said. "It's been years since I had such a time."

In spite of all the holiday excitement, the incident

ALMOST HEAVEN   155

with the delivery truck still preyed on Angel's mind. "Cora?" she said, her tone serious. "A strange thing happened to me yesterday. I didn't want to mention it to Jim, but I need to talk to someone."

"I'm all ears," Cora said. "What happened?"

"You know the delivery van that wrecked those cars out in front of the house?"

Cora nodded. "I didn't see it for myself, but the whole town's talking about it. Sure was lucky no one was hurt."

"It's lucky no one was *killed!*"

Cora leaned closer. "What do you mean?"

Angel stared down into her coffee cup, unable to meet Cora's eyes. "Only a second before that van went out of control and hit the curb, I was standing in that very spot, about to cross to the house."

"My lord! What saved you?"

"A little girl, maybe five years old. A child I'd never seen before. She cried out and I turned, then ran to her. She'd fallen down and was screaming."

"Looks like her mother would have been tending her."

Angel shook her head. "No. She seemed to be all alone out on the Mall."

Cora gave a disgusted snort. "The way some people let their children roam all over nowadays!"

"That isn't the end of the story, Cora."

"No?"

"When I heard the crash from the street, I turned away from the child to look. Only a second later, I turned back to say something to her, but she was gone."

"She probably ran on home."

156 *Becky Lee Weyrich*

"That couldn't be. She wasn't out of my sight for more than two seconds. If she'd been anywhere on the Mall when I looked again, I'd have seen her. She was wearing a bright red snowsuit, and it wasn't dark yet. She just vanished in a blink."

"Are you saying you think she was some sort of Christmas angel—that she just appeared there to keep you from getting hurt?"

Angel laughed, embarrassed when Cora stated the possibility so bluntly. "I don't know what I'm saying or what I think. All I do know is that if she hadn't called to me, I would have been right in the middle of that crash. It gives me goose bumps just thinking about it."

Cora covered Angel's hand with hers. "Stranger things have happened. I have a nephew, a fisherman, who had something like that happen to him. It was in the fall of the year, 'bout twenty years ago now. He figured on setting out to the fishing grounds early that morning, getting a jump on the other boats. But when he got to the dock, there was a big sign up that the fishing grounds was closed for the next week—something about a mercury scare. He cussed a good bit, but turned and went on back home. Later that day, he found out everybody else had gone out. Nobody knew nothing about a sign or a mercury scare. What they did know by then, though, was that a hurricane had been headed out to sea after slapping into the mid-Atlantic coast, had veered back in and picked up strength. Of all those boats that went out that day, only one made it back in and it was near sunk. There was a terrible loss of life. But that sign out of no-where—a sign nobody else saw—saved my nephew's

ALMOST HEAVEN 157

boat and maybe his life. He got religion right fast, I can tell you."

"But what does it mean when something like this happens?"

Cora shook her head. "I reckon only the Almighty knows that. I figure there's a big plan for the whole universe and everything and everybody in it. Somehow, that day with my nephew and yesterday with you, the plan went off course. It wasn't your time yet. There's things you still have to do—like raise that sweet daughter of yours. So some force intervened to set things back on the right track. Sounds to me like that's what happened to you."

"Then you believe in predestination?"

"Don't know. I do believe that there's a time for everything and an order to everything. And if you were truly saved by some Great Power from getting hit at that curb, then there's a reason for it."

"What should I do?"

Cora shrugged. "If I was you, I'd send up a little prayer of thanks, and make every day count like it was my last from now on."

Angel nodded. "I prayed, all right! But the little girl . . . ?"

"Maybe she was some sort of guardian angel."

Angel smiled, feeling a warm glow at Cora's words.

"All shoveled and salted," Jim called from the hallway. "When do we eat?"

Christmas dinner was followed by a rollicking, frolicking sleigh ride. They sang "Jingle Bells," called out to friends and strangers, and laughed until the cold air rang with the sounds of their gaiety.

By nightfall, exhaustion took its toll. They fixed turkey sandwiches for supper. Tucked Hope into bed. Saw Cora off to her apartment. Once the house was quiet, Angel and Jim collapsed on the sofa in front of the fire.

He kissed her tenderly, then smiled into her eyes. "Thank you, darling."

"For the sweater? You're more than welcome."

"For Christmas. For loving me. For giving me a daughter. For being my own special angel."

She wrapped her arms around him and sighed. "Oh, Jim, isn't life grand?"

For a long time, they embraced in silence. Angel guessed that Jim was going over every detail of their day in his mind. But her thoughts were once again on the little girl on the Mall and how close she had come to missing this whole, precious day.

Chapter Seven

Winter set in for real after Christmas. Early January brought gray, snowy days and cold, cold nights. The weather got so bad that Jim had to drive to work instead of walking the short distance. He bought a second car so Angel would have transportation. Nothing fancy—a used compact, but it ran okay and had brand-new snow tires.

Angel laughed at her little red car and teased Jim for buying it. "If you think I'm driving in this weather, you'd better think again."

"It's just in case of emergency, sweetheart. I don't like leaving you stranded all day."

The emergency came in mid-January.

Hope had been fretful all night. In order to let Jim sleep, Angel spent most of the hours between midnight and dawn in the nursery. For a long time she'd walked the floor, back and forth, back and forth, whispering reassurances to keep Hope from screaming and waking Jim. When Angel could no longer put one foot in front of the other, she'd dropped into the rocking chair, singing in a tired, hushed voice, trying to silence

160 *Becky Lee Weyrich*

the infant's pitiful wails. Angel couldn't remember a longer, more painful night. Each time she'd think Hope was about to drop off to sleep, the baby would jerk herself awake and give another feeble, anguished cry.

The lazy winter sun was coming up before Hope, then Angel finally fell into exhausted slumber.

When Jim peeked into Hope's room before leaving for work that morning, he found his two girls sleeping, Hope clutched tightly to her mother's breasts.

He leaned down and kissed Angel's cheek. "Darling?" he whispered. "Have you been up all night? Come back to bed."

Angel roused slowly, stretching one cramped arm far over her head while the other remained protectively around her daughter. "What time is it?"

"Almost eight-thirty," Jim answered. "Is Hope sick?"

"I don't think so." Angel tried to sound reassuring even though she was worried. "All babies have a bad night now and again, just like grownups do. She's usually so good, she's spoiled us, that's all. Still, she did feel a little feverish earlier."

"It wouldn't hurt to take her to the pediatrician, just to be on the safe side."

Angel nodded. "That's exactly what I was thinking. The doctor may not be able to do anything for Hope, but having him take a look at her would certainly make me feel better."

She handed the sleeping baby to Jim. "Take her for a minute, honey, and I'll go fix your lunch."

Jim took Hope, but insisted that Angel forget about

ALMOST HEAVEN 161

making his lunch. "I'll grab a bite at the cafeteria. Don't worry about me."

"Oh, Jim, you know you hate institutional food." She fully intended to dash straight down to the kitchen that very minute and bag him a sandwich, some sliced carrots, and one of the luscious apples they'd bought from Bea and Tom Fair's farm over in Litchfield. But when she rose, her knees went rubbery. She had to admit that another hour or so of sleep in her own bed would feel wonderful.

"Come on, sweetheart," Jim urged, leading her out of the nursery and across the hall to their bedroom. "You climb back under the covers for a while. I'll put Hope right beside you, and you can nap until she wakes."

Angel hardly knew when her head touched the pillow. She made a habit of giving Jim a big hug and kiss before he left for work each morning. Her final words to him as she sent him on his way were always, "I love you." But not *this* morning.

By the time she woke up an hour later, he was already in the middle of his first class of the day. "Oh, no!" she moaned. "I hate it when he leaves while I'm still asleep. My day never goes right."

Then another thought struck her. She always put the dry cleaning in on Fridays and Jim picked it up Mondays. "I forgot to tell him I changed cleaners. He'll go all the way out to Mere Point Road for nothing, while our cleaning's waiting at Cook's Corner." Even as she was dialing the pediatrician's office to make an appointment for Hope, she was making a mental note to call Jim's office later and leave a message about the new dry cleaner.

162   *Becky Lee Weyrich*

"Yes, Mrs. Rhodes, Dr. Stalling can see Hope." Mrs. Davis, the receptionist, sounded so cool and unruffled it was reassuring. "I'm afraid we'll have to work you in, though. The office is filled this morning. Can you come around two this afternoon?"

"Yes, we'll be there."

"Mrs. Rhodes, are you all right? You sound so tense."

Angel tried to laugh, but the sound died in her throat. Panic had set in. "First baby, first month, first illness, that's all. I'll be okay, and I'm sure Hope will be, too. I just have new mother jitters, I guess."

"Of course Hope will be all right. Now, don't you worry, Mrs. Rhodes. It's probably a simple case of cholic. Nothing serious in the least."

"I know," Angel answered. "But it's still scary."

The receptionist, a motherly sounding woman in her forties, said, "Wait till your Hope is a teenager. That's when it gets scary, take it from one who knows. Late nights, fast cars, and faster boys!"

Just now, Angel couldn't even imagine her Hope as a teenager. In fact, it was the last thing she wanted to imagine. She decided at that very moment that Hope would never be allowed to date—too dangerous. Still, she couldn't imagine being more afraid for her child than she was right then. The fear was like a huge black cloud, pressing down on her, smothering her, and making her heart ache.

"I guess it's just that she's so little. If only she could tell me what hurts her, what she wants or needs."

"Ah, isn't that always the way of it," Mrs. Davis said. "When they're little and would tell you, they can't. When they get older, they could tell you, but

ALMOST HEAVEN 163

they won't." The woman sighed deeply, obviously thinking about some problem in her own family with her own children. "We'll look for you and Hope at two, then, Mrs. Rhodes. If there's a change, call us immediately. And do drive carefully on your way to the office. Those roads are like glass out there this morning."

"I will, Mrs. Davis. Thanks for the warning. We'll be there at two or before."

Angel should have felt some relief when she hung up the phone. Only a few more hours and Hope would be in the capable hands of her physician. But her feeling of depression, of something ominous, refused to go away.

Hope seemed perfectly fine over the next few hours. But Angel knew if she canceled the appointment, Hope would get sicker than ever the minute Dr. Stalling closed his office for the day. In spite of the bitter cold, the icy roads, and Hope's decided improvement, Angel bundled her up at one o'clock to head for the doctor's office out on the old Bath Road.

Her glum mood should have lifted when she left the house and got into the car, but instead it became as dark and grim as the weather. Zinc-colored clouds had closed in completely since noon, making it look like five o'clock rather than midday.

"We're going to get more snow," she muttered as she strapped the baby securely into the well-padded infant seat on the passenger side. "I sure hope we can see the doctor and get home before it starts."

Cora Shute came slipping and sliding along Park Row as Angel was about to get into the car. "What are

164   *Becky Lee Weyrich*

you doing, taking that child out in weather like this?" she called.

"Doctor's appointment," Angel answered. "What're you up to?"

"I decided to come over and take The Monster for a walk. I didn't figure you'd be wanting the baby out in this cold. But me and that fine mutt of yours thrive on it. Why don't you leave Hope with me? I'll stay till you get back."

"Thanks for coming. I know Monster will appreciate a romp, but the appointment's for Hope. She was awake all night fretting."

Cora offered Angel an indulgent smile. "Just cholic, most likely. But if it makes the mother feel better to run to the doctor, then it'll help the baby, too. You know Hope can sense your every mood. If you're upset about something, she'll know it and feel it, too."

"Really?" Angel frowned. She had been upset last night, but she'd had no idea why. Had she actually kept Hope up all night instead of the other way around?

"Ayah! Hope's not been out of the womb long enough yet to separate herself from your emotions and feelings. It's like she has ESP where you're concerned, Angel. Why, if she could talk, she could tell you your every thought. Baby's and animals have that with their people. It fades as children get older."

"I never thought about that," Angel said. "But it sounds possible."

"Possible? It's God's own truth. Ayah!"

Angel glanced at her watch. "Oops! Gotta go! I don't want to be late. Thanks for thinking about Monster. Stay till I get home and we'll whip up some sup-

ALMOST HEAVEN 165

per together. In fact, why don't you stay for the night? We'll have a snow party."

Cora cocked a wintry eye at the darkening sky, and nodded. "We'll have snow all right—party or no. I'll stay till you get home. You drive careful now, you hear?"

Angel waved and slowly eased her foot down on the gas. The car's first movement was far from reassuring. The back end skated to and fro on the ice.

Angel gritted her teeth. "Easy now," she said. "Just get it in motion and don't make any fast moves."

The car inched at a snail's pace along Park Row to Maine Street. Angel breathed a sigh of relief. The heavier traffic along the town's main thoroughfare had melted some of the ice. The salt used on the main roads had turned the sheet ice into a mixture of dirty sherbet and dishwater. But at least her snow tires seemed to be getting a better grip.

The moment Angel eased her strangle-grip on the steering wheel and let go of the breath she'd been holding, Hope, solemnly silent before, made the little trilling noise she reserved for her mother. It was like a signal that everything was all right between them.

Angel laughed and glanced at her daughter. "Hey, maybe Cora's right. You do seem to sense what I'm feeling. Well, you just relax, sweetie. We'll be at Dr. Stalling's office soon and everything will be fine. You'll see. Mommy will take good care of you. That's what I'm here for; that's my job—to take care of my baby."

Everything might have been fine, as Angel had promised Hope, if the snow hadn't started the minute they turned into Bath Road. Angel had seen her share of snow while they were living in New York—enough to send yellow cabs sliding crazily along Broadway and keep most cars locked up until warmer temperatures thawed ice and snow to black slush. But she had never seen a storm like this. It came on suddenly, blindingly. Huge, fat, wet flakes plastered the windshield. The busy road was lined with cars, not speeding, but traveling at a healthy clip when the snow-out hit. There was no possibility of plows getting out to clear the road because of the suddenness of the storm and the extent of the traffic. Frantically trying to see where she was going, Angel flipped on wipers, defrosters, and headlights, but they were no match for the snow descending. As her anxiety level rose, she became conscious of Hope's whimpering. But she dared not take her eyes off the road for an instant.

"It's all right, Hope. Mommy will pull off as soon as we reach a safe spot."

But there were no such spots. All Angel could do was grip the wheel, lean forward squinting her eyes into the strange afternoon darkness, and try to stay in the ruts of the car ahead of her. She was so tense, she began sweating inside her heavy clothes. Her hands ached all the way up to her shoulders from gripping the wheel so tightly.

"We'll be okay," she murmured as much to herself as to Hope. "We'll have quite an exciting tale to tell Daddy tonight at supper. Poor Daddy! He'll have to walk home unless they plow out the college roads."

At that moment, Angel would have given anything to be walking. She would gladly have walked the two miles home in the storm, carrying Hope, to be out of this dangerous traffic.

A car ahead missed the ruts, hit ice, and slid down

ALMOST HEAVEN 167

the embankment on the right side of the road as if it were moving in slow motion. The dark compact came to a stop, its front fender crumpled against the fence of the Naval Air Station property. Angel felt almost envious of the driver. He was out of it, off the road, uninjured. He was lucky!

That instant's diversion heralded disaster. The cars directly ahead of Angel's speeded up slightly to close the gap where the compact had been. She stepped on the gas, too. Stepped down without thinking. Stepped hard. Beneath her, her tires screamed on the ice. Frightened by the strange sound and the sickening fishtail motion of the car's rear end, she hit the brake with all her might—a reflex action.

She heard a scream. Was it her own or Hope's? There was no time to answer the question. No time for anything now.

Again, a sense of slow motion overcame Angel. She felt the car buckle and jerk when she slammed on the brakes, like a wild horse enraged by the kick of its rider's spurs. Then it seemed they were airborne—flying, flying, flying endlessly. Some alarm mechanism in Angel's brain warned her that if they were in the air, they would soon come down with a dangerous impact. Fighting to get out of her seatbelt, she flattened her body over Hope's car seat, shielding her baby as best she could. And just in time. She saw a telephone pole racing right at them.

Next Angel heard metal grinding and glass breaking. Then she felt pain. Thick and black and nauseating.

She tried to call out to Hope. But she couldn't

168 *Becky Lee Weyrich*

speak, couldn't see, couldn't feel anything beyond the hot, agonizing pain.

She had to know that her baby was all right, that she had saved her. *Dear God,* she prayed silently, urgently, *save my baby! Take me, not Hope!*

As if in answer to her prayer, she heard Hope's feeble cries. A blinding blue light flashed for an instant, long enough for her to see Hope's eyes, wide, staring directly into hers.

Then, only silence. Only a dead, vacant silence and suffocating blackness. No more pain. No more anything.

Suddenly, blinding lights pierced the seemingly impenetrable blackness. Flourescent lights that glared all around Angel and even through her. At the same time, sharp, metallic sounds broke the dead silence. The clicks of machines, the squeaking of gurney wheels, the beeps and hums of computers. Bleeding through the confusing assault on her senses came the smells of alcohol, anesthesia, and institutional cleaning compounds.

Then came the voices—a towering confusion of men's and women's—all talking at once in hushed tones. To Angel it seemed they were inside her head, screaming and moaning. As hard as she tried, she could neither shut them out nor make any sense of them. She tried desperately to will them away.

"Give me peace!" she begged, but she couldn't hear her own words above the din.

One voice finally drifted loose from the tangle of

ALMOST HEAVEN 169

noise. "I want to see my wife. Where is she? Where's my baby? You can't keep them from me."

"Jim!" Angel cried.

But a woman's voice drowned Angel's out. "Dr. Rhodes, please take this. The emergency physician prescribed it for you. It will help you calm down."

Angel stared down from above—near the ceiling, or so it seemed—as Jim dashed a tiny paper cup from the nurse's hand. "I don't want your pills. I want to see my wife. *Right now!* Dammit, what have you done with her?"

"I'm up here, Jim," Angel called. "Just look up, darling. It's okay. I'm right here with you." She tried to reach out and touch him, longing desperately to give him some comfort. But she was too far away. Try as she might, she could not close the distance between them. It seemed almost as if some invisible veil kept them from each other.

Jim obviously couldn't hear her, didn't know she was there. He kept calling her name, begging for someone to take him to her. It made Angel's heart ache to watch him. He seemed lost, alone, destroyed. Tears streaked his pale cheeks and his wonderful eyes looked empty and glazed. His broad shoulders drooped like those of an old man. From time to time, his whole body shook with dry sobs.

A short, rotund doctor, his face a mask of forced calm, took Jim's arm and led him down the hospital corridor, talking to him in a quiet voice. Angel hovered above, swimming in air after them. She could just make out what the doctor was saying to Jim.

"We're doing all we can, Dr. Rhodes. You must try to help us by staying calm. Your daughter has been

170   *Becky Lee Weyrich*

through a rough time. It will only upset her if she senses your agitation. Try to get hold of yourself, for your little girl's sake."

"Your daughter!" The doctor's words stopped Angel in midhover. Where was Hope? What had happened to her?

Bits and pieces of the dreadful scene were coming back. She remembered the car, the snow, the sickening motion as they slid, out of control, faster and faster, down the embankment. Then the awful grinding of metal and shattering of glass as they struck the power pole. She'd heard Hope's wails even as she used her own body as a shield to protect her child. Then came blinding pain as her head struck something. Bright lights . . . then total blackness and no more pain.

Was she in pain now? She stopped to think about it for a moment. No. The pain was gone. She must be all right, then.

While Angel let her thoughts drift back over the horrible crash, the doctor led Jim farther down the long, fluorescent-lighted, neutral-carpeted, antiseptic-smelling hallway. She had missed some of the conversation between them. They turned a corner and Angel lost sight of them.

"Wait!" she called. "I'm coming. Wait for me!"

Taking the corner at top speed, Angel narrowly missed a sprinkler head suspended from the ceiling. Actually, she didn't miss it, but flowed right through it without feeling a thing.

She caught up with them just in time to see the doctor motion toward a closed door. "You daughter's right in here. She's bruised and shaken up a bit, but she'll be fine. As good as new in a few days. Her

ALMOST HEAVEN

171

mother saved her life. She shielded Hope with her own body. She's one lucky little girl!"

"Where is my wife?" Jim asked again in a subdued monotone.

The doctor didn't give him a direct answer. Instead, he said, "Go see your daughter first. I'll wait for you out here."

Angel entered the room with Jim. Hope's tiny form looked almost lost in the big hospital bed.

Jim hesitated just inside the door, but Angel hurried to hover over the bed, gazing down at her baby, anxious to see for herself that Hope was all right.

Hope stared straight up, her blue eyes going wide. Then she flailed her tiny fist and made the soft trilling sound she always sang for her mother.

"Oh, God," Jim moaned. "My poor little girl!"

He moved to the side of the bed and stared down into Hope's eyes—*Angel's eyes.* The baby continued her little song of welcome, the sound she reserved for her mother alone. Angel could tell that Jim recognized it, and that it was tearing him apart. At the same time, her own heart soared as she realized that even though Jim had no idea she was there with them, Hope knew.

"Shhh!" Angel cautioned her daughter. "Don't make Daddy sad, precious."

Hope stopped the sound immediately. She turned her head slightly to stare directly at her father. She smiled.

"Baby, oh, my precious baby," Jim murmured. Then he broke down completely when Hope curled her tiny fingers around one of his.

For a long time, Jim sat beside Hope's bed, letting go of his emotions completely. Angel tried talking to

172   *Becky Lee Weyrich*

him, tried soothing him, but it was no use. The veil separating them remained. Angel's spirits sagged. Something terrible had happened, but what?

When Jim was able to get control once again, he leaned over and kissed Hope's cheek. "Don't you worry, little sweetheart. Daddy's going to take care of you from now on. I love you twice as much now as I did before. You're my best girl, my little love."

Angel smiled, thinking how sweet it was for Jim to talk to their daughter that way. But then, the meaning of his words sank in. Why should Jim have to take care of Hope? And why should he love her more now than before? Unless . . .

"Unless!" Angel said to herself. "Oh, no! It can't be! I *can't* be *dead!* It's not possible."

The door opened and the doctor stuck his bald head in. "Dr. Rhodes? If you'll come with me now, you can see your wife."

Angel did a cartwheel over Hope's bed, making the infant smile at her midair antics. *"Yes!"* Angel cried. "I'm alive! Jim, it's okay. Can you hear me, darling? I'm alive! I'm injured and they've been treating me. That's why they wouldn't let you see me before. But I'll be all better soon, you wait and see. Come on now, Jim! Follow the doctor. He's going to take you to me."

The fact that Jim showed little enthusiasm at the prospect of seeing her, dampened Angel's excitement somewhat. Hadn't Jim been begging to see her all this time? What was wrong with him now? Why was he dragging along the corridor, looking as pale as the well-scrubbed walls?

The doctor led Jim to another part of the hospital, away from the emergency area. This section seemed

ALMOST HEAVEN

173

somehow cold and deserted. Angel shivered as she skimmed the low ceiling above the two men.

The doctor paused outside the door, gripped Jim's sagging shoulder with one hand, and lowered his head. "I'm sorry," he murmured.

Jim said nothing, but a new spasm of silent sobs passed through his body.

"Come on, Jim. It's not that bad. I'll mend." But Angel's voice this time didn't sound very convincing, not even to her own ears.

The scene inside the room confirmed her worst fears. The lights were dim. No window relieved the gloom. There was no furniture, not even a bed. Only a stainless steel gurney covered with sheets sat in the center of the room. Angel held back. But as Jim moved closer, she glided along with him.

An involuntary gasp escaped her when she saw who lay on the gurney. The pale, obviously lifeless form, wore her own red hair, her own faint freckles, her own tipped-up nose. But this person was a stranger. An unsmiling stranger with the ashen pallor of death. A deep, ugly gash marred her high forehead. As for what other injuries she might have sustained in the crash, they were covered by the sheet pulled up to her chin.

"That's why Jim can't see me or hear me. I'm nothing, no one, thin air. So much for all that talk of souls and afterlife!"

When Angel spoke those words, she felt herself begin to fade. Jim and the sight of her own lifeless body lost substance. It was like thick fog closing in around her.

"No, wait!" she cried.

At that moment, Jim untucked the sheet and took

her left hand in his. She watched silent tears slip down his face as he bent and kissed her cold fingers.

"Angel, oh, my darling. How am I going to go on without you? You were *everything* to me. I never knew—I never imagined that I could love anyone so much. And now . . ."

If the gash in her head had caused pain, that was child's play to the hurt Jim's words brought. She hadn't even kissed him goodbye that morning, hadn't told him she loved him.

Jim continued talking to her and weeping, kissing her hand and then her still lips. Angel had to do something. This might be her last chance. If they had to say goodbye, she wanted to be a part of it. She wanted to feel his kiss and return it. One final gesture, one final touch.

Willing herself with a power beyond her own understanding, she forced her spirit back into the cold, still form on the gurney. She braced herself to endure the awful pain again. But the pain never came. What she did feel was Jim's warm hand squeezing hers, Jim's soft lips on her mouth, Jim's tears on her face.

Angel tried with all her might to return his caresses. "Just one small movement," she begged. "Just let him know I hear him." But it was no use. Even though she could sense the slightest pressure of Jim's touch, he could feel only the chill of cold, final death.

"I'll never love anyone else, Angel. You were my one and only. My *everything.*"

"Jim, listen to me. Don't go! There's so much I have to tell you. I love you, too, more than you could ever imagine. And I've failed you. I've left you without any notice. There are so many things you need to know.

ALMOST HEAVEN

For starters, I'm sorry I didn't make your lunch this morning. I should have done that instead of going back to bed. And the dry cleaning. I meant to leave you a note or call your office, but I was so worried about Hope, I forgot. And you'll need to check with the doctor about Hope's formula. And The Monster has to go to the vet for his shots next Wednesday. "Oh, Jim, listen to me! *Hear me! I love you!*"

But it was no use. Already, Jim was distancing himself from the still form on the gurney after first tucking the cold hand back under the sheet. Worse yet, Jim was fading, losing substance before Angel's very eyes. Quickly, she fled the body, hoping that would help. But the thick fog continued to close in.

"Jim!" Angel wailed in vain.

Then a thought came to her. Maybe Jim couldn't see her, but Hope could. She knew that for a fact. She'd go to Hope, enlist her help with Jim. The moment she thought about Hope, she found herself once more in her daughter's room. The baby smiled up and sang her trilling little song.

"Yes, darling, it's Mommy. I have to talk to you and you must listen very carefully. I don't think I'm going to be able to stay with you and Daddy. There are a lot of things I should tell you like don't kiss on a first date, a little brandy in warm water is good for cramps, don't wear makeup until you're at least sixteen. Oh, there are so many things! But I suppose I'll have to count on you to make the right choices. Daddy, however, is another matter. He's a very special man. He needs someone to take care of him. Since I won't be here, I'll have to turn the task over to you, precious. Now remember these things. Never put pepper in his

176 *Becky Lee Weyrich*

food. Make sure his socks match before he leaves for work in the morning. Don't rumple his paper before he gets to read it. And tell him I changed dry cleaners and the dog needs his shots and he must pick up a case of formula for you before you go home."

At those last words, Angel's spirits sagged. Hope was only a baby, an infant barely a month old. Even if by some miracle she understood every word her mother had told her, there was no way she could communicate the messages to Jim. It was useless, hopeless.

"Never mind, darling. Mommy will take care of Daddy. You just get well quickly and have a wonderful life. I'll be watching over you all the time. I love you, my little sweetheart. I always will. But, I promise you, I'll find someone to take care of you and Daddy. Someone special who will love you both almost as much as I do."

All of a sudden, a voice boomed out of nowhere, *"It is time now!"*

The voice of God? Angel wondered.

"Time?" She looked around, befuddled. "Time for what?"

"Time for you to leave this place. Your earthly cares are done."

As Angel saw it, her earthly cares weren't done by a long shot. She had a family to take care of and a mission to accomplish before she'd be ready to go anywhere.

"Now, you just hold on until I—"

Angel never got to finish her sentence. A brilliant flash of light, much brighter than the fluorescent hospital fixtures, blinded her. She felt a rush of warm air, a sensation of flying, and then . . . nothing.

ALMOST HEAVEN 177

But in the distance, she heard music playing. Music so sweet it made her ache to sing. The sound was like a million golden harps and a chorus singing all the beautiful songs in the universe, all rolled into one haunting, inspiring melody. She knew she wanted more than anything in the world to fly to that faroff place of light and music. Only her own stubbornness, her earthly memories of Jim and Hope, and her plans for them kept her from melding with that sweet, welcoming light that beckoned.

Chapter Eight

To Angel it seemed she'd come through some sort of time warp. Once again she was back where she'd started, in the midst of a dark void, staring at the unearthly light that came close to blinding her. However, this time she knew she wasn't alone. She could feel Alexander's presense—a comfort, somehow—even before she saw his glow.

"So, that's my story," she said. "All of it. Now do you see why I have to go back? They really can't manage without me."

Alexander's voice was quiet, thoughtful. "I see that they need someone. But there are alternatives, you know."

"Like what?" Angel was getting truly exasperated with the man.

"Think about it. I believe you'll see the light."

Angel was in no mood after all she'd just been through. "Oh, don't give me that stuff about the light again."

Still, she mulled over his words for a time. Something had changed. Her companion wasn't trying to

ALMOST HEAVEN

give her the bum's rush now. He wasn't trying to convince her to go into the light, only to *see* the light. What was he getting at? Half-closing her eyes, she stared at the brilliant orb that pulsed down from on high. When she did, she heard that music again—harps playing so sweetly that tears came to eyes. The sound and the light were calling her name, pleading with her to come. Seconds before she might have lost herself completely in the light, she jerked back mentally.

"It won't work. I know what you're trying to do. You think you can hypnotize me and make me do your will. It's all a trick. Well, Alexander, I'm not buying in!"

"Why, I'd never try to trick you, Angela. The very idea! We don't operate that way up here."

"Then tell me what I have to do to go back."

He sounded almost regretful when he said, "I'm truly sorry, but that isn't possible. Earlier, we might have managed a near-death experience for you, but you've been on this side too long for that now."

"What? I could have gone back? Why didn't you tell me? I don't believe this. I demand to speak to whoever's in charge. Right this minute!"

"Shhh!" he cautioned. "If you don't lower your voice, She'll hear you. Remember, your temper is already in question. I do believe there's someone you need to talk to, however."

"Well, it's about time! Now we're getting somewhere."

"Follow me, Angela."

"Hey, no tricks, now! I'm not going into any light."

"I told you, we don't do tricks here. Come along

180   *Becky Lee Weyrich*

with me to the garden. I believe you'll be able to find
him there."

Angel had barely moved when suddenly the darkness changed. She found herself alone, standing beside a peaceful stream that widened in the distance into a vast river.

"The River of Time," she whispered, wondering how she knew its name.

Everywhere around her flowers bloomed, perfuming the air. But these were like no blossoms she had ever seen before. They glowed with vivid colors. Even the leaves looked neon green. And as if it were a mirror, the silvery surface of the stream reflected the beauty of the setting. An ornate silver bridge spanned the still waters to a beautiful gate that led directly into the bright beam. Once again, Angela heard the sweet harp music and felt its lovely, calming influence.

But something marred this perfect picture. All kinds of junk littered the lovely garden. Heavy keys on a rusting chain lay under a flowering bush. A Roman gladiator's iron helmet with a fierce face mask sat near the bridge. A torn, jeweled veil drifted along the ground like a bright cloud that had lost its way. She could see an old sailing vessel in the distance, wrecked on the river's far bank, its sails rotted to tatters. A Civil War saber stuck out of the ground near her feet, and nearby sat a chest of pirate gold. She reached down and picked up a set of Spanish castanets. Fitting them in the palm of her hand, she clicked out a musical rhythm and did a quick, expert flamenco step.

"That's odd," she said. "I never could get the hang of castanets, and I'm sure I never learned any Spanish dances. I wonder who all this stuff belongs to."

ALMOST HEAVEN
181

She shrugged and glanced in the other direction. In the shadows down along the bank of the stream, she spied an old junked car. Its red body was horribly mangled. Through the shattered windshield she saw an infant seat on the passenger side.

Suddenly, she recalled a painful scene—Jim weeping, saying goodbye to her.

"But it wasn't really me," she assured herself. "I'm here. That woman was just a pale, cold shell of the real me. Wasn't she?"

Did she still look so gray and dead? Angel wondered. Was that ugly wound still there? She leaned down over the silvery water to look at her reflection. Her first reaction, relief that she was no longer disfigured, was soon replaced by wonder.

She was more or less the old Angel she remembered, if you discounted the fact that she was almost transparent. Her whole form glowed with a ghostly shimmer. Gone were her earthly clothes, replaced by a flowing white robe. Stardust twinkled in its folds. And at her shoulders, she glimpsed little, feathery tufts— the first sprouting of wings yet to be grown.

"Actually, they don't grow," said a voice from behind her. "You must win them."

"What?" Still staring down at her reflection, she saw another image that hadn't been there a moment ago. The tall figure of a man.

"Your wings. You must prove to the Power-That-Be that you are worthy to wear them."

She jerked around so quickly that she almost lost her balance.

"I'm glad you've arrived at last, Angela." He smiled at her—a dazzling, blinding smile. If they'd been on

Earth, she might even have thought it a sexy smile. "I bid you welcome, love, and peace."

She knew that voice. Moving closer, she found herself staring into the most beautiful face she had ever seen on a man. For a fleeting instant, she recognized him, but then she couldn't think who he was. She'd never met him before, she decided. She would have remembered someone so tall, with that long black hair and dazzling smile. Still, there was something about his eyes—eyes that were brilliant but at the same time as dark as any night sky. He was dressed oddly, not in heavenly robes but in a flowing cape of scarlet brocade. He wore short pantaloons and long, tight stockings with his high black boots. His mustache and goatee were as dark as his hair.

Sensing her confusion, he said, "You don't remember me yet, but you will."

"Remember you? Who are you? And why don't you clean up this messy garden? Just look at all this junk!"

"*You* brought all this into the garden, Angela. It's clutter from your lifetimes past. As for who I am, you'll know when the time is right."

"I hope I don't have to start at the beginning again and tell you my life story."

"No. That won't be necessary. I know everything about you, Angela. More than you know about yourself."

"Then you know that I have to go back to Jim and Hope." She let out a long breath. "That's a relief. Finally, someone who understands my problem."

"I know that you *want* to go back to your husband and daughter. But not all things are possible, Angela, not even in Heaven."

ALMOST HEAVEN

"That's your final answer, then?" She was growing too weary to argue.

"Nothing is ever final in Heaven. Think about it. There might be another way."

Angel sank down to a grassy spot and plucked at the shining blades. "Another way," she murmured. "Another way to be with Jim and Hope?"

In a flash of clarity, those words took on a terrifying meaning for Angel. She sprang to her feet. "No!" she cried. "You leave them right where they are! Jim's too young to die and Hope hasn't even had a chance at life yet."

"Angela! Angela! Calm down. I certainly wasn't suggesting anything so drastic. Jim has many years left and much to accomplish. As for your daughter, she is a special child who has a magnificent purpose in life."

"A purpose? What kind of purpose?"

He only nodded in response. "You'll know in time."

"Well, if you weren't talking about bringing them up here, what did you mean? I don't understand."

When he smiled his whole, beautiful face lit up. "I think you do. Stop concentrating on what you want, and consider instead what Jim and Hope need."

Angel, her mind whirling, was slow to respond. When she finally spoke, her words came quietly, evenly. "Jim *needs* a wife. Hope *needs* a mother." She looked directly into the man's compassionate eyes. "But, don't you see? That's the problem. Jim won't marry again, not ever. We promised each other on our wedding night that we'd never love any others. So poor little Hope will never have a mother." Her voice broke and she looked away. "Why did I make him promise? It wasn't fair. Why did I do it?"

184   *Becky Lee Weyrich*

"At the time, you had no way of knowing what the future held. You were both young and in love," he answered gently. "Besides, on that night you both seemed immortal. You aren't the first to make that mistake, and you won't be the last. Don't punish yourself, Angela."

She shook her head sadly. "If Jim won't take another wife, he needs a guardian angel to get him through this."

When the man beside her made no comment, Angel turned to look at him. He was smiling broadly, nodding his head.

"A guardian angel," she mused aloud. "That's it! Just like in that old movie *It's a Wonderful Life.* I'll be Jim's Clarence!"

He chuckled, a deep husky sound. "That was a great movie, wasn't it? But it was only a story, Angela. It doesn't work exactly like that in reality. Guardian angels don't really go back in the flesh, except for brief periods in extreme emergencies. Jim wouldn't be able to see you or hear your voice."

Angel looked perplexed. "Then what good would I be to him?"

He glanced about as if trying to figure out how to explain this to her. Finally, he asked, "Did you see the movie, *Always*—the one about the fire-jumpers, starring Richard Dreyfuss?"

Angel mumbled through a frown, "Yes, I saw that one."

"What? You didn't like it?"

"Oh, yes! I loved it! When it was *only* a movie, it was great. But are you suggesting that I go back down and find another woman for Jim—*another wife?*"

ALMOST HEAVEN

185

"Don't tell me that thought hasn't crossed your mind. Remember what you told Hope right before you left her?"

Angel lowered her gaze. "Oh, that. Yes, I did promise her a new mother, didn't I?" She looked up at him, a pleading expression in her eyes. "But it's hard—real hard—to think of some other woman taking my place in their lives."

"I'm not actually suggesting anything of the sort. It's strictly up to you. I'm merely pointing out that a guardian angel can exert a great deal of influence on the lives of earthbound loved ones. It's something to think about, Angela."

"Yes, it is, isn't it?" To divert the conversation, she demanded, "Tell me how I know you. When have we met before?"

He uttered a weary sigh. "You're always so impatient, Angela. Why can't you ever allow things to take their natural course? My identity and our former relationships should be revealed to you gradually. Otherwise, the shock—"

"Former relationships! What are you saying? I was a good, faithful wife to my husband. I never had any relationships while Jim and I were married."

He shook his head. "Must you always take such a narrow view of reality?"

"Oh!" Angel exclaimed, her cheeks warming with embarrassment. "Then you didn't mean *sexual* relationships."

"Not while you were married to Jim."

She took a step back. "You *did* mean sexual relationships?"

"Don't sound so shocked, Angela." He couldn't

help chuckling at her reaction. "Do you think you've spent all your other lives as a virgin in a nunnery?"

"This is getting way too deep for me," she admitted, looking at him askance.

"Your own stubbornness is at fault. Any *normal* new arrival in this place would go immediately into the light and know all the answers to the universe in one brilliant flash. But you cling to your ignorance as if it were some cloak of honor. So, I suppose I'll have to show you what you need to know."

"Alexander!" she cried suddenly. "That's you, isn't it? You're the same person. The only difference is that now I can see you clearly. But you look so different, not at all like Al. Except for your eyes."

"We are all many different people, Angela, as you will soon learn. As for you and I, we have worn numerous identities through time. But always we have sought each other out. Our incarnations have coincided until now."

"Until now? What do you mean?"

"You spent your time below alone in your most recent life. I was too weary to return when you chose to be reborn. I promised I would wait for you. I knew you would return in time."

"Hey, you're making me crazy! I don't understand any of this."

"You will. Be patient for once, Angela."

And then Alexander did something Angel would never have expected from any heavenly being. He came to her, took her into his arms, and kissed her, fiercely, deeply.

"It's been so long." Angel heard his words inside her mind and heart. He couldn't have spoken aloud.

ALMOST HEAVEN

He was still holding her, kissing her. And, oh, it felt good!

To her own surprise, she slapped him sharply across the face when he let her go, and a stream of Spanish curses flew from her lips.

He only smiled—a slow, lazy expression that kindled in his jet eyes and then spread over his wickedly handsome face. "Ah, Gelina, how your fury fans my fires! You are mine now. Perhaps I should have 'Property of Alejandro Gonzalez' branded on your lovely breast."

She tried to claw his olive-dark cheek. "You wouldn't dare!"

"I dared to love you. I dared to steal you. It will take little courage to dare the rest."

The garden had vanished. The year was 1540. Gelina in her seventeenth summer was many leagues distant from her childhood home, a prisoner of the dashing pirate known as the Sea Dragon—a man she both desired and feared.

The ship carrying them away from Spain rolled suddenly in a fitful sea. Gelina fell into Alejandro's strong arms. He held her, laughing deep in his throat.

"You're a monster!" she raged. "I hate you!"

"Is there such a vast difference between love and hate, my little dove? And if you loathe me so, why, then, did you flash your lovely eyes my way when you danced the flamenco for your father's guests last night? Your movements alone were enough to light fires in my blood, but the look in your eyes—ah!—that told me so much more."

"I told you *nothing!*"

"You've refused all other suitors. Your father

188   *Becky Lee Weyrich*

wanted to be rid of you. I had a bulging chest of gold and nothing better to do with it. So, you see, little wench, instead of marriage papers, your name is now on a bill of sale. You belong to me."

He kissed her again and again until she felt the fight go out of her. She had flirted with this great, dark pirate—yes! She had wanted him since their eyes first met. But to submit after being sold to him! It was unthinkable!

Alejandro's warm mouth strayed from her lips, down her neck, to the tops of her breasts. In spite of herself, Gelina sighed. Would it be so terrible a fate to have the great Sea Dragon as her lover? To sail the world with him? To spend tropical nights beneath his hard, beautiful body?

He cupped her breast. She gasped softly. With one finger, he drew an imaginary brand on her tender flesh, then singed the spot with the tip of his tongue.

Gelina might have responded at that moment. Her own Spanish fire had been kindled as never before, and she was about to return his caresses when he abruptly released her.

"The storm above is growing fiercer than the storm of your temper, my little cockleshell. I will leave you now to think things through. Mark my words, I *will* have you. Time, the sea, and passion are all on my side."

Gelina had been ready to ask him to stay. Not to *beg,* mind you, but at least to invite. His next words dashed her fires and stayed her tongue.

"I paid a pretty price for you. More than I have ever paid for a whore. I mean to collect on my investment."

She managed to hold back her anger and hurt until

ALMOST HEAVEN   189

the cabin's door slammed after him. Then she collapsed on to the captain's bunk and poured out her heart, all the while remembering the many hours she had spent haunting the high turret of her father's castle near the sea, watching for the green sails of Alejandro's ship, dreaming of the day when he would come to claim her. But those had been a child's dreams, and now she was a woman.

A woman without a man! she reminded herself painfully.

Gelina's Spanish blood raged with fiery passion. If given the chance, she vowed she would put everything into loving him, just as she had put everything into dancing for him and fighting him.

While she lay weeping in his cabin, Alejandro paced the deck above, searching his own soul. He had handled things badly. Fighting with Gelina was the last thing he desired. He had wanted things to turn out differently. They, he felt, were fated to love each other to the end of time.

His face still burned where she had slapped it. He touched the spot with his open palm. Even a painful smack from Gelina was more precious to him than the most tender caress of any other woman. He had been sorely tempted to force himself upon her, to recoup her price by stealing her precious virginity. But what a waste of gold. He wanted her body—yes! But he wanted so much more from his Gelina. Yet how could she ever love him now?

Far past the hour when he normally went below, Alejandro manned his post, occupied with going over the events of the past days. Seven years had passed since his last stop at the castle in Málaga. His business with Gelina's father had been handled by agents located near Gibraltar during all that time. But as he was sailing homeward, the urge had come over him to pay a call on the old man after all these years, to see how his youngest daughter had ripened. He'd found Gelina still unwed. She was the angel of the family, with her burnished hair and flashing eyes, her fiery spirit and passionate heart. He would have stayed to woo and win her had her father not tricked them both.

When Alejandro had ventured cautious questions about Gelina's future and any plans for her marriage, the old man had spat out, "Gelina, bah! Wicked girl! She should be wedded, bedded, and birthing babies by now. But not that one! She laughs in the face of Spain's finest young noblemen. To be rid of her, I may have to sell the flighty wench. But who'd buy such a package of trouble?"

The man was old and sick and into his cups when he made those statements; Alejandro realized all that. The truth be told, he'd had more than his share of strong Spanish wine that night, too. Perhaps that was why he'd made his outrageous offer. Still, he had imagined that Gelina would be flattered by his gesture. He had decided to call the old bastard's bluff.

"I'll give you that chest of Aztec gold I brought back from the Americas," he offered brashly. "Your Gelina is worth that and more."

"Done, Captain Gonzalez!" Cordoba had said with a greedy smack of his lips.

Later that evening, during the afterdinner entertainment, Gelina had danced a fiery flamenco. Alejandro imagined that she danced for him alone. Her tiny feet tapped and stamped so rapidly that his heart beat

ALMOST HEAVEN

faster just watching. Back arched, breasts jutting proudly, castanetes clacking in her elegant fingers, she had looked almost wanton as her scarlet skirts flew about her, offering him brief glimpses of her lovely limbs. No wine could addle his brain like the vision of her bright hair tossing about creamy white shoulders and her mysterious eyes sending him secret, woman-to-man signals. By the end of her performance, Alejandro had been afire with the bulge in his crotch.

He had meant to go to her that minute, declare his love, and ask her to be his wife. But his aroused condition had made that impossible. Before he dared rise, her father had stood, drunkenly, and made his announcement, shocking and shaming Gelina.

Turning toward Alejandro and raising his goblet of Aztec gold, Cordoba had said, "I give you my daughter, Captain Gonzalez, along with her bill of sale." The inebriated old lecher then produced a document penned in the flourished hand of a scribe. He read it aloud before passing it about for all his guests to see. Gelina stood frozen in horror. The beautiful eyes that had showered Alejandro with the promise of love as she danced, bored into him with pure hatred the moment before she fled the stage in tears.

Alejandro went after her. He caught her on a balcony overlooking the moonlit sea.

"Please, let me explain," he begged.

"No!" she spat. "Get away from me! I thought you cared for me. Fool that I am, I thought you might even love me."

He captured her in his arms. She spat and clawed like a wildcat. He subdued her with long, hard kisses. He had meant to be gentle with her, but her anger dashed his reason. His kiss became one of mastery, of explosive passion. For a moment, she responded to some unbidden longing deep within, yielding to her own secret desires. But an instant later, she bit him hard on the lips, drawing blood.

"You little witch!"

"You bastard!" she countered. And then she was gone.

Alejandro stayed for a time, alone on the balcony. His lip hurt, but that pain was nothing compared to the ache in his heart. He had spent the rest of the night wrestling with his conscience. As dawn broke, he knew what he must do. He must risk stealing Gelina and having her hate him forevermore. If she remained at the castle, her life would be a living hell. She would be whispered about, laughed at, and taunted from every quarter. Worse yet, she would be forced to remain unwed now, consigned to a life at the castle, caring for her wicked, aging father.

Unwittingly, Alejandro had ruined the life of the woman he loved. Now it was up to him to make amends in the only way he knew how.

Convinced that in time he could make her love him, he stole into Gelina's room in the blood-light of sunrise, cast a tapestry over her, and hauled her off to his ship. Her release was not a pretty scene. She cursed and fought. Her anger sparked his, making bad matters far worse. He'd said cruel things to her and treated her roughly.

He sighed deeply, wishing he could start over. Now, he must go back to his cabin and face her once more, try to set things right.

Instead of bursting in on her, Alejandro knocked

ALMOST HEAVEN 193

softly, then waited for Gelina to answer. Only silence. A second rap of his knuckles, a bit harder, brought the same lack of response.

"Gelina?" he called softly. "May I come in, *cara?*"

He leaned close to the door, pressing his ear against the smooth wood. But he could hear no sound within. Sudden fear gripped him. Had she taken her own life rather than submit?

The instant Alejandro shoved the door open, his fears fled. Gelina lay sleeping on his bunk, her white night robe draped about her like a sea of lace, her fiery hair spread fanlike over the pillow. She looked more angel than woman.

"Gelina," he whispered. "My love, my heart, my soul! If only you knew how sorry I am. If only you knew how I adore you."

Silently, he strode across the room to kneel beside the bed. He reached out, longing to stroke her silken tresses. The feel of the strands in his fingers was like the cool slither of quicksilver. He brought a lock to his lips. It smelled of lime and ginger flowers. He was so close to her, he could feel her breath upon his flesh. Letting his gaze travel down her body, he stared hungrily at the dark rosettes of her nipples that strained at the sheer fabric of her gown. He reached out to touch, but drew his hand back when she stirred in her sleep.

He knelt there for a long time, gazing down at her. With each passing moment, he wanted her more. Finally, he could no longer keep his distance. Slowly, carefully, and with great tenderness, he leaned down to kiss her softly pouting lips.

To his enormous delight, Gelina responded. Her arms came up to twine around his neck, drawing him so close that he could feel her warm breasts pressed to his chest. She parted her lips and her little tongue, with motions as quick as her castanets, darted in and out of his mouth until he thought he would surely lose any particle of control he had left.

"Alejandro," she whispered between kisses. "Oh, my dearest, can this be real? Can this be love?"

He touched her breast with a lover's gentle fingers and kissed her open mouth with a lover's caressing wonder.

"Gelina, my love, forgive me," he begged. "I meant to woo you, win you. I never would have shamed you so. I love you with all my heart."

"Then show me, Alejandro. Show me this great love you possess."

She caught her breath sharply. As they stared into each other's eyes, making visual love for the first time, he stripped the gown from her shoulders and covered her breasts with his horn-hard hands. Still holding her with his mesmerizing gaze, he let his fingers tease her tender flesh. Wildfires licked through her body at the feel of his intimate touch. He caressed, fondled, and stroked until she thought she would lose her mind with wanting him.

"Patience, my Gelina," he whispered, smiling down at her. "We have waited so long for this, you and I. I knew in my soul the first time I saw you that this day would come for us. I've dreamed of you, lonely nights at sea. I've seen your eyes in blue, tropical skies. I've heard your voice in the trade winds. And each time this happened, I would stiffen with my longing for you. But you were never there to ease me. Are you really here now or only a dream?"

ALMOST HEAVEN 195

To assure him that she was indeed there, Gelina let her hand stray to his bulging crotch. Her stroke told him all he needed to know. He moaned deeply.

As if he meant to force a similar reaction from her, Alejandro leaned down and let his tongue lazily circle her plump, ripe nipple. Her reaction did not disappoint him. She thrashed and moaned and pleaded, but he held her fast, his hands gripping her shoulders. On and on went his tender, loving torture. His rough velvet tongue stroked and flicked and dragged over her flesh until she felt her breast would burst with pleasure.

He drew away. She sighed—partly with relief but more from disappointment. A moment later, it began again with his attention focused on her other breast.

"Alejandro, I burn for you!" she begged.

"And I blaze for you!" he countered.

Releasing his grip on her shoulders, but maintaining his suckling hold on her breast, Alejandro let his hands stray over her body. He stroked her neck, spanned her waist, then brushed over her belly to reach his final goal. When his eager fingers found her tender spot— all moist and swollen—Gelina gave a cry of surprise. But surprise soon turned to hot, molten pleasure. By the time Alejandro left off pleasuring her to remove his boots and britches, Gelina lay quivering all over, murmuring his name between gasps of desire.

He made short shrift of her tangled gown. When he covered her body with the hard, hot length of his, she was more than ready to receive him. All her life she had been saving herself—saving her heart, her soul, her body for one lover. For Alejandro Gonzalez, the great and magnificent Sea Dragon.

196 *Becky Lee Weyrich*

His first thrust brought a quick, sharp stab of pain. But that sensation quickly changed to the most exquisite pleasure. He rode her gently at first, waiting for her to capture his rhythm. Then faster and faster, harder and harder, deeper and deeper, until Gelina felt as if they had left their bodies behind to soar through the starry heavens, locked in an eternal embrace. When they reached the limits of the outer universe, a burst of stars shot all about them, setting their souls afire.

"Alejandro! Don't leave me!" she cried.

"Never!" he answered. "Not ever, my darling angel."

After the sudden star shower, Angel found herself back in the garden, still breathing hard. Alexander stood close beside her. She couldn't bring herself to meet his eyes. The smells of sea and sweat and sex were still in her nostrils. She could even feel her taut breasts straining at her star-dusted robe. As for Alexander, he looked himself once more—long, golden hair and heavenly robes. But his glow was considerably brighter than it had been before and perspiration glistened on his brow.

"Well?" he prompted, his voice none too steady.

Angel tried to laugh it off. "That's quite a yarn you've just spun. You should have been a writer."

"I was, in one of my lives. But that was no yarn, Gelina."

"Don't call me that!" she snapped, flushing to the roots of her red hair. "My name is Angel."

He shrugged, causing his shining wingtips to brush

ALMOST HEAVEN 197

the neon grass. "Not Angel yet. But Angela, Gelina, what's the difference? The soul is the same."

The hair rose on the back of Angel's neck, and she trembled, gazing at Alexander—an *angel,* for cripe's sake!—and realizing that he had been Alejandro and had, in that guise, reduced her to a quivering mass of passionate jelly.

"Wow!" The single syllable was more a reaction than a word. Words were impossible; she was speechless.

"Ours was a great and tragic love in that life." He uttered a deep sigh. "A truly eternal passion."

"Why was it tragic? It seemed like a happy ending to me."

Angel could have sworn she saw a hint of tears in his eyes. Quietly, he said, "A storm at sea that very night. The ship went down with all hands. We ended our lives as Alejandro and Gelina. We died in each other's arms, then returned here together."

"You mean . . . ?"

He nodded sadly. "Such perfect lovers only to share one time together." Then, almost to himself he murmured, "One glorious, rapturous hour of passion!"

"That *is* sad!" Angel agreed, feeling Alexander's contagious gloom.

He waved a hand in the air as if to dismiss that long-ago sorrow. "Well, that's all in the past. We'd better get back to your immediate problem."

"My problem?" Angel looked at him blankly. Their brief voyage back in time had managed to chase all else from her mind. "What problem?"

"You want to find a wife for Jim, don't you?"

Suddenly, another love scene flashed through Angel's mind—her wedding night with Jim. With it

198 *Becky Lee Weyrich*

came something else—a strangling feeling of jealousy at the thought of him with any other woman.

"Angela?" By Alexander's warning tone, she knew that he sensed what she was feeling. "Angel candidates must learn to control such wayward emotions."

"Yeah! Right!" She nodded, shamed by his scolding. "Jim needs a wife, a mother for Hope."

"Then we'll begin with your guardian-angel lessons immediately."

She tilted her head and stared up at the tall, handsome angel. "Can I ask you a question before we start?"

"Yes? What is it?"

"You and me—you said we'd been together a lot. Were there other times like . . ." She faltered. "You know. Like when we were Alejandro and Gelina?"

Alexander smiled and for just an instant Angel thought she glimpsed some flickering shadow of the Sea Dragon's passionate, black eyes. "Oh, yes! Many, many times. But we'll cover all that later, when you're better prepared to deal with your past."

She shrugged. "Well, sure! I mean, I'm curious, of course. But I wasn't trying to rush you. After that bit with Alejandro, I'm not sure I'm up to any more strenuous . . . ah . . . I mean, it probably would be a good idea to wait, or not get into bed with . . ."

Embarrassed to the core and unable to stop babbling, Angela stumbled over the words. Alexander just let her suffer for a time. Then he threw back his head and laughed; it was definitely Alejandro's laugh.

He put an arm around Angel's shoulder and gave her a quick hug. Then he leaned down and whispered, "It *was* fine, wasn't it? But we'll save the rest till later."

Chapter Nine

Angel was eager to get off the subject of the two Spanish lovers. She didn't know Alexander well enough yet to know him *so well.* So she forced her thoughts and the conversation back to matters on Earth.

"You said I could see Jim and Hope?"

"You can see anyone you like down below. Anytime you wish to."

Angel's initial excitement changed to sudden anxiety. A lump formed in her throat. After a time, she asked, "How? How do I do it?"

"Go to the wishing well. Make your wish, then look down into the water."

"There's no wishing well," Angel argued. But the minute she turned, she saw it. It was the very well that had stood on her parents' property when she was a child. Shingled roof over it, a rope and bucket alongside.

As a kid, she'd thrown pennies down into the darkness and waited to hear the faint splash before she made her extravagant wishes. As a bride, she'd tossed

200   *Becky Lee Weyrich*

in her "sixpence" and made her wish on her wedding day. But this well was slightly different. It shimmered with a faint silver light and seemed to hover inches above the neon grass on a cloud of shining, iridescent mist.

She started toward it, then paused. "What will I see?" She was more than a little apprehensive.

"You'll be able to view whatever is going on at this very moment."

Angel hurried to the well, eager now to look in on Jim and Hope. Probably, they'd be at home—Jim in his study, working on his play, and Hope sleeping in her crib, surrounded by wallpaper angels. General Joshua might even be there, watching over his tiny charge as he rocked in his favorite antique chair while The Monster lay stretched out on the rug.

When Angel touched the cool stones, they vibrated under her hands. She watched, amazed, as the well's soft glow traveled up her arms and over her body. Warmth followed in the wake of the light. She closed her eyes and thought long and hard about her husband and daughter. She could see their faces. Hope's sweet smile. Jim's loving eyes. A wealth of emotions swelled in her heart.

Somewhere in the distance, a familiar bell tolled. Angel opened her eyes. She was no longer at the Gates of Heaven by the River of Time, but inside the chapel on the Bowdoin campus. Her invisible form hovered near the back of the sanctuary. From the pulpit in front came the black-robed minister's solemn voice. He was praising someone to the skies, saying what a wonderful wife and mother she had been, what a loving daughter, what a special friend. Angel looked to-

ALMOST HEAVEN

201

ward the flower-banked altar. A casket of beautiful cherry wood sat among the baskets, sprays, and wreaths. The cover was closed. She wondered . . . then with a chilling certainty, she knew.

"Angela is still with us," the minister said. "She will live on forever in the hearts of those who loved her, of those whose lives she touched. We should not mourn her passing, but rejoice in the knowledge that she has gone to a new and better life. Now, if you will turn to page fifty-seven in your hymnals, we will sing the 'Song of Joy'—joy that even in death, we will all live anew."

"No!" Angel cried. But not a soul in the church heard her. "This isn't what I wanted to see. Take me back! Alexander? Do you hear me? Where are you? Get me out of this place!"

After a moment of blind panic, Angel looked around to find herself standing near Jim. She spoke his name, but he didn't hear. She tried to touch him, but it seemed that an invisible curtain separated them. Her parents were there, looking out of place with their Florida tans, yet in tune with the deep sorrow of the occasion. Her cousin Tory, eyes red-rimmed from crying, stood between Angel's mother and Jim. Hope, wearing the dress Angel had bought her for Christmas, with the little gold locket around her neck, her bright eyes wide with wonder, nestled in Cora Shute's arms. In the silence, before the organ music swelled, Angel heard another sound—her daughter's little trilling song, the one she always reserved for her mother.

"Oh, Hope, my baby—darling!" Tears flooded Angel's eyes. "It's Mommy, sweetheart. I'm right here. You can see me, can't you?"

202 *Becky Lee Weyrich*

Hope answered with a smile.

Angel's spirits soared. She turned back to Jim. "I'm here, love. Look at me. It's all right. I'm still with you. Jim? Jim, answer me."

Jim's shoulders shook with suppressed sobs. Tory held her hymnal so that he could read the words of the "Song of Joy," but he uttered not a sound. He looked pale, ill, lost. Angel's heart broke at the sight of his grief.

"Oh, Jim," she begged, "don't mourn for me. It's going to be all right. You'll see. I've worked things out so I can stay with you. I'm going to be your guardian angel."

But her silent words fell on deaf ears. Only Hope seemed to realize she was there. Angel tried to talk to her mother and father. They, too, ignored her, bravely attempting to sing words of joy when they had lost their only child. Cora, who always said she could sing about as well as a bullfrog, spent her time whispering softly to Hope, trying to quiet her. Only Tory sang out with sweet determination, head up, teary eyes bright, voice almost angelic.

As the benediction was pronounced, Jim reached for Hope. He took his little daughter in his arms and buried his face against her soft neck. Angel heard a sob escape him. Hope clung to her weeping father as if she knew she must comfort him. All eyes turned on the sad sight of the man and his child, alone now except for each other.

And then the service was over. The family filed out, into the pastor's study. Soon everyone else left too, talking in whispers and wiping their eyes as they exited

ALMOST HEAVEN 203

the church. For a few moments, only Angel and the body in the casket remained.

Angel was glad the casket was closed. She didn't think she could bear to look at that shell of herself that she'd left behind. What did life mean, what was it all about if it could be snuffed out so quickly, so tragically? Had she been put on earth only to make those she loved the most suffer?

"It isn't fair!" she cried.

As tears filled her eyes, she felt a hand on her arm. It was a gentle, soothing touch, almost a caress.

"Come now, Angela," Alexander pleaded. "Come back where you belong. You mustn't dwell on their grief."

Angel closed her eyes and let go of all her earthly feelings. Alexander was right. What good would it do her to stay here? If she couldn't comfort Jim, she was no use to him. Better to return to the serene garden with its loving light and sweet music. She felt the weight of their sorrow slipping away.

When she opened her eyes again, she was back by the shining bridge that spanned the calm, silver stream. The warmth she sensed came from Alexander's glow. His light became a heavenly embrace. She relaxed and let him ease the last of her pain. After a time, she was herself again.

"Your return was poorly timed. That's my fault," Alexander said quietly. "Forgive me, Angela. I should have anticipated what you would find. I should have waited before I let you go back. I'm sorry. If it were up to me, I would keep you safe from all pain . . . forever."

Angel gazed up at her tall companion. At the moment, the tarnished gleam of his eyes held the sadness of the universe, the love and caring of all eternity.

"It isn't your fault," she said. "I'm always too impatient. I wanted to go back. I *needed* to go. I don't think I realized that any of this was real. I had to see for myself."

"There are difficult times ahead. Do you still want to be there for Jim and Hope? You don't have to go back, you know. If you choose to go into the light, you'll know nothing but bliss as long as you remain on this side. You'd never have to trouble yourself with the earthly cares down below. However, once you make your decision, there's no turning back. Which will it be, Angela? The light or the wishing well?"

Angel remained silent, thoughtful. The light's promise of love and comfort was tempting. But what about Jim and Hope? Finally, she asked, "What would you do, Alexander, if you were me?"

"There would be no choice for me, but my case is different. You see, you have no eternal obligation to James Rhodes."

"What do you mean? He's my husband!"

Alexander nodded, his face solemn. "He *was* your husband. And you did all that you could do to give him love and comfort during the time the two of you spent together. But your bond had been severed now. Your responsibility, Angela, has ended—unless you choose otherwise."

"I still don't understand."

"Remember the words on your wedding day, 'until death do us part'?"

"Well, yes, but that's only a ceremony. Everyone says that. It doesn't mean that I can just dump Jim and

ALMOST HEAVEN

Hope because I happened to die before my time." She stared hard at Alexander, silently daring him to dispute her conviction. "They still need me. You looked after me; you told me so."

"I had no choice, but I'd never have had it otherwise," he answered quietly. "I had to watch over you while you were down there. This was our first time apart. I felt as if I had only half a soul while you were on Earth. But you see, Angela, you and James Rhodes were not joined at the soul, only at the heart. There's a vast difference. The times I came to you, I could not have stayed away."

She looked at him quizzically. "You mean that you came to me more than once? I don't remember any other times—only when you came as Al to return me to my parents when I was lost."

He smiled, realizing that Angela had a long way to go before she would gain full understanding. "I took many forms. But when you needed me, I was there for you. In moments of sorrow, uncertainty, or danger."

His words brought something to mind. All of a sudden, Angel remembered the little girl in the red snowsuit. "Could you take the form of a child?"

He nodded solemnly. "If the need was there."

"What need?"

"The need to save you from danger."

"Then *you* were the little girl in the red snowsuit— the one who saved my life on Christmas Eve. But why? If I was to die so soon afterward, why bother to save me then?"

His heavy brows drew down, and his eyes flashed with angry lights. "It wasn't fair!" His voice boomed through the heavenly silence. "You needed that one

Christmas with your daughter and your husband. Nothing could be more tragic than to lose a loved one at such a happy time. I stated my case before the Power-That-Be. She said if I could think of a way to save you, She would not interfere."

"But why a child? Why didn't you have Al simply call a warning to me?"

"I wasn't sure that would work. Many friends called greetings to you as you crossed the Mall. You might have turned to wave without moving from that deadly spot at the curb. Your thoughts were on getting home, on Christmas, on your daughter and your husband. I knew the anguished cry of a child was the only sure way to move you to action, to get you away from the street."

Angel nodded. "You were right." Experiencing a rush of warmth and love, she looked up at him, her eyes misting with tears. "You saved my life. You gave me that happy time with Jim and Hope. How can I ever thank you, Alexander?"

He reached out and touched her cheek. "I need no thanks. Knowing I gave you happiness is all I ever wanted." He paused then, seeming uncertain of his next words. Finally, gazing at her with more love than she had ever seen in any man's face, he said, "Only promise me one thing."

"What, Alexander?"

"That when we go back again, we'll go together. We belong together, Angela. We always have. I was called back before you the last time. The Power-That-Be thought I needed rest and rejuvenation. We had created problems on Earth for each other that seemed insurmountable at the time."

ALMOST HEAVEN 207

"You and I were together then?" Angel still found the idea of reincarnation and of Alexander as her soul mate hard to credit.

He nodded, looking sad and almost ashamed. "We were together, but separated by hurt and misunderstanding. So much so in fact that when your time came to join me here, you refused to leave the earthly plane."

"What do you mean?" Angel stared at him as if he were speaking some foreign language, his words being so difficult to decipher.

"Of course, you wouldn't remember. Ghosts have no memory."

"What?"

He looked away, obviously embarrassed. "It's hard to talk about. Ghost-time comes to all of us sooner or later, but it's only the radicals of spirit who cling to their unearthly shadow form as long and as determinedly as you, Angela."

"When was I ever a ghost?" She didn't believe a word of it. "Where? Why?"

"I can't go into that at present." His tone held a hint of anger. "It was an extremely painful time for me. And it lingers even now."

"Are you saying that part of me is still a ghost? Get serious! I'm here. Look at me!"

"Look at yourself, Angela." He took her arm and led her to the mirrorlike stream.

She stared down. Beside her, Alexander's image looked solid as a rock. He was real. He was all there. By comparison, her own reflection was nearly transparent. She seemed to waver as if she might disappear entirely without a moment's warning.

208 *Becky Lee Weyrich*

"You see the difference?" he asked. "Part of you is still down there, still waiting for something. I want you whole again. I want you with me, Angela. Heaven has been a sort of Hell for me without you here. I must have all of you again. Then when we return to life on Earth, we'll go back together. I couldn't bear it any other way. And we'll make things right this time. I swear it to you!"

Angel felt her soul pulse at his words. "When will that be?"

He shook his head. "I can't tell you. But when the call comes, I want you—*all of you*—with me."

Angel nodded, too choked with emotion to speak. She didn't quite understand what he was telling her, but she shared his deep emotions, his deep need to make things right.

"I want that, Alexander." Her voice was little more than a whisper. "What can I do?"

"You have a mission to accomplish," he said. "You must find someone to take your place down there. A wife for Jim. A mother for Hope. And it won't be an easy task."

This was what Angel had *said* she wanted all along. But at Alexander's words the old jealousy crept into her. It involved thoughts of Jim with another woman, but she also suspected Alexander had more on his mind than the mending of their souls. If she and Alexander were truly soul mates, as he claimed, why did he seem more concerned with earthly matters than with having her all to himself again? Something was fishy here!

"They'll be all right," Angel snapped. "They have Cora Shute to look after them."

ALMOST HEAVEN
209

"There you go again! You should be ashamed of yourself, Angela. Would you have Jim spend the rest of his long life—and it *will* be long—alone and without love? We should begin your guardian-angel instruction immediately for the good of everyone involved. The sooner you set things right on Earth, the sooner you and I can get on with what we must do."

"And what's that?"

"You'll know in time," he answered cryptically.

"I want to know *now.*"

A slow smile curved his wide mouth and his glow throbbed a passionate, scarlet-tinged purple. "Always so impatient. Always so quick with anger and with love. You never change, do you, Angela? I can't fault you, though. It seems I never change either. I want you just the way you are."

Angel opened her mouth to ask what he meant by the word "want," but thought better of it. He had her brain muddled as it was. Until she could figure out some of this heavenly maze for herself, she wasn't sure she'd be wise to ask in just what way Alexander wanted her. This might be Heaven and he might be an angel, but she was beginning to suspect that the old Earth rules still applied, at least where the chemistry between a man and a woman were concerned. And Alexander—spirit or whatever—was very much a man!

"All right," she said resignedly. "Tell me what I have to do."

"The rules are simple. As a guardian angel, you can manipulate the lives of your loved ones to make sure they go in the right direction. But, remember this—it's important. You may use only your mind and your

210 *Becky Lee Weyrich*

heart to lead them in the right direction. No trickery, no gadgetry, no sleight of hand. You're not a magician; you're an angel. Or you will be once you've earned your halo, your wings, and your starry crown.''

The warning annoyed Angela. "I'm not going to try anything tricky. Why should I? Just tell me how to begin."

Alexander stared at her, silent and pensive for a few moments. He'd waited so long to have her return. The day on the Mall, Christmas Eve, he'd had to pray long and hard to make himself save her. He'd been hellishly tempted to tamper with her fate so she would return to him sooner. Only some mystical sort of heavenly intervention had forced him to do what he knew was right—to leave her with her Earth-husband and child for a few more days. Now she was here—beside him—so close he could wrap her in his glow and feel the throb of her heart and the pulse of her soul. He wanted her. He needed her. But still the spark was missing that would allow them to remain together forevermore. Until she soothed the pain of those she had left behind on Earth, her soul would not be whole, would not be his. Soon now, he would have to make her remember everything about General Joshua and Lexie. It would be painful for both of them. But he knew that the end result would be worth the heartache.

"Well?" Angela interrupted his thoughts. "What do I do? How do I start? I don't think I'll have much luck interesting Jim in another woman at this point. He's a traditionalist. He'll mourn for me at least a year."

"Go to the wishing well," Alexander advised. "I think you'll see that nearly a year has passed down there."

ALMOST HEAVEN

"You're kidding!" Angel cried. "But I just got here."

"Time passes differently on different planes. Look. See for yourself."

Angel went to the well, but hesitated to touch it. She glanced back at Alexander. "I'm afraid."

"You've nothing to fear," he assured her.

"Last time it was awful. What if I see something like that again?"

"That's all in the past down there. You needn't worry. It's autumn already. The new school year has begun. Everything will seem normal to you. Don't you want to see how Hope has grown? She's a toddler now, speaking her first words. A bright, beautiful child."

Only Alexander's mention of Hope gave Angel the courage to reach out and touch the glowing stones. Again vibrations traveled up her arms. Again she saw and felt the glow of the magical well infuse her soul. She closed her eyes against the swirling, shining mist that enveloped her. She seemed to be flying, coursing through the heavens.

As her flight slowed, then finally stopped, she opened her eyes. To her utter shock, she found herself staring into the grim blue eyes of General Joshua. He gave no indication that he was aware of her presence, but kept up his steady rocking in the chair beside Hope's crib.

Moving quickly away from the ghost, Angel went to hover near her sleeping baby.

"Hope," she whispered. "My precious. My little darling."

She reached out to touch the soft red-gold curls that now framed her daughter's tiny head like a glowing

212 *Becky Lee Weyrich*

halo. The child turned and her eyes opened. She smiled and reached up toward her mother. The trilling song Angel remembered so well now sounded more like attempts to form words, even sentences.

"I'm here, Hope," Angel whispered. "I'll always be here for you. But I have to go to Daddy now. You sleep. I'll be back."

Just then, Cora Shute tiptoed into the room. Her lined face warmed with a smile. "Well, you're awake, are you, Miss Hope. High time! Your breakfast is ready and getting cold."

For a moment, Angel thought what a wonderful mother Cora would be for Hope. But the idea paled when she tried to picture Jim and Cora in the same bed. She shook her head. "Not likely," she whispered.

Leaving Hope in Cora's capable hands, Angel willed herself to Jim's office. He would be there or in class at this time of the morning. Jim was not at his desk, but he was on campus. His heavy parka hung from a hook on the coat rack. Angel went to the jacket and tried to caress it. The sense of touch failed her, but she could still smell. She breathed in deeply, drawing in the scent of evergreen aftershave, pipe smoke, and Jim. The sensation made her feel closer to him than she'd been in so long. She leaned into the coat for a long time simply breathing in his essence. Finally, dizzy with longing, she moved away.

While Angel waited for him to return from class, she had time to study his office. Pictures of her and Hope were everywhere—on the desk, the bookcases, and hanging on the walls. One caught and held her interest. She had never seen it before. It must still have been in the camera when she'd died. Jim had taken it on

ALMOST HEAVEN

New Year's Eve. He had surprised Angel as she came down the staircase, dressed in a black satin gown for the faculty party that night. There was no doubting it was a good likeness of Angel, but what caught her eye was the other image on the staircase. She was sure that to Jim the figure looked like nothing more than a beam of light from some unknown source. But within that blur at the head of the stairs, Angel could make out the face of a man—a bearded man, General D'Angelo Joshua.

She was still staring at the ghostly photo when she heard the door open. She turned, beaming, expecting to see Jim. Instead, a buxom woman in her thirties in a too-tight, too-short black skirt and a blouse that strained over her ample breasts tiptoed in as if she were on some covert mission. Angel narrowed her eyes, trying to think of the woman's name. She'd seen her before around the campus—one of the secretaries. Who could forget that big head of hair that shone like patent leather or that wide mouth painted the same blood red as those inch-long lacquered fingernails? Yes, Angel remembered now! She and Jim had joked about the woman and wondered how in the world she ever typed with those talons. Rhonda Tillinghast—that was her name.

Rhonda of the big hair and bigger boobs closed Jim's door silently, then hurried to his desk. She rifled through his papers, looking for something. What? Angel wondered. The woman continued her search, opening drawers and finally going through the pockets of Jim's coat. Resentment welled up in Angel as she watched those red daggers dig into the pockets of her

214 *Becky Lee Weyrich*

husband's jacket—the one that smelled so wonderfully of Jim.

Triumphant at last, Rhonda fished a scrap of pale blue paper out of a pocket. Grinning broadly, she picked up the phone, dialed a number, and tapped the desk with her nails until someone answered.

"Hello? I'm calling for Dr. James Rhodes. Could you tell me if his dry cleaning is ready?"

She paused while the person on the other end spoke.

The grin that spread over her face at that point could only be described as joyously wanton. "Well, fine! I'll pick it up during lunch for him. Thanks."

Rhonda, still beaming, replaced the receiver, then picked it up again and dialed another number. "Stormy?" she whispered.

Stormy Weston, Angel surmised. The secretary everyone on campus called The Love Storm. Rhonda herself was known as The Man-Eater.

"It worked like a charm. I found his laundry ticket. I'll get his cleaning during my lunch hour. He'll have to at least buy me a drink to thank me for saving him the trip. Yeah! Maybe even dinner. This is going to be like taking candy from a kid. He's lonely, depressed. He wanders around like he's in a fog all the time. A little TLC from his secretary and he'll be a new man."

Rhonda paused, giggled, then said, "Sure you can be one of my bridesmaids. Hey, you're the one who fouled up the computer and got me accidentally-on-purpose transferred to his office. Oops! Gotta go! He'll be back from class soon. I want to have coffee waiting when he gets here, and I picked up some of those bear claws he likes at the bakery before work this morning. You know what they say about the way to a man's

ALMOST HEAVEN

heart being through his stomach. Well, I think there's a shorter route, but I mean to cover all the bases."

"Bitch!" Angela yelled. She was seething, and if she'd been angel enough to have a glow, it would have been pulsing in a shade of putrid and bilious green. Centering in on Rhonda, Angel now focused all her energy into destructive channels and filled the office with a foul odor.

"Phew! What *is* that?" Rhonda groaned, holding her perky nose.

Then as a run in her stocking crawled up the length of her leg, she moaned and reached down. In so doing, the tip of one bright red nail was caught by the desk's edge, tearing it down to the quick. Rhonda shrieked in pain.

"Take that . . . and that!" Angel roared indignantly, though silently. "You leave my husband alone or I'll break all your claws and snatch you bald-headed besides, you home wrecker, you tart, you wh—"

Angel never got a chance to get out the rest of the word or to see Jim. Some watchful force dragged her back to the Gates of Heaven before she could do any more damage. Her flight was rough, fast, and gut wrenching. When she opened her eyes and gasped for breath, Alexander was standing before her, his arms crossed angrily over his broad chest and his aura brilliant with rage.

"How dare you break all the rules in your first attempt?"

Angel was still gasping as if she had been yanked backward through a wind tunnel at hundreds of miles per hour. Her very soul hurt.

"But I—"

216   *Becky Lee Weyrich*

"*You* hold your tongue and listen! You've managed to cost us months of work in only a few moments." One long arm shot out, pointing toward the stream. "Go look at yourself—see what you've done. I don't know if the damage can be repaired. You're likely to be called up before the Angelic Board for this. And if you go, they'll chastise me as well. I can't believe what you just did. How could you, Angela?"

"That Rhonda's a bitch!" Angel shouted back, struggling to spit out each word.

"Go look at yourself!"

Angel struggled over to the stream, dragging her torn and tangled robe and limping from her rough landing. She pushed her hair out of her face and stared down at the mirrorlike surface. Tears filled her eyes.

"My pretty robe," she moaned. "What happened? It was all white and sparkly. Now it's a dull gray, streaked with dirt."

"It's not dirt," Alexander corrected in a gruff voice. "It's tarnished stardust to mark you as a tarnished angel candidate. I warned you, Angela. Why couldn't you listen?"

Even now, Angel wasn't heeding him. Determined to wash the ugly black streaks out of her ragged robe, she waded into the crystal clear River of Time, pulling off her filthy gown as she went.

"Here, now! What do you think you're doing?" Alexander's shouts rumbled like thunder, making the ground shake. "Get out of the river! Put your clothes back on right now!"

Angel bobbed in the water, oblivious to the tempting eyeful she was giving Alexander. Her breasts shone like twin moons barely below the surface. Ignoring his

ALMOST HEAVEN

217

agitation, she continued scrubbing at the stains on her tarnished gown.

"Angela, do you hear me? We can't have this sort of behavior in the garden. Nakedness isn't allowed!"

She gave him an amused glance. "What's all the fuss? Eve went naked in the garden. Adam didn't seem to mind."

"Don't blaspheme! You're a far cry from Eve."

She turned and gave Alexander a sardonic smile. "But you're not so different from Adam. Is that what you're trying to say? That just because you're an angel doesn't mean you can't be tempted like any other man?" She turned slightly so she was facing Alexander, her proud breasts in clear view.

For a moment, his fiery gaze caught and held them. She watched smugly as his expression of anger changed to one of blatant desire. She could feel the heat of his aura even though he stood several feet away. He took a step toward her, another, then with an exasperated groan turned away.

"You're incorrigible, Angela! I don't know why I even bother with you. The easiest solution would be simply to cast you out."

"But if you and I are truly soul mates, then what would *you* do?"

"Heaven only knows!" he groaned. "In all likelihood I'd go running after you, chasing along all the way to Hell just to be with you."

"What do they do down there?"

"Don't ask! You don't want to know."

"You're saying we wouldn't exactly enjoy the experience?"

"I think that's a fair statement. But you're drawing

218   *Becky Lee Weyrich*

me off the subject. The question under discussion is how we can get you back into the good graces of the Power-That-Be."

"She's angry, I take it."

"Outraged!"

Angel sighed. "If it had been *Her* husband that vamp was plotting to steal, I doubt She would have acted differently."

Alexander gazed upward and spread his arms in a gesture of supplication. In a whisper to Angel he said, "Can't you hold your tongue? Do you want to earn us both a one-way ticket straight down? And for God's sake, put your clothes on!"

Angel chuckled as she squeezed the water from her robe. "Don't you mean for *your* sake, Alexander?"

She slipped the wet fabric over her head and walked out of the water. The effect of the clinging robe was little better than total nakedness, but it seemed to lessen Alexander's distress.

"That's better," he said, trying not to look directly at her, although it was clear he wanted to.

"Well, what now?" Angel asked.

He rubbed a hand over his chin and slowly shook his head. "You'll have to make amends of course. The question is how?"

"If you're thinking of asking me to go back down there and help that bit— witch trap my husband, forget it! I only wish he'd caught her rummaging through his personal papers."

A slight smile quirked one corner of Alexander's mouth. He didn't want it to show, but he couldn't help himself.

ALMOST HEAVEN

219

"What is it?" Angel demanded. "You're keeping something from me."

He drew his lips into a grim line, trying to force the smile to vanish. "You're a bad influence. You always have been. And I've never been strong enough to resist your antics." The smile finally won out.

"Tell me, Alexander! What are you hiding?"

"Jim caught her all right."

"Hot diggity!" Angel whooped. She slapped her knee and danced a little jig. "I wish I'd stayed to see that."

"It wasn't a pretty sight, believe me. I'm almost ashamed that I allowed it to happen, but you seemed so upset."

"You mean, *you* kept her there? You made her get caught to please *me?*"

Alexander avoided Angel's grateful grin and shining eyes. "At the time, it seemed the thing to do. As I said, you're a bad influence, Angela."

He tried to sound stern again, but Angel could tell he was barely controlling the urge to chuckle right along with her.

"So, what happened?"

"Jim informed Ms. Tillinghast with cool politeness that she was to clear out her desk and be off the Bowdoin campus within the hour."

"Way to go, Jim!" Angel cried. Then she gave Alexander a quizzical look. "But I don't understand. She'd already found his laundry ticket. Why did she stick around?"

Alexander rolled his eyes and his aura blushed with shame. "Irippedherskirt." He ran all the words together and spoke them in a tiny, hurried whisper.

220 *Becky Lee Weyrich*

"You did *what?*"

"You heard me. Don't make me repeat the nature of my crime. When Dr. Rhodes came in, she was once more searching his drawers, trying to find enough safety pins to hold it together."

"Oh, you're *bad,* Alexander!" Angel could hardly control her giggles just imagining the sordid scene. "I'll bet Jim thought she'd done it herself, and was planning to blow the whistle on him and claim sexual harassment. It's happened before."

Alexander shook his head. "I don't think he even noticed her skirt. All he saw was his secretary rummaging through his things. He's a very private person, you know."

Angel nodded, her laughter turning almost to tears as she remembered how Jim used to be—how he was even now.

"I'm not going to put him through this again, Alexander."

"What are you talking about?"

"He's better off alone than with some scheming woman like Rhonda Tillinghast. I can't find him a wife. He has to do that for himself. I'm not even sure Jim wants to marry again. Maybe he'd be better off single."

"Did you notice his socks at your funeral?"

Angel bit her lip, not wanting to remember that scene. She couldn't bring herself to visualize Jim at all.

When she didn't answer, Alexander said, *"Brown!* And he was wearing a charcoal suit. I'm sure everyone noticed."

"Forget his damn socks!" Angel exploded. "I'm not going to do this. I've made up my mind and that's that!

ALMOST HEAVEN 221

Jim will be fine raising Hope alone. Besides, he has Cora Shute to help."

"You simply don't understand, do you?" Alexander shook his head, then bowed it tragically and sighed. "But then, you have no experience with deep loss that you can recall. And for a man it's worse. We may be the stronger sex, but we're the more vulnerable, too. We depend more than you could ever understand on our loved ones. Your husband will suffer all his life from losing you, Angela. But with someone else to love, although he'll still suffer, his burden will be lighter. Give him that. If you loved him, set him free to love again."

Alexander looked directly at Angel, searching her face with eyes that glowed with compassion, with pleading.

"No!" She whirled away from him and covered her ears. "Don't do this to me! It's not fair. I don't want Jim to love anyone else. There! I said it. Now are you happy? Just quit pushing. It's no use."

She was trembling all over with an eruption of emotions. She hated herself for being so jealous, but at least she was being honest with Alexander, and with herself, at last. She wouldn't help Jim find a new wife because she simply couldn't. Maybe she didn't have the stuff it took to be a guardian angel. She'd loved Jim too much for too long to simply let go and turn him over to someone else. Someone who would take her place in his life, in his bed, and in his heart.

"No," she murmured again. "I can't do it."

Sensing the extent of her torment, Alexander enfolded her with his warmest aura until they both

222 *Becky Lee Weyrich*

glowed bluish silver. Not until she was calm and quiet
did he speak.

"I'd been putting this off, Angela. I've dreaded having you remember. But it seems there's no choice now.
It's time you found out about General Joshua. Maybe
once you've learned more about him, you'll understand what Jim Rhodes is going through."

"No, please," Angel whimpered, afraid though she
didn't know why.

"It will be all right. Close your eyes now and let
yourself feel it all. Don't fight it. It's always been the
same and always will be, Angela. When our souls
touch, sparks fly. But there's always been warmth,
there's always been love. There will be again, I promise
you."

Angel tried to relax in the security of Alexander's
glowing embrace, but something told her she would
not be pleased by this journey back in time.

Chapter Ten

"Where are you taking me?" Angel's voice lost force and form in the fierce psychedelic hurricane that enveloped them as they began their flight back through time.

"... *far*..." was the only word she caught in Alexander's answer. The howling wind swallowed all the rest.

She decided further conversation would be useless until they reached their destination—wherever that might be. She should have demanded answers from Alexander before she'd agreed to come on this wild excursion. She *hadn't* agreed, as she recalled. Alexander hadn't given her a chance. He was always accusing her of being impatient. Well, maybe she was, but he was twice as stubborn and bullheaded. The man—angel or not—was a chauvinist. He seemed to think because Angel was *only* a woman, he could do whatever he liked without consulting her. She was sick and tired of getting pushed around and yelled at by this heavenly hunk. And the minute she could make him hear her again, she meant to tell him so. She had to admit,

224   *Becky Lee Weyrich*

though, that something about him did pluck her harp strings.

As they continued whirling, swirling, tumbling through space, Angel's thoughts gyrated and jigged with the same erratic motion. Then their flight began to slow. The howl of the wind settled to a dull moan. At the same time, the vivid clouds, like splashes of Easter-egg dye, turned dark and ominous—purple, gray, and finally deepest black. When all the colors had faded completely, their motion ceased as well. They seemed suspended inside a death-dark void. Even Alexander's aura lost its glow.

And the silence! The silence was so complete that Angel was sure she could have heard her own heartbeat, if it hadn't stopped beating that snowy day in Maine—the day of her fatal accident.

"Where are we?" she whispered.

"Shhh!" Alexander cautioned. "Wait for the transition."

"The *what?*"

"The final transformation from our present identities back to our entities from the past."

"You mean we're about to change into different people again, like when we were that Spanish couple who died in the shipwreck?"

"Alejandro and Gelina. Yes."

The psychedelic fog cleared from Angel's mind suddenly and she recalled Alexander's final words before their wild flight. "Don't tell me—we're going on a ghost hunt. We are, aren't we? We're going to find General Joshua. But why? What good will that do, Alexander?"

"I hope it will bring you new understanding," he an-

We've got your authors!

If you seek out the latest historical romances by today's bestselling authors, our new reader's service, KENSINGTON CHOICE, is the club for you.

KENSINGTON CHOICE is the only club where you can find authors like Janelle Taylor, Shannon Drake, Rosanne Bittner, Sylvie Sommerfield, Penelope Neri and Phoebe Conn all in one place...

...and the only service that will deliver their romances direct to your home as soon as they are published—even before they reach the bookstores.

KENSINGTON CHOICE is also the only service that will give you a substantial guaranteed discount off the publisher's prices on every one of those romances.

That's right: Every month, the Editors at Zebra and Pinnacle select four of the newest novels by our bestselling authors and rush them straight to you, usually *before they reach the bookstores*. The publisher's prices for these romances range from $4.99 to $5.99—but they are always yours for the guaranteed low price of just *$4.20!*

That means you'll always save over 20% off the publisher's prices on every shipment you get from KENSINGTON CHOICE!

All books are sent on a 10-day free examination basis, and there is no minimum number of books to buy. (A postage and handling charge of $1.50 is added to each shipment.)

As your introduction to the convenience and value of this new service, we invite you to accept

4 BOOKS FREE

The 4 books, worth up to $23.96, are our welcoming gift. You pay only $1 to help cover postage and handling.

To start your subscription to KENSINGTON CHOICE and receive your introductory package of 4 FREE romances, detach and mail the card at right *today.*

We have 4 FREE BOOKS for you as your introduction to KENSINGTON CHOICE

To get your FREE BOOKS, worth up to $23.96, mail the card below.

FREE BOOK CERTIFICATE

As my introduction to your new KENSINGTON CHOICE reader's service, please send me 4 FREE historical romances (worth up to $23.96), billing me just $1 to help cover postage and handling. As a KENSINGTON CHOICE subscriber, I will then receive 4 brand-new romances to preview each month for 10 days FREE. I can return any books I decide not to keep and owe nothing. The publisher's prices for the KENSINGTON CHOICE romances range from $4.99 to $5.99, but as a subscriber I will be entitled to get them for just $4.20 per book or $16.80 for all four titles. There is no minimum number of books to buy, and I can cancel my subscription at any time. A $1.50 postage and handling charge is added to each shipment.

Name _____

Address _____ Apt. _____

City _____ State _____ Zip _____

Telephone ( ) _____

Signature _____

(If under 18, parent or guardian must sign)

Subscription subject to acceptance. Terms and prices subject to change.

KC0595

We have
4
FREE
Historical
Romances
for you!

(worth up
to $23.96!)

Details inside!

KENSINGTON CHOICE
Reader's Service
120 Brighton Road
P.O.Box 5214
Clifton, NJ 07015-5214

AFFIX
STAMP
HERE

ALMOST HEAVEN 225

swered. "I also hope it might restore the lost spark to your soul."

Hearing this, Angel got so excited she nearly fell off the black cloud which seemed to be the only thing that kept them from tumbling down and down through the dark tunnel of time and space.

"You mean you're going to bring me back to life?" She threw her arms around Alexander and hugged him soundly. "Oh, thank you, thank you! Then I can go back to Jim and Hope and everything will be just the way it was before."

Alexander clung to Angel, accepting the unexpected embrace as he would any other unanticipated gift from God. It was a wonder to have this happy, bubbling spirit so close after all their time apart. Yet he was pained on two counts as he listened to Angel's excited chatter. First, because she misunderstood completely what they were about to do and it would be up to him to provide an explanation that was certain to bring her crushing disappointment. Second, because even though she was in his arms, she *still* longed to return to the husband she had loved both emotionally and physically down below.

A tremor of longing gripped him. It had been so long for him that even thinking about the act of physical love between a man and a woman set his desires raging. Angela still did not look on him—Alexander, Alejandro, Lexie Joshua—as her partner through eternity. What a terrible mess they had made of things their last time on Earth. His only hope was that by going back he might make Angela understand and forgive him for that one crime, that moment of misplaced passion. He'd never meant to hurt her. *Never!*

226   *Becky Lee Weyrich*

"It will be so wonderful to pick up right where I left off after Christmas. A new year, a new life, a new chance," Angel enthused. Then she turned thoughtful, frowning. "But how will you do it, Alexander? You can't just drop me back into the picture. How would I explain returning from the dead after so long? This is going to be tricky, isn't it?"

Alexander stared at her, his eyes filled with gentleness and compassion. He was about to speak, to correct her mistaken idea with words he hoped would comfort her. But before he could think of what to say, she hurried on.

"I know!" she cried. "You don't have to tell me. I've figured it out for myself. That's why you said we had to travel back in time. You've turned the clock back, haven't you? When I return, I'll bet it will be the night before the accident, but something will be different. Maybe Hope won't be sick. Or maybe I'll figure the weather is too threatening to take her out. Or it could be the doctor—maybe he won't have any appointments. Whatever . . . I won't go out, so I won't have the wreck. I won't die!"

Angel was breathless, too excited to go on. She felt like Dorothy, about to be sent back to Kansas after such a long time. Without even thinking about what she was doing, she closed her eyes, tapped her heels together, and repeated several times, " 'There's no place like home! There's no place like home! There's no place like home!' "

Unfortunately, Angel wasn't wearing Dorothy's ruby slippers.

"Take me home, Alexander," she begged. "Home to Maine."

ALMOST HEAVEN 227

Sure enough, after the wind kicked up again, then calmed, and the colors swirled, then faded, Angel found herself back in Maine. But she wasn't in the house on Park Row, on the Mall, or even in Brunswick. She found herself standing on a windswept, snowy hill overlooking a frozen river. Gray clouds laden with more snow threatened and the copperish cast to the air signaled that a storm was gathering.

Angel pulled her heavy woolen cloak closer, turning up the collar for protection from the icy wind. Half-frozen, the hair on her head was as stiff as her beard. One hand was bare and tingled with the cold. Angel looked down to see if she'd dropped a glove. Yes, there it was, lying on the ground near the toe of her boot.

The moment she reached down to retrieve it she realized that the "transformation" Alexander had mentioned had obviously taken place. Stunned, she rubbed her big, bare hand over her rough face.

"A beard?" She jumped at the sound of her own deep voice.

Even as she wondered at this transformation, she realized that her woman's will was losing ground to decidedly male thoughts and feelings. He was cold, weary, and obviously disappointed about something. But, oddly enough, he wasn't angry. He'd half expected to be disappointed.

"She's not coming," he muttered to himself. "You were a fool, D'Angelo Joshua, to think she would. A bigger fool to imagine that she might care for you. She's young, beautiful, and a rich man's daughter. What could she possibly see in an old soldier of fortune with barely two coppers to rub together?"

The wind sighed through a nearby stand of birches,

making a sound almost like a human voice. He cocked his head, listening, hoping, on the verge of praying.

"Mr. Joshua?"

He turned. Surely the birch trees couldn't be calling his name. And then he saw her, tripping over the icy crust on the snow as lightly as a new fawn. Lexie Mallette, her silvery eyes dewy with excitement, her long hair whipping in the wind. His heart beat faster. His body heat rose despite the winter chill. Was there ever a lovelier woman, a sweeter voice, a dearer smile?

"Lexie," he murmured, hurrying toward her. "You came."

She waited for no greeting, but went straight into his strong arms. "Oh, D'Angelo! You're near frozen, aren't you? I'm sorry. I had to wait until Papa took the sleigh to Wiscasset before I could slip away."

"Then he hasn't changed his mind about me."

She clung to him, shivering more with emotion than with cold. "He will. He must!"

She looked up at him, staring into his rugged face, his cobalt eyes. The pucker of her perfect, bow-shaped mouth begged for his kiss. He did not disappoint her. Drawing her close to his hard body, he covered her cold lips with his, drinking in her sweetness at the same time that he warmed her and fanned her innocent flames.

Lexie came away breathless. "You never kissed me like that before."

"We've never been alone before. I've had to steal my moments of bliss."

She smiled, a quivering smile that threatened to produce tears. "D'Angelo," she whispered, "I've never known anyone like you before. You make me feel"—

ALMOST HEAVEN 229

she paused, trying to think how to express herself—"like a woman."

He opened his cloak and wrapped her tiny form inside, closer than ever. So close he could feel her heart fluttering against his chest. "If only you'll marry me, Lexie, I'll see to it that you never forget what it feels like to be a woman. I love you. If you don't know that by now, I don't know how I could put it plainer."

She blushed. Her long, honey-gold eyelashes fluttered and she looked away. "I love you, too, D'Angelo, with all my heart. But what can we do? Papa is so set against our marriage. He makes so many unreasonable demands."

"What sort of demands?" A vague sense of hope began to rise in D'Angelo Joshua's heavy heart. "Do you mean that he's set conditions for your suitors to live up to?"

Lexie nodded, shy and embarrassed. "Impossible ones! You see, it isn't *you* Papa objects to, D'Angelo. He doesn't want me to marry anyone—not ever. He's told me many times that since I'm his only daughter, I should remain by his side to take care of him in his old age."

"Preposterous!" D'Angelo could hardly believe his own ears. How could any man be so cruel as to order his daughter not to follow her heart? "Your brothers? What do they say of this?"

"Papa is the head of the family. They abide by whatever he says."

Joshua wanted to curse, but held his tongue so as not to offend Lexie. Instead, he said, "That's easy for them, with their comfortable lives, their wives and

230   *Becky Lee Weyrich*

children. Don't they want the same happiness for you, their little sister?"

"You can't fault them, D'Angelo. They want most of all not to have to deal with Papa. He can be difficult at times."

D'Angelo gave a mocking laugh. "The man can be impossible!" Then he kissed Lexie ever so gently and held her close. "Tell me his demands. By God in Heaven, I'll meet them—all of them—to have you as my wife."

Lexie looked up through misty eyes at the man she loved. "You'd do that for me?"

"I'd crawl to hell and back on my knees for you, Alexandra. I've been all over this country, all over Europe. I've sailed the seven seas. But never have I met your equal. Our love was written among the stars at the beginning of time. Without you there is no love, no life. Now tell me what I must do."

Lexie swallowed back tears of love and gratitude before she could answer. "Papa says the man I marry must be richer than he is. He says any man who wishes me for his wife must build me a fine home and fill it with lovely things."

D'Angelo began to feel a ray of hope. "I've made and lost three fortunes in my lifetime. I can make another. And once I'm rich again, I'll build you the finest mansion between Bangor and Boston. Is that all I have to do to make you my bride?"

"No," Lexie answered with a chill in her voice. "The last thing is the most difficult of all."

"Then tell me, love. Out with it. I'll do *anything!*"

"Papa says that the man I want to marry must leave me for two long years."

ALMOST HEAVEN

"Two years? Why in God's name would he wish such a thing?"

"He says the only way to prove true love is to test it. He says any man who wants me, who loves me with all his heart, must be able to endure such a separation. He claims that any man who cannot endure it is not fit to be my husband."

Tears streamed down Lexie's face. She knew that D'Angelo Joshua was perfectly capable of making money. He was a shrewd and capable businessman. She knew, too, that he was a man of fire and passion, a man who needed a woman. She had no delusions that she was his first. She only hoped that if they married she would be his last, his one and only from that time forward. To tell such a man he must live like a monk for two years, unable even to see the woman he loved, was like telling a man dying of thirst that he could not drink sweet water from a deep, cool well.

"You see," she said in a small, agonized voice, "it's impossible."

He forced the stricken frown from his angular face to smile down at her. "Unpleasant, my love, but not impossible. Haven't I told you about the time I was kidnapped by Barbary pirates and kept in chains for three years without ever so much as laying eyes on a woman the whole time?"

She smiled back through her tears, sure that he was making up the tale to soothe her fears. "Maybe you managed in chains. But this time you'll be a free man, able to go after any woman your heart desires. Any woman but me."

He cradled her close and kissed her damp eyelids. "Ah, little love, you have my heart in chains already.

232 *Becky Lee Weyrich*

There's not another woman in all creation who could touch it now that I've fallen in love with you."

"Where will you go? What will you do?"

He thought about it, seriously, for a time. Then with a smile broad enough to melt the winter snow, he said, "I'll get a ship. I'll set to sea. Maybe I'll sail to the coast of Africa and back again. I hear there's a fortune to be made in the black ivory trade. And in every port I hit, I'll buy exotic treasures to fill your mansion, my wedding gift to you, my beloved. Then, when I return, what a homecoming it will be."

"You truly mean it, don't you?" The quiver in Lexie's voice held wonder and more than a touch of awe at this magnificent man who loved her enough to make such extravagant promises.

"Of course. Every word of it. But by the time I return, I'll be an old man past thirty years and you still a maid. Can you live with such a fall and spring match, my darling?"

"Oh, D'Angelo, you'll be forever young to me. I love you so!"

Just as they embraced, they heard the jingle of a sleigh and old Mallette's voice booming through the cold air at his team.

"Let's beard the lion in his lair this very minute," D'Angelo proposed.

Lexie shivered in his arms, afraid of her father's wrath, but more afraid of losing the man she loved. "Then you'll be going away afterward?"

"Take heart, my dearest. The sooner I leave, the sooner I'll return to you."

* * *

ALMOST HEAVEN 233

The touching scene dissolved in a swirl of flying snowflakes and neon splashes of Easter egg–colored clouds. When Angel opened her eyes again, she was staring at Alexander.

"What's going on?" she demanded.

"Tell me what you think is happening. Explain to me what you've learned so far."

Before she answered, she glanced about. Gone was the frozen river, the stand of birch trees, the windy hilltop. She and Alexander were once more standing on a cloud or hovering within it, she wasn't sure which. She realized she knew a lot more than she had before she met D'Angelo and Lexie, but she wasn't sure if it had all been real or just some sort of vision provided to test her.

"Okay," she said, concentrating on her new knowledge. "What have I learned? I know we were watching a scene that took place sometime before the Civil War."

"Were you only watching?"

Angel gave this some thought. "No, I guess not. I was part of what was happening. I knew what D'Angelo was feeling and thinking. I know a lot about him, too. Things he never mentioned during his meeting with Lexie."

"Such as?"

"I know he was born in Brunswick, Maine, in 1825, October third, to be exact, in a log cabin his father built. Eli Joshua was a trapper. He spent much of his time away from his wife and son, in the mountains or the deep woods." Angel looked off into the distance as D'Angelo's most painful memories came flooding back and with them D'Angelo Joshua's persona. "Pa

234 *Becky Lee Weyrich*

was off working his traps when Mama disappeared. I never quite got over what happened to her. And I never got over blaming Pa."

"Tell me about your mother."

"She was beautiful—had long black hair and flashing eyes. She and Pa met in Boston not long after she came over from Naples, Italy. Pa bought her indenture so he could marry her. I remember he always used to say, 'One look into them volcano-black eyes and I was a goner. I had to marry her or die from wanting to.' Mama's name was Carmina D'Angelo. She gave me her name when I was born."

"Can you tell me what happened to her, D'Angelo?" Alexander's prodding was as gentle as possible.

"It still hurts, but I can tell it now. For a long time I couldn't. The Indian troubles were supposed to be long over by then. But from time to time a raiding party would sneak into one village or another to do mischief. Some Abenaki braves stole into Brunswick of a winter's night and set upon the settlers. Mama heard the alarm and saved me. Our cabin was finer than most. We had a wood floor instead of packed earth. Mama pried up one of the boards and made me climb down under the floor. I'd hardly wriggled into position before the Indians were beating down the door. You should have heard my mama! She yelled and screamed at them in Italian, calling them every kind of name. I could see a little through a crack between the boards. It was all I could do to keep from hollering at those redskins when they shoved Mama around and tied her hands behind her. They didn't seem to hurt her, though. They plundered our belongings and took whatever they wanted. When they left,

ALMOST HEAVEN   235

they took Mama, too. As they were pushing her through the door, she called out to me in her native tongue, knowing that I'd understand, but they wouldn't. She told me not to come out of hiding until daylight. And she promised she'd come back."

"And did she?"

"Yes, but after years and years. And then it wasn't my mama who came home, but some stranger. She'd aged way beyond her years, and her mind was gone. She didn't remember me or Pa."

"Where was she all that time?"

"Up in Canada—Quebec City. Seems the Frenchies would pay the Indians cash money for any pretty women they stole. Then they'd take them over the border and resell them to brothels. So my mama spent my growing-up years way off in the North, against her will, as a whore. By the time Pa found out where she was and went after her, she wasn't his wife or my mama anymore. She was some crazed stranger who never knew who we were. She didn't live a year after Pa brought her home."

"That's a sad, sad tale, lad," Alexander said with deep sympathy. "What happened to her?"

"One night while Pa and I were sleeping, she just up and left. It was snowing hard and as cold as it gets. We started searching as soon as we discovered she was gone. But we didn't find her body until the spring thaw. She was sitting up—real lifelike—under her favorite elm tree. Pa said she used to go to that very spot to sit in the shade and dream her dreams when she was carrying me. So I like to think that right there at the end she remembered me and that she was my mama."

"You had a hard life, didn't you, lad?"

236   *Becky Lee Weyrich*

Angel perked up and gave Alexander a broad grin that looked for all the world like D'Angelo's. "Those days are long gone. I'm a man now, living a man's life. And I'm here to tell you I've found myself a woman almost as sweet and pretty as my mama. Maybe you know her—Alexandra Mallette. She lives up Wiscasset way. She's got a pa who's tough as horseshoe nails, but I mean to meet his conditions and marry my Lexie. And you know where I'm going to build her a house? Right smack-dab where the old cabin used to set."

Alexander smiled and nodded. "I wish you well, D'Angelo. And I wish you and your Lexie all the happiness in the world."

"Well, I'll see you around, friend. Right now, I'm headed up to the Mallette house to make my peace with Lexie's pa. I mean to have that girl!"

"You'd better go to Papa alone, D'Angelo," Lexie insisted. "He's not an easy man to deal with, and he'll be worse if I'm there. He likes to show off."

They were coming down the hill, arm in arm. In the distance, they could see the portly Mr. Mallette climbing down from the sleigh, with the aid of two servants.

"I'll go around the back way and sneak into the kitchen," Lexie said. "As soon as he's inside, you go to the front door. It wouldn't do for Papa to find out we've been alone together."

Lexie, her cheeks rosy with anticipation as much as the cold, went up on tiptoe and kissed D'Angelo quickly. Then she hurried off into the woods.

D'Angelo paced back and forth in the snow, watch-

ALMOST HEAVEN 237

ing and waiting while old man Mallette made his way to the house.

"Old ogre," he muttered. "Pompous wind bag! Rotter!"

He made himself wait even after Mallette disappeared within. He meant to be firm with the man, but he didn't want to rile him. If he was to be successful, he needed to proceed as if this talk were gentleman to gentleman, no matter what he thought of Mallette. He forced all bad thoughts from his mind and tried to think of this man as Lexie's father, his prospective father-in-law.

"Whatever happened to the good old days when a man could expect a dowry instead of having to provide one?" he mused. He knew, though, that paying the price for Lexie was no hardship. Waiting two long years to claim her was.

When it finally came time, D'Angelo strode purposefully up to the front door and rapped sharply. One of the servants, a tall fellow who looked suspiciously as if he might have Abenaki blood, answered, unsmiling.

"I wish to see Mr. Mallette immediately. Tell him Mr. D'Angelo Joshua is here to pay a call."

The tall Indian-looking chap disappeared into the gloom of the house and kept D'Angelo cooling his heels for some time before he returned.

"Mr. Mallette wishes to know the nature of your business."

D'Angelo smiled with a cordiality he did not feel. "Tell him matrimony is the nature of my business."

Moments later, D'Angelo heard the old man roar

238   *Becky Lee Weyrich*

from his study, "Tell him to go away! Take the musket to him if he refuses."

But it was too late for that. D'Angelo had let himself in and was standing in the doorway of the study before the servant had a chance to deliver the message to him.

"You'll hear me out, Mr. Mallette. I've come to ask for the hand of your daughter in marriage, and I won't leave until I have what I came for."

The fat old man sat sprawled in a huge chair, its proportions barely handling his bulk. He made an attempt to look the dandy in his powdered wig and fancy waistcoat, but his fake hair sat askew on his round head and his brocades were stained with wine and food. Everyone knew that Mallette was the richest man in Maine. They also knew that he came from the humblest beginnings. It was rumored that he bore his mother's name because his father's remained a mystery.

"Alexandra has no wish to wed. She's a frail child, not up to the demands of a husband."

"Not all husbands make such demands on their wives that they send them to their graves." D'Angelo could have bitten off his tongue. He'd meant to remain civil, but the old bastard irked him so. Still, he shouldn't have alluded to the gossip that poor Florence Mallette had succumbed to her own husband's lust after repeated pregnancies, the bearing of a child every spring for many years.

"A man has his rights!" Mallette bellowed.

"And a woman has hers. The right to marry the man she loves and the right to refuse him if his demands become unreasonable."

D'Angelo saw a shadow move in the hallway and

ALMOST HEAVEN

knew that Lexie was hidden there, listening. He guessed that if things did not go well, she would spring into the room to state her own case and fight her own battle. Brave girl! He smiled.

"You think this a laughing matter, sir?" Mallette demanded. "This is my daughter we're discussing. The dear, sweet, innocent child of my heart. She's far too good for you." He sipped at a brandy without offering one to D'Angelo, then chuckled. "She's also far too rich for you. I'd never allow my daughter to marry *down*. Besides, everyone knows the sordid tale about your mother."

D'Angelo ground his teeth, bit his tongue, and clenched his fists. He must hold his temper. But right now, he would like nothing better than to strangle the old lecher with his bare hands. How could such a miserable fool have raised a dear person like Lexie?

After swallowing several times, trying to rid himself of the taste of angry bile, D'Angelo said in an even voice, "I realize that I must have a place to take my bride. I own a prime piece of land in Brunswick. I intend to build a fine house for her there. The finest in all the town. I promise you, sir, your daughter will want for nothing."

"Ha! Do you think I'm a fool?"

D'Angelo realized in the nick of time that this was a rhetorical question. He held his silence.

"You may have made a fortune in the spice trade with India, but rumor has it that you lost your last cent gambling."

"I am not a gambler. I risked my fortune, hoping to treble it, on land in the Indies. There was no way anyone could have known of the slave uprising to come."

240   *Becky Lee Weyrich*

"A wise man keeps his money at home, in timber, fishing, furs. A wise man also keeps his daughter at home. No, Mr. Joshua, you may not have my Lexie!"

The shadow in the hall moved quickly, materializing in seconds in the study. Lexie's eyes gleamed, but not with tears. Determination was written on her face and in every move she made.

"Mr. Joshua already has me, Papa. I love him, you see. And there's no way on earth you can keep us apart."

"Out! Out!" Mallette shouted. "This discussion is not for your ears."

"I will not go!" Lexie not only stood her ground, but stood it with one arm linked through D'Angelo's, daring her father with her actions as well as her words to try to keep them apart.

"Lexie's right, you know," D'Angelo said, smiling down at her. "When love is the bond, it's not easily severed."

A long silence followed. The old man looked from one to the other of them, then gave an angry snort. "You know my conditions, Alexandra."

She nodded. "I do, Papa, unfair as they are."

"Then send him away. This minute! You'll not set eyes on him for the next two years. And when he returns, he'll return a rich man or he'll not be a part of this family."

"Then you agree?" D'Angelo asked, a mixture of relief that they had won and regret at the thought of leaving Lexie making him almost weak.

"I agree to *nothing!*" the old man shouted. "Get out of my house, out of my sight! You'd better tell him

ALMOST HEAVEN 241

goodbye now, Alexandra. He'll be dead or wed to another before two years have passed."

In the shadowy hallway, D'Angelo stole one last kiss from his Lexie before he set out to seek his fortune.

"Where will you go? What will you do?" she murmured through her tears.

"For now, love, I'm off to Boston. I know a man there who's in dire need of a ship's master. I mean to strike a deal with him to take his vessel to Africa for half the profits. But before Boston, I'll go back to Brunswick to arrange for work to begin on your house. By the time I return, have your wedding gown ready. I won't be a patient man, my darling."

They kissed again, one last long sweet meeting of their hearts and their souls. Then D'Angelo Joshua set off into the gathering twilight of the snowy afternoon. He turned and waved, etching into his memory this last picture of his beautiful Lexie, his love.

Chapter Eleven

When Angel became herself again, she felt like a different person. Two people, actually. She could still recall her life as the wife of Jim Rhodes, the mother of Hope. But another personality seemed to have taken over the broadest realm of her consciousness. The most startling change was that she no longer thought like a woman. Instead of worrying about what she would do if this happens or that doesn't work out, she found herself meeting problems head-on with a determination to make things turn out the way *he* wanted them to or to know the reason why. There was not a great deal of contemplation in D'Angelo Joshua's acts. He simply charged ahead, bent on getting through his two years without Lexie and piling profits upon profits so that he could have her at the end of their enforced separation and provide for her in grand style.

The one overwhelming surprise to Angel was the enormity of D'Angelo's love for Lexie and his total, hellbent drive to have her. She had thought she couldn't love anyone more than she loved Jim. But this

ALMOST HEAVEN 243

obsession of D'Angelo's for Lexie was over and beyond any kind of human affection she had ever imagined.

He ached for Lexie with a pain that only grew as the time went by, but a pain he willingly endured in order to make her his wife. He dreamed of her at night, thought of her every minute of every day. He imagined her dressed in fine gowns of brocade and silk. He thought of the pleasure he could bring her with trinkets of silver and gold. He admired her. He adored her. He worshipped her as if she were a goddess or the queen of Heaven.

"You find such total love hard to understand, don't you, Angela?" Alexander was there beside her again as they drifted aimlessly through the heavenly sunset skies.

"I never knew such love existed." Her voice was hushed with awe. "What will happen to D'Angelo if he doesn't get to marry Lexie? What if she should die before he returns? What if she marries someone else?"

Alexander chuckled softly. "There you go, thinking like a woman again. The whole purpose of this journey through time is to reacquaint you with yourself as a man. You've been a woman for so long, you've forgotten how deeply we men feel, how unreasonably we trust, how totally we love."

She rounded on him and demanded, "Are you saying that a woman doesn't know how to love properly?"

"Not at all. I know Lexie's feelings for D'Angelo, and they are powerful indeed. All I'm pointing out to you is that a man loves differently. When he gives his heart totally, as D'Angelo has given his to Lexie, as

244   *Becky Lee Weyrich*

James Rhodes gave his to you, he never thinks of the future without her. In his mind, she simply becomes his other half for his entire life from the moment he falls in love. He never considers how he might go on without her should tragedy strike. In guarded moments, a wife might think about a time without her husband. Could she support herself and her children? Could she bear the loneliness? Could she find another husband who would love her and protect her? But not a man. Never would a man consider that distant point in time when he might have to go on without the woman he loves. So, if the worst happens and his wife is taken from him, a man is left to drift aimlessly in the sea of life. He can see no future without her, only a long parade of dark days and darker lonely nights."

"Jim," Angel whispered, putting her own husband into the grim scenario Alexander had just painted.

"Yes, Jim," Alexander replied. "If you are to understand his feelings, you must first experience those of D'Angelo Joshua. You must remember what your life was like when you were a man who loved a woman with such all-consuming passion that nothing else in your existence mattered. His was a man's love, a man's pain."

Angel looked up at Alexander, who stood tall and proud against the darkening sky. Her eyes misted with a woman's tears. "Tell me, Alexander," she begged, "if we're really soul mates, as you claim, have we ever had a happy life together?"

"We've been happy, you and I. We knew happiness as Alejandro and Gelina."

"Only briefly," she reminded him. "The blink of an eye and it was over for us."

ALMOST HEAVEN 245

"Ah, but even happiness that short-lived is much to be desired over long years without love. What's that old saying your mother is so fond of repeating? 'It is better to have loved and lost than never to have loved at all.' She's right, you know."

"What about D'Angelo and Lexie?"

"Close your eyes and see for yourself. Experience it now as you did so long ago."

Two years had passed—the most difficult of D'Angelo Joshua's life. Captain of an illegal slaver out of Boston, he had spent his time plying the stormy seas, putting in, at New England, West Africa, Cuba, Jamaica. Had he allowed himself to dwell on his unholy mission, it's likely he would never have survived. Only his obsessive love for Lexie kept him sane. Black nights on rough seas, nights filled with the tortured moans of humans suffering in the ship's fetid hold, and long, scorching days of endless, blinding sun reflected off the restless ocean made life aboard the *Sea Ghost* near unbearable, even considering the comparative comfort provided the vessel's master. But that comfort was purely physical. It did not extend to his soul. Captain Joshua made a fortune on his voyages, but he earned every pence with his blood. By the time he returned to Maine and his beloved, he was a changed man. Older, wiser, jaded, but still in love with all his heart and soul.

Lexie had passed her two years under only slightly more favorable circumstances. Her father had made it his business to remind her daily that she would likely never see D'Angelo Joshua again.

246   *Becky Lee Weyrich*

"He's no doubt lost at sea," he'd assure his daughter with a knowing smile. "Or boiled in a cook pot and eaten by some wild tribe of savages. And even if he's survived, I vow he's found some tall, dark Ashanti princess and taken her as his woman. Those wild, black heathens need no vows or sanctions in order to wed and bed. They need naught but a woman—willing or no—to lie beneath a man until his seed is planted."

Lexie did her best to ignore her father's words and set herself to more productive pursuits.

Like Penelope, who wove her tapestry while she awaited the return of her Odysseus from Troy, Lexie set herself the task of weaving a coverlet for her marriage bed. A bed she vowed to share with none other than her dear D'Angelo. The work, although tedious at times, kept her mind off her father's constant doom-saying. When she wearied of work at her loom, she turned to sewing the delicate silk of her wedding gown. By sunlight or lamplight, she measured each tiny stitch religiously—exactly three threads of the fabric between each thrust of her needle so that to the naked eye the seams were invisible, as if sewn by some fairy magic. Each prick of her needle became a sacred symbol to Lexie, an affirmation of her love. In spite of all odds, she would never give up hope that in time D'Angelo would return to make her his wife.

That day came in early April of 1861. On a morning fresh with dew and soft with spring, in the bower of lilacs beside the house on Park Row, Captain D'Angelo Joshua took Alexandra Mallette to have and to hold from this day forward.

Until the very moment when Lexie, veiled in lace and weeping happy tears, stepped down from the car-

ALMOST HEAVEN 247

riage to walk slowly toward the garden altar and her groom, their reunion had been thwarted by old Mr. Mallette. D'Angelo had returned from the sea nearly a month before. After settling his affairs in Boston, he'd taken the fastest stage north. He paused only briefly in Brunswick to inspect his fine new home, before hiring a horse at the stable to ride with all haste to Wiscasset.

He dismounted in front of the Mallette house and tossed his reins to a brawny, young stableman. Only as he started for the door did he realize his heart was in his throat. He knew his first fear in two years. He had faced hurricanes, mutiny, and savages with far more bravery than he felt at the thought of facing the woman he loved after so long a time.

He seldom prayed, but the moment seemed appropriate. "Dear God," he murmured, "please let her be well. Please let her still love me."

His knock was answered by the same servant who had guarded the door for decades. The man was older now and looked unwell.

"Please inform Mistress Mallette that she has a caller."

A plump, arthritic hand shot out from the shadows of the hallway and shoved the servant aside. Mr. Mallette.

"My daughter no longer receives callers," he bellowed. "Begone with you!"

D'Angelo managed to wedge the toe of his boot in the door before the old blackguard could slam it shut.

"She'll receive me," he bellowed back. "She'll do more than that. She'll *marry* me!"

He put his shoulder against the door and shoved it open.

248   *Becky Lee Weyrich*

"What's the meaning of this?" Mallette demanded.

D'Angelo faced the man fiercely. "You know full well. It's been two years. My purse is filled with gold as are my bank accounts in Boston. And there's a shining new mansion in Brunswick, which will soon be filled with the most elegant furnishings I could find in the world. All that's left is for me to stand with Lexie before a parson and be wed in God's eyes as we have been in our hearts since the first day we met."

Mallette's eyesight had failed over the years. He leaned closer, squinting to get a good look at D'Angelo's face. Only when he heard what his unwanted visitor had to say did he realize the full import of this intrusion.

"You expect my daughter to marry you when she hasn't so much as laid eyes on you in over two years? You fool! A woman's heart is fickle. She's drifted on to other loves."

For an instant, D'Angelo felt a terrible pain in his chest. Then he rallied, remembering the old man for the liar he was.

"Never!" D'Angelo exclaimed. "It's not possible for Lexie to love another while my heart still beats for her alone. Call her down here. We'll see what her true feelings are."

Mallette smiled—a look to freeze hearts. "She's not here, as it happens."

Again, D'Angelo felt his chest tighten. Again, he offered up a prayer. Surely her father couldn't mean that she had died while they were apart. But no. D'Angelo loved her too much. He would know if anything had happened to her. He would feel it in his soul.

"Tell me where she is, then. I'll go there. I'm not a

ALMOST HEAVEN 249

patient man, Mallette. I've waited two years already. Now each moment without her is like a century."

"You still mean to marry her, then?"

"Are you mad, man? Of course I do! And I won't be kept from her a minute longer."

D'Angelo started for the stairs, but at a slight motion from Mallette the servant moved to bar the way.

"I won't have you invading my private quarters, Joshua. I told you, she's not here."

"Where have you sent her?" D'Angelo demanded in a threatening voice.

"I sent her nowhere. She went of her own free will to visit a cousin in Kittery."

"Kittery," D'Angelo breathed. If only he had known, his stage passed right through there on the way.

He looked down at Lexie's father through narrowed eyes. "How soon will she return?"

"Next week . . . next month. How should I know? She'll come home when the spirit moves her."

D'Angelo was at a loss. What now? He knew Mallette would not send word of her return, nor would he tell his daughter that her fiancé was back. Short of camping out in the front yard, there would be no way to greet Lexie upon her return. He could ride down to Kittery and search her out. Yes, that was the best idea. D'Angelo turned to leave, without another word to Mallette.

He was mounting his horse for the ride back to Brunswick when the servant who had barred his way called to him in a harsh whisper from the corner of the house.

"Wait, sir!"

250 *Becky Lee Weyrich*

D'Angelo turned. "What now?"

The tall, sickly man beckoned. D'Angelo urged his horse closer.

"It's about Miss Lexie," the servant said. "He lied to you. She's not gone to Kittery, but to Camden. She's due to return the day after tomorrow."

"By damn! I should have guessed he'd try to send me off on a wild-goose chase. Probably by the time I got back from Kittery, he'd have hustled her off to some other distant point." He looked to the servant pleadingly. "How is she? Is she well?"

The man smiled. "Well and ripe and counting the days till her wedding, sir."

"Then she still loves me," D'Angelo said with relief. He felt such joy that he feared his chest might burst. "Will you give her a message for me upon her return?"

The man nodded, then glanced toward the front door. "Yes, but quickly, sir. His Honor will be calling for me at any time now. He'd not take kindly to my talking to you."

"Tell Miss Lexie that I came. Tell her that I'll send a carriage to bring her to Brunswick on Friday, the day after her return. And tell her that her house is ready, all it needs is a bride and a groom."

The servant grinned and nodded. "I'll tell her all that, sir, and I'll see that she gets into your carriage and away before her father knows she's gone. May I come with her?"

D'Angelo gripped the man's hand. "We'd be pleased to have you. What's your name?"

"Willum, sir. Willum Stiles."

"Well, Willum, if you'd like to stay on with us in

ALMOST HEAVEN 251

Brunswick, we'll be needing a fine butler to oversee the servants in our new home."

Tears of gratitude gathered in the old fellow's eyes. "I'm much obliged, sir. I've only stayed on here to watch over Miss Lexie like her mother asked of me before she died. And might I bring along my son? He's good with horses, sir, and he can chop a cord of wood in jig time. He's a strong one, ayah."

D'Angelo remembered the fair-haired lad he'd seen driving old Mallette's sleigh. A young man of brawn, with a quick sureness to his stride.

"The lad's name?" he asked.

"Cabot," answered the servant with a father's pride in his smile.

"Willum, you and Cabot must bring Lexie to Brunswick, to the wedding. And here's a pouch of gold, an advance on your wages."

On the morning of his wedding, D'Angelo waited inside the house on Park Row as long as he could. In the past two hours, he had paced the length of every room, peered out every window, opened every cupboard with restless, pent-up energy.

Would she come? Could Willum and Cabot sneak her away from the house without interference from her father? What if the coach broke down? What if one of the horses went lame?

"I should have gone for her myself," he muttered. "Never mind that old wives' tale that a groom is not supposed to see his bride until the hour of the wedding. I've lived without the sight of her for far too long already."

252 *Becky Lee Weyrich*

Finally, unable to contain himself a moment longer, D'Angelo strode down the gleaming stairway and out into the garden. He'd wait in the fanciful white arbor he'd had built among the lilacs—a tiny chapel for his love.

Already the townspeople were gathering, curious to see the fabled Captain Joshua give up his freedom at last to wed his shy, young bride from Wiscasset. Everyone had heard the gossip about this pair—how old man Mallette had sent Joshua on his way, demanding that he not return in less than two years, and then only if he'd made a fortune in order to support his Lexie in high style. For well over a year now, they had all watched the progress on Joshua's fine mansion as it went up, board by board and brick by brick, in the heart of town. They had wondered at the cost of such a showplace, then had gasped collectively when they saw the lavish European furnishings—carved rosewood and mahogany pieces, huge gilt-framed mirrors, tapestries, and paintings—being carried into the house. Did Joshua mean for his bride simply to live there or had he in mind for her to reign there as a queen?

The old-timers in Brunswick still remembered the rude log cabin that had once stood on the site. They told and retold the tales of the tragic Joshua family, the Indian raid, the madwoman who had come home from Canada to her husband and son only to freeze to death one cold night. They wished D'Angelo Joshua and his bride well, but whispered ominous warnings that history and grief had a way of repeating themselves.

D'Angelo felt all eyes on him as he walked out into his garden. He was not a man to welcome undue atten-

ALMOST HEAVEN 253

tion. He'd spent his life as a loner, drifting about the world in relative anonymity. He liked it that way. He coveted his privacy. Too many people and too much attention made him edgy—gave him the itch to take off to the north and lose himself in the deep woods as his father had done so often long ago.

But this morning, after his initial nervous reaction to the curious crowd, D'Angelo realized that these were *his* people, neighbors, hometown folk who wished him only the best. They had come, not to gawk, but to share in his happiness as he wed the woman he loved. His heart brimmed with goodwill toward his guests. He moved through the smiling throng, shaking hands, exchanging greetings.

Suddenly, a hush fell over the crowd. All heads turned toward the Bath Road where a cloud of dust in the distance signaled the imminent arrival of a coach. Then they saw it—the shiny forest green carriage with D'Angelo Joshua's initials entwined in gold, like a crest, on the doors.

"The bride!" An awed whisper went through the crowd.

Minutes of silence followed before cheers rang out from every quarter. "The bride! Hooray! She's come!"

Never in D'Angelo's life had he experienced such a moment. The happy shouts of his guests faded to jubilant whispers in the back of his mind, overwhelmed by the thunderous beating of his heart. It seemed that everything he had ever worked for, ever dreamed of, ever imagined was at this instant rushing to greet him. He stood frozen for a time, watching his love draw ever closer. Only when the coach rolled to a halt in his drive was he able to shake off his trance.

254   *Becky Lee Weyrich*

In long, purposeful strides, he covered the distance
to it. Willum sat on the box next to his handsome son
Cabot, who held the reins in his strong hands. D'Angelo nodded to the two men, but the main focus of his
attention remained on the figure in white inside—his
Lexie.

He had the sudden urge to wrench open the door,
scoop her into his arms, carry her into the house and
up to their bed. Never mind the curious crowd, the
waiting parson, the vows, the sanctity of the occasion.
For two long years, D'Angelo had played the role of a
monk, turning down the alluring offers of whores from
Maracaibo to Marrakesh. He'd been no more interested in the dark princesses of the Nile or the pale god-
desses of the Thames. Love had kept him on the
straight and narrow path to this day, to this woman.
But now it seemed that passion and desire might over-
ride his pure, soul-deep affection. He wanted her,
needed her, he could not live another moment without
her. And, by God, he would *have* her!

A soft voice—like angels' song—brought him back
to his senses. "D'Angelo?" Lexie whispered from the
deep shadows within the carriage. Her voice trembled
with emotion as she spoke his name. "Can it really be
you or is this just another of my lonely, wishful
dreams?"

Out of a sea of white silk and lace, he saw a small,
elegant hand reach toward him. He opened the door
and clasped her cool fingers in his.

"Lexie," he whispered, a catch in his voice as they
touched for the first time in so long. "Ah, dearest, I
thought this day would never come. Do you love me
still?"

ALMOST HEAVEN 255

He held his breath, waiting for her reassurance.

"How can you ask?" she murmured. "I love you more than ever, D'Angelo. With all my heart. You own my soul."

"Then you'll be my wife?"

She gripped his hand more tightly, sending warmth coursing through his body. "I'll be your wife, your partner, your friend—your lover—my dearest, from now through all eternity."

D'Angelo burned at her words and their passionate delivery.

"Then let us be done with formalities," he said in a husky voice. "Here, let me help you, my love."

He handed her out of the carriage, careful not to snag her lovely gown. In the sunlight, he could see the tears glistening in her eyes through her veil. Tears of joy. Tears of love. He bent slowly and brought her dainty hand to his lips.

"Are you ready, then?" he asked, still hesitant to believe that their moment had finally come.

Her answer made his heart sing. "I have been ready for this day since I first drew breath. Quickly now, my love. Our long wait is almost over."

The ceremony itself seemed no more than a blur of color and light and sound to D'Angelo, a mingled vision of purple lilacs, white lace, and tall, green pines whispering overhead. All his concentration remained focused on his bride, on her slight form beside his towering height, her sweet voice, her shy answers to the parson's nuptial queries. How could someone so slender and fragile make a man his size tremble and quake? How was it that she had conquered him and become the center of his universe, his moon and stars, his one and only hope for happiness?

And then it was done. They were man and wife, joined at the soul for all eternity.

Carefully, as if she might break, D'Angelo lifted the veil and took her into his arms. For a moment before he kissed her, their eyes met. The impact of her silvery gaze set new fires ablaze within him. Never had he desired a woman so totally. Never had he felt the need to protect and cherish another to such a degree.

Their kiss was sweet and brief, as if they both realized that anything more would cast them over the brink and into the stormy sea of their own desires.

"My *wife*," he whispered.

She pressed her soft, warm hand to his weathered cheek. "My own dear husband," she answered with a sigh.

Her words and her touch brought D'Angelo a moment of such joy that he wondered how he could bear it. He clung to her, murmuring her name over and over again, trying to make himself believe that this was true, that Lexie was really his at last.

D'Angelo's fondest wish would have been to sneak away at that moment, to take his wife into their new home and make it theirs by performing the very act that would make her his. But the guests were ready for a real chivaree. They spread blankets under the trees and brought out baskets and boxes of food. D'Angelo passed the word to Willum and Cabot to bring out casks of wine and pipes of gin from his well-stocked cellar for the celebration. Some of the sailors in the crowd produced a fiddle and hornpipes and began to

ALMOST HEAVEN 257

play a lively tune. Soon the younger bucks were dancing, passing Lexie from partner to partner.

D'Angelo picked at his food, swilled his wine, and stood by, impatient to claim his bride again. When finally she whirled into his arms, the guests gathered round, clapping and stomping, demanding a dance from the bride and groom. This was all a part of the wedding fun. Steal the bride away from her man to dance with every other. Make him wait. Make him anxious. Then give her back. Let him hold her for a time and dance with her until his trousers are near-bursting with his need. Then steal her again and leave him in misery.

The dance worked its charms on poor D'Angelo as the grinning guests all knew it would. They demanded the "Kissing Dance." Whirls and turns and bows and skips, and a kiss from the groom each time they touched. D'Angelo's kisses at first were mere pecks. But urged on by the laughing, cheering crowd, he became more bold. He kissed Lexie's lips in passing a few times. Then he caught her in his arms for a long, smoldering kiss, and then another and another.

He was more than ready to end this frolic for more intimate sport in bed when the crowd brought out their pots and pans and wooden spoons. As they set up their din of noise, several of the women stole Lexie right out of D'Angelo's arms and whisked her off to the house.

The groom's loud protests were met by a circle of men, who cut off his passage. They offered him more wine and told him off-color jokes. They teased and jeered and suggested things he might do to pleasure his bride.

258 *Becky Lee Weyrich*

While the women were inside making Lexie ready for her husband, the men primed D'Angelo for his coming performance. After nearly an hour of wine and lusty talk, they escorted the slightly tipsy groom into his house and up the stairs.

"You'll get a son on her this very night," one of the burly sailors shouted, loud enough for the bride to hear. That was all part of the game.

Another called out, "Mind you don't scare her to death with that big stallion's tool."

"She's a wee thing," another warned. "Careful you don't grind her right into the mattress."

Just then, the women threw open the bedroom door. D'Angelo could see Lexie cringe at the sight of the drunken men, himself included.

"Go home!" he begged. Then he demanded. "Leave us in peace!"

"Not till the deed's done," one of the men shouted back.

The women all clutched at D'Angelo and hustled him toward the huge bed he'd purchased for his bride. Lexie lay, wide-eyed, propped up on lacy pillows, the coverlet she'd woven pulled up to her chin. Still tugging at D'Angelo, the ladies removed his coat, vest, and shirt. Then they stole his boots. When they went for his trousers, he turned on them.

"Out, I say! I can do it myself!"

This brought whoops and guffaws from the men, but it served the purpose. The women shoved him down on the bed next to Lexie, but then left the bedroom, shooing their men ahead of them.

At last, D'Angelo and Lexie were alone. Still

ALMOST HEAVEN

259

sprawled across the bed, his broad, bare chest heaving with exertion, he looked up at his bride and smiled.

"Did they frighten you?" he asked.

Lexie's lips trembled, but she managed to return his smile. "Perhaps a bit. Not the women so much as the men."

"You can't be afraid of *me?*"

"I'm not," she whispered, easing the coverlet down from her breasts.

D'Angelo tried not to stare, but he couldn't help himself. The sheer batiste of her gown did a bad job of hiding her beauty from his hungry eyes.

From outside in the garden came the sounds of the merrymakers still rattling their pots and pans, still shouting their coarse jokes. D'Angelo rose and closed the window. The uproar faded to a faint hubbub.

"There! That's better," he said. "Forget about them, my darling. This concerns only you and me."

"Then come here," she invited, lifting her arms to him.

D'Angelo needed no second invitation. He climbed onto the bed and went into her arms, cradling her close to his hard, bare chest.

"Ah, Lexie," he breathed. "You smell of warm honey and wild flowers." He kissed her, tenderly at first, then harder. "And you taste of everything wonderful in the world. Ambrosia, the nectar of the gods."

They lay together for a long time, she under the covers, he on top of the coverlet. Afternoon sun streamed in the window, warming D'Angelo's shoulders, bringing a flush to Lexie's cheeks.

D'Angelo knew he had had too much to drink. For that reason, he moved slowly with her. He knew his

260 *Becky Lee Weyrich*

own eagerness and his own desire and power. Lexie seemed as delicate and fragile as a spring violet. He must handle her carefully. He must treat her tenderly. He must love her with care.

For now, he wanted to fill his senses with her so that he could believe that she was really here and really his. He stared at her face, touched her shining dark hair, kissed her cheeks, her eyelids, her throat.

She sighed, then sighed again. Her hands inched up over his back. D'Angelo trembled with a pleasure so deep that his body ached and breathing came hard.

"Oh, Lexie! My Lexie!" he moaned. "There's so much we need to say to each other. There are so many days we need to fill in. Where do we begin?"

"My days without you had no meaning. They aren't worth discussing. My whole life began today, with you."

His gaze went once more to her breasts—sweet, heaving peaks there within his grasp. But would his touch startle her? He reminded himself once more of the need to take things slowly and gently.

As if sensing his thoughts, Lexie took his hand and brought it to her breast. As his fingers crushed her gown and closed over her tender flesh, she sighed and closed her eyes.

Made bold by Lexie's action, D'Angelo slipped the gown from her shoulder and feasted his eyes on her for the first time. He touched her nipple with one finger. It puckered and hardened as if begging for more. He leaned down and kissed it, then drew the soft flesh into his mouth and stroked it lazily with his tongue.

Lexie moaned his name.

For a long time, she lay back on the pillows with her

ALMOST HEAVEN 261

eyes closed, seemingly content with what he was doing to her. But then her hips began to move and her moans became more urgent.

D'Angelo knew that he could not wait much longer. He was considering how to go about undressing and climbing under the covers when he felt a tug at his britches. He looked down to see Lexie's fingertips gripping his waist anxiously. He rose and she flipped the covers back, exposing his place beside her, offering herself to him.

He glanced at her face. Her eyes were no longer closed. She was staring at him, the glitter of desire in her silver gray eyes. Her lips were parted. He watched the tip of her tongue glide out to moisten them.

Not a word was needed to tell D'Angelo what his bride wanted. Hadn't they both waited long enough. Boldly, he stepped out of his britches. Even more boldly, Lexie stared at his naked body, his firm erection. She showed not a flicker of fear.

He started for the bed, but Lexie held up a hand to stop him. "Wait!" she commanded.

Puzzled and disappointed, D'Angelo stood his ground. His disappointment was short-lived. While he watched, Lexie pulled her gown up, over her head, then tossed it aside.

"There!" she said. "That's better."

D'Angelo stared at her, fascinated, amazed, aroused. Her breasts were like twin mounds of the purest snow. Her torso was slender, her skin as softly gleaming as satin. She had a narrow waist, only the hint of hips, and long, shapely legs. His gaze was drawn to the dark triangle at the top of her thighs, like an arrow pointing the way. He longed to touch her

262 *Becky Lee Weyrich*

there, kiss her there, then sink to his hilt in her softness.

"I burn for you, Lexie," he warned her.

She cocked her head and stared straight into his eyes. "And am I not allowed to burn, simply because I'm a woman?" She raised her arms to him.

D'Angelo went to her, stunned and in awe. He'd been with many women before he met Lexie. He'd seen all types from bold, brazen whores to weeping, thin-blooded virgins. But never had he approached anyone like his bride. She knew neither shame nor fear. Her first act when he lay down beside her was to clasp him boldly with her small, cool hand.

"Oh, God!" he moaned. "Oh, my Lexie!"

Encouraged by her power to arouse him, she tempted him more, nipping at his shoulder, biting his neck, darting her little tongue into his mouth. He took her splendid torture for as long as he could bear it. Then he turned the tables on her, returning her passion in kind. Soon *she* was whimpering, moaning, and begging. Emboldened by their game of love, he touched her where he knew she most desired to be stroked. A tremor shook her body. And then he kissed her there, letting his tongue have its way with her.

Lexie gave a fierce shudder, then shot up in bed. She grabbed his shoulders and buried her face against his chest. When he felt her tongue drag over his nipple, all games were canceled. Forcing her down, he covered her body with his.

He captured her lips in a hard, fierce kiss. At the exact moment of his first thrust, he stabbed with his tongue as well. Lexie's slender hips pitched forward,

ALMOST HEAVEN 263

driving him deeper. He swallowed her whimper of pain, then her pants of desire.

They moved together as if they had been created for this one act. Two long years of dreams and longing exploded into a starburst of mounting pleasure. Lexie clawed at his back, urging him on—deeper, harder, faster. Every moment, it seemed to D'Angelo that the ecstasy would reach its peak, then the next instant the feeling would grow and expand until he felt ready to explode.

Lexie clutched his waist, then gripped his buttocks, pulling him into her, begging for more. And then it happened! Like a million fireballs bursting in his groin to scorch his whole body. He heard Lexie gasp. He felt her body shudder against his. Then she went limp in his arms with the happy exhaustion of a satisfied bride. His own body, still pulsing with erotic vibrations, began to relax.

Lexie was the first to speak afterward, although her words were weak and halting. "Papa always warned me about this night."

"Warned you?" Had he hurt her, then?

"He said it would be a horror like none other, short of childbirth. He said I would find it demeaning and horribly painful."

"I'm so sorry . . ."

She cut off his apology with a soft laugh. "Papa lied! Nothing I ever imagined could have been so wonderful, my darling."

D'Angelo buried his face against her breasts. "Lexie," he murmured against her hot flesh. "Oh, Lexie, at last! We'll never have to be apart again. I promise to love you for as long as we live and even beyond the grave."

"I don't ever want to be alone again, D'Angelo. You've made my life worth living at last. Don't ever take that away from me."

"Never, my love, never! I'll be here with you from now on. Nothing, no one can separate us."

Little did either of them suspect that shortly before D'Angelo Joshua made his promise, a cannon had been fired, aimed at a manmade granite island in South Carolina called Fort Sumter. An American flag was torn, a mule was killed, and D'Angelo's promise to his bride was instantly shattered.

Chapter Twelve

"Wow!" Angel exclaimed. "I thought women back in the nineteenth century were supposed to be shy and retiring. I thought they hated *that.*"

"Hated what?" Alexander asked innocently.

"You know." Angel could feel herself blushing and was glad the sunset heavens acted as camouflage. "Sex," she whispered, not sure she should utter such a word aloud to an angel.

"Hey, I'm sorry! Okay? Don't blame Lexie. That was my first time on the bottom. I'm used to being on top. And I'm not much of an actor. I wanted the same thing you wanted, maybe wanted it more. After all, you might have waited two years, but I'd been waiting Lexie's whole life."

Angel glanced up at him through lowered lashes. "Was it good for you?"

"Yeah, real good!" Alexander threw back his head and laughed, then asked with the feigned timidity of a recently unfrocked virgin, "But did you still respect me the next morning?"

Angel chuckled and winked at her eternal lover.

266   *Becky Lee Weyrich*

"You want to know the truth—I don't remember much about the next morning. I was worn out. We were at it all night."

"I always was a frisky little wench."

By now, Alexander had Angel laughing so hard she was afraid she might get the hiccups. "Hey, cut it out! You're an angel, remember? Show some respect." She giggled some more, then added, "Man, you shocked the socks off me!"

"As I recall," he answered with mock decorum, "you weren't wearing any."

"Stop it! Stop it!" Angel howled. "Be serious, Alexander. D'Angelo and Lexie were very much in love."

Alexander reached out and touched her cheek. His fingertips trailed lightly along the soft curve of her chin. *"You and I* were in love, Angela. We still are unless I'm mistaken."

She looked at him, all seriousness now. "You've changed, Alexander."

"If I have, it's because of you, Angela. Until you arrived, I'd forgotten what it was like down on Earth. I'd forgotten the challenges, the changes, the highs, the lows. Up here everything stays pretty much the same from century to century."

"I thought you told me Heaven was perfect."

Alexander nodded, unsmiling. "It is. That's my point. Even perfection can get boring after a while. When everything's perfect all the time—no bumps, no bruises—you tend to just level off and glide like you were on autopilot—unless you have someone to keep you grounded and plugged in to real life."

"So I'm sort of your extension cord to Earth, eh, feeding you juice from down below?"

ALMOST HEAVEN

He smiled at her. "Something like that. Having you here with me again is like an awakening. It's a sign, too."

"What kind of sign, Alexander?"

"It's my notice from the Power-That-Be that I'll be leaving here soon, going back."

"Are you ready?"

"Oh, yes! More than ready."

"Then what's keeping you here?"

"You are. You and D'Angelo Joshua."

"I don't understand."

"You will. We aren't done with D'Angelo and Lexie yet. He's still haunting the house on Park Row. You must recapture his spark before either of us can return to new lives."

Angel shook her head and frowned at her solemn companion. "You're not making a lot of sense, Alexander. Can't you tell me what I'm supposed to do?"

"Not yet. You'll know in time. You'll see it all clearly, and you'll understand about Jim, too. You'll realize what you must do."

Angel felt ashamed of herself for letting Jim's plight slip her mind for the moment. "He still needs a wife, doesn't he?"

"Need you ask? Think about it, Angela. How would D'Angelo feel if Lexie was suddenly taken from him?"

Angel closed her eyes tight and let D'Angelo's spirit slide back into her soul. After a moment, she answered in his voice, "I'd be devastated, destroyed. I couldn't go on without her. But why are you troubling me with such nonsense? Nothing will happen to my Lexie."

"One can never be sure of the future."

When Alexander answered, it seemed to Angel that

268 *Becky Lee Weyrich*

his voice came from far away. They were drifting again, traveling the heavens back through time. Far off, she heard faint rumbling, like thunder, but different somehow.

"Is that cannon fire I hear?"

"You know it is. Its echo is coming from the very date on which you married Lexie."

"That was the twelfth of April, 1861, the day we wed."

"That date has another significance. Think harder."

She did think, very hard. When she looked at Alexander again, she had tears in her eyes. "Fort Sumter. The beginning of the Civil War. Oh, no . . ."

Her words were swallowed up in the whirlwind of time.

Three days after the attack on Fort Sumter and little over a month after President Lincoln's inauguration the call went out from Washington for seventy-five thousand volunteer troops to help quell the "insurrection." When the news reached Maine, D'Angelo Joshua felt the call of his conscience.

"You can't go! I won't let you." Lexie wept.

D'Angelo put his arm around his bride of only weeks to comfort her. Overhead the Bowdoin Pines sighed as if they too were grieving for the Union and for all the lovers about to say farewell.

"It's only for three months, darling. Then it will be over and I'll be home. I couldn't live with myself if I didn't volunteer."

She whirled away from him. "And I can't live with-

ALMOST HEAVEN

269

out you, D'Angelo. You said you'd never leave me again. You promised!"

Never had a man felt so torn. D'Angelo had made that promise to his wife. But his country was in peril. And, although he'd never say such a frightening thing to Lexie, he feared his sanity was at stake. No one in the government admitted it yet, but D'Angelo believed that the unholy practice of slavery was at the heart of the insurrection. He held himself accountable for his part in this madness. He had built his fortune by transporting enslaved human beings. He would never be a free man—free of nightmares, free of guilt—until the last slave from his ship was free.

"Come, Lexie. It's getting late. We can talk more when we get home."

"I refuse to talk about it. I refuse even to consider your leaving. If you go in spite of my wishes, I can't be held responsible for what happens."

D'Angelo, mistaking her meaning, said gently, "I'll be all right, dear. And should anything happen to me, no one would hold you responsible. You've made your thoughts on the subject quite clear."

The rest of their afternoon stroll passed in silence. That night for the first time since their wedding, Lexie Joshua turned away from her husband in bed, refusing the comfort of his arms, the pleasures of his body.

D'Angelo lay awake long into the night, doing anguished battle with himself. He could feel Lexie's warmth in their bed, but her back was turned to him. How could he even think of going away and leaving this woman who meant so much to him? It would be so easy simply to forget about those battles waging far to the South. What business was it of his what happened way down in the Carolinas, Tennessee, or Georgia? He had a wife to care for, and maybe a baby on the way. Lexie had broken the news to him only two days before.

"A baby," he murmured. "Maybe a son to carry on my name. Or a little daughter as beautiful and sweet as her mother."

His thoughts shot ahead to a scene his imagination conjured up. He and his son, a young man in his teens, were talking in his study. The lad was tall and well built, his silver-blue eyes gleaming with intelligence.

"Tell me about your days at sea, Father. That's how you made your fortune, Mother says."

And what would the great Captain Joshua say to his son? Could he bear to tell his boy how he had bought human beings from the Africans who sold them, had crowded them in the dark hold, had chained and nearly starved this human cargo?

"No, by God!" D'Angelo swore softly.

He broke into a sweat. His eyes burned. His head ached. He *had* to go to war or he could never face his own son.

D'Angelo reached out in the dark for his wife. He needed her closeness, her comfort, her love. Lexie, her mind dulled with sleep, forgot her anger and responded to his caress. Soon the two of them were locked in a lovers' embrace, moving smoothly with a well-practiced rhythm.

After a swift, sweet trip to the stars, Lexie said drowsily, "Then you've changed your mind, darling. You'll stay."

He couldn't bring himself to tell her the truth. In-

ALMOST HEAVEN 271

stead, he kissed her and said, "I love you. Go back to sleep now."

Not until midday did Lexie learn her husband's true intentions. She'd spent a busy morning, singing happily while she baked in the kitchen, sure that all was well, that D'Angelo had given up his foolish plans.

But by noon, he could keep his secret no longer. He sauntered into the kitchen from his study and sat down at the table.

"We have to talk."

Lexie's singing broke off in midnote. When she turned toward him, her face was ashen. Her eyes brimmed with tears.

"It's only three months," he began. "I'll be back before the baby comes."

"If you return at all," she replied in a stony voice.

"Darling, I *must* go! Don't you see?"

"All I see is that you tricked me last night. Well, it won't happen again. If you persist in this madness, you can sleep in the guest room until you leave."

And so he did. Three long, lonely nights he spent in an empty bed. On the morning of his departure, Lexie wept to break his heart. Relenting at last, she kissed him and clung to him, all the while begging him to change his mind.

The last sight D'Angelo saw as he rode off to war was his beautiful wife, sobbing in the lilac arbor where they had been wed such a short time before.

He joined up with a Maine unit in Portland. The troop took trains down to Boston, then on to Washington City. All the while, D'Angelo regularly wrote let-

272 *Becky Lee Weyrich*

ters home to Lexie. Each time after he apologized for disappointing her, and swore his unwavering love, he would go on to describe his present circumstances . . .

We marched from the train station through Washington. In passing the White House, I got a glimpse of the President, a tall, gaunt fellow, indeed. I hope he is up to the task of bringing our country together again. The city itself is an unlovely sight—mud holes everywhere that streets should be, pigs routing and wallowing, some fine houses but more shanties. We soldiers are bunking wherever we can. The Rhode Islanders are camped out at the Patent Office. The New York regiments have an easy life, sleeping on the carpeted floor of the House of Representatives and making speeches to while away their time. I am at present with a group of Massachusetts boys. We've spread our bedrolls in the rotunda of the House and are cooking our meals in the furnaces down in the cellar. The locals don't seem to take this invasion too kindly. And I can see their view. Some of the "soldiers" are of a very low caliber and think nothing of desecrating the beauty and art of our Federal city. But we'll be moving out soon. We'll make our point, then head back home. It won't be long, darling. Keep me in your thoughts and prayers as you are in mine.

Lexie tried. She *really* tried! She, too, wrote long letters, begging her husband's forgiveness for the way she'd acted, and swearing her enduring love. In September she received word from her husband that he would not be home in three months as he had prom-

ALMOST HEAVEN 273

ised. "Perhaps in time for Christmas," he wrote. The following week, she lost the baby. Had it not been for that sad event, all might have been well. As it was, her miscarriage seemed the final blow.

After spending long weeks in bed, Lexie simply gave in to her weaker, darker side. Since there was no safe harbor for her love now with her baby gone and her husband far away—dead or alive, she knew not—her loneliness deepened into depression. Happiness seemed only a dim memory far in the past. In one final attempt to amuse herself and make the time go faster, she bought a horse. She rode her fine mare every day, out Mere Point way or along the banks of the Androscoggin. The townspeople whispered about her—a lone woman riding out that way. But Lexie didn't care. She was past caring what people thought or said. Her rides were not solely for entertainment. She was searching, searching for something—perhaps love, perhaps her own sanity.

The fateful day came in mid-May. D'Angelo had not returned for Christmas, and his letters came seldom and erratically now. Reports of bloody battles and many casualties reached Brunswick almost daily. And every day, Lexie scanned the posted lists, searching for D'Angelo's name and praying that she wouldn't find it on the black-bordered pages. As she finished with the list that fine May morning, she murmured a prayer of thanks that her husband had survived one more battle. But the thought that he could be in the heat of another fight at this very moment or lying dead on some distant battlefield sent her spirits plummeting.

She mounted her horse and headed for the river.

274 *Becky Lee Weyrich*

How could she know that the banks of the Androscoggin would be both her salvation and her downfall?

Lexie rode slowly down a wooded path above the falls. Her troubled mind ignored the beauty of the day—the delicate violets winking in patches of deep shade, the tiny pristine Quaker ladies like bits of white lace on the path, the forsythia bursting with golden blooms. When she reached a shady glen at the head of the falls, she reined in her mare and dismounted. Settling on a large, smooth rock, she took a slim volume of poetry from her pocket and read the love sonnets aloud. Somehow it seemed that the wind and the water might carry her words of love to her husband.

She had no idea that her words of passion were falling on other ears. When she heard the crunch of a boot nearby, she looked up from her poetry. There stood young Cabot Stiles, her groom and childhood companion, with his thatch of golden hair, his sea green eyes, and a look of concern on his handsome face.

"Cabot!" she said. "You startled me."

"I'm sorry, Mrs. Joshua. You were gone so long that I came to look for you. I was afraid you might have had an accident."

She stared right into his eyes, unsmiling. "Tell the truth, Cabot. You've followed me, haven't you? Were you afraid I might throw myself into the river? Well, don't think it hasn't crossed my mind."

"It'd be a sin to destroy such beauty," he said quietly.

"Don't talk to me of sin!" she countered. "This war is a sin. Losing my baby was a sin. Being alone when I need my husband so desperately is a sin."

She was still staring into his green eyes. Eyes that

ALMOST HEAVEN 275

seemed to speak to her of something far different from the sadness that had been her constant companion these past months. Just looking at him brought back a rush of memories—the best memories of her childhood, when she and Cabot had sledded together in the winter, gathered wild flowers together in the spring, and fished together in the summer. And they had laughed—it had been the only laughter in her father's house. She had fancied Cabot as they grew older. But then they had grown apart. After all, he was only a hireling and she was the master's daughter. The Mallette Princess, people had called her.

She patted the rock. "Come sit beside me, Cabot. Do you remember the time you fished me out of the frozen river back home? I'd ventured out too far on the thin ice and it broke with my weight. I might have died that day."

Cautiously, he took the spot beside her on the sunny rock in the secluded glen. The veiled look vanished from his eyes. Lexie was startled when she saw the intensity of his gaze.

"I would have died myself that day before I would have let you drown, Lexie."

This was the first time in years that Cabot had called her by her given name. The sound of it from his lips seemed as intimate as a kiss. Lexie grew uncomfortably warm suddenly. Was it the springtime sun or was it Cabot's nearness?

She smiled at him. "There are better memories," she said. "Like the day we went exploring in the deep woods, searching for Indian arrowheads."

Lexie could hardly believe what she was saying. That day was the one and only time Cabot had kissed her. They'd been in their early teens, playing a game of pretend. Cabot was the brave warrior returning from battle, and Lexie had played the part of a faithful Indian maid welcoming the conquering hero back home. The kiss had shocked them both. They hadn't planned it; it had simply happened. For weeks afterward, they had avoided each other, too embarrassed ever to speak of it again. Until this very moment. Why on earth, Lexie wondered, had she brought it up now?

For a time, Cabot didn't answer. He stared down at the smooth rock, drawing invisible designs with one finger. When he looked at her again, his eyes were like green fire.

"How could I ever forget *that* day? I was so in love with you, Lexie." He paused and heaved a heavy sigh. "Please don't hate me, but I have to confess it. I still am."

His words shocked her so deeply that she could think of nothing to say. He didn't give her time. Before Lexie could utter a word, Cabot turned to her, took her in his arms, and kissed her for the second time in their lives. But this kiss was far different, deep and lingering and passionate.

And for the brief time they spent in the woods, Lexie forgot her unhappiness. Cabot made her feel like a woman again. A whole woman, loved and cherished, and—dear God!—*satisfied.*

But they were hardly done with the glorious act before Lexie's guilt set in. It gripped her soul like some horrid black demon.

She sat on the rock afterward, sobbing, cursing herself, wishing that she had thrown herself into the river before she'd let this thing happen.

ALMOST HEAVEN 277

Cabot rose from the rock, a towering shadow over his weeping lover. "You'll be wanting me to leave, I expect."

"Yes! I mean, no!" Lexie cried. "I don't know what I mean. I'm so ashamed."

"I never meant to cause you more pain. I never meant to do what we did. I'm sorry. I'll go."

Cabot Stiles went straight back to the house on Park Row, packed his belongings, and said goodbye to his father. Lexie never saw him again. But he left her a lasting momento, one that would change her life and D'Angelo's life forever.

Two months later, on a fine July day, Brigadier General D'Angelo Joshua finally came home, more dead than alive. His field promotion had come in the bloody, smoky peach orchard near a little church called Shiloh in Tennessee. He'd taken three Reb bullets, one from his own troops; and he'd given up his right arm to the field surgeons. As happy as Lexie was to have him home again, her guilt only intensified at the sight of him. She suspected by now that Cabot Stiles had given her more than simply his love.

D'Angelo was a changed man. Not only was he pale, thin, and ill, something in his soul seemed altered by his battlefield experiences. He'd always been gregarious, laughing, talking, filled with life. Now, when Lexie tiptoed into his darkened room to see to his needs, it seemed to her that he had left more of himself than his arm back there. She had dreamed and planned so long for this joyous homecoming. How different it was!

"Is that you, Lexie?" D'Angelo asked in a thin voice that sounded far older than his years.

"Yes, dear," she answered.

"It's not time for my supper, is it? Or my medicine."

"No," she whispered, fighting tears, battling guilt. "I only want to sit with you and hold your hand."

He made a noise that sounded like something between a growl and a groan. "I needn't ask *which* hand."

Once again, Lexie had said the wrong thing, reminding him of his loss. She took her place beside the bed and clasped his only hand in hers. She tried to think of something to say, but no words came to mind.

"I'm sorry about the baby," D'Angelo said. It was the first time in the week since his return that either of them had mentioned her miscarriage. "It must have been rough on you. Worse because you were all alone. I should have been with you."

"Don't blame yourself, dear."

"Hard not to. I should have come home in August like I promised instead of signing on for another hitch. I got my payback, though. Damn near got myself killed for breaking that promise. Serves me right. But it wasn't fair to you. Can you forgive me, Lexie?"

The tears she'd been fighting won the battle. She only hoped D'Angelo couldn't see her crying in the darkness of the room.

He didn't have to see. She was his wife; he knew. He knew more than she could have guessed. He'd sensed a tension in her since the moment of his return. Something had happened while he was away. Something more than her losing the baby or him losing his arm.

ALMOST HEAVEN 279

He felt an invisible wall between them, a wall that he couldn't penetrate.

"You still haven't forgiven me for leaving you, have you, Lexie? I can't say as I blame you."

She clutched his hand tighter. "Of course I forgave you. Long ago, darling. I wrote to you. I told you I forgave you. Didn't you get my letters?"

"Some of them. Mail took a while catching up with us. Some never did, never will. But wives don't write bad things to their husbands during wartime. They make everything sound rosy so their men won't worry. The shock comes when a fellow gets back home."

A spear of cold tension shot through Lexie. He knew. Somehow, he knew!

"What shock?" she asked, trying to sound casual.

"I don't know. It's hard to explain. But things are different now between us, and I have a feeling they'll never be quite the same again."

A sob escaped Lexie. "Don't say that!" she cried. "Once you're well, everything will be just the way it was. We'll be happy again. We'll have a child. We'll be a family."

D'Angelo made no reply. He could tell by the desperate tone in Lexie's voice that she didn't believe a word she was saying. Trying to change the subject, wanting to get on some topic that might calm her, he asked, "Where's Cabot? I haven't seen him since I got home."

Lexie nearly jumped out of her chair at the mere mention of the name. She let out another sob and gripped D'Angelo's hand in both of hers.

"Gone," she said in a gasp, her body trembling violently. "Gone for good!"

"You mean he just took off?" D'Angelo sounded angry. "How could he do such a thing, leaving you here all alone with only Willum to tend to the place and look after you. That young scoundrel! I'll have his hide next time I see him."

"It was for the best," Lexie said. "He couldn't stay. Not after . . ." She caught herself in the nick of time. It was bad enough living with her guilt without having D'Angelo know.

"Why couldn't he stay?"

Panic-stricken, Lexie rose. "That's enough talk for now, darling. You need to rest. I'll go and see to supper."

She hurried out of the room before D'Angelo could ask any more questions.

Her husband improved remarkably over the next few weeks. But his somber mood remained. Lexie grew frantic. He suspected something, she was sure of it. Her own suspicions that she might be carrying Cabot's child became positive knowledge, so as she saw it, her only hope of saving her marriage was to make love to her ailing husband, then convince him that the baby was his when it arrived. Time was not on Lexie's side.

D'Angelo had been home for over a month when she decided she could wait no longer. Soon there would be no hiding her condition from her husband. She chose her time well, the middle of the night so that he couldn't see her rounding belly and full breasts.

She had been sleeping in the guest bedroom since her husband's return. He'd insisted she would be more comfortable in another room—his nights were restless, disturbed by pain and nightmares caused by the war.

ALMOST HEAVEN 281

But on this particular night, she slipped into his room and climbed in bed next to him.

He grunted and groaned, then reached out to touch her. "Lexie? What's wrong?"

"I couldn't sleep," she whispered. "I needed to be close to you, darling. I'll lie here with you for a bit, if that's all right."

She recognized the well-remembered huskiness in his voice when he said, "It's more than all right. I've been trying to work up the nerve to ask you to come to me for a while now."

"Work up the nerve? What are you talking about, darling? I'm your *wife!*"

"But I'm not the husband I used to be. I wasn't sure you still—"

She cut off his words with a long, deep kiss. A kiss that enflamed her blood as well as D'Angelo's. When caresses were no longer enough, Lexie mounted him, slowly, carefully.

She hadn't realized the level of her desire. What had been a plot to trick her husband, soon turned into an interlude of erotic, passionate wonders. A short time later, when they reached that blissful pinnacle in unison, Lexie found herself weeping once more. Her tears this time were tears of love and thanks and hope. Maybe there was still a chance for them after all.

"I've never loved you more than I do at this moment," D'Angelo said in a grave whisper. "You are my life, Lexie. Without you, I'm nothing."

She clung to him, hoping against all hope that his love would allow him to forgive her and believe her when the time came for her to convince him that Cabot's child was his.

282   *Becky Lee Weyrich*

                         *   *   *

Lexie's labor was long and difficult. With the doctor
and the town midwife in attendance that cold Febru-
ary morning, D'Angelo stayed below in his study,
wincing each time he heard his wife scream. Surely, he
thought, the baby would not survive. Lexie's labor had
come far too early. Even if he had impregnated her the
first time they made love after his return, the child
shouldn't have come until spring crocuses were breaking through the last patches of snow.

He paced and fretted, poured himself a brandy to
calm his nerves; then he paced some more.

Long shadows stretched across the study late that
afternoon before D'Angelo heard a new sound from
upstairs—the strong, loud cry of an infant.

"Thank God!" he cried, heading for the stairs.

He burst into the bedroom and went straight to
Lexie. She looked as pale and small as a sick child
there on the bed.

"Darling," he said between kisses, "it's over at last.
Are you all right?"

"She's fine," the doctor answered. "She came
through it like a trooper. And you have a fine, strong
son, General Joshua."

D'Angelo turned, shocked at this news. "A son?
You mean he lived? But the baby came too early by
months."

"This baby's not one day early," offered the midwife, hefting the squirming bundle in her ample arms.
"My guess is he's a good nine-pounder."

D'Angelo went to the woman to see for himself. He

ALMOST HEAVEN 283

peered down at the infant. "My God!" he breathed. "He's so big."

"That's why Mrs. Joshua had such a hard time," the doctor explained. "It takes a good deal of effort for so small a woman to be delivered of such a large baby."

"But . . ." D'Angelo broke off, not wanting to voice his doubts in front of outsiders. He glanced at Lexie. Her eyes were closed. She looked as pale as death.

"She'll be all right?" he asked the doctor. "You're sure?"

He nodded. "With rest and plenty of nourishment. She should stay abed for the next few weeks, though."

"Yes, of course," D'Angelo answered, glancing back at his "son." He didn't want to know, but questions kept nagging at him: If this wasn't *his* son, then *whose?* What had happened here while he was away? What had Lexie done to him?

As hard as D'Angelo tried over the next days and weeks, he could not bring himself to go near the child again. When Lexie suggested that they name their son for D'Angelo's father, he told her coldly, "No!"

"Then what shall we call him, darling? He must have a name."

"You choose," he told her, then strode out of the nursery where she was sitting in a rocking chair, nursing the baby.

It took little imagination to understand the source of D'Angelo's barely suppressed rage. After all, he was not a stupid man. He could count months and dates quite accurately. Lexie prayed that somehow he would find it in his heart to love this beautiful golden-haired, green-eyed child as his own. But as time passed, her husband only drew farther and farther away from her son and from her. Even months later, when Lexie had long recovered from the rigors of Mallette's birth—she'd finally chosen to give him her own name—D'Angelo kept his distance from his wife. She remained in the guest bedroom, near the nursery, and her husband made no move to come to her, nor did he invite her to share his bed. He spent his time in long, brooding silences or hid out in his study, writing his war memoirs, so he told her. He never asked the name of Mallette's father. He never accused Lexie aloud. But his constant, silent accusation was an unending torture.

Finally, when Mallette was nearly a year old, Lexie taught him to say, "Papa." Surely, no man could remain hostile toward such a charmer. Lexie adored her son. He was so bright, so beautiful, so sweet. She was certain that D'Angelo could come to love the boy, too, if only he would give the lad a chance. Certainly this man, who had once been so warm and loving, would not turn from a child who thought of him as his father.

If Lexie was in agony, D'Angelo was enduring a living hell. He still loved his wife. But the boy was a constant, living reminder of Lexie's indiscretions. Worse yet, the whole town knew. They probably even knew her lover's name, a fact that still eluded D'Angelo. He was almost afraid that he would find out some day. He'd had more killing than he could stomach during the war. But if he ever found out the identity of the boy's father, he was sure he would strangle him with his bare hands.

All these thoughts were tearing at D'Angelo's heart on the cold, snowy afternoon that Lexie quietly opened his study door and sent Mallette trotting in, crying, "Papa! Papa! Papa!"

ALMOST HEAVEN

285

The toddler caught D'Angelo about the boot tops and continued his happy chant.

"Isn't it wonderful!" Lexie exclaimed, beaming on the outside, but shuddering with fear in her soul. "Mallette's first word. 'Papa.' "

Shaking the boy off his leg, D'Angelo turned a fierce gaze on his wife. "Don't you think it would be more appropriate if you took the little bastard to his real father with this new trick you've taught him?"

Lexie clutched her throat and tears sprang to her eyes. In spite of everything, she had convinced herself that through her son she could win D'Angelo over. That hope died in an instant.

"You know," she gasped.

"Lexie, I lost my arm in the war, not my wits. Who ever heard of a nine pound premature baby? You're my wife, and if you wish to stay here and continue this charade, I'll permit it. But don't expect me to be a father to the fruit of your adultery. Now, get him out of my sight!"

Lexie grabbed Mallette up in her arms and fled the study. All the while, the boy's proud little voice sang through the house, "Papa! Papa! Papa!"

D'Angelo had never felt such self-loathing in his life. He started to go after Lexie, to apologize for being so cruel. He loved her. He always would. And the boy was part of her. So why couldn't he love the child simply as an extension of the woman who owned not only his heart but his soul?

Yes, he decided. He would go and make amends, the very next morning, he would talk to her, apologize for his unpardonable behavior, and then he would do everything in his power to make the three of them a real

286   *Becky Lee Weyrich*

family. But for tonight he would allow Lexie a few more hours to think about her sins.

"Yes," he assured himself. "The very first thing tomorrow."

But *tomorrow* came too late.

Long after dark, Lexie sneaked Mallette out of the house on Park Row. She saddled her horse and headed for the river, not sure of her destination, only sure that she must leave with her son.

The snow was almost blinding, but Lexie knew those trails by heart. She'd ridden them often enough while D'Angelo was away at war. She headed for the bridge across the river. She'd heard not long ago that Cabot had been seen in one of the villages on the other side. Maybe she could find him. She would never love him the way she loved D'Angelo, but Cabot was the boy's father. Surely, he would take them in.

The horse balked at the bridge. Lexie urged her on, pressing the stubborn beast to more speed. They'd freeze to death if they didn't find shelter soon. Midway across the river, the horse's hooves hit a patch of ice. Lexie heard the animal's scream of terror, then felt herself flying through the air. Down and down and down with the frozen river rushing up to meet her.

D'Angelo was sleeping when someone pounded at his front door before dawn. Still groggy, he stumbled down the stairs, cursing under his breath at this early intrusion.

He found the town constable waiting on his stoop. The man's face looked drawn and grim. In his arms he carried what seemed to be a bundle of rags.

ALMOST HEAVEN 287

"Well, what is it?" D'Angelo demanded in a less than cordial tone.

The man doffed his hat. "If I might come in, General?"

D'Angelo made an impatient gesture with his hand, then slammed the door against the cold wind and snow.

"Now, if you'll state your business, I'd like to go back to bed."

Just then, a faint whimper came from the rags. D'Angelo looked closer and saw the golden down of Mallette's head.

"My, God!" he exclaimed.

"It's your son, General Joshua. He's cold and wet, but seems to be all right."

A million questions were crowding into D'Angelo's head all at once. What was the constable doing with Lexie's son? How could he have gotten out of his crib? What the hell was going on?

"Lexie!" D'Angelo shouted up the stairs. "Lexie, come down here quickly!"

"Beg pardon, sir, but your wife's not up there."

D'Angelo turned disbelieving eyes on the constable. "What do you mean? Of course, she's upstairs. She's sleeping like any normal human being is at this time of night."

"No, sir," the man muttered. "She's dead. I'm sorry to have to bring the news, but someone had to tell you and fetch your boy home."

D'Angelo could never remember exactly what else the constable said. Something about Lexie's horse and the river and a fall to the ice and a broken neck.

"But God looks out for innocents," the constable

288   *Becky Lee Weyrich*

continued. "Your son here fell only to the bridge and
he was wrapped up in so many blankets that he wasn't
hurt. You've that to be grateful for, sir."

Torn with grief and guilt, tears streaming down his
face, D'Angelo reached out and took the child in the
crook of his arm. For the first time he held Lexie's son.

"Papa," the baby whimpered.

D'Angelo cradled the cold little bundle against his
chest and wept. "Son," he murmured. "It's all right
now. You're safe. You're home. Papa won't let anything happen to you."

All through the rest of his long life, D'Angelo
Joshua mourned his wife and wore the hairshirt of his
own guilt. If Lexie had sinned, at least her sin had been
productive. She'd given her husband as fine and loving
a son as he could ever have desired. D'Angelo's sin
was so much greater—the sin of an unforgiving heart.
He had to live with the guilt of Lexie's death on his
conscience for the rest of his days. Only Mallette made
D'Angelo's life bearable.

That dark dawn, as D'Angelo tucked his motherless
son into bed, he swore to the child and to Lexie, wherever she was, that he would love Mallette and care for
him from that day forward. And he kept the promise.
Many was the night D'Angelo sat in the rocker in the
nursery, soothing his son's troubled dreams or simply
watching him sleep and thinking of how their lives
might have been.

At General Joshua's death, many years later, when
he finally went to lie beside his Lexie once again, a single guilty spark of his soul remained on Earth, refusing
the comforts of Heaven to watch over the nursery's

ALMOST HEAVEN 289

tenants—his son's children and then their children and finally the child of James and Angela Rhodes. He felt a special kinship to little Hope. Poor little motherless Hope.

Chapter Thirteen

The silence in the clouds was deafening. Angel, who till now had had a ready retort for every situation, huddled in the gray mists, unable to find her voice. In her short stint as D'Angelo Joshua, she had experienced every human emotion, from the heights to the darkest depths. The aftermath left her dazed, near paralyzed.

"So now you know all the secrets of your life as D'Angelo and mine as Lexie," Alexander said quietly. "As a great writer once wrote, 'It was the best of times. It was the worst of times.' And, Angela," he added, "it will be our *last* time together unless you can recover the soul-spark that anchors the ghost of D'Angelo Joshua forever to that past life."

"But *how,* Alexander?" she begged. "How am I supposed to do that?"

"Think, Angela! You must find the answer for yourself. I've shown you all I'm allowed to. The final resolution is up to you."

When she didn't answer, he said, "Please. . . . You must determine how to proceed. If not, our time is at

ALMOST HEAVEN 291

an end. What did you learn from D'Angelo? What did his mistakes show you?"

Slowly . . . slowly the light dawned, like the majestic sun rising over the distant horizon. "I learned it isn't enough for D'Angelo to forgive Lexie. He must finally, after all this time, forgive himself. I must forgive *myself.*" She stared up at her tall, rough-hewn angel through tear-starred eyes. "I loved you so much when I was D'Angelo. The blame lies wholly with me for any mistakes you made, Lexie. And what a precious gift you gave me in Mallette. He was all I had left of you. I could never have gone on without that part of you that remained alive in your son—in *our* son." She became agitated suddenly. Her voice deepened, grew husky. "My sweet Lexie. It's all my fault. I drove you away. I caused your death."

"Angela, stop it!" Alexander grasped her shoulders and shook her. "You're slipping back. Get a grip on yourself or all will be lost. You're not D'Angelo any longer—not completely. And I'm Alexander, not Lexie. Lexie is gone entirely. Angela, can you hear me? Do you understand?"

She nodded and blinked rapidly. "I do understand. I'm Angela Rhodes. But I'm not whole, am I? A part of me is still down there, still walking the halls of the house on Park Row, still watching over Hope, still grieving for Lexie."

"Don't you see, though? There's no reason for you to grieve for Lexie any longer. I'm here with you, darling." Alexander cupped Angel's tear-damp cheeks in his palms and kissed her. "D'Angelo and Lexie are long dead, but their love—*our* love—lives on. We must

292   *Becky Lee Weyrich*

leave them now, let them rest, and move ahead in time."

"Ahead?" she said wistfully. "What lies ahead?"

"You know. *Think!*"

"Jim," Angel whispered. "This is all about him and Hope, isn't it?"

Alexander let out a long, relieved sigh. "Yes! You *do* understand."

"I never realized before how it feels to be a man in love, a man who feels he's lost everything when that love is taken from him. Poor Jim! Poor dear Jim! How can I help him, Alexander? Show me the way."

"You know the way. It was your idea, even before you came back to me. A wife," he answered gently. "By finding a new wife for Jim, you'll not only ease his pain, but release D'Angelo as well. It's the only way, Angela."

Angel glanced about, searching for something. She saw the blue-velvet clouds of evening, a million glittering stars, but no garden, no wishing well.

"What is it?" Alexander asked.

"I want to see Jim. I need to look in on him and Hope. Where's the well?"

She had no more than spoken the words when they were once more in the beautiful garden at the Gates of Heaven. Without a word to Alexander, she hurried to the wishing well, placed her hands on the smooth stones, and closed her eyes. The familiar sensation of flying returned. A moment later, she heard her own voice, an echo from the past.

"Good morning," she heard herself say. She saw her image sitting in the rocker, nursing Hope. The room was filled with sunlight and warmth.

ALMOST HEAVEN 293

The video tape, she realized. The film Jim had shot that long-ago morning when all seemed right with their world.

Off camera, Jim said, "It is a good morning, isn't it? The best morning ever. Turn your head just a little to the right, darling, so Hope's face isn't in shadow."

Then, her vision changed. As if a camera had suddenly zoomed back for a broader view, she saw the whole scene. Jim was sitting in a chair in the living room, watching old videos. His eyes looked red and puffy. His cheeks were damp with tears. He needed a shave and a fresh shirt. Beside him on the table sat the remains of a peanut butter sandwich. His dinner, Angel guessed. It was dark outside, and besides the light from the TV screen, the only other illumination in the room came from the Christmas tree. All the beautiful ornaments had been hung—the ruby slipper, the old glass Santa, the silver airplane, even the iridescent ball with the angel on top and the baby inside that Jim had given her the year before. And on top of the tree sat the red satin angel with her gold lace wings.

Angel glanced about. On the floor near the tree lay a small bulb in a socket and an extension cord. Just like last year, Jim had tried to light the angel on top of the tree. Obviously, his attempt had failed again.

The sight of him sitting in front of the television, staring at the old videos of their one Christmas together was more than Angel could bear. Thanks to D'Angelo Joshua, she could feel Jim's pain as never before. It was something black and horrible and agonizing. When the happy, laughing shots of the two of them making snow angels came on the screen, she had to leave the room. She couldn't bear Jim's grief a mo-

294   *Becky Lee Weyrich*

ment longer. It was the same soul-wrenching pain she had known as D'Angelo Joshua.

Quickly, she wished herself away. She moved through the house, checking to see if anything had changed. What struck her most was an overall atmosphere of untidiness and neglect. Her beautiful old home on Park Row looked exactly like what it was—motherless and suffering from it. Dirty dishes were stacked in the kitchen sink and on all the counters. Cupboard doors stood open. The Monster's water bowl needed washing and filling. The lovely jade plant Cora had given her the day they moved in—the same plant that had thrived so under her tender care—now looked shriveled and sad as if it, too, were in mourning.

"Jim doesn't have anything against jade plants," she whispered to the poor, withered thing, "he just can't remember to water and feed you."

Leaving the sorry mess in the kitchen, Angel hurried to the nursery. A night light chased the dark shadows from the room. She could see the faint outline of D'Angelo's ghost sitting in the rocker, but he disappeared the moment she entered. She went to the crib and stared down at her sleeping daughter.

"My, how you've grown!" she whispered.

Hope's golden lashes fluttered, then her eyes opened. She stared up at her mother and trilled a greeting. Reaching up, she said, "Mama. Angel Mama."

The sound of her child's voice thrilled Angel, but brought tears to her eyes. "Darling, you can talk. How wonderful!"

She reached down to touch her baby. She ached to

ALMOST HEAVEN 295

hold Hope close. But her hands passed right through the child's body. For a moment, she felt the tingling warmth of contact, but it passed so quickly that she wondered if she had only imagined it.

The great, black dog she had rescued from the pound ambled into the nursery. He stood and stared at her, cocked his head this way and that, then circled on the rug before settling with a sigh.

"Good boy, Monster," Angel said. "You take special care of Hope for me. Okay?"

His ears pricked up as if he heard and understood every word she said.

Hope drifted off to sleep again. As much as Angel dreaded it, she knew she had to go back to Jim. She had to do something to help him. When she returned downstairs, he was still sitting in the same hunched-over position, still staring at the television screen.

"Jim?" she ventured. "Jim, can you hear me? It's Angel."

"I love you so much," he murmured. "How could you leave me?"

For a moment, Angel's spirits soared. He could hear her! Then with a sinking heart she realized he was talking to her video image on the screen.

"Christmas!" he said. "Everything was so perfect this time last year. We were all together and so happy. I thought it would go on forever. Why didn't I realize how quickly things could end—how quickly I could lose you?"

"Jim, don't!" Angel begged. "I'm still here with you. It's not the same, I know, but I'm here. I still care about you and Hope. I want you both to be happy."

296 *Becky Lee Weyrich*

She leaned down and kissed his rough cheek. Jim glanced up, then brushed at a tear.

"Damn!" he muttered. "Damn it all to hell! What am I going to do? How am I going to go on?" He leaned down and put his face in his hands, his shoulders shaking with silent sobs.

Angel had the sudden urge to flee—back to the Gates of Heaven, back to Alexander. Jim's grief tore her apart. She couldn't bear it. The pain was worse than when she was dying. But she knew she must bear it, she must be strong for him, for Hope. What could she do to reassure him? She needed to give him some sign.

"The satin angel," she said, glancing up at the Christmas tree.

She closed her eyes and imagined what she wanted to see. She strained her will and stretched her powers to make it happen. When she looked again, she had made it so. She smiled. The beautiful red satin angel with her gold lace wings glowed softly atop the tree, as if with some inner light.

"Look, Jim," she whispered. "Look, darling. Merry Christmas!"

Jim turned slowly away from the television screen, unable to watch the happy scenes any longer. When he saw the tree, he frowned.

"What the . . . ?"

He stood up and walked over to the bulb and extension cord he had discarded in frustration. He picked up the useless contraption and stared at it, then looked back at the angel. There was no light, no electric cord, yet a soft glow surrounded the pretty ornament.

He said nothing for a time. He simply stood there,

ALMOST HEAVEN 297

gaping. But his tears dried and the slightest hint of a smile eased his pained expression.

"Angel, can you hear me?" he said at last. "I don't know how you managed this little miracle, but I hope you can see it. Merry Christmas to you, too, darling!"

The sun was coming up. Jim climbed the stairs to get Hope. She was awake, waiting for him. He picked her up and held her close, kissing her forehead and whispering to her softly.

"Santa came, sweetheart," he said. "And we had another visitor, too. A very special visitor—a Christmas angel."

Still talking to Hope softly, Jim carried her downstairs. The moment he entered the room, Hope made a trilling sound and reached toward the tree, more specifically toward the softly glowing angel atop the tree.

"Angel!" she cried. "Mama Angel!"

Satisfied that she had helped at least in a small way, Angel left Jim and Hope unwrapping packages and went back to the nursery. She found the rocking chair empty, but she could feel D'Angelo Joshua's spark somewhere near.

"You can hear me," she said. "I know you can because you're a part of me. Show yourself, D'Angelo. We need to talk."

She waited. Only silence, but she knew he was there.

"D'Angelo, listen to me. The time has come for your vigil to end. Lexie and Mallette are no longer here. Jim and Hope are *my* responsibility. I need your help. Yes. But we must work together, not separately. I need your spark; I need your strength and your endurance. I can't do this alone. We have to come together once more."

298 *Becky Lee Weyrich*

She felt something behind her. When she turned, she saw the shimmer of his outline at the door. She flew toward him, determined to merge with his shadow and become whole again. But he moved away.

"I've a duty here." She heard the faint rumble of a deep male voice—D'Angelo's voice—even though his image had vanished.

"We both have a duty here. But don't you see? You've accomplished yours. Now it's my turn. I need my whole soul to make things right for Jim and Hope. *Please!* Merge with me! Help me!"

"Your plan?" he demanded.

"To find a mother for Hope, a wife for Jim."

"He'll not marry again." His voice sounded gruff, jealous. "I never took a wife after Lexie, yet I raised a fine son."

"Were you happy?"

A long silence followed Angel's question.

Finally, in a faint, heartbroken voice, D'Angelo said, "I deserved no happiness. I lived only for Mallette."

"Was *he* happy, growing up without a mother's love?"

"Dammit, woman, that's none of your business!"

"Oh, but it is! You see, I don't need an answer from you because I know the truth. Mallette suffered all his life from the same sort of guilt that tortured you. He always felt that his mother lost her life trying to save him, didn't he?"

"He never said any such thing!"

"No, he never did. He suffered in silence, just as you did. Just as you're still suffering. It's pointless, D'An-

ALMOST HEAVEN 299

gelo. Come with me! Help me! We can put an end to all this pain.''

His image shimmered before Angel for an instant, giving her cause for hope. Then it faded.

"I won't do it! I mean to stay here where I belong." His words came like an echo, then faded into nothingness.

Disheartened, Angel, too, faded, returning to Alexander with a heavy heart.

"D'Angelo was always a stubborn man," Alexander told her. "Give him time. He'll come around. Until he does, you'll have to go on alone. There's really no time left to waste arguing with that bullheaded old spark."

Angel shook her head hopelessly. "I really don't know where to start searching for a wife for Jim."

"Start close to home," Alexander advised.

"How close?"

"Why not try the Mall?"

Even as Alexander spoke the words, Angel found herself back in Brunswick, Maine. But the Christmas snow had melted. The tall elms were lacy and vivid with their summer-green leaves. Children played on the swings and seesaws or climbed the jungle gym. Angel spied Jim, lounging on a bench, his long legs clad in washed-out jeans, his feet sockless in sneakers, and his rumpled white shirt open at the neck. His hair was a touch too long and his beard needed trimming. He'd lost weight in the months since she last saw him. But his eyes shone with love as he watched Hope picking violets a few feet away.

Just then, a little blond girl not much older than Hope came racing past, her brother chasing her.

A lovely, tall woman in beige slacks and a blue

300 *Becky Lee Weyrich*

sweater exactly the color of her eyes called to them. "Samantha! Garrett! Come back here!"

The two children ran over to see what Hope was doing. Samantha began picking her own bouquet of violets while brother Garrett, about six, continued to taunt her.

"Garrett, *please,* darling, leave the girls alone."

The handsome, but sullen-faced boy, shot a glance at his mother, then ambled over to the jungle gym and hung upside down, making faces at the two little girls as they picked flowers.

"I don't know what I'm going to do with him." The woman was speaking only to herself, but she was standing close to Jim's bench.

"Talk to her, Jim," Angel begged.

Jim chuckled nervously and glanced at the woman. "Boys are like that," he said. "Before you know it, he'll grow out of this phase and start chasing girls for other reasons."

She sighed and sank down on the bench beside him. "I know, and how I dread *that* phase! He's been difficult ever since his father passed away two years ago."

Jim nodded. "It's not easy being a single parent. You have my sympathy."

"You, too?" she asked gently.

"My wife was killed in an auto accident a little over a year ago."

"Heart attack," she answered, even though Jim hadn't asked.

"That's my little girl, Hope, playing with your Samantha," Jim said, pointing with pride at the strawberry blonde in her pink sunsuit.

"She's adorable."

ALMOST HEAVEN

"Thank you," Jim answered, smiling. He offered his hand. "James Rhodes," he said. "I haven't seen you around the Mall. Are you here on vacation?"

She smiled warmly and took Jim's hand. "Francine Lawrence," she answered. "I've rented a cottage out on Bailey's Island for the month. I can't bear the heat in New York this time of year. When Warren was still alive, we always went to Capri in midsummer. But that's out of the question now. I feel I need to keep the children closer to home."

"Hey, how about that? My wife and I lived in New York for several years before moving up here. I'm with the college. We live right over there." He pointed out the lovely old house on Park Row.

Hovering nearby, Angel watched all this with growing interest.

"Alexander?" she said excitedly. "Can you hear me? Are you watching what's happening here? This could be perfect. She seems nice, and Hope looks enough like Samantha and Garrett to be their real sister."

Alexander, not wanting to butt in, didn't answer. So Angel turned her attention back to Jim and Francine. By now the pair had progressed to the point where Jim was sporting a boyish grin and calling her "Fran."

Fran, Angel learned, was a fashion designer. "Well, that's obvious," Angel muttered to herself. "Even her casual clothes are expensive looking, and everything matches. And look at all that gold she's wearing—chains around her neck, watch and bracelet, rings, even a gold circle pin. Warren must have been loaded."

302   *Becky Lee Weyrich*

Angel sniffed the air. "Joy!" she said. "Fran's wearing Joy perfume, the real French stuff, too. Not the watered-down version you buy in the States. I'm impressed!"

Meanwhile, Jim and Fran's conversation had moved on to their favorite New York restaurants. Angel noted with some chagrin that Jim failed to mention the Shark Bar on the Upper West Side, her own favorite place for ribs, barbecue, and greens. But then Fran didn't exactly look like the soul-food type. Angel would be willing to bet her sprouting wings that never had a turnip green passed Francine Lawrence's perfect, peach-tinted lips.

"What's this?" Angel said, hovering a bit closer.

Jim and Fran had discovered a mutual friend in the Arts Department of NYU.

"Yes," Jim was saying, "I knew Norton well. In fact, if I'd stayed in New York, he'd planned to help me find a backer for my play."

"You're a writer?" Fran sounded seriously impressed.

Jim dug the toe of his sneaker into the grass and lowered his gaze like an embarrassed teenager. "Well, I dabble a bit. I've been working on this one piece for years. But with Hope to look after and all my college duties, I don't have much time to write anymore. I'll probably never finish it."

"Oh, you mustn't give it up!" Fran exclaimed. "I'm so impressed with anyone who can put his thoughts down on paper. I can't even write a decent letter."

Jim grinned at her. "I guess that makes us even. I can't design a dress."

They both laughed. Angel frowned. She'd heard Jim

ALMOST HEAVEN

303

laugh that way a long time ago, back when they were dating.

"The next thing you know, he'll be hauling out the Johnny Mathis records," she fumed.

Sure enough, before they left the park bench, Jim and Fran had made a date to meet at Cook's Lobster Pound that evening for dinner.

Any delight that Angel had felt over Jim's meeting someone vanished in that moment. The old jealousy returned with a vengeance. Taking advantage of a crow that just happened to be flying over the Mall at that moment, Angel steered his flight toward Fran and gave him a sudden, undeniable urge.

"Oh, no!" Fran groaned, holding the soiled sleeve of her sweater away from her with the tips of two fingers.

"Yuck!" Garrett said, grinning with mischief and a glee that was all too obvious. "He sure got you good, Mom."

Trying to make the best of a bad situation, Jim declared, "Some days you need an umbrella out here—and I don't mean for rain."

Fran gingerly wiped at the stain with a tissue. "Well, we'd better head back so I can soak this. What time tonight, Jim?"

"How about six-thirty? I know that's early for dinner by New York standards, but Hope gets sleepy if I keep her out too late."

Angel thought she saw a flicker of something in Fran's gorgeous blue eyes when Jim mentioned bringing Hope. But giving the woman the benefit of the doubt, she told herself she had been mistaken.

"I *hate* lobster!" Garrett announced with a grimace.

304 *Becky Lee Weyrich*

Jim laughed and ruffled the boy's towhead. "How about hot dogs? You don't hate them, do you, pal?"

"Hot dogs? Wow!" he cried. "Mom, am I really going to get to eat hot dogs tonight?"

Fran gave Garrett the look strict mothers reserve for children who have displeased them. "We'll see," she answered noncommittally.

"Six-thirty, then, Fran. We'll see you there."

Jim ambled over and scooped Hope up in his arms. She stuck her bunch of violets under his nose, then yawned expansively. To Angel it seemed that Jim's step was lighter than usual as he jogged across the Mall with Hope in his arms. Gone, too, was the soul-wrenching grief she had felt from him at Christmas. He seemed almost light-hearted.

"That was not nice—what you made the bird do to Fran," Alexander said the moment Angel returned to their heavenly garden.

"Me?" she asked, all innocence. "How in the world could I make a bird do that?"

"Obviously, you know very well how it's done! Picked up a few tricks along the way, have you?"

"Well, it wasn't like I dumped her in the duck pond or something. Just a tiny little stain. It'll come out in cold water."

"You'd better hope it does, Angela."

She shrugged. "What difference does it make?"

Without saying a word, Alexander pointed to Angel's robe. She looked down.

"Oh, no!" she cried.

Her pretty, sparkling robe, which had finally re-

ALMOST HEAVEN

turned to its normal brilliant color, was spattered from head to toe with droppings. It looked like she'd been dive-bombed by a flock of crows that had been eating a steady diet of blackberries.

"Yuck!" she said, echoing Garrett.

"What goes around comes around," Alexander said. "But don't worry. It'll wash out with cold water."

Angel glared at him and headed for the stream.

Angel spent the next few Earth-weeks scrubbing her robe in the River of Time. Alexander, she noticed, made himself scarce. It was just as well. She was damn mad at him and he knew it. No doubt he was off plotting the next trick he'd use to complicate her life.

"My *life*," she said with a snort of contempt. "I don't have a life any longer. I might as well be in limbo."

"Don't ever say that!" Alexander's deep voice boomed behind her.

"So you decided to come back, did you? Where have you been?"

"Watching over things down below while you washed away your latest sins."

"That wasn't sin, that was bird poop. You ought to know, you put it there."

He only smiled. "No, Angela. If that were the case, it would be angel poop, wouldn't it? And we don't do that sort of thing. One of the minor miracles of Heaven."

Angel turned away from him to hide her smile.

306 *Becky Lee Weyrich*

He reached out and touched her shoulder. "Look at me, Angela. Please."

Her smile faded the minute she saw his serious expression.

"What's happened, Alexander?"

"Much! It's time you went back to see for yourself."

The tone of his voice frightened her. Without a word she hurried toward the wishing well.

"Angela?" he called. "Take care, won't you? And be nice. Jim likes the lady."

"Hey, that's great!" She tossed the words back over her shoulder. She didn't feel like it was great. And she didn't want Alexander to see her face. Then he would know her gut reaction. How could Jim do this to her? They'd been so in love. They'd meant so much to each other.

Her jealousy only increased as she flew through the dark heavens, like an arrow aimed directly at Brunswick, Maine.

The first sounds she heard, even before she reached Earth and the house on Park Row, were the sweet, melancholy strains of Johnny Mathis crooning "When I Fall in Love." Tears blurred her vision. From high above town, she stared down on the moon-silvered autumn leaves of the Mall, the dim lights in the tall windows of her house, and the silhouette on the shade in the living room. There was no doubt as to what the couple were doing. And there was no doubt in Angel's mind as to who they were.

Jim and Fran!

Angel watched, frozen in midflight at the tree line, as the two forms melded into one, then swayed sensually to the music.

ALMOST HEAVEN

307

"Jim," she murmured in a whisper filled with heartache, "that was *our* song. How could you?"

Miserable, and regretting the fact that she had let Alexander talk her into this, Angel let her spirit sink lower and lower, toward the house. Even if she didn't want to know, she had to find out what was going on between Jim and Fran.

Alexander, she reminded herself, had said, "Jim likes the lady."

Well, it appeared to Angel that whatever had developed, it went a lot further than *like*.

"Okay," she told herself. "Let's list the good points. Francine Lawrence is definitely classy—sharp looking, well groomed, intelligent, educated, and probably a great mother to Samantha and Garrett. The kids are a point in her favor, too. They'd be good company for Hope. She's the perfect faculty-wife type. She'd be right in her element at alumni teas as well as hockey games—in a designer sweater, of course. The point is, she'd be good for Jim, for his career. And a good mother for Hope."

Angel had herself psyched up to accept Fran until she entered the house. First, she checked on Hope, who was fast asleep upstairs with Monster and D'Angelo standing watch. Actually, the dog was sleeping through his duties, but the General was alert as ever.

Sensing the arrival of Angel's spirit, the old man tried to vanish. But she nailed him. "Don't you dare fade on me!" she warned. "We still have things to talk about."

"You've no right here," he snarled. "This is *my* house!"

"Maybe it was a long time ago. But that's *my* baby

308   *Becky Lee Weyrich*

sleeping in the crib. When are you going to give up and put our soul back together as it should be?"

"When hell freezes over!"

"You stubborn old coot! I'm trying to help you. Don't you realize that? If we can come to an understanding, we can live again."

"Who wants life?" he snapped. "Life is too painful. A pox on life!"

"Hey, so we had a bad time of it once. It will be different next time."

"Say's who?"

Angel looked straight into his eyes—her own eyes—and said gently, "Lexie told me. She's waiting for us to join forces so that she can be with us again. She says in our next life on Earth we'll know the happiness that was denied us in the past."

Tears watered the old ghost's eyes. "Lexie said that?" he whispered. *"My* Lexie?"

"Our Lexie," Angel corrected gently. "She wants us back—both of us as one loving soul. Until we do what she asks, she can't return to Earth either. She's begging, D'Angelo. She misses you so."

He seemed befuddled and confused. Staring at Angel with pleading eyes, he said, "I need a bit more time. Will Lexie wait?"

Angel shrugged. "She has no choice."

"Do tell her I'm coming, won't you, and that I still love her?"

Angel smiled at the fading image. "She knows that. She's always known it."

Without willing herself to go there, Angel found herself an instant later in the living room with Jim and Fran.

ALMOST HEAVEN 309

"Jim, you look great!" she said, surprised to see that he'd put on weight, that his hair was trimmed and his beard was clipped and neat. The living room was immaculate, except for the dishes and wine glasses still on the coffee table from the intimate supper Jim and Fran had shared.

Angel checked the scraps and raised an eyebrow. This was no fast food or takeout. Fran must have cooked. "Lobster bisque, seafood Newburg, wilted spinach salad, and, Jim's favorite, German chocolate cake, for dessert."

The music ended and Angel turned her attention to Jim and his "date." Just thinking of Fran in those terms smarted. Angel told herself it wasn't *really* a date. After all, they hadn't gone out anywhere. Fran had simply dropped by to cook Jim a decent meal.

"Who are you kidding?" she then asked herself. "This is *more* than a date." With a sudden pang she realized that in all likelihood the two of them would soon go upstairs to make love. She groaned.

She sent a frantic message back to the garden. "Alexander, I can't take this. What am I supposed to do? Why don't you go ahead and beam me up or something?"

Alexander characteristically turned a deaf ear to her cry for help.

"You can't imagine what this evening has meant to me, Fran."

Jim's voice brought Angel up with a start. He was sitting next to Fran on the sofa, holding her hand, playing with her long fingers. Perfectly manicured of course.

Fran's soft, sexy laugh floated on the silence. "Oh,

310   *Becky Lee Weyrich*

Jim darling, it was nothing. I love to cook, especially for a man who appreciates good food."

He leaned closer, until his forehead was touching hers. "You know I'm not talking about supper, although it was delicious. I mean *you,* Fran. You're so perfect in every way. I've never met a woman like you."

"Now, wait a minute, pal!" Angel fumed. "This is *me, your wife,* up here!"

"I'll bet you say that to all the girls, Jim. Your Angel sounds like she was the be-all and end-all in the perfect department. I've never heard a man speak of a woman with such tenderness and devotion."

"Well, that's better!" Angel said, deciding that Francine Lawrence wasn't such a bad Joe after all. She felt even better when she saw Jim's eyes go misty.

He shook his head. "You're right. There was never anyone else in my life or in my heart before Angel. I loved her deeply. I always will."

Angel puffed herself up and did a little strut around the living-room ceiling. "He loved me! He loves me!" she sang silently.

Then in the very next instant, Jim burst her pretty bubble. "Angel was the love of my younger days. She was crazy and fun and passionate, but—"

Fran didn't let him finish. She leaned over and kissed his words away. Then in a deep, husky voice, she whispered, "I can be passionate, Jim."

Angel groaned and hid her eyes. She couldn't bear to watch. But she couldn't bear not to either. A moment later, she moved in closer to make sure this was a dry, formal kiss instead of a wet, mushy kiss. It started dry, but then she saw Jim's lips part.

ALMOST HEAVEN 311

"Oh, God!" she cried. "Jim, what are you doing? Have you had this woman checked? She might be carrying anything—rabies maybe!"

The kiss went on and on. Soon they had their arms around each other and were half lying on the sofa. Angel lapsed into a sulky silence, thinking how she'd trade her own budding wings for a passing crow about now.

Alexander caught that thought and responded. "Be nice!" boomed inside Angel's head.

She glanced menacingly heavenward and shot him a bird.

Think, Angel, think! she told herself. If you don't do something fast, they're going to be upstairs in bed in another few minutes.

Just then, the grandfather clock in the hallway chimed midnight.

Fran pulled free of their embrace and looked at her watch. "Oh, Lord!" she cried. "I promised the sitter I'd be back by eleven-thirty."

"Don't go," Jim begged.

Fran leaned over and kissed him one last, sweet time. "You know I don't want to, darling. But I must. There's always tomorrow night."

"I'm so glad you decided to stay in Maine till the end of the month."

They walked to the front door, arm in arm. There in the shadows, Jim gave her a long, lazy, wet kiss that sent chills through Angel. That had been her favorite kind of kiss. She could still remember how it felt, how Jim tasted.

Fran left. Angel had Jim all to herself at last. She

312 *Becky Lee Weyrich*

tried to touch him, tried to kiss him, but it was no use. He couldn't feel her. He had no idea she was there.

Or did he?

Returning to the living room, Jim pulled out a photograph album from under the end table. The snapshots documented their entire life together. Jim started at the beginning, when they were dating.

Angel was peering over his shoulder, smiling at her out-of-fashion clothes and frizzy hairstyle, when Jim spoke to her.

Pointing at a photo of the two of them on the Maryland campus, he said, "Remember the day this was taken? It was the first week you were in my class. You told me it was for the school yearbook or some such nonsense. But you kept it. I didn't find out you had it until after we were married."

She answered, even though she knew Jim couldn't hear her. "You didn't know either that I slept with it under my pillow every night. I was so in love with you, Jim, I could hardly stand it."

"And here we are at our wedding reception," he said, "out by the wishing well. Oh, look! There's Tory in the background." He chuckled. "She was just a kid then. It's hard to realize our wedding was that long ago."

Snapshots of New York City came next—Angel at the Statue of Liberty, Jim at Washington Square, the two of them beside Cleopatra's Needle in Central Park. So many happy days, so many treasured memories.

"I think I'd give my soul," Jim said, "to be able to step into one of these photos and be with you again, sweetheart." He closed the album and sighed. "What

ALMOST HEAVEN 313

am I going to do, Angel? I wish you could tell me. I don't love Fran the way I adored you, but I do have some strong feelings for her. She's a good person. She'd be a wonderful mother to Hope." He looked down at his hands and shook his head. "I'm lonely, Angel. So lonely, I hurt. And I need someone who cares for me. Someone to sort out my sock drawer and make me feel like a man again. Can you understand that? Can you forgive me for wanting to feel alive again? Tell me, darling! Tell me what I should do."

Angel whispered through the lump in her throat, "That's simple, Jim. You're going to marry Francine Lawrence and live happily ever after."

It took every ounce of Angel's heavenly understanding to whisper those words in Jim's ear. She knew it was the right thing to say, but, oh, how it hurt!

In typical Angel fashion, the instant before she fled back to Heaven, she whispered a P.S. in Jim's ear.

"Just don't sleep with her till after you're married!"

Chapter Fourteen

When Angel reached the garden again, she found Alexander waiting for her, garbed as a Roman gladiator, wearing the hideous iron mask. She grinned and gave his bulging muscles a whistle. He looked like Mister America in his short tunic, his bare chest gleaming golden with sweat.

"Don't tell me we lived in ancient Rome, too?"

"That we did, slave girl!"

Angel rolled her eyes. "Come on now. Give me a break! You a gladiator and me a slave wench? Why couldn't we have been an emperor and his wife or something?"

"You live the lot you draw," he answered, flexing his muscles and giving his spiked iron ball a practice swing. Then he removed the mask, grinned at her, and winked. "Actually, this is a reward for you. You handled yourself nicely down there. Looks like Jim and Fran are all set."

She eyed him suspiciously. "What do you mean by *reward?*"

ALMOST HEAVEN 315

"We had it pretty good as the great gladiator 'Iron Face' and his slave mistress Acte."

Angel thought for a minute. She'd heard the name "Acte" somewhere before—read it in a history book, maybe. It came to her in a flash.

"Hey, wasn't she Nero's mistress?"

"Yes, you were. But you were in love with me. And we had a fine life after Nero died. Since you behaved so well down below, I thought I'd have a little treat waiting to reward you."

Angel looked askance at him. "Didn't Nero's mother, Agrippina, try to poison Acte?"

"On a number of occasions. But she was never successful. You outwitted her each time. You and I lived a long and happy life together in Pompeii after we gained our freedom."

She gave him a more careful inspection, then grinned. "You look good in that. Sexy!"

He bowed. "All for you, my darling Acte. Now, if you're ready to begin . . ."

She held her hands up to stop him from taking her back in time. "Wait a minute, please. I need to ask you some questions, Alexander."

"Questions? There's no need for that. You'll remember everything as soon as you become Acte again."

"Not those kinds of questions. I need to know if I did right about Jim and Fran. How can I be sure she's the one for him? What if they get married, then find out they hate each other?"

"They seemed happy enough tonight. Don't worry about it, Angela."

"I can't help worrying," she said stubbornly.

316 *Becky Lee Weyrich*

"We're talking about the woman who's planning to marry my husband. My daughter Hope's new mother. You just can't be too careful these days. And there's something about Fran that still bothers me."

"What?" Alexander demanded, impatient to be off to their ancient love nest.

"I don't know. Call it instinct. Call it ESP. It's just a feeling I have that she's not what she seems."

"You'll get another opportunity to watch the relationship develop after we get back."

Distracted, Angel asked, "Back from where?"

"Pompeii, of course, in the year 79 A.D. Nero is long dead and you and I are free. We live and love in a white stone villa on the shore of the bay. Oleanders are in bloom, perfuming the air. The wine is the best Falernian. The figs are ripe and sweet. And you have a body created for love. Life is good, Acte. Take my hand. Come with me. I'll show you."

Her eyes closed, Angel could see and feel the lovely images Alexander's words evoked. When he gripped her hand to lead her back in time, she could sense his love, his need for her. Any moment now, they would sail off through the heavens in a swirl of neon clouds and shimmering stardust. They would make passionate love as Acte and her tender giant Iron Face. The thought was, oh, so tempting.

But the instant before their flight, Angel pulled away.

"Angela, what are you doing? Take my hand," Alexander demanded.

"No. I'm sorry, but I can't leave right now. Something's wrong down there. I can feel it."

"What could have gone wrong? Jim loves Fran,

ALMOST HEAVEN

Fran loves Jim. They'll be happy together. You've already given this match your blessing, Angela. Come with me now. Accept your reward."

She shook her head, feeling a terrible sense of dread possess her. "I was too hasty. I should have waited and watched. I'm going back down, Alexander."

He sighed, the disappointed, martyred lover. "There's nothing I can do to stop you, but I wish you'd reconsider."

He trailed his fingers across her cheeks, sending a shiver through Angel. Then he drew her close and kissed her ever so softly. He almost won her over. Had it not been for a vision that flashed through her mind—a vision of her dog, The Monster—she might have left Jim and Fran to themselves and flown off to Pompeii to make love. But the sight of her dog, who had a heart as big as his paws, staring pitifully at her from behind bars was too much. She pulled out of Alexander's embrace.

"Something's happened to Monster. I have to go. Right now!"

"Angela-a-a!" Alexander's anguished wail followed her through time and space.

The flight to Earth was bumpy, with whipping winds and cutting cold. Angel was sore and shivering by the time she reached the house on Park Row.

To her vast relief, she found Monster curled up beside Jim's chair in the study. Jim was working on his play, occasionally reaching down to pat the dog's huge head.

As relieved as Angel was at this warm, domestic scene, she was confused as well. She knew what she had seen before she left the garden—Monster staring

318   *Becky Lee Weyrich*

at her with great, soulful, pleading eyes. She'd heard
the frightened yelps and pitiful whines of other dogs in
the background. The sounds and smells of the place
had struck a chord in her memory.

The pound! she'd realized suddenly. But she
couldn't have been remembering the day they rescued
The Monster and brought him home. He'd been just a
puppy then, granted a very large puppy. The dog she
had seen in her vision was full grown, Monster's size
now.

Jim stopped work at his keyboard and glanced at his
watch. "Uh-oh! Time for you to go out back, old boy.
Fran will be here soon, and you know how she feels
about dogs underfoot."

In utter horror, Angel followed along. She watched
Jim take her great, gentle beast out to the backyard,
where he tied him to a post. She would *never* have allowed such treatment.

She tried to pull at Jim's hands. "You stop that!
Don't you dare leave Monster tied up out here.
Look!" She pointed up at the dark clouds overhead.
"It's going to rain. If Fran doesn't like dogs underfoot,
why don't you bring her out here and tie her up?"

Jim heard nothing. But he did pat Monster's head
and say, "I'm sorry, old pal. But as Fran says, you're
just a dog."

"Just a dog, my foot!" Angel fumed. "That's *my*
dog you're mistreating! I won't stand for it!"

Fully aware of her presence, Monster looked directly into his mistress's eyes and whimpered softly.

"It's okay, boy," she said. "I'll get you out of this."

She tried and tried, refusing to believe that just because she was dead she couldn't untie a simple knot.

ALMOST HEAVEN

319

Completely exasperated, she gave up at last, admitting defeat only grudgingly. She floated down to the ground beside her beloved dog and attempted to put her arms around him.

"Oh, Monster, what are we going to do? I've made a mistake. A *big* one! And it's going to take more than a passing crow to get us out of this fix. If I could undo the rope, you could run over to the duck pond and muddy your feet, then jump on her designer suit when she gets here." Angel paused and thought for a minute. "No, that's no good. Number one, I can't untie the rope. Number two, that would just get you in trouble. It wouldn't do a thing to break up Jim and Fran's romance."

The Monster whimpered as if he understood every word she was saying and sympathized with her pain.

"Gotta go now, boy," she said, patting him one last time and giving his ear an angel-kiss. "I'll think of some way to fix things. Trust me."

Inside, Angel found Jim at the kitchen table, feeding Hope. She babbled with excited baby talk the moment Angel entered the room.

"Come on," Jim begged. "I don't have much time. Eat your carrots. You know how upset Fran gets when I'm late."

Hope, her red-gold curls tousled and her cheeks smeared with carrots, continued her trilling sounds and baby words while she reached out to her Angel Mama.

The phone rang just then. Jim leaned over Hope to reach it. When he did, he knocked the plate of baby food off the high chair's tray. Orange, green, and purple mush splattered all over the kitchen floor.

320   *Becky Lee Weyrich*

"Damn!" he fumed. Then, into the phone, "Hello!" in a voice that was far from cordial.

"Jim? This is Fran. Is something wrong?"

"No. Not really. Hope and I just had a little accident, that's all."

"Oh." He could almost hear her shudder through the phone. Messy kids were not Francine Lawrence's cup of tea. She insisted that her two stay immaculate at all times.

After a moment's silence, she continued. "I'm calling to tell you there's been a slight change. That old woman who hangs around, Mrs. Shute, called me a few minutes ago. She said she was supposed to sit with Hope tonight, but she's ill and can't come."

Concerned, Jim asked about Cora, but Fran brushed his question aside, obviously less than interested in Mrs. Shute's ailment.

"Way to go, Cora!" Angel cheered.

She stifled her joy over Jim and Fran's broken date to hear the rest of what the woman had to say.

"I really don't know why you insist on having Mrs. Shute stay with Hope. She's so unreliable. At any rate, I took the liberty of calling one of the sitters I use for Samantha and Garrett. Tiffany will be there at seven-thirty."

"Tiffany?" Jim said. "I don't know, Fran. Maybe we'd better just cancel tonight. Angel and I never let anyone but Cora stay with Hope. Hope's used to her."

"For goodness' sake, Jim, Hope's a *baby*," Fran said in an exasperated voice. "She'll be sleeping most of the time we're out. It won't make the least bit of difference to her who's there. And I won't even con-

ALMOST HEAVEN 321

sider canceling. I've been dying to see this performance at the Brunswick Music Theater."

"How old is this Tiffany?" Jim asked suspiciously.

"Oh, how should I know? She's in high school, and she's had no problems with Samantha and Garrett. As you know, they can be a handful. If she's capable of supervising them, she can certainly handle one baby."

"Well, I suppose it will be all right, just this once."

"Of course it will. You haven't a thing to worry about. I'll be at your house at seven sharp so we can have a martini before the performance. I'd thought we might walk over to the theater, but it's going to rain. We'd better take a car. Then afterward we can go to the Stowe House for a drink with the others from the college. They're dying to hear our wedding plans. Wait till I tell you my idea for the reception. You'll love it, darling! I'm going to ask the Bowdoin wives to help serve. The president's wife, of course, will keep the bride's book."

Jim rolled his eyes. Seeing his reaction and knowing him as she did, Angel guessed that he'd have preferred a quick trip to a justice of the peace.

"You'd better go now, darling, and get ready. I'll bet you're not even dressed yet, are you?"

"Almost," Jim lied.

"I love you, Jim," Fran chimed brightly.

"Yeah, love you, too." He delivered his reply with such a pronounced lack of enthusiasm that Angel grinned.

Then he glanced at the kitchen wall clock that had the face of a smiling daisy. Its petals were creeping toward six-thirty already. Taking a damp dish towel, he gave the kitchen floor what Angel's mother used to

322 *Becky Lee Weyrich*

call "a lick and a promise" then scooped Hope out of her high chair and headed upstairs.

"Only time enough for a quick rinse off tonight, sweetheart," Jim said to Hope as he headed for the bathroom. "Your old dad's got to get ready on time or he'll be in hot water."

As they passed the nursery, Angel peered in. There sat General Joshua, a bleak look on his face. He never looked happy, but tonight he seemed perfectly miserable. She paused a moment at the doorway.

"High time you got yourself back here!" he growled. "Where have you been?"

She pointed heavenward. "You know. Up there."

He sneered. "Fooling your time away. Playing a bloody, gold harp or some such. While here I sit, helpless, watching all hell break loose under my own roof."

Angel started to argue with him about whose roof it actually was, but decided that would only get him more agitated. Besides, neither of them could claim it. It was Jim's roof now.

"What's the matter?" she asked instead.

"Like you didn't know! *That woman* is what's the matter. She's got poor James twisted around her little finger, and she's twisting him tighter every day. She comes up here and coos and chortles over our baby to make him think she's got a true mothering instinct. Bah! I can see right through her kind."

Angel found herself in the peculiar position of trying to defend Fran. "She is a mother. She has two children of her own. And what woman doesn't adore babies?"

"*That woman!* That's who! She never wanted chil-

ALMOST HEAVEN 323

dren. It was her husband who insisted on a family. She's had herself fixed, you know."

"What?"

"Prime, healthy breeding stock like her, and she's gone and had herself spayed like a hound bitch so she won't have any more babies."

"I didn't know," Angel answered, shocked. "Does Jim?"

"Not likely. I heard him say something to her about having a brother for Hope once they're wed. She passed it off, let him believe she was able and willing. She's not right for him. They're headed for heartache, and it's all *your* fault."

Angel rounded on him. "Sure! Blame *me!* That's the easy way out, isn't it? If you'd given me your spark when I asked you to, we would have been whole again and strong enough to stop this. But you'd rather sit there in that old rocker and pretend you're guarding *my* baby than return to me where you belong and help me fight her."

"Then you plan to help?" He brightened, going from miserable to simply grumpy.

"Are you going to join me?"

For a moment, the old ghost-spark remained still and thoughtful. He tilted his head and squinted up at the ceiling. "What's it like up there?"

"If you mean, in Heaven, I can't tell you. I'm not allowed to go through the gate and into the light until I'm whole again. But I can tell you this—there's someone waiting up there who loves us. *Both of us!*"

"Lexie," he whispered.

Angel nodded, thinking it would be too difficult to explain that Lexie was now Alexander, who at this

324 *Becky Lee Weyrich*

moment was dressed in the soul and tunic of the gladiator Iron Face.

As if testing the truth of her statement, General Joshua called, "Lexie! Lexie, can you hear me? Say something. Give me a sign if you're there."

Angel's hopes died. She'd felt that he was right on the verge of melding with her, making her spirit whole again. As the silence lengthened, she realized he'd never give in unless Lexie urged him to.

Please, Alexander! Give him a sign, Angel prayed silently.

A moment later, a soft voice floated on the air. At first, it was so low that Angel wasn't sure she heard it. Then it gained strength and volume.

"D'Angelo," a woman's sweet voice murmured. "D'Angelo, my dearest. I'm here waiting. Won't you come to me? Please! I miss you so."

Angel held very still, watching the old man. Tears glistened in his eyes, then dribbled down his pale, hollow cheeks. Without a word, he rose and came toward Angel. When he gripped her hand, she felt a tingling sensation all over. It was like some magnificent force touched her, became a part of her.

"We'll join, then," he whispered. "Now and forevermore. Enough of this sad place . . . Earth!"

Angel closed her eyes. She felt her spark return, felt D'Angelo Joshua become whole again in body as well as spirit, felt her own soul expand and rejoice. When she looked again, the ghost was gone. She called his name. There was no answer. The only sign left of him was within her in the form of a new and stronger determination to put a stop to Francine Lawrence's plans.

"She won't get away with this," Angel said.

ALMOST HEAVEN 325

From somewhere within her, old General Joshua's voice replied, "No, she won't. Not now!"

It was the last time she heard from the old ghost-spark, but his power and determination were giving her strength from that day forward.

The long-awaited melding accomplished, Angel flew with new speed to Jim's bedroom. Hope lay, clean and sweet, between two pillows in the middle of the bed. Angel could hear the shower running in the adjoining bathroom.

An instant picture came to mind—a flash from the past. She saw herself with Jim in that very shower, his body gleaming with steaming droplets of water while he soaped her breasts luxuriously. She clung to her hover-spot close to the ceiling, trying to will temptation away.

It was no use. An instant later, she found herself in the shower stall, pressed close to Jim. She tried to touch him, to caress him. To her frustration, he never knew she was there.

"Jim," she begged, "can't you feel me here with you? Don't you remember that night we made love on this very spot with the water beating down on us?"

The water! Her gaze went to the shower head. Some new awareness had come to her when her soul became whole again. She realized that she could expand or contract her spirit at will. She knew, too, that she could become one with fire, air, and *water*. Telescoping in on herself, she squeezed through the tiny holes in the nozzle. Immediately, she felt herself turn liquid and hot. The next moment, she came pouring back out, coursing over Jim's hard body. She dashed against his back, smoothed over his shoulders, down

326 *Becky Lee Weyrich*

his chest. She washed over his belly—lower, lower—fondling him, teasing him, bringing him, with her watery touch, the memory of past ecstasies.

Jim closed his eyes and moaned softly. "Oh, God! If only Angel were here."

She slipped down his buttocks and licked at him with hot, watery kisses, telling him silently that she was with him and that she remembered, too.

Suddenly, Jim crossed his arms over his belly, bent forward, and let out a long, low groan. Angel felt what he was feeling—the love, the relief, the euphoria.

She was still reeling with wonderful sensations a moment later when he turned off the shower. Bliss turned to panic as Angel found herself pooling on the shower floor, then flowing down the drain.

"I ought to put the stopper in and not let you out!" a voice boomed in her head. Alexander's voice. "Shame on you, Angela!"

"Oh, please!" she begged, her voice echoing up out of the dark, soap-scummed drain. "I didn't mean to do it. It just happened. I'll behave. Just let me out of here! I don't want to wind up in the sewer."

"Don't give me any ideas," Alexander warned. "Who told you you could turn into water anyway? You weren't supposed to know that yet."

"I guess it was D'Angelo Joshua. It seems I know a lot more things now that he's with me."

"You did it!" Alexander gave a victorious cry, his anger forgotten for the moment. "You actually convinced that old spark to return?"

"Yes!" She felt herself propelled up out of the drain and back into the steamy bathroom. "Didn't you know? Why, I thought you knew everything."

ALMOST HEAVEN   327

Sheepishly, Alexander replied, "I slipped away to Pompeii for a quick look, to make sure everything was ready for us just in case." Then in a hurt tone, he added, "But I guess you're out of the mood now."

Just then, Angel heard the doorbell ring. "Listen, Alexander, I've got to go. We can talk about Pompeii later. Right now, I have work to do. That's Fran at the door. I can't leave her alone with Jim for a minute."

"I'll be keeping an eye on you," he warned. "It seems I can't leave you and Jim alone for a minute."

Ignoring his sarcasm, Angel quickly purged the last of the soapy water from her spirit and flitted into the bedroom. She caught her breath at the sight of Jim.

"A tuxedo?" she gasped. If memory served, he hadn't worn a tux since their wedding, and that one had been a rental. On several occasions in New York, he'd had ample opportunity to dress up—she'd begged him to—but he'd absolutely refused. "For *dear Fran* you'll wear one, eh? Well, we'll just see about this!"

Ignoring Angel, since he could neither see nor hear her, Jim hurried Hope off to her crib, then dashed down the stairs to greet Fran.

"Oh, my Great-aunt Fanny!" Angel moaned when she saw the woman.

Francine was gowned in a revealing designer original of beaded champagne satin. It must have cost more than Jim made in a year, and it clung to every curve it didn't expose. She'd had her shoulder-length hair done in long waves, Veronica Lake style, so that it almost covered one eye, making her look mysterious and vampishly sexy. She'd also had her hair tinted, the exact shade of her gown.

Fran went immediately into Jim's arms and sort of

328   *Becky Lee Weyrich*

melted against him, clinging like a fair-haired vampire.

After a lingering kiss that set Angel's miniwings flapping with fury, Jim stepped back and let his gaze take in the whole, luscious picture.

"Wow, Fran! You look good enough to eat!"

Angel hovered at his ear and hissed, "Don't try it! Her beads would stick in your teeth, and her hair dye would probably poison you. Besides, you might choke on her silicone boobs."

Jim gave a nervous laugh and glanced over his shoulder.

"How about that martini now, darling?" Fran asked, inviting herself into the living room, not waiting for Jim.

He headed for the bar cabinet by the fireplace. "Coming right up!"

While he stirred the pitcher of martinis he kept glancing over his shoulder at Fran. As much as it galled Angel to admit it, she couldn't blame him. On the best day of her life, she *might* have looked one-quarter as sexy as Fran did on this night.

"I've really got my work cut out for me," she moaned.

"Chin up, Angela," she heard Alexander say. "You're much better looking than she is."

"Oh, yeah? How so?"

"Well, you're *sturdier.*"

"Thanks a lot, buddy!"

"And you have a sweeter spirit. Besides, I've always been partial to redheads. Don't give up. Just keep telling yourself that you can do it. You have to! We're laying bets on this thing and my money's on you."

"You can't gamble in Heaven!"

ALMOST HEAVEN   329

"I'm not in Heaven. I'm in Brunswick, Maine. Me and the guys at the checkerboard have placed a few small wagers."

"You're gambling with *live* guys?"

"No, dead ones. Some of the old-timers have hung around to see how the game comes out."

"The checker game?"

"No. The Game of Life. Talk to you later. Go for it, Angela!"

Angel turned her attention back to Jim and Fran. "Just like Alexander," she said, "to let me know he's watching my every move."

Martinis in hand, the couple were now snuggling on the sofa—their favorite spot. "Used to be *our* favorite spot!" Angel grumbled.

"I've reserved the Marble Collegiate Church for our wedding, darling. Isn't that wonderful?" Fran enthused. "We were lucky to get it with so little advance notice. Usually you have to make arrangements up to a year ahead of time. But the Trump affair was canceled so we were able to slide right in."

Jim moved slightly away and stared at Fran. "You mean, we're going to get married in New York?"

She fingered his lapel and drew him closer again. "Of course, darling. Why, all of my friends and business associates are there. We couldn't expect them to fly up here, could we? Besides, the Bowdoin Chapel would hardly hold them. It's so small. So provincial. Then, too, I'm sure you have family and friends you'll want to invite."

Angel puffed herself up. "Listen, sister, if the Bowdoin Chapel was good enough for my funeral, it's

330 *Becky Lee Weyrich*

good enough for your wedding. That is, *if* there's going to be a wedding. And there *isn't!*"

Still caressing Jim's tux, Fran cooed, "Darling, I just can't get over how handsome and dashing you look tonight. I knew you'd look wonderful in this Armani, but I had no idea what an effect you'd have on me. I can barely wait till the evening is over. We'll have our own after-party party."

"Don't you touch him *there!*" Angel shrieked uselessly and too late. *"That does it!"* she fumed, glaring at seeing Fran's long fingers on Jim's thigh. "Now you've really made me mad. If it's the tux that turns you on, I can fix that."

She'd done it with water, so why couldn't she do it with booze? Sucking herself in, Angel slid down into the martini pitcher. A moment later, Jim poured her into his glass. She sloshed about giddily, wondering why she'd never tried a martini when she was alive to enjoy it. Quickly, though, she forced her thoughts back to her plan. As Jim tilted his glass to take a sip, Angel leaped. She splashed herself all over his bow tie, his crisply starched shirt, his cummerbund, and finally sloshed his crotch, getting Fran's fingertips wet in the process.

Jim jumped up and began brushing her off his new tux. "Oh, no!" he groaned. "How did that happen? I guess I'll have to go change into my suit."

Angel gathered herself from the scattered droplets and grinned.

"You'll do no such thing!" Fran exclaimed. "It will dry before we get to the theater, and if you smell a bit like martini, everyone will simply think you've found some new, expensive cologne."

ALMOST HEAVEN

331

"Drat!" Angel fumed.

Fran glanced at her glittering diamond watch. "It's seven-thirty now. Where could Tiffany be?"

As if on cue, the doorbell rang. Fran continued sipping her martini while Jim went to answer it. Angel was right behind him, anxious to see what kind of sitter Fran had chosen to stay with Hope.

When Jim opened the door, he found a leather-clad blonde with a green streak in her hair lounging against the door frame. She wore headphones attached to a cassette player. The crack of her chewing gum was the only sound interrupting Jim's stunned silence.

"You Dr. Rhodes?" the blonde demanded, freeing one ear to hear his reply. "The one with the kid named Hope?"

He nodded mutely.

"I'm Tiffany. Ms. Lawrence called me."

"Come in," Jim said in a hesitant, barely audible voice.

Angel tried to bar the doorway, but such a feat was not within her powers.

Tiffany bopped in to the beat of the rap music bombarding her brain. Without missing a beat, she gave Fran a half-wave and a nod. "How you doing, Ms. Lawrence? Did you order me a pizza like always?"

The next few minutes sent Angel into a frenzy. Surely Jim wouldn't leave their precious baby with this gum-snapping, boot-scooting, leather-clad delinquent.

When Tiffany bumped and ground her way into the kitchen to "check out the fridge," Jim held a quick, quiet conference with Fran.

"I don't think she's right for the job."

332 *Becky Lee Weyrich*

"Don't be silly, Jim. Tiffany sits for half the people in town. You've nothing to worry about."

"But her hair—it's *green!*"

"It's only streaked. That's a fashion statement among teenagers today. Besides, Hope will be sleeping. She won't care if Tiffany's hair is purple and puce."

"That's not the point," Jim argued. "With those headphones on, she won't be able to hear Hope if she cries."

Fran glanced impatiently at her watch. "Jim, it's late. We don't have time to argue about this. She's here and she'll be fine. You're such a worrier."

"All right," he grudgingly conceded, "but I don't like this, Fran."

"You've already made that quite plain. Now, can we go?"

Angel was pleased to see Fran fuming over the delay while Jim went to Tiffany, made her remove the headphones, then gave her all the usual baby sitter's instructions. He showed her the bottles, the diapers, the emergency numbers, and the baby, who was sleeping sweetly.

When they'd finished the tour, Tiffany asked, "Where's the phone, Doc?"

Naively, Jim took this as a good sign, thinking that Tiffany wanted to be prepared, in case of emergency.

"Your pizza will be here shortly," Fran assured Tiffany as she hustled Jim out of the house. Then she sent him back in. "It's starting to rain. Get your umbrella for me, won't you, darling?"

For Angel, the rest of the night was sheer chaos. Once Jim and Fran drove off, Tiffany removed her

ALMOST HEAVEN 333

headphones and turned her rap tapes up full blast. The blaring sound was almost, but not quite loud enough to block out the sound of the pouring rain. Angel heard a howl from out back.

"Monster!" she cried. "He's going to drown in this downpour."

She flew to the kitchen door and peered out. Her poor dog was huddled miserably in a puddle of mud, trying to shield his eyes and nose with one soggy paw. Angel hurried out and tried to untie him again but it was no use. The names she called Francine Lawrence at that moment were unprintable.

Then, from inside the house, she heard Hope crying. She tore off to the nursery, assuming that Tiffany would be there already. She was not. Downstairs the music blared and the pizza delivery boy was pounding on the front door.

"It's all right, precious," Angel soothed. "Mama's here."

Hope had cried so long and hard that she had the hiccups. Angel continued talking to her until the child calmed down and finally dropped off to sleep.

Downstairs again, Angel found Tiffany and the pimply-faced delivery boy smooching in the hallway, the hot pizza box pressed between their even hotter bodies.

"Dammit! I'm putting a stop to this right now. One way or another, I'm getting Jim home."

The theater was dark when Angel arrived moments later. She could see Fran's dress glittering with the reflection of the footlights. The curtain was about to rise. But before it did, a spotlight illuminated one sec-

334 *Becky Lee Weyrich*

tion of the stage. Actor/producer Bernard Wurger stepped into the spot to a smattering of applause.

"Good evening, ladies and gentlemen." He bowed slightly, a powerful presence on stage even out of costume. "Welcome to the final performance this season of the Brunswick Music Theater. We have an announcement to make this evening before we begin. You all know about the contest to choose an original play to be produced here next summer." With a theatrical flair, he waved the paper in his hand high in the air. A hush fell over the audience. "I have here the name of our new playwright."

He paused dramatically and let his commanding gaze wander over the hushed audience. Then his deep voice boomed in the silence. "Is Dr. James Rhodes here tonight?"

"Stand up, Jim!" Fran urged.

For a moment, Angel forgot about the chaotic scene back at the house. She stared at Jim, tears gathering in her eyes. "Oh, Jim," she whispered, "you did it! You won! I'm so proud of you."

Jim took a bow, but refused to go up on stage. He was clearly moved, shaken by the announcement. Angel could sense conflicting emotions battling within him. One of his thoughts came through loud and clear: *I wish Angel were here to share this night. It's not the same without her.*

Wurger grinned and laughed. "Stage fright, eh, Dr. Rhodes? Well, you'll get over that. Congratulations! Your play, *No Other Love,* will be performed right on this stage next season, on the Fourth of July." Once again Wurger smiled at the audience and gave a casual bow. Then he exited, stage left.

ALMOST HEAVEN

Angel went to Jim. She hovered near, trying everything she could think of to get him to understand the problems at Park Row. But it was no use. Fran kept a firm grip on his arm all through the performance. So Angel had a busy night, flying back and forth from the theater to the house.

By now Hope was sleeping peacefully, but in the few moments during the evening that Tiffany wasn't on the phone, gabbing with her friends, she had on her headset, blasting her brain with obscene lyrics and bad music. She couldn't have heard a bomb go off.

The last time Angel dashed to the theater, she found it dark. The musical was over and everyone was gone. Vastly relieved, she hurried back to the house. But Jim and Fran hadn't returned. Then she remembered Fran's plans to go to the Stowe House after the play. She zoomed over to Federal Street.

Jim was the center of attention in the lounge. His friends from the college were there, all talking excitedly and congratulating him on writing the winning play. Jim acted shy and slightly embarrassed by so much sudden adulation.

Fran seemed to be encouraging him and enjoying the fuss. But after a while it became clear that she missed having the limelight to herself. That was when she began telling the group about their wedding plans.

Angel was all ears.

"We've set the time and the place," she confided to an intimate group of fifty or more. "The Marble Collegiate on December fifteenth, with a reception at the Plaza afterward."

Oohs and aahs went up from the crowd. Someone asked, "How about the honeymoon?"

336   *Becky Lee Weyrich*

Fran trilled a laugh. "That's a secret. Only Jim and I know."

From the look on Jim's face, Angel could tell that he did not. Fran hadn't let him in on *her* secret yet.

"I can tell you this, though," Fran continued. "We'll be away for a month, returning just in time for the winter term. Then next summer, after we've moved back to the city, Jim and I will take an extended trip to Europe. That will be our real honeymoon."

Jim leaned close to Fran and whispered, *"Moved?* What are you talking about?"

She pressed his cheek and smiled. "Darling, you can't expect me to live up here—away from the *real* world. I have a business to run. Besides, now would be a terrible time to try to sell my apartment—it will be much easier to sell the house on Park Row. And I recently redecorated, had all new white carpeting put in. Which reminds me . . . about the dog—"

"The dog!" Jim jumped from his seat, overturning his drink. "I left Monster tied out back, and it's been raining all night."

"So?" Fran had a grip on Jim's arm, trying to tug him back into his seat.

"I have to get home."

"Leave now?"

"Yes! *Right now!*"

"But I'm not ready to go."

Fran and Jim locked gazes—hers demanding, his defiant.

"Yea, Jim!" Angel cheered.

"What were you about to say regarding the dog?" Jim asked suspiciously, still standing, poised to leave.

Fran shrugged and laughed nervously. "Only that

ALMOST HEAVEN 337

we can't take him to New York with us. It wouldn't be fair to the animal to keep him penned up in an apartment. The Humane Society can find him a suitable home."

"And besides, you just got white carpets, right?" Jim accused.

"Well, that too."

"And tell me this, what were you planning to do with Hope while we're on our extended honeymoon in Europe? Put her in a kennel?"

"Oh, darling, don't be silly! I have a fine nanny in the city who lives in. She can certainly look after three as easily as two. Hope will be well taken care of."

"But she won't have a mother, will she?"

Fran drew back, her eyes wide with shock, her palms flattened to her chest. "You expected *me* to take care of the child?"

Without another word, Jim started to leave. He turned, as an afterthought, and asked, "Are you coming?"

"No," Fran answered, a cold light in her beautiful eyes. "I think I'll stay."

"Fine!" Jim left.

When he got home, he found music and television blaring, Tiffany asleep on the sofa with pizza scraps strewn about, Hope crying hysterically, and Monster wet and howling in the backyard. Like a man possessed, he tossed the green-haired teenybopper into the night, went up to change and calm his abandoned child, then brought Monster in and gave him a good rubdown and an extra dish of food.

"You're quite a dog!" he said to Monster as the big Lab devoured his midnight treat. "I never thought I'd

338   *Becky Lee Weyrich*

say it, but I'll take you over Fran any day. You're part
of this family, part of the legacy of love Angel left here.
I won't give you up any more than I'll give Hope's care
over to a nanny so I can go gallivanting around the
world with Ms. Lawrence's jet set." Jim glanced
about, looking at the drooping jade plant, the yellow-
and-white curtains at the windows, the daisy clock. He
watered the plant. "And the very thought of selling
this house! This is home. This is where all the memories are. This is where Angel is. You *are* here, aren't
you?"

Angel answered with a silent, teary, "Yes, Jim, I'm
here."

He shook his head as if he were just coming out of a
dream or a nightmare. "I guess Fran's next surprise
for me would have been that instead of changing her
name to mine, she'd want me to become Dr. James
Lawrence." He ruffled Monster's damp head. "Well,
we won't have to worry about that now, will we, old
pal?"

Jim was right. It was over. He received a curt phone
call from Francine Lawrence the next morning, in-
forming him that all bets were off. She was leaving
within the hour for New York and she wouldn't be
back.

Angel cheered until she felt the emptiness that crept
into Jim's heart when he hung up the phone. She'd
been so busy worrying about Hope and Monster and
herself that she'd forgotten to worry about him. Now,
she realized, he was more miserable than he'd been
before. Her scheme had backfired at Jim's expense.
Happiness had seemed to be within his grasp. Now his

ALMOST HEAVEN

339

hopes were dashed. And in addition to his loneliness, he was bitter, turned against love.

"Don't worry, Jim," Angel whispered. "I'll find you someone. Someone who's everything you ever dreamed of. I made a mistake with Fran. I'm sorry. But don't give up. Don't *ever* give up on love!"

Chapter Fifteen

Angel spent the next four months—from September through most of January—in a determined effort to find the *right* wife for Jim. First, she sent a lady vet who made house calls when The Monster caught a head cold. Dr. Betsy Blocker was thirty-one, pretty, bubbly, blond, and wonderful with animals and with Hope. But she struck out with Jim. He looked on her as a mere convenience to keep him from having to load Monster in the station wagon to drive him all the way out to the animal hospital. After Dr. Blocker, Angel tried tempting Jim with the new French teacher at Bowdoin, a young divorcee who moved in down the street, the mayor's daughter, the fire chief's niece, and even the first female assistant pastor at one of the local churches. But after Francine Lawrence, it seemed that Jim had donned permanent blinkers. He wasn't about to let himself get burned a second time. There was nothing Angel could do to budge him.

Finally, spiritually drained, Angel let Iron Face lure her away to Pompeii "for a rest." On the morning that things started popping back in Maine, she was in bed

ALMOST HEAVEN 341

and far too preoccupied with what the great gladiator was doing to her to be tuned in to Earth. As he moved deep inside her and kissed her breasts, the passionate fire building between them was enough to make her forget about the imminent eruption of Mount Vesuvius. As for Jim, he was way back on the very edge of her consciousness, hardly a speck in the vast distance of time.

To Jim the four months since Fran's hasty retreat seemed more like four years. She'd given him just the right taste of happiness to make him miss female companionship all the more. Yet he was afraid now. Afraid of making another mistake. He couldn't take any more pain, especially now with the second anniversary of Angel's death fast approaching.

Another Christmas had passed, his third in Maine. Even though Angel's parents had come to see their only grandchild, the holiday had been dreary and joyless for him. His dark mood lingered into the doldrums of a snowbound January.

Jim was lying in his rumpled bed, staring at the ceiling when the phone rang early that blizzardy morning. He reached listlessly toward the bedside table and removed the receiver more to stop the annoying sound than out of any curiosity as to who might be calling. Probably only his secretary, to remind him of some early morning meeting he'd forgotten.

Forgotten hell! He just plain didn't care anymore. He should have guessed when he lost Angel that he'd never find anyone like her. He'd spun beautiful dreams—fantasies, he knew now—around Francine Lawrence. She'd urged him along every step of the way, pretending such an interest in Hope, cooking him

342   *Becky Lee Weyrich*

special meals, trying to make him believe that life could be wonderful again. At least he'd learned the truth about her in time.

"Jim! Jim? Are you there?"

A woman's voice, distant, called his attention back to the phone. The sound was coming from the receiver still dangling in his hand. Lost in his misery, he'd forgotten about the caller.

"Yes, Jim Rhodes here. Who's this?"

"It's Tory, Jim. How're you doing?"

Jim smiled in spite of his depression. Angel's cousin, Victoria Cason, always had that effect on people. On him anyway.

He propped up in bed. "Hey, Tory. What's up? You haven't called in months. I was beginning to think you'd run off and gotten married or something."

Her laugh was bright and cheery. "No such luck! I've been working steadily and taking acting and voice lessons on the side. I haven't had time for much else. But something's come up, Jim, and I need to ask a favor."

"Sure, Tory. Shoot!"

She hesitated before she spoke again. "Well, I don't want to impose, but . . ."

"Come on, Tory. This is old Jim you're talking to. What you ask would never be an imposition. Speak and it's yours."

"Okay, but don't feel obligated if it's a problem. I've landed a job at the Brunswick Music Theater for the summer. I plan to drive up in late April, and I'll need a place to stay for a couple of days. Just till I can find an apartment—something small and cheap." She laughed

ALMOST HEAVEN 343

again, the sound making Jim forget his troubles for the moment. "I can't afford anything fancy," she added.

"The Brunswick Music Theater," Jim repeated.

"Yes," Tory said. "That's where I'll be working all summer."

"This is *so* weird!"

"What do you mean, Jim?"

"The BMT is going to produce my play this summer. They plan to do a special presentation on the Fourth of July."

"You finished it? After all this time? Oh, Jim, that's wonderful! I can't wait to see it performed."

He laughed and the sound surprised him. He hadn't heard his own laughter in a while. "Don't get too excited, Tory. It could be the world's biggest flop."

"Never! Remember, I read the first act in New York several years ago. I told you then I thought it was super. I'm sure it's even better now."

"Well, maybe." Jim grinned. "Bernard Wurger read it, and he thinks it has merit. Do you know him?"

"Of course, I do. He's the one who picked me for this job. Why, he's an institution with the BMT. He's been there for over thirty years—producer, director, and one of the finest character actors I've ever seen on stage. Have you seen him as Tevye or Ben Franklin or Judd Fry in *Oklahoma? Magnificent!*"

Jim chuckled. "Sounds like you have a crush on the guy."

"Just hero worship. To tell you the truth, he scared me at first. But he was too nice for me to stay intimidated for long. I hope to learn a lot from him while I'm working in Brunswick."

"You will. He's certainly taught me a few things

344   *Becky Lee Weyrich*

about writing plays. So, when will you arrive, Tory? I can't wait to see you."

"It's all right, then?" She still sounded hesitant. "You don't mind my coming?"

"Mind? Having you here will be great. God, Tory, you don't know how lonely this big house gets."

Tory paused, then said cautiously, "I thought you and Fran Lawrence were keeping each other company."

Jim was flabbergasted. "That ended months ago. How on earth did you hear about me and Fran? Don't tell me you know her."

"Not personally," Tory admitted. "But she designs clothes for the wife of one of my directors. The scuttlebutt's been that you and Fran might be headed for the altar. Just theater gossip, eh?"

"For a time it looked like more than gossip. It didn't work out."

"I'm sorry, Jim," Tory said softly.

He had to force his laugh this time. "Don't be! We were all wrong for each other, but too blind and desperate to see that in the beginning. Loneliness plays strange tricks on the heart. Still, in spite of how it turned out, I consider her a lovely lady. A real class act, even if she doesn't like dogs and kids."

"No broken heart?"

"Naw! Angel was the love of my life. I guess until Fran and I got involved I just didn't realize what a hard act Angel was to follow."

"Hey, don't count yourself out. There's another love for you out there somewhere. And Angel would be the first one to want you to find someone else. She was like that, you know."

ALMOST HEAVEN 345

"You're a sweetheart to say that, Tory. But I don't know. I'm a tough guy to live with."

"Well, at least I'm warned," Tory said. "Looks like I'm fixing to be the next woman to try it."

The slave girl Acte came to sudden, shuddering orgasm. Iron Face joined her, bellowing his pleasure until the villa's walls seemed to shake. Afterward, they lay still and silent in each other's arms. Heat and sweat fused their bodies. The smell of sunlight and oleander blossoms wafted in through the open window. With the sweet scent came something else.

"What was that?" Angel rose up on one elbow and listened. "I heard something."

"Just cicadas in the bushes outside."

Iron Face tried to pull her back down to him. He was ready to make love again. But one glance at her face told him Acte was gone. Angela was back, worrying about things on Park Row. With a sigh and a wave of his hand, he transported them back to the garden just in time to listen in on the last of the conversation between Jim and Tory.

Alexander glanced at Angel and gave her a broad grin.

"What are you smiling about?" she demanded.

"Looks like we have a new development here. This could be love! I do believe your wings are starting to grow again."

Angel glanced over her shoulder, then tossed her bright hair to cover her wing sprouts. "Don't be ridiculous! I had nothing to do with this."

346 *Becky Lee Weyrich*

"Maybe not, but you can't deny the attraction between them. It's so obvious."

"They can't get together unless I say so. Besides, they've always been fond of each other. She's my *cousin,* for cripe's sake!"

"Ah, but a very distant cousin. And who says Jim needs your help to find love?"

"Love? What are you saying? Jim doesn't *love* Tory. He can't!"

"Oh, can't he? What you still don't understand, Angela, is that there is a pattern to the whole universe and everything and everyone in it. You and Jim both consider Francine Lawrence a mistake, a bad call. She wasn't, you know. She crossed Jim's path for a reason—not to become his wife, but to bring him back to life again, to pull him out of your grave. She served a secondary purpose as well."

"And what might that be?"

"She managed to fire Jim up about his writing again. His play's finished, Angela. It's going to be produced, or had you forgotten? You've been so busy trying to play Cupid. And not only is it finished, it's good. He won the competition at the college, and you didn't even have to bribe any judges."

"Me? Bribe judges? I'd never!" She wasn't fooling anyone. They both knew the only reason she hadn't tried it was because she hadn't thought of it in time.

"Don't you see, Angela? Jim's lovelife is exactly like his play. He didn't need your help to succeed in winning the contest, and he doesn't need your help winning Tory's love. You don't need to bribe anyone. Trust in Jim. He has talent. His play is good, really good. And his life with Tory will be just as good."

ALMOST HEAVEN 347

Angel bristled. "You're getting way ahead of things here. Tory's only coming to stay a couple of nights. Nothing will happen between the two of them. They've been friends for years. That's all! *Friends!*"

"It seems to me you're getting very defensive about this affair."

"It is *not* an *affair!*" she shrieked. "Don't use that word!"

"All right! All right! Don't get your wings in a flap. Let's change the subject. Tell me about Jim's play."

"It's a love story," she said thoughtfully, in a much calmer tone. "He was working on it when we first met. In New York he never had time to write. He got back to it when we moved to Maine, but it took him a long time to finish."

"It was too painful for him to write about love after he lost you, Angela. But that's where Fran came in. She gave him hope again. In her own way, she gave him love. Most important of all, she made him believe that love might be possible again, and that's what gave him the courage to finish the play."

"Okay, so Fran wasn't a total zero. But what about Tory? What do you suggest I do now?"

"Nothing! Absolutely nothing. I think you'd better stay completely out of it this time."

"What? You mean I can't even go down and keep an eye on things?"

He smiled at her and touched her hand. "There's still our villa in Pompeii. We could go back for a time. I really wasn't ready to leave, you know. We could return there until things get farther along down on Earth."

348 *Becky Lee Weyrich*

"I don't think so, Alexander! Didn't you say when we were there a while ago the year was 79 AD?"

He nodded, looking a bit uncomfortable.

"Well, if memory serves, that was the year Vesuvius erupted and destroyed Pompeii and killed most of its citizens."

"We didn't suffer," Alexander pointed out. "And we were making such beautiful love when it happened." He sighed, remembering.

"Ha! Some fun *vacation!* Go to Pompeii for love and the hot lava baths!"

"It wasn't lava that covered the town. It was a mixture of ash and rain."

"Oh, that makes a *big* difference! I think I'd rather go back down to Maine and keep an eye on what's happening between Jim and Tory."

Alexander sighed and shrugged. "Suit yourself. But you have to promise not to interfere."

Angel was all innocence. "*Me?* Interfere in Jim's life? When have I ever—?"

"When have you ever *not?*"

Despite Alexander's misgivings, Angela left for Earth moments later. Several Earth-months had passed while the two of them were arguing. She arrived just in time to see Tory moving into the house on Park Row.

Tory bounded out of the old Volkswagen in which her things were packed as tight as a tick on a dog's ear. She'd brought most of her belongings with her, and was now dressed in tight jeans and a red-on-black tee shirt that read, DOWN WITH YUPPIE SCUM! Her light brown hair, cut smooth and short, bobbed about her smiling face. The Monster came bounding out of

ALMOST HEAVEN

the yard, almost knocking her down in his excitement.

"Hey, fellow, take it easy!" she said, laughing. "It's good to see you, too, but don't muss my party clothes."

Hearing all the commotion outside, Jim peered through the front door. His bearded face split in a grin.

"Hey, Tory! You got here!" He bounded down the stairs, almost matching Monster's enthusiasm, and scooped Tory off her feet in a bear hug, swung her around.

"Does this mean I'm welcome?" she asked, laughing and trying to struggle to her feet.

"Welcome as the first of May," he said. Then he stepped back and gave her a long silent look before grabbing her again. "Lord, you look good!"

She pulled out of his embrace. Hands on slender hips, she said, "Well, you don't! You've lost so much weight I wouldn't have recognized you. What have you been living on, bean sprouts and water?"

He shrugged. "I'm not much of a cook. Frozen dinners mostly."

"Well, I'll fix that." She looked toward the house. "Where's Hope?"

"Out jukin' with a bunch of three-year-old swingers. She runs with an older crowd. It's a birthday party down the street. Cora should bring her home any time now. Come on in. I'll help you unload later."

"You're on! A cold beer would go real good about now."

Jim threw back his head and laughed with sheer glee. Suddenly, with Tory's mention of a beer, the image of Francine Lawrence had flashed through his

350   *Becky Lee Weyrich*

mind. She'd hated beer—said it was the wine of the lower classes. Well, he guessed he knew where that put him!

They went to the kitchen and popped the tops on two icy brews. Jim took a long swig, then smacked his lips.

"Man, that does taste good!"

Tory clinked her can against his. "Cheers!" she said. "Here's to kissin' cousins!"

Jim looked into Tory's sparkling hazel eyes, all flecked with gold and green. He looked at her wide, smiling lips. Little did she suspect the ideas her words brought to mind.

"Yeah," he said. "To cousins!

Tory seemed oblivious to the tension in that moment. She glanced out the window and spied the tilled earth. "You're putting in Angel's garden. Good! I can help. I love planting stuff, but there's no room in New York." She turned back to him, her face serious now. "God, it's good to be here, Jim! To see you again . . ."

What might have turned into an intimate moment did not, for the front door banged open.

"Tory! Tory! Tory!" Hope cried as she raced through the hallway to the kitchen.

"Who is this?" Tory demanded when the bright, golden-haired beauty in the yellow polka-dot pinafore grabbed her around the knees. "I don't know this person, Jim."

Hope tilted her head back and grinned up at Tory. "I'm Hope!" she said firmly.

"No!" Tory said. "Hope's a little baby. She doesn't wear fancy dresses and go to parties."

"I am, too, Hope!" the child insisted, stamping her

ALMOST HEAVEN   351

tiny, white patent-leather shoe. "And I can prove it."
She pulled at the gold locket around her neck. "See
this? My Angel-Mama gave it to me when I was just
little, and it has her picture in it." Hope opened the
heart to show Tory the small photo of Angel.

Jim and Tory exchanged glances, both with moist
eyes.

"That's my girl!" Jim said, picking Hope up and
giving her a hug.

Tory shrugged. "Well, I guess I was wrong." She
scooped the child out of Jim's arms. "Come here to
me, precious, and give me some sugar."

Hope dissolved in giggles as Tory rained kisses all
over her cheeks and around her soft neck.

Jim stood back watching. He experienced a roller
coaster of emotions in those few seconds. It was so
good to see Tory again, so wonderful to have laughter
ringing through the house. Yet having her here made
him miss Angel all the more. Of all the women he'd
ever met, Tory was the most like Angel. Physically,
there was no resemblance. Angel had been tall, blue-
eyed, with exotic hair the color of a brilliant sunset.
Tory was petite and almost tomboyish with her short,
smooth brown hair, her lightly freckled nose, and
sparkling hazel eyes that always looked wide with
wonder.

So what made Tory seem so much like Angel? Jim
wondered. He realized in a flash of clarity that it
wasn't the women who were alike; it was their effect on
those around them. For the first time in over two
years, the old house on Park Row felt like a home
again. The very walls came alive to Tory's presence.

Tory glanced at Jim. He was so quiet and thoughtful

352   *Becky Lee Weyrich*

all of a sudden. She smiled and he smiled back. Then quickly, they both looked away, both for the same reason. They could feel the emotions, feel the chemistry, knew they would have to fight hard to keep their distance.

"I'm glad you're here," Jim admitted.

"Hey, don't get nervous. I won't be underfoot for long. I'll be out of your hair just as soon as I can find my own place."

"No hurry," Jim said, and he meant it.

But they both knew there was a need for haste. They felt equally guilty over how wonderful it was being together, like a family. The family Tory had always longed for. The one Jim had missed for so long, so desperately.

"There, you see?" Alexander said. "I know you can sense it as well as I can."

"Sense what?" Angel asked with an air of innocence, a pout on her pretty face. "Sure, Jim's glad to see Tory. They've always enjoyed each other's company. And she adores Hope."

"It's more than that and you know it. Why don't you admit it, Angela?"

"Oh, Alexander, you always jump to conclusions. Tory just got there. She and Jim haven't seen each other in over a year. It's a happy *family* reunion. That's all!"

"I believe you've struck the very heart of it. Family. They *act* like a family. They *are* a family. Tory is perfect for Jim!"

"Don't get ahead of yourself." She gave Alexander

ALMOST HEAVEN 353

a scorching glance that flamed with the jealousy she was trying desperately to hide. "And, for goodness' sake, change out of that gladiator's garb. It looks ridiculous up here."

He glared right back at her. "You liked it well enough when we were in Pompeii."

"That was then. This is now. What will people think?"

"They won't think anything. This is Heaven, remember? Up here we dress as we please—whatever makes us happy."

Angel was about to suggest that he get back into his robe. Then she glanced down and gave a startled cry. "Oh dear! My robe! What's happened to it? It's lost its pretty colors and its sparkle. It's a dull greenish gray."

"It's your attitude."

She fired him a sizzling look. "I don't have an attitude. What are you talking about?"

"You're jealous of Tory and Jim, that's what I mean. You might as well admit it, Angela. Your robe tells the whole tale. You didn't bring her to Jim, so you can't stand their being together, can you? You have a lot to learn before you earn your halo and crown."

"Stop it!" she cried. "I can't help the way I feel. Tory walks in and it's like I was never even there. Jim and Hope have forgotten I existed. How would that make *you* feel?"

Angel's shoulders were shaking. Alexander touched her arm, trying to soothe her. "I didn't mean to make you cry. I'm sorry, Angela. If you weren't so stubborn, you wouldn't be blind to how right they are for each other. Can't you see? This is what we've been waiting for. Tory is the answer to our prayers. She'll make Jim

354 *Becky Lee Weyrich*

happy and she'll be the best mother Hope could ever have."

The angry fire was back in Angel's blue eyes. "Better than me?"

"Of course not," he said gently. "No one could be a better mother than you were."

"Well . . ." Angel still felt resistant to the match.

"Why don't we just sit back and watch—see what develops?"

Angel agreed, but she didn't promise anything. She sank down, silent and glum, trailing her fingertips in the mirror-surface of the stream, staring at her dull greenish robe.

Things would have progressed at a much more rapid pace between Jim and Tory if it hadn't been for Angel's attitude. The two of them held back, refusing to admit they could ever be a real couple, because of the guilt Angel's jealousy transmitted.

Tory couldn't help recalling a certain conversation she'd had with Angel years ago. It was the night in New York when Angel and Jim had had that terrible argument and he had walked out, leaving her hurt and furious.

"Want to swap lives for a few days?" Tory had asked Angel. She'd gone on to say that she'd gladly take Jim Rhodes to fix dinner for and have quiet conversations with when he was in the mood to talk. She'd finished by asking her cousin, "Is life with Jim so bad?"

Angel had been quick to admit that she loved Jim and could never live without him. Now, every time

ALMOST HEAVEN

355

Tory began thinking of herself and Jim as a couple, she was so overcome with guilt that she immediately backed off.

Little did she suspect that the same thing was happening to Jim. Though he was happier than he had been since right before Angel's death, his very happiness almost made him hate himself. What right had he to be enjoying life when Angel was no longer around? He had been miserable ever since she died, and that's exactly how it should be, he reasoned. He'd told her on their wedding night that he could never love anyone else, and he'd meant it. He might have been attracted to Francine Lawrence, but he had never really loved her. Not the way he'd loved Angel. As for Tory, he reasoned that the way he felt about her really had nothing to do with Tory herself. It had to do with the fact that she reminded him of happier days with Angel.

Still, it was hard to deny the warm feeling he got every morning when he woke up to the smell of coffee and breakfast cooking downstairs. And more often than not, Tory was singing as she worked. She filled the old house with joy and warmth, made the whole place come alive again and Jim with it. As for Hope, she had blossomed from a shy toddler into a bubbling child under Tory's influence. How could Jim *not* be happy under such circumstances? How could he *not* want Tory to stay forever?

A month after Tory's arrival in Maine, she was still with Jim and Hope. Each time she found a place that she thought she might rent, Jim would take a look at it and pronounce it "too small, too depressing, too expensive." Then Tory would go back to Park Row and

356   *Becky Lee Weyrich*

begin her halfhearted search all over again. In truth, she didn't want to move out any more than Jim wanted her to go. She adored the old place and loved every minute of keeping house for Jim and Hope. At times, she even caught herself pretending that she belonged there.

One evening in late May, they put Hope in her stroller and headed out to the Mall. It was the first truly balmy night of the year. The brilliant sunset was fading to deep scarlet and purple as they left the house. The evening star was already twinkling brightly. It was soon joined by millions of others in the blue-velvet night sky. Lightning bugs blinked amorously in the lilac bushes and among the roses on the fence.

"I wonder what the peasants back in New York are doing this evening?" Tory said with a little laugh. "If they knew about Maine, they'd all flock up here."

Jim grinned at her. "Then there wouldn't be room for the rest of us. And we'd have garbage strikes and gridlock and panhandlers on every corner."

Tory shivered. "Don't even talk about it! Oh, Jim, it's just so perfect here. I love it!"

He stared at her smiling face in the dim starlight. It was on the tip of his tongue to say, "And I love *you,* Tory." But the old guilt flamed up inside him. What right had he to say that to her? They hadn't so much as held hands or shared a kiss since she'd arrived. She'd be shocked if he admitted his feelings.

The moment passed. They walked on in silence.

Tory knew that Jim had been ready to say something to her, something that he'd decided to keep to himself. She wondered what it could be. The look on his face at that moment she had seen before. He had

ALMOST HEAVEN 357

looked at Angel that way. Had he been thinking about her? Or had he meant that look for Tory herself? If he only knew how he made her feel. If he only knew how much she loved him . . .

The thought came as a shock to Tory. She hadn't admitted it to herself before. But it was true—*and* hopeless. Her heart ached painfully as she realized how useless it was for her to hope. She decided then and there that she would find an apartment before the week was out. As wonderful as her life was right now, it was becoming too painful to live with Jim, caring for him the way she did and knowing that it could never come to anything.

They were walking side by side, both gripping the wide handle of Hope's stroller. Jim moved his hand, making contact with Tory's. She jumped with surprise as heat shot up her arm. She meant to move her hand away, but the feel of Jim's flesh touching hers was too exciting, too wonderful. They walked on, still touching, while Tory's heart sang a sad little song of love.

"Tory, I've been thinking." His voice sounded very loud in the silence. "It's great having you with us, but . . ."

Before he could finish his statement, Tory's heart sank. She was sure he was about to say, "But you said it would be for only a few days. Don't you think it's about time you found a place of your own?"

Instead, he continued, ". . . it's driving me crazy, not knowing if I might come home one day and find you packing to leave. I'd like it very much if you'd stay. Hope's so happy having you with us. And I have to admit that I like having order in my life again. It gives me such a feeling of security to come home at night to

358   *Becky Lee Weyrich*

a tidy house, with the smell of supper cooking and you singing in the kitchen. And there's my paper beside my chair and the dog's been walked and the laundry's done. Won't you stay with us? Please?"

Tory smiled up at him. "If any other man said things like that to me, I'd consider him a first-class chauvinist. But I know you mean well, Jim. And you want to know a secret? I guess I'm old-fashioned, but I love doing those things—keeping house, cooking, taking care of Hope . . . and you," she added.

"Then you'll stay?" There was joy and wonder in his husky voice.

"I think Angel would want me to," she said softly.

Jim's guilt swelled at her words. Was she staying only because she was Angel's cousin, out of a sense of responsibility? He had hoped she'd stay for him, because she enjoyed being with him.

"Hope's fast asleep," Tory whispered. "We'd better head home and get her to bed."

Jim smiled warmly. "Home," he repeated. "That sounds so good the way you say it. And now I don't have to worry every morning that you might be gone by the time I come home in the evening. I'm so glad you're staying."

"Me, too," she answered in a whisper. For some reason she couldn't explain, she was on the verge of tears. Maybe because Jim saw her as a housekeeper instead of a possible lover or wife. She chided herself for such thoughts. She should be happy with what she had instead of wishing for the moon and stars.

Back home, they tucked Hope in, then went down to the kitchen for coffee. Jim sat at the table, gazing out over the moonlit backyard.

ALMOST HEAVEN

"Penny for your thoughts," Tory said as she cut him a piece of cherry pie, still warm from the oven.

"I was just thinking it's about time to get to work on the garden. This weekend, for sure."

Remembering the pitiful jade plant she'd found in the kitchen window and how long it had taken her to nurse it back to health, Tory smiled.

"Can I help?" she asked.

He glanced up at her and grinned. "Sure thing! I'll need all the help I can get. Angel was the gardener in the family. I don't know my hollyhocks from my snapdragons."

Tory sat down next to him and took a bite of cherry pie. She chewed in thoughtful silence. "Needs a touch more cinnamon."

Jim had finished his already. He shook his head. "Nope! It was perfect! If you weren't such a fine actress, Ms. Cason, I'd hire you to cook for me."

"And I'd take the job." She wasn't smiling any longer.

"What's the matter, honey?"

Tory focused on his eyes for a moment, trying to figure how he meant that "honey." Was he just feeling mellow and calling her that in the way he often called Hope "sweetheart"? Or did he mean it as a true endearment—man to woman? Probably the former, she decided, disappointed.

"The matter is, I've just been cast as the lead in your play."

"Tory! That's great!" He grabbed her and hugged her enthusiastically, the way he sometimes hugged The Monster after the beast had performed one of his tricks. Still, Tory enjoyed it immensely.

360   *Becky Lee Weyrich*

"It's not so great, Jim. That's an extremely demanding role. I'm not sure I'm a good enough actress."

"Of course you are! You're perfect for the part."

"It's such a touching love story, I'm not sure I can get all the emotion into it. I usually play comedy roles. Every time I audition for a dramatic piece, the answer is always the same: 'You're a lightweight, not right for anything this heavy. Come back when we're casting a comedy.' I'm scared, Jim," she admitted. "I don't want to ruin your play."

"You couldn't ruin anything if you tried, Tory. Don't you realize how good you are? I slipped into the theater last week and watched you rehearsing for the part of Luisa in *The Fantasticks.* You were absolutely brilliant!"

Tory blushed she was so pleased. "But that is the role of a girl. Margo in your play is a mature, married woman. She's also extremely passionate. I'm just not sure I can play her convincingly."

"I have an idea. What if I help you? We can read lines together here at home. I *know* Margo. I created her. So I think I can turn you into her. It'll be a challenge for me. It will be fun! How about it?"

"Oh, Jim, I don't know. You stay so busy. When will you have time?"

"I'll make time for this. I just can't believe that neither you nor Bernard told me you got the part."

"I only found out this afternoon. I've been trying to think how to tell you. I wasn't sure you'd be happy about it."

"Happy? I'm ecstatic! We'll get to work right away."

Without thinking what she was doing, Tory gripped

ALMOST HEAVEN   361

Jim's hand. "Oh, thank you! This will make all the difference, Jim."

Only one person guessed exactly what a difference it would make. Angel stared down, frowning, as Tory took Jim's hand.

"Don't do that, Angela," Alexander warned from behind her. She didn't know he was watching her watching them.

"Do what?" she asked innocently.

"You think I don't know what's in your mind? You're scheming again. Why can't you just leave them be? They're happy! They're in love!"

"That's not love. They're only holding hands."

"Because that's all *you* will allow. Shame on you, Angela! You've been in love. You know what they want, what they need. Let them have it. Let *me* have what *I* want."

"And what might that be?"

"You, Angela! You're all I've ever wanted. We're so close now. The Gates of Heaven are ready to swing open. But they can't until you let go."

Alexander's words made Angel feel ashamed. She knew she wanted everything her own way. Why couldn't she do as Alexander wished? Just let go of her control of Jim and Tory and let them realize their love? She wanted to be happy, and she wanted them to be happy. It seemed so simple, so easy.

She stared down at her reflection in the mirror stream, at Alexander's powerful image next to hers. Then her cheeks flamed with embarrassment, knowing that he saw the same thing she was staring at. Her robe now glowed like dirty green fire. Try as she might, she could not conquer her festering jealousy.

Chapter Sixteen

Seriously worried about Angela, Alexander tried his best to distract her. He lured her away from the garden and her preoccupation with Earth by drawing her back in time to other lives they had shared.

He showed her Constantinople when it had been a center of intrigue and mystery. Angel had been an exotic dancer, the most beautiful woman in the world in that ancient time. She had performed the dance of the veils for him, her rainbow-colored drapes flowing, her sapphire eyes flashing, the gold coins at her hips and ankles jingling as her luscious body swayed in sensual rhythm to the throbbing music of drums and mandolins.

Alexander had been a handsome merchant prince, rich enough to buy his way into her bed and eventually into her heart. They had shared a clandestine affair for nearly a year before an evil, lusting potentate burst into their curtained chamber late one stormy night and murdered them both while they lay in each other's arms. But death could not end their everlasting love.

From Constantinople, he flew her far back in time

ALMOST HEAVEN 363

to the isle of Crete, to the court of King Minos. In that beautiful, decadent kingdom of lilies, great palaces, and fierce bulls, Angela was a spirited young virgin, torn from her family in Athens and enslaved as tribute to the island king. She was destined to leap the bulls in the arena for the entertainment of the bloodthirsty throngs of Crete. If she survived, she would go below to the dungeons in the infamous labyrinth of Knossos to await her next turn with the bulls. Ten leaps and she would be free.

But in centuries of the gory sport, only one bull leaper had survived, the horribly disfigured keeper of the dungeon, who ministered to his charges with kindness and understanding. Alexander, that lone survivor, had been Angela's mentor, the one who taught her the tricks she needed to live through the ordeal.

Once a handsome youth from Athens, like Angela carried to Crete on a ship with black sails, he was now only a shell of the strong man he had been. He masked his face to hide the ugly scars left by the bulls, and walked with a shuffling limp. He was so hideous that the tender virgins turned from him in fright. All but Angela. Only she could see beneath the horribly ravaged flesh into the dungeon master's tender heart.

They came to love each other in a spiritual way. The only way they could. The bulls had robbed him of his ability to love her as a man should love a woman. But a truer affection never flourished. Before her tenth leap, the two made plans to leave Knossos together that very day. They would share a hut beside the shining sea, spend the rest of their lives together. They would never again face the horrors of the bulls. They would live a gentle, easy life together—fishing, gather-

364 *Becky Lee Weyrich*

ing saffron, talking quietly for hours of the gods and the universe. Theirs was a love for all time.

After her tenth performance, when Angela lay dying in Alexander's arms, pierced through by the horn of a bull, their tears mingled and they vowed to search for each other in another, kinder life.

Alexander knew it was cruel to make Angela face and relive those terrible times, but he hoped in doing so he would make her realize once again the depth and dedication of their love for each other.

When they returned to the garden from Crete, Angela was weeping. Alexander's heart ached at the sight of her tears.

"It's over now," he said gently. "We're back."

She stared at him as if she expected to see the horrible face of the bull leaper again. *"Why?"* she moaned. "Why have we had to suffer so, Alexander?"

"With soul mates it is often so," he answered. "Without the painful times, would we appreciate the joy of life? Our day *will* come, Angela. It's waiting for us now. You have only to believe and accept your new life and my love."

"I'm afraid," she admitted.

He touched her hand and smiled. "You have nothing to fear. All the bad times are behind us."

"How do you know?"

"I know," he said simply. "We are both old souls now, with a vast amount of understanding. We won't repeat our past mistakes. Trust me, Angela."

"If we go back to Earth together, who will we be?"

He shook his head. "That I can't tell you. That is not in our hands."

"Then how will we find each other?"

ALMOST HEAVEN 365

"The same way we were drawn together in Spain, in Constantinople, in Crete, and in Maine. The lure of our souls will bring us together again. We'll look into each other's eyes and suddenly we'll know."

"Will we remember everything from the past?"

"No. All the painful memories will be washed from our minds. We'll begin fresh—be two new people, finding love as if for the first time."

"It scares me."

"It shouldn't. Are you ready to go now?"

"Not yet," she answered quickly, forcefully.

He glanced toward the wishing well. "You're going back down there, aren't you?"

"Please, Alexander." There was entreaty in her words, her voice, her eyes. "I must!"

"I'll be waiting here for you, Angela. Come back to me soon."

His tone was so hurt, so grieving that Angel went to him and slipped her arms around his waist. She leaned her head against his chest and sighed.

"I wish I could stay here with you. I don't know why I feel compelled to go back." She stared up into his solemn face. "Why don't you order me to stay?"

"It's not for me to command you. You must settle things in your own mind and heart before all will be right between us. Go *now* if you must. Don't make this parting more painful."

Angel sauntered uncertainly toward the well, glancing back over her shoulder time and again at Alexander. He was so strong and steady, so tall and handsome and loving. Why couldn't she simply forget about everything else and go with him through the Gates of Heaven?

366   *Becky Lee Weyrich*

"I'll be waiting," he assured her one last time.

Before she even realized what was happening, Angel found herself back in Maine, hovering over her garden behind the house on Park Row.

A large gold-and-black butterfly fluttered by. Angel, weary from her time travels with Alexander, hitched a ride on its broad wings.

Hope was standing near where Jim and Tory were spading and planting. When she saw the butterfly, she hopped up and down, crying "Mama! Mama! Angel-Mama!"

Jim looked up and wiped the sweat from his forehead, leaving a smear of dirt. He said, "No, Hope. That's a butterfly."

"Mama!" Hope replied stubbornly. "Not bubberfly!"

"Have it your way, sweetheart." Jim went back to his digging.

Tory, however, continued staring at the large monarch as it swooped over their heads, dancing in the air. She watched Hope's rapt attention. The little girl was smiling, positively glowing. The child held up her hand to the butterfly. It landed in her outstretched palm and rested there. Its wings opened and closed in lazy fashion. Tory listened closely to Hope, who was whispering to the pretty creature.

"I miss you," Hope said.

Then the child cocked her head as if she were listening to an answer.

She bobbed her red-gold head in an affirmative nod. "Yes, Tory is nice. We play games, sing songs. And Daddy smiles now."

Another listening pause.

ALMOST HEAVEN 367

"Blueberry pancakes," Hope said, as if in answer to a question from the butterfly. "She makes them so good!"

Tory smiled. She had begun a tradition of blueberry pancakes for Saturday morning breakfast. Hope loved them. Tory nudged Jim and whispered, "Your daughter has quite an imagination. She thinks the butterfly just asked her what she had for breakfast."

"It's in the genes," Jim replied. "Angel used to talk to plants." He went back to digging a hole for a dahlia bulb.

The Monster raced from across the yard as if he meant to snatch Hope's butterfly. But instead, he settled beside the child, as still as a statue, except for his tail, which was wagging in welcome.

Hope turned to the dog. "See, Monster, it's Mama."

The great black beast wagged his tail harder.

With a flutter of wings, the butterfly lifted from Hope's hand and landed again, this time on Monster's damp nose.

Tory watched, fascinated. She knew that Monster had an on-going vendetta with the insect world. No grasshopper, cicada, beetle, or fly was safe if he was anywhere in the vicinity. Tory rose quickly, ready to rescue Hope's butterfly before Monster swallowed it whole. But the dog sat very still, allowing the creature to perch there unmolested. He was still wagging, still docile.

"Mama says you're a good dog." Hope reached over and patted Monster's head.

Tory couldn't stand it any longer. She got up and went over to Hope. She knelt down beside her.

"Who's your friend?" Tory asked.

368   *Becky Lee Weyrich*

The butterfly was on Hope's shoulder now.

"It's Mama," she said matter-of-factly.

"You mean your mama's turned into a butterfly?"

Hope giggled. "No, silly! He's just letting Mama have a ride. She says she's tired and her wings don't work right yet."

Tory stared at the butterfly. "Angel?" she said under her breath.

Hope grew solemn. "Yes, she's an angel now, or almost. She lives in a pretty garden, but she comes to see me a lot."

"Really?" Tory couldn't think of anything else to say.

Hope nodded vigorously, delighted to have an adult believe her. "Um-hum! You know the angels in my room?"

"You mean the wallpaper?"

Another nod. "When Mama comes, they sing to me. They play their harps and sing so sweet. They sing me to sleep at night." With a full head of steam, Hope rushed on. "And you know the man who used to stay in my room? He was real sad—I guess because he only had one arm. He used to make me feel sad, too. So Mama came and took him away. Now I'm not sad anymore. Mama does wonderful things."

"And she's here now?" Tory wanted to make sure.

Hope frowned at Tory and put her tiny hands on her hips. "I told you she is! She wants to see what you and Daddy are doing and what you're planting in her garden. She says sweet peas are nice. She wants sweet peas." Hope looked up at Tory, her whole pretty face a question mark. "What are sweet peas? Do you eat them?"

ALMOST HEAVEN 369

Tory hugged Hope and laughed. "No, darling. Sweet peas are pretty flowers in rainbow colors that look like tiny angels with their wings folded."

"Oh! That must be why Mama wants them then."

That night, after Hope was in bed and Jim had planted sweet peas, at his daughter's request, Tory and Jim were in the living room having iced tea and oatmeal cookies while they went over her part in his play.

"What was all that business with the butterfly today?" Jim asked.

Tory looked up from the script she was studying. "Hope thought Angel was there, that she'd hitched a ride with the butterfly to see how the garden was coming."

Jim scowled. "You shouldn't encourage her, Tory."

"What harm can it do? She misses Angel. If she thinks her mother's with her, it makes her happy."

"Angel's *not* with her! Angel's dead! Gone for good!"

"Can you be sure she's gone?"

Jim's frown deepened. "What are you talking about? Don't tell me you saw Angel today too."

Tory shook her head. "No, I don't think grownups can see angels. Just innocent children and animals are allowed that privilege."

"Animals? What do you mean?"

Tory put the script down and leaned closer to Jim. "Didn't you see the butterfly land on Monster's nose?"

"Bye-bye, butterfly!" Jim said with a short laugh.

Tory shook her head. "No. Monster sat there as still as a statue and cocked his head as if he were hearing a voice he knew."

370 *Becky Lee Weyrich*

"And that *proves* Angel was really there? Come on, Tory! I've been working you too hard."

"I only know what I saw this afternoon and what your daughter told me."

Tory paused, waiting for Jim to respond, but he didn't. Instead, he picked up the script she'd laid aside, his way of putting an end to the conversation. But she wasn't ready to end it.

"Jim, do you know anything about a one-armed man?"

He thought a minute, then nodded. "Oh, you must mean General Joshua. He built this house. Lost his arm in the Civil War, so the story goes."

"Does Hope know about him?"

"Of course not. I don't think he's ever been mentioned since she was born. I heard his story the day we first came to look at this house. Angel had kind of an obsession with this guy. She told me once that she thought she'd seen his ghost. She was given to flights of fancy, though. I dismissed the whole thing, and she never mentioned him again. Why do you ask? Don't tell me you've been seeing ghosts, too."

Tory sighed, almost sorry she'd brought up the subject. But there was no stopping now. "I haven't seen him, but Hope has."

"What?" Jim jumped up and tossed the script aside.

Tory repeated to Jim everything Hope had said about the unhappy, one-armed man and how Angel had taken him away so he wouldn't make Hope sad anymore.

"This is outrageous! Who's been feeding Hope all this garbage?" He thought for a minute. "Cora Shute! I'll bet she told Hope about General Joshua."

ALMOST HEAVEN   371

Before Tory could stop him, Jim dialed Cora's number even though it was nearly midnight and the elderly woman was sure to be fast asleep.

"Ayah? Who's calling?" Cora answered in a groggy voice.

"It's Jim, Cora. Sorry to wake you. But something's come up with Hope."

"Oh, Lordie! You want me to come right over? How high's her fever?"

"No, no! Hope's fine. It's just that this afternoon she said something to Tory about seeing a one-armed man in her room. Have you told her about General Joshua?"

"Land, no! I wouldn't tell that child ghost stories and give her nightmares."

"Ghost stories? What are you talking about, Cora?"

"Well . . ." She hesitated, remembering how upset Jim had been when Angel had mentioned seeing the ghost. "I know you don't believe it, but there's been tales for years about the general's ghost being in that house. Angel saw—"

Jim cut her off. "I know what Angel *said* she saw. Angel always had a vivid imagination. You're *sure* you never mentioned this to Hope."

"Positively!" Cora said firmly.

"Well, thanks. Sorry I woke you."

When Jim turned back to Tory, he had a puzzled expression on his face.

"It's all right, Jim. Hope said he's gone now."

"No, it's not all right! Maybe I should take Hope to see a child psychologist."

Tory smiled at his overreaction. "Don't be silly,

372   *Becky Lee Weyrich*

Jim. There's nothing wrong with Hope. All children have imaginary playmates."

"Not one-armed Civil War veterans!"

Tory tugged at his arm. "Sit down. Calm down! Angel certainly didn't mean to upset you."

He glared at her. "I wish you'd stop talking as though Angel's still here—in this very room with us."

"I believe she is. Think about it, Jim. We both loved her. She's still in our minds and our hearts, so how could she not be here?"

"But you don't mean *physically?*"

Tory laughed softly, trying to soothe him. "Of course not! I just mean that her spirit will always be with us."

He thought for a minute, then nodded. "Yes, I can accept that."

"Good! I'm glad that's settled."

Suddenly, Jim turned and stared at Tory, puzzlement in his eyes. "Why did Hope ask me to plant sweet peas today? She doesn't know a sweet pea from an artichoke."

Tory avoided Jim's direct gaze. "No, she doesn't know what they are. She said Angel wanted them in the garden."

Jim threw his hands up in total frustration. "Great! Now we've got talking butterflies who are partial to sweet peas. What next?"

"Maybe we'd better just call it a night," Tory suggested.

He sighed and patted her hand. "I think you're right. I sure can't concentrate on the play now."

* * *

ALMOST HEAVEN 373

The tender greens of spring soon turned to deeper and more vibrant summer shades. On the Mall the Farmers' Market flourished again, while in the garden behind the house on Park Row, giant sunflowers lifted their faces to the heavens and Hope's sweet peas blossomed in a delicate rainbow of pinks, lavenders, and yellows. The Fourth of July was fast approaching.

High-school majorettes were practicing for their prance down Maine Street. Musicians were tuning up for their concert in the band shell on the Mall. Volunteer firemen were polishing their shiny red engines. And the mayor was writing his patriotic speech.

In the gray stone Picard Theater, however, the home of the Brunswick Music Theater, the focus was on Jim's play, especially on its star.

"Try it once again, please, Tory." Although he spoke quietly, Bernard Wurger's deep voice boomed in the tense silence.

He sounded so patient—*too* patient, Tory thought. She'd been blowing her lines all morning. She guessed the director was nearing the breaking point. The thought made her all the more panicky. She *must* get it right this time.

Somewhere in the back of the theater a man cleared his throat. She glanced up, but couldn't see him. She didn't need to see; she knew who it was. Jim was back there, sitting in on the rehearsal, probably squirming with discomfort at the way Tory was butchering the beautiful lines he'd written. Knowing he was there made her even more nervous and uncomfortable.

"Where do you want me to start?" she asked, feeling like a total novice instead of a seasoned professional.

"Why don't you pick it up right before the kiss?

374   *Becky Lee Weyrich*

Where John says, 'I knew the minute you spilled wine on me at that stuffy party that I was in love for the first time in my life.' Then Margo comes in." Still looking at the script, Bernard pointed at Tory.

" 'Darling, you shouldn't read so much into that. I spill wine on whomever I choose. I don't have to be head over heels to ruin a fellow's suit.' "

"Much better," Bernard encouraged. "I think you've got it. Margo needs to sound very sure of herself. Sophisticated, almost flippant. But you have to make the audience realize that she's teetering on the brink. She's in love with John, too, but she doesn't want to admit it, least of all to herself. John says, 'What are you trying to do? Make me jealous, Margo?' "

" 'Jealous?' " Tory uttered a laugh that held just the right sense of forced humor mixed with uncertainty. " 'If it will make you happy, darling, I'll christen you with a whole magnum of Dom Pérignon.' "

" 'That's not what I want and you know it.' " Wurger moved in on Tory and slipped an arm around her waist. " 'This is what I want.' "

Margo's next line—the all-important words before their first kiss—flew right out of Tory's head. She had memorized this script backward and forward. Not only did she know all her own lines, but everyone else's as well. So why, each time she got to the kiss, did she draw a blank?

"I'm sorry," she whispered, her eyes filling with tears.

"Let's take a break," Bernard said, his voice totally controlled, totally without emotion, and all the more

ALMOST HEAVEN 375

frightening for his calm. Tory wished he'd soothe her conscience by yelling at her.

Instead, leaving her alone in the middle of the stage, he walked back to the darkest part of the theater. Tory stared after him, squinting, hoping her gaze would penetrate the shadows. She knew Bernard had gone to confer with Jim, probably to suggest that they put the understudy in her stead. Tory didn't want that. With all her heart and soul she wanted to play this role. She wanted to play it for Jim.

Out of nowhere, the line suddenly came to her. She yelled it at the top of her voice, determined that the two men should hear it. " 'If it's *me* you want, darling, why didn't you just say so? I'm not that hard to get.' "

Tory stood frozen on the stage, body tense, eyes and ears straining to pick up the slightest movement or sound from the back of the theater. Nothing! Her heart was thundering. More than anything, she longed to dash from the stage and hide. She knew they were out there. She knew they were watching her. She felt naked and vulnerable and afraid.

She saw a movement in the shadows. Jim emerged into the light. He was staring at her. He wasn't smiling. Still without a word, he mounted the stage steps and came toward her. The expression on his face was that of the dominant male, yet his eyes held sadness, real pain.

The theater seemed to vanish. Tory and Jim vanished with it, leaving only Margo and John, locked in an atmosphere of sexual tension and passionate confrontation.

" 'You said that to hurt me, didn't you, Margo? Admit it! You can't bear the thought that I might re-

376 *Becky Lee Weyrich*

ally love you. That would require some response, some commitment on your part. Well, I'm not like all those other guys. I'm not interested in a one-night stand.' "

Tory managed to get past the lump in her throat to utter Margo's sultry laugh. " 'Darling, you'd sell your soul to the devil himself for a one-night stand with me. We both know that. And why should I expect anything more?' "

Wurger materialized out of the shadows, moving slowly toward the stage, his hypnotic gaze focused on Tory and Jim, Margo and John. When he reached the front row, Tory turned and glanced down at him.

"Go on!" he urged in a stage whisper.

The next line was John's. " 'I'll show you why.' " The next action was also John's—the kiss.

When John drew Margo into his arms, she quickly became Tory again. Tory, pressed close to Jim—the man she loved, the man she desired. Was this passionate kiss, a kiss that set Tory's heart racing and her blood sizzling, only a stage kiss meant to convince Margo? Or was Jim feeling the same sensations now raging through Tory like a runaway fire? Was this John drawing her close to his hard body, lingering over her lips, teasing her with his tongue, or was it— please, God!—*Jim,* wanting her as much as she wanted him?

Applause echoed through the empty theater, breaking the spell. "That's perfect, Tory," Bernard said. "You delivered those lines with just the right inflection and with *real* feeling. I *believed* you were Margo."

Jim stepped away. He was no longer touching Tory except with his eyes. His gaze seemed filled with wonder and puzzlement. "So did I," he said quietly. "You

ALMOST HEAVEN 377

were Margo, the very woman I created. You made her come alive, Tory. Thank you."

Tory's heart sank. Jim hadn't been kissing her after all. He'd been on the verge of making love to Margo. All that feeling and passion had been inspired by a totally fictitious woman. A woman she could never be. It was all she could do to hold back tears.

Silence lingered in the theater. Jim was still staring at her. He hadn't moved and she dared not either. The tension between them now was tenuous, fragile. She longed for the moment to go on and on.

"Okay!" Bernard said, looking at his watch. "It's after three. Why don't we wrap it up for today. You and Jim work on that together at home. Tomorrow I want to see the same scene with the same perfect feeling between you and the real John."

Bernard's words banished all sexual tension and jerked Tory back to reality. She wouldn't be playing this scene with Jim. Her leading man was a young actor named Dave Strom. Dave was much better on stage than Jim. Tory only hoped she was a good enough actress to make the scene believable with someone other than Jim.

"See you guys tomorrow," Bernard called as he headed out of the theater. "I've got to go home and feed my cat."

"Are you ready?" Jim asked. "Hope will be glad to have us home early for a change."

Tory was sorely tempted, but she couldn't go with Jim right then. She needed some time away from him to sort out her feelings. She'd known since she was a teenager that she was crazy about him—a kid's crush, that's all. But now things were different. That kiss

378   *Becky Lee Weyrich*

might have been meant for Margo, but Tory had been
the recipient and Jim the giver. It had opened cham-
bers of her heart and soul that she never knew existed.
If it was true that everyone in life had a soul mate, then
surely James Rhodes was hers. But what about Angel?
Where did she fit into the picture? She and Jim had
been so much in love.

"You go on," Tory said. "I'll be along in a little
while. I need to run some errands in town."

He nodded and started to leave, then turned back to
her. He was frowning, "Tory, about just now. I feel I
ought to explain . . ."

He was talking about the kiss. Tory didn't want to
discuss it. She just wanted to savor the memory. She
didn't allow him to go on.

"It's okay, Jim. Don't give it another thought. I'll
see you back at the house later."

She tore off the stage and out of the theater as if the
place had suddenly caught fire and she was racing for
her life. Outside, the Bowdoin campus was so green it
almost hurt her tear-glazed eyes. Bernard Wurger
hadn't gone home to feed his cat. She found him
lounging on a stone bench under a tree, staring at her
through his ever-present aviator sunglasses. He was
dressed much like Tory herself—jeans, tanktop, sandals. It seemed to be the summer uniform among the
actors in Maine.

"Hey?" he called quietly. "You want to talk about
it? I may not have any answers for you, but I'm a good
listener."

Tory clamped a hand over her mouth, trying to hold
back a sob. It escaped in spite of her.

"Come on," Bernard said. He motioned her toward

ALMOST HEAVEN 379

the bench. "Tell me what's eating you, Tory. We've got a play to put on, remember?"

She nodded, fighting for control. At length, she said, "I'm sorry."

"You've got nothing to apologize for. You were terrific in there just now. Jim wasn't bad either for a playwright. I'm half tempted to give him Dave's role."

The mention of Jim's name brought a new flood of tears.

"What'd I say?" Bernard looked puzzled even though his shades hid his eyes.

"Nothing!" Tory cried. "It's not you. It's . . . it's Jim!"

Bernard nodded silently. "Yeah, I could see that. He's really smitten. And you don't feel the same way, right? But you don't know how to let him down easy."

Tory laughed through her tears. "If he's smitten, it's Margo he's fallen for. I'm the one who's caught Cupid's arrow. Bull's eye! Right through the heart! But Jim doesn't have the slightest inkling how I feel. I'm finally in love, and I've never been so miserable in my life."

"So that's the problem." Bernard shook his head, laughing, until his reddish hair fell over his forehead. "Hey, I think you two guys need to sit down and have a serious talk. I've known Jim since he and Angel first got to Maine. I saw the way he looked at her, like he couldn't keep his eyes off her—*ever*. Then after the accident he drew into a shell and I didn't think he'd come out again. But now he's back—same old Jim. And that look he gives you is the one he used to reserve only for Angel."

Tory stared at him, seeing her own reflection in his

380   *Becky Lee Weyrich*

silvery glasses. "You're serious, aren't you? You're
not just making this up so I'll feel better?"

"No way! You don't kid around with people in love.
Go home. Talk to him."

Tory gripped his hand in both of hers and smiled.
"Thanks, Bernard. Thanks for everything!"

She left then, but she didn't go straight home. She
had to think things through before she saw Jim. If he
really was in love with her, then why hadn't he said or
done anything to show it? Sure, they were close. How
could they help it, living under the same roof? But it
was a casual closeness, with none of the intensity of
love. He treated her like Angel's cousin. And she
tried—oh, how she tried!—to treat him with the same
distant concern and affection. What else could she do?

Tory walked and walked, never looking to see where
she was going. She wound up in the deep, cool shade
of the Bowdoin Pines. There was an otherworldly silence among the tall evergreens. The wind made the
treetops whisper overhead, but otherwise all was still.
She crossed her arms over her breasts, hugging herself.
She felt as if someone were here with her, some presence she couldn't see.

"Angel?" she whispered after a time. "Angel? Is that
you?"

Of course, she received no answer. That in itself
made her feel brave enough to go on.

"Angel, I need to talk to you. It's about Jim. And
you're not going to like it much. I'm in love with him,
see? I can't help it. I tried not to be. But there it is."
Tory paused and drew in a deep breath before going
on. "Bernard thinks Jim loves me too."

Without even thinking about what she was doing,

ALMOST HEAVEN

Tory shut her eyes tightly and steeled herself for a blow. Nothing hit her. But she jumped when a pine cone struck the ground at her feet.

Trembling slightly, she went on. "So, I guess I'm sort of asking your permission. I feel awful guilty about what's happened. I mean, he *was* your husband, and I know how much you loved him. But now *I* love him. And he needs to be loved, Angel. He's been so unhappy and lonely since you died. If I'd planned and schemed to get him, it would be different. Then I could see how you'd be mad. But, honest, Angel, it just happened. And there's not a damn thing I can do to undo it. I love him! I want him! And, with or without your permission, I'm going to let him know how I feel."

Tory paused and waited. Then in a pleading voice, she said, "Can you hear me, Angel?"

In the garden high above, past the Milky Way and beyond the Big Dipper, Angel was listening. Her gown had never been greener.

"Let me talk to her," she begged Alexander. "Just let me go down there for a minute and tell her what I think."

Alexander held her in an embrace that might have been passionate if she hadn't been struggling to get away.

"No!" he said simply.

"Why not?"

"Because you'll do exactly that—tell her what you think. And just look at yourself. You're in the middle of a jealous fit. You couldn't be greener if you were that grass down on the Mall. And that wasn't nice,

382   *Becky Lee Weyrich*

what you did with that pine cone. It's a good thing
your aim is bad."

Angel ignored the remark about the pine cone she'd
launched at Tory. She didn't know Alexander had
caught onto that little trick.

"Tory asked my permission. The least you could do
is let me give it."

"That's what all this is about, isn't it? It galls you
that she and Jim fell in love without your help. Well,
that's just the way it works sometimes, and you're
going to have to live with it, Angela."

"I don't see why."

"You don't?" His voice was calm and steady now,
as if he were explaining something to a very small
child. "I'll tell you why. Because I've been waiting a
long time to get you back and I'm not going to let your
petty jealousy come between us now."

"Petty? I hardly think it's petty of me to want my
husband to have the right wife."

"If that's so, then why don't you let Jim and Tory
be. Sit back and see what happens. If they're meant to
be together, all will go well. If not, Tory will pack up
and go back to New York."

"You know that for sure?"

He nodded. "I do. But the only way things are going
to work out for them is by your staying out of it."

"All right," Angel answered.

"Promise?"

After some thought, Angel said, "Promise! Will you
let me go now?"

"No," Alexander answered.

"Why not? I promised, didn't I?"

"Because I'm not ready to let you go. If you won't

ALMOST HEAVEN

go back to Pompeii with me, I guess I'll have to steal a kiss here and hope no one's watching us."

"What difference does it make if someone sees us?" Angel wasn't fighting him now. She was no longer being held against her will, but with her own full approval.

"Because heavenly kisses are special," Alexander whispered. "They're sweeter than any other kind. So, like wings and halos and crowns, they're reserved for angels with full status. I could get into serious trouble for kissing you here in the garden."

"And you're willing to risk it?" Angel closed her eyes and lifted her chin toward his lips. She had no way of seeing the transformation when her robe turned from green to a passionate rose.

Alexander's lips touched hers. Angel heard music. She didn't just hear it, she felt it. Singing vibrations filled her, making her whole being tingle with sweet, wonderful sensations. She was the harp string and Alexander became the strong, gentle fingers plucking heavenly sounds from her soul. She was the violin and he was the bow, making her heart sigh with desire. Together they became an erotic, frenetic drumbeat reverberating through the heavens.

Her eyes were still closed, yet she could see all of their lives together, past and future. She could feel all the tears and smiles and pain and joy and love they had shared and were yet to share. With his kiss, Alexander opened his soul to her. He drew her in and made a warm, safe place for her.

Never was there such a feeling. Never was there such a kiss.

384 *Becky Lee Weyrich*

"Now do you understand?" Alexander whispered. "Tory is Jim's soul mate, just as *you* are *mine.*"

Alexander's words stunned Angel. But her state was far too blissful for her to worry about Tory and Jim. She closed her eyes and sighed, waiting for another of her soul mate's heavenly kisses.

Chapter Seventeen

Jim knelt at the edge of the inflated, blue plastic wading pool in the backyard, recovering Hope's rubber ducky each time it swam out of her reach. It was a simple task, a good task for him at the moment. He couldn't have handled anything much more complicated right now. Jim was confused. His trigger-action brain seemed to be malfunctioning.

"Bewitched, bothered, and bewildered . . ." The words of the old song kept swimming round and round in his head, imitating the motion of the duck in the pool.

His confusion might have begun on stage two hours ago when he'd kissed Tory—as Margo—but it had certainly intensified. Something had happened to him when his lips had pressed Tory's for the first time. Something unexpected. Something wonderful. Something almost scary.

One thing was sure. He wasn't the same man now that he had been when he woke up that morning. He might look the same on the outside, but inside he'd changed. Everything around him seemed different,

386   *Becky Lee Weyrich*

too. The sun shone brighter. The colors of the flowers in the garden were definitely more vibrant. The gentle breeze was cooler and more refreshing. Even Hope had changed. She was still wearing her tiny, pink bikini, and the damp red-gold curls still clung to her pretty face, but her laughter suddenly sounded as sweet as the song of an angel.

He glanced around, grinning like a kid. "The whole world's perked up all of a sudden. I feel so young, like a college boy with his first real crush."

"Don't let that child stay in the pool too long," Cora Shute called from the kitchen door. "She'll catch cold or get sunburnt or both."

"Okay!" Jim called back.

He looked down at his beautiful daughter. She was a happy child for one who had suffered such an early tragedy.

"You'd be a lot happier, though, if you had a real mother, wouldn't you, sweetheart?"

In answer, Hope, who had a strangle hold on the wayward duck, smashed him into the water, sending a shower all over Jim.

"Hey, watch it!" he said, pulling his wet shirt away from his chest, laughing his head off.

Hope pointed and giggled. "Daddy's wet!"

He peeled off his shirt and tossed it on the grass. "No harm done, kitten. It'll dry."

He leaned back, bracing his arms behind him, to let the warm sun dry the droplets on his bare chest. Hope immediately wriggled out of the top of her bathing suit in imitation of her dad.

When Tory reached the edge of the yard, she found father and daughter both basking bare-chested in the

ALMOST HEAVEN 387

sunshine. She stood at a distance, staring at Jim. He *never* went shirtless. The effect of seeing him this way for the first time was far more arousing than it should have been. She felt as if she'd come upon him naked.

The spell was broken by Cora's shrill voice. "Jim, you'd better bring that child in here."

"Coming, Cora," he called back.

"You stay right there," Tory said as she approached them. "I'll take Hope inside."

Jim smiled at her lazily, his silver gray eyes reflecting darkly in the bright sun. "Why don't you come back and join me? It's sure nice out here this afternoon."

Tory, her heart beating madly, smiled back. "You've got a deal. Want a beer while we sun?"

He winked at her. "Sounds good!"

Tory scooped Hope up and wrapped her in a towel. "There you go, missy. Have a nice swim?"

She giggled and snuggled close to Tory, her eyes drooping with happy weariness. "Duck wet Daddy. Bad ducky!"

Tory glanced back at Jim. "I don't think your dad minded, honey. He looks pretty contented to me. How about you? Are you ready for a nap?"

Hope closed her eyes completely and rested her damp head on Tory's bare shoulder. "Will the angels sing me to sleep?"

Carrying the child gently, Tory whispered, "I think they already have."

After handing over the sleeping child to Cora, Tory grabbed a couple of icy beers from the refrigerator, then headed back out.

She sensed a change in Jim. She'd wandered around in the Bowdoin Pines for over an hour, waiting for

388   *Becky Lee Weyrich*

some sign from Angel that this was okay by her, that she wouldn't hate them both for all eternity if they let themselves give in to love. Tory hadn't known what kind of sign she'd expected. Maybe the talking butterfly would come back and speak to her this time. Or Angel might have made a rainbow without any rain. She might even have spoken directly to Tory. But there had been no sign from on high. Finally, she'd given up, telling herself that once people were gone they were *really* gone and couldn't care less what was happening down among the living.

Now Tory knew that she'd given up too soon. Her sign had come all right, but not beneath the Bowdoin Pines. She'd found what she was seeking under the lilac bushes, on the green, green grass, beside the wading pool. The sight of Jim had been her sign. The feelings she got when she saw him stretched out, shirtless, on the grass, worshipping the sun and smiling at his baby daughter—they were the only sign she needed. If she hadn't felt love, truly and totally, at that moment, then she would never feel it. As for getting to love Hope in the bargain, that was an extra added bonus. What woman wouldn't welcome a darling child like Hope to mother.

Tory was glowing as she approached Jim.

He reached up for one of the beers, then took her hand and tugged gently. "Pull up a piece of lawn," he invited.

Tory tried hard to come up with something perfectly marvelous and witty to say to him. Nothing came to mind. She was too giddy to think straight. Instead of talking, she just kept smiling and blushing.

Jim patted the leg of her jeans. "Hey, you were great

ALMOST HEAVEN

389

this afternoon. You really put some soul into Margo."

Tory nodded her thanks. "You weren't so bad yourself. Bernard told me afterward that he was tempted to hand you that role."

Jim slapped his bare chest. "Me? No way! I get butterflies on stage. I'd freeze up and make a fool of poor old John for sure." He touched her bare arm with his cold beer can, lightly, affectionately. "But you and Dave are going to be great."

"I'm going to give it my all," Tory answered in a quiet voice. "I don't want to disappoint you, Jim. Not ever."

They both knew that her last two words had nothing to do with the play or her role as Margo. Tory's "not ever" sort of floated on the air between them like a verbal butterfly—pretty, delicate, something to be appreciated, but not touched.

After a time, Jim reached over and took Tory's hand. He didn't look at her, didn't say anything. He only held her hand gently in his.

The warmth and innocence of his gesture set Tory's heart raging again. She'd had her share of boyfriends and lovers. But no man had ever touched her the way Jim did. He wasn't simply holding her hand. He was holding her heart. He was telling her without words that she was special to him, that they might have a chance. And even the barest chance with Jim Rhodes meant more to her than all the promises from all the men she had ever known.

Jim tilted his head back and stared up at the sky— all crystal blue except for one cloud puff drifting by. "This is about the prettiest afternoon I've ever seen. In fact, the whole day has been damn near perfect."

390   *Becky Lee Weyrich*

"Does it scare you when things seem this good?"

He looked at her, his handsome face solemn now. "No. I don't think so. What about you?"

"Sort of," she admitted.

"Why?"

She tried to laugh it off. "I don't know. I guess I'm just a worrier by nature. But it seems when things get too good, I must be building up to a fall. *A dark moment!*" she added dramatically.

Jim laughed and squeezed her hand. "Drink your beer, Tory. You've been spending too much of your time around those theater people. You're beginning to think and talk like them."

She forced all dark thoughts from her mind. What was she worried about anyway? she wondered. She had done well at rehearsal and she was confident now that she could play Margo convincingly, perhaps even with a touch of brilliance. She was here on this beautiful day, in this beautiful summer with a man she adored. So what in the world could go wrong?

The summer will end! she thought suddenly. *That* was what worried her. And what then? Would Jim wave goodbye and let her drive out of his life forever? She couldn't bear that.

As if sensing her thoughts, he asked, "What do you have lined up for the fall? Any big deals brewing in New York?"

Tory answered him honestly. "I don't like to think that far ahead."

"Take it one step at a time, eh? That's not a bad idea. I was never one for long-range planning either." He leaned back, rested his head on one arm, and sighed. "Besides, who can think of anything serious on

ALMOST HEAVEN 391

a day like this? Blue sky, soft breeze, cold beer, and a pretty woman beside me. That should be enough for any man."

And there they left it. For another half-hour they simply enjoyed each other's silent company. Tory would have given anything to know what Jim was thinking as he stared up at the softly sighing pines. Was he thinking about their one kiss? Was he wishing, as she was, that they could try it again, see if the same rush of feelings came a second time?

Before she could find out, Cora Shute called from the kitchen to tell them supper would be ready soon.

Jim sat up and pulled on his shirt. "Guess I'd better go wash up."

"Me, too," Tory answered reluctantly. She wasn't hungry. She could lie there beside Jim forever.

Before Jim got up, he turned to her, his face serious. "Hey," he said quietly, "about this afternoon—at the theater."

Tory blushed and avoided his gaze. "You don't have to explain, Jim."

"I just wanted to tell you, Tory, that kiss might have been meant for Margo at the start, but somewhere along the way you intercepted it. I'm glad. I'd been wanting to kiss you all summer."

Without giving her time to reply, Jim got to his feet and headed for the house. Tory sat alone for a few moments, feeling herself glow as she followed Jim with her eyes.

"My sign," she murmured. "Jim would never have mentioned the kiss on his own. Something or someone prompted him to say that." She glanced up at the sky.

392   *Becky Lee Weyrich*

"If you did that, Angel, thank you. Thank you from the bottom of my heart."

"Angela!" Alexander warned. "Don't do it!"

Angel turned to him with a shy smile, but he could see the cunning in her eyes. "Do what?" she asked innocently.

"I don't know—a pine cone, a crow, a snake in the grass."

"A lot *you* know! There aren't any snakes in Maine. And I wasn't going to do anything. Besides, Tory is taking this whole situation far too seriously. She always was one to jump to conclusions."

The two of them were stretched out on a lush patch of neon grass beside the silvery stream, much as Tory and Jim had been moments before. Alexander, like Jim, was shirtless. Angel was convinced the man was too vain to be a first-class angel. But she had to admit he looked good in his gladiator's tunic, his bare torso rippling with muscles. He must have been something when he fought in the Circus Maximus.

"I don't think Tory's jumping to conclusions," he said. "And I don't believe you think that either. You know Jim better than anyone else. He's coming around, isn't he? I think he's beginning to realize he's in love with Tory."

Alexander watched Angela's robe closely. Only a faint green aura pulsed when he mentioned love. He smiled. Angela was the one who was coming around whether she was willing to admit it or not.

"You needn't look at me that way."

"What way?"

ALMOST HEAVEN

393

"Like you expected me to turn into a pea-green harpy at any minute and swoop down on Tory with a fury. I care about her. She's my cousin."

"Your *distant* cousin, remember?"

"How can I forget? You keep reminding me. But we were more than that. While Jim and I were in New York, Tory and I became very close—best friends. I suppose, if Jim does decide to marry again, she'd be a good choice."

Alexander reached out and drew Angel close. His hug was warm and tender. "I knew you'd see the light. Look! Your wings are growing again. And, although I wouldn't swear to it, I think I can see the faintest glimmer of a halo forming over your head."

Pleased, Angel grinned and touched the air above her head. "I think you're right. It feels warm." She stood and turned her back to the stream, looking over her shoulder to get a glimpse of her wings. "Oh, look, Alexander! They're definitely longer and the feathers are all silvery."

He rose to stand beside her, then slipped his arm about her waist and smiled down at their shining reflection. "Before you know it," he said, "you'll be wearing a glittering rainbow robe, full wings, and a glowing halo. When you do, we can go through the Gates of Heaven into the light. And then . . ."

She looked up at his beautifully handsome face. "Then what?" she whispered, almost breathless with anticipation.

"Then we'll go back, to start all over, to live again."

"Together?" Her voice was a trembling whisper.

He nodded. "Together!"

The thought both thrilled and frightened Angel.

394   *Becky Lee Weyrich*

There had never been any doubt in her mind that Tory would be a wonderful mother for Hope. She also realized now that her cousin was right for Jim. But what would happen when the crucial moment came? *That moment!* Jim hadn't really loved any other woman since Angel's death. Could she bear it when the time came? There was no way of knowing.

Angel was soon to face that test. Two days after that earth-shattering rehearsal kiss, Tory played Margo during the Fourth of July production, played her as if she were the woman Jim had created. The production proved a triumph for all involved.

As the curtain came down on the final scene, not a sound could be heard in the audience. Then the applause erupted. The rafters shook with it. The sound echoed over the Bowdoin campus.

Tory was moved to tears by the crowd's reaction. She received a standing ovation—through seven curtain calls—and a huge bouquet of red roses from the playwright. Finally, Jim joined Tory and the rest of the cast on stage. The cheers rang out, stronger than ever. He clung to Tory's arm for support. She could feel him shaking inside his tuxedo—the same tux Angel had anointed with gin months ago.

"I can't believe this," Jim kept murmuring over and over.

"You wrote the perfect play. They loved it!" Tory squeezed his arm.

He smiled down into her wide, dewy, hazel eyes. "They loved *you,* sweetheart. Who could resist you? I've never seen such a moving performance."

ALMOST HEAVEN 395

In that moment, it seemed to them that the other actors, their cheering audience—all the world—vanished. Only Jim and Tory stood on the stage, enveloped in the scent of roses and the euphoria of love. Before it happened, they both knew it was coming, building like the tension in the play and the applause that followed the final curtain.

To Tory, it seemed to happen in slow motion. She watched Jim's silver gray eyes go dark with emotion. He tightened his arm about her waist, drawing her closer, crushing the roses. Then slowly . . . ever so slowly . . . he bent down to her.

"This one's for you, darling," he whispered.

When their lips met, Tory was suffused by the most wonderful heat. She seemed to glow with it. Dropping the roses, she slipped her arms around Jim's neck and they held each other. So long the audience grew still again . . . watching, waiting, wondering.

After a long, deep kiss, they drew away from each other. Yet their eyes still held—hazel gold staring into silver. The audience broke the spell with more applause and shouts of "Bravo!"

Behind his salt-and-pepper beard, Jim's flushed deeply. He turned to the audience with a boyish grin. "Didn't you love her, too?"

"Too?" Tory stared at him. Was this Jim's roundabout way of telling her that *he* loved her?

As if in answer to her unspoken question, he beamed down at her. "I *do* love you, you know. I've been meaning to tell you."

Tory clung to him. "Oh, Jim!" she cried softly. "I didn't dare hope— This is wonderful. I've loved you for so long."

396 *Becky Lee Weyrich*

There was no time to say any more as the cast gathered around to shake Jim's hand and give Tory hugs and kisses. Bernard Wurger beamed on them both and told them what a great team they were. Tory would always remember this night as the most exciting and exhilarating of her life. Jim, on the other hand, would recall it as the night that almost ruined the rest of his life.

The after-theater party was a formal picnic on the Mall, catered by the Stowe House. The tables set out were covered with white linen cloths, and each had its own silver candelabrum with glowing candles. The buffet was set up near the band shell. While the chamber music ensemble from the college played, the guests feasted on cold lobster, clams on the half shell, rare roast beef, and a wide array of salads and pastries. Champagne flowed like water.

As befit the occasion, Tory had changed into a strapless summer evening gown of silver tissue and lace. She gleamed as bright as starlight as she moved among the other guests, Jim by her side all the while.

Near midnight, everyone settled back to watch the fireworks over the river. Tory felt like one of the skyrockets bursting into bright sparks of red, silver, and blue. Jim sat beside her, one arm around her bare shoulders while he held her hand. She guessed, with mounting pleasure and anticipation, that their evening would end with fireworks of a very different sort.

An hour later, after the last bomb had burst in the air and the last guest had said good night, Tory and Jim strolled home. All the way, Jim kept his arm around her.

"What a night!" he said over and over again. "I

ALMOST HEAVEN

can't believe it. It was just too good to be real." He bent down and kissed her. *"You* are too good to be real! Why did it take me so long to realize how much I love you, Tory?"

"Say that again," she begged.

"I love you, Tory. So much!"

Cora Shute met them at the door. She'd taken Hope to see the play, then brought her home immediately after the performance.

"She's sleeping like a lamb, Jim. I'd best be going now."

"Can I walk you home?"

Cora laughed. "What? So I won't get mugged? This is Maine, remember? We have better manners up here."

"Well, if you're sure."

"I'll be fine. I do enjoy a brisk walk across the Mall this time of night, when I've got the place all to myself. Good night now."

Jim leaned down and gave her a peck on the cheek. "Thanks, Cora. I don't know what I'd do without you."

"Oh, go on with you!" she blustered.

A moment later, Jim and Tory were alone. They stood in the hallway just gazing at each other.

"I guess it's bedtime," Tory said at last, hoping against all hope that Jim would have a better idea.

He didn't disappoint her. "I'm too charged up to sleep. Let's have a nightcap."

Tory smiled and nodded. She didn't really want another drink, but she'd gladly sip one more glass of champagne just to be with him.

Once they had their wine, Jim suggested they go up

to the sitting room on the second floor so they could hear Hope if she woke. The room was cozy with its Victorian furniture and lace curtains. Angel had added romantic touches, candles in sconces on the walls, a ceiling fan, and vases that were always filled nowadays with fresh flowers cut from the garden.

Jim lit the candles, but left the lights off, and they sat on the red plush sofa, both sighing contentedly.

"I can't get over it," Jim said.

"It was quite a night," Tory agreed.

He set down his glass, then took Tory's from her. "I don't mean the play or the party. That was all wonderful. But *you*, Tory! I just never believed I could fall in love again."

He turned her slightly toward him so he could look into her eyes, stroked her bare shoulders lightly with his fingertips. Chills of pleasure shivered all through her.

This is it! she thought. *There's no turning back now.*

But then, she didn't want to turn back. She wanted to rush head on to love, to Jim, to happily forever after.

He leaned down and kissed her neck, sending more tremors through her. A moment later, his lips were on hers and his hand was on her breast, gently fondling the silvery fabric. Tory could hardly keep from moaning with her need. Her head was spinning, her heart pounding, her desire rising with his every touch.

Then she heard the sound of the zipper easing down the back of her gown. Jim's warm palm was on her bare back. She must have stiffened slightly. He drew away.

ALMOST HEAVEN   399

"I'm sorry," he whispered. "I haven't acted like this since I was a college kid."

She snuggled closer, giving consent with her body language. "I was always partial to college men," she whispered.

Taking his cue, Jim's hand returned to her zipper. This time he slid it all the way down. Tory's bodice gaped wide.

With one finger, he traced the thin lace at the top of her strapless bra. Tory closed her eyes and gave a shiver of pleasure.

"A bra, huh?" he said. "Haven't seen one of those in a while."

He began fumbling at the back, feeling for the hooks.

"It fastens in front," Tory whispered breathlessly.

She could have undone it herself, but she was infinitely glad she hadn't offered to do so when she felt Jim's hands working between her aching breasts. Having a man—the man she loved—undress her was a whole new experience. A wonderfully blissful experience. Her whole body was glowing with pleasure.

Seconds later, the stiffly boned bra slipped away allowing cool air to soothe her hot flesh. Then Jim's hands were touching her. Tory caught her breath. She'd never felt anything like this. His fingers stroked with such gentleness, yet such power. When he leaned down and touched one nipple with the tip of his tongue, Tory couldn't help herself, she moaned aloud.

"Oh, Tory. Tory." Jim murmured between kisses. "Let me love you. *Really* love you!"

In answer, she caught his face between her warm

palms and kissed him—a long, deep, wet kiss that set them both on fire.

The sofa was too narrow. By mutually tacit consent, they rose and headed for Jim's bedroom, shedding clothes as they went. The bed was waiting, all silver in the moonlight. Clinging to each other, savoring the contact of bare, burning flesh, they slid down together. But neither of them seemed in any hurry. They had all night to kiss, to touch, to caress, to explore.

If they had been in haste, things would probably have turned out far better. As it was, Angel had time to come between them. When Jim turned on his side, ready at last to make love to Tory, he caught a glimpse of the picture on the bedside table. It was a wedding picture—his wedding. Angel was smiling, hugging him. He was glowing with happiness and pride. All the old feelings came rushing back. All the old guilt.

"Jim?" Tory whispered. "Is something wrong, darling?"

He drew away from her. Lying on his back, he stared up at the dark ceiling.

"What is it?" Tory was really worried. Was he ill? Having a heart attack maybe?

He was definitely having an attack, but not that kind.

"I'm sorry," he groaned, not knowing if he was apologizing to Tory or to Angel. Maybe to both of them.

Tory glanced at the photograph and knew instantly what had happened. Her whole body ached with wanting him, but that pain was nothing compared to the ache in her heart. It wasn't going to work between them. Jim wasn't ready.

ALMOST HEAVEN 401

"It's okay." She managed to hold back her tears just long enough to get the words out. She knew exactly what Jim was experiencing. She felt it herself—a soul-deep guilt, a feeling that they were somehow betraying Angel.

Before Jim could do or say anything else, Tory hurried from the bed and out of the room. She spent the next hour crying and packing.

Alexander was in a towering rage. Angel had never seen him so angry. "How dare you? The other pranks you've pulled were bad enough, but *this!* To take away a man's strength when he is most in need of it. To leave him limp and useless at such a moment! No angel has ever done such a thing. That is the work of the Devil himself! I never knew you were so spiteful, Angela. I'm ashamed of you. You'll have to go before the Power-That-Be on this one. And don't expect me to defend you. In my opinion, there is no defense. I am a man, after all!"

Angel had been sleeping in a patch of heavenly clover near the wishing well. She'd been dreaming lovely dreams of butterflies and sweetpeas and darling little cherubs with red-gold curls. Alexander's tirade brought her out of her blissful repose in a snap.

"What are you yelling about?" She rubbed her eyes and looked around. "What's happened?"

"Don't play the innocent with me," he stormed. He was no longer the gladiator, but a fierce, towering spirit in dark robes that whipped in an angry wind. "I'm talking about Jim and Tory as you well know.

402   *Becky Lee Weyrich*

Their moment finally came and you ruined it. You ruined *everything!*"

Still baffled, Angel rose and went to the well. She placed her hands on the stones. A moment later, she saw Tory dressed only in an oversized tee shirt. She was throwing things into her suitcase and sobbing her heart out.

"Where's Jim?" she said, her anxiety mounting.

Next she saw the bedroom they had shared as man and wife. Jim was sprawled naked on the bed, one arm thrown over his eyes. He was moaning softly—no words, just the sounds of someone in grave pain. Their wedding picture lay beside him on the rumpled sheets.

Angel turned back to Alexander. "What's been going on down there while I was napping? Why didn't you wake me? Is Tory leaving? What's wrong with Jim?"

"As if you didn't know!" Alexander shot back at her with utter contempt.

"I *don't!* Tell me!"

Alexander stared at her, wondering if she could be faking this innocent act. As he calmed down, his robes went from night-black to a more gentle hue. The fierce wind died to a soft breeze.

"You didn't interfere?"

Still staring into the well, experiencing Jim and Tory's pain, Angel shook her head.

"You swear it, Angela?"

When she turned to answer, tears were streaming down her cheeks. "How could you of all people, Alexander, suspect me of bringing such sorrow to people I love? What can I do?" she cried. "There must be a way

ALMOST HEAVEN 403

to get them back together. They need each other. They love each other."

As Alexander watched, Angela's robe turned all rainbow colors. Stardust sifted down from the Milky Way to settle in its soft folds, making her glow with a heavenly light.

"I'm sorry, Angela." His voice was quiet, sincere. "I misjudged you. As for what you can do to help, I'm afraid—"

"Sh-h-h!" Angel held a finger to her lips to silence Alexander. "Did you hear that?"

"What?" he whispered.

"Someone called my name."

She stared back into the well. Jim was holding their wedding portrait, talking to Angel's image.

"Angel, what am I going to do?" he said in a voice husky with emotion. "You know I loved you. I always will. But you're gone. I need someone. I need Tory. I love her, but you know that. You probably knew it before I did. I've always been slow on the uptake."

He set the picture back on the table and glanced about the room.

"I know you're here, Angel. I've felt you with me— so close sometimes, so very close. Maybe Hope, as young as she is, is the wise one in the family. She's comfortable with your presence. She talks to you and you make her smile. She says you talk back. Can't you talk to me, Angel?" he begged. "Can't you at least give me some kind of a sign that it's okay with you? That I won't dishonor your memory or anything like that by marrying Tory?"

Jim heaved a heavy sigh, then turned on his side to

404   *Becky Lee Weyrich*

stare at the picture again. He seemed utterly defeated, totally miserable.

Angel called down the well, "Jim? Jim, can you hear me? It's all right. I want you to marry Tory. Don't let our life together interfere with your life now. I want you to be happy. I want you to be loved."

Jim sighed again, sounding just as miserable as before.

Angel turned to Alexander. "He can't hear me. What can I do?"

Alexander only shook his head sadly. "Children and animals can sometimes hear angels, but seldom does an adult have the faith. Grownups simply refuse to believe what they cannot see."

"That's it!" Angel cried. "I'll make Jim see."

Angel concentrated all her powers on the wedding portrait. If she could turn herself into water or even a martini, she could certainly become that picture. And once she was a part of the paper, she could change its appearance.

"I'll be back," she called to Alexander.

The next instant, it seemed, she felt strange—flat, squeezed into a narrow space. When she opened her eyes, she was looking out through the glass in the picture frame directly into Jim's face. He still looked miserable, sad, and lost.

"All right," she muttered to herself. "This is it. Make it good!"

Again, she focused all her powers of concentration. She thought of Tory's slight form, her short, shiny brown hair, her large hazel eyes, her pixie grin. She laughed Tory's laugh, smiled Tory's smile, and felt the depth of Tory's love for Jim.

ALMOST HEAVEN 405

Suddenly, Jim grabbed the frame. He let out a cry of shock that quickly turned to a laugh of pure delight. He kissed the cold glass covering the picture.

"Oh, Angel, I don't know how you did it. I don't even care. All I know is that I have my sign from you, sweetheart. I love you, darling. But now I know I can love Tory, too."

For just a moment before the illusion faded, Angel caught sight of her heavenly trick in the vanity mirror. No longer was she standing beside Jim in the wedding picture. Instead, Tory's arm was linked in his and Tory, as a bride, smiled up at her adoring groom. Even as Angel watched, the picture changed back to its original form. Her spirit expanded once more, and she was back, standing beside the well.

"Nice!" Alexander complimented. "Your powers are growing as fast as your wings."

"Uh-oh!" Angel said, staring down into the well. "Sorry! No time to chat. Things still aren't going so well down there."

As she watched, she saw Jim pull on his robe and dash toward Tory's room. He was aglow with happiness. Short-lived happiness. When he opened the door, she was gone. Packed and out of there.

A scribbled, tear-stained note was propped on her pillow. "Jim, I'm sorry, but I have to leave. Kiss Hope goodbye for me. By the time you read this, I'll be on my way back to New York. Thanks for everything. We've had some wonderful times. Tory."

Jim crushed the note in his fist after reading it. Then he sank down on the bed and buried his face in his hands.

406   *Becky Lee Weyrich*

"Wait right there!" Angel told him. "I'll get her back. I promise!"

Angel found Tory speeding through the night in her old Volkswagen, crying so hard she could barely see the road.

"Pull over!" she demanded, perching herself on a suitcase in the backseat.

Tory ignored her.

"You're speeding! I'll call a cop," Angel warned.

The speedometer needle inched closer to seventy. Angel couldn't spot a police car for miles.

"Tory, listen to me," Angel pleaded. "Jim loves you. He wants to marry you. You can't just go running off like this. Isn't it bad enough that I died and left him? Do you want to break his heart till it can't be mended? Turn around, Tory. Please! Go back!"

But Tory couldn't hear. Her mind and her heart were too wrapped up in her own misery. To make matters worse, a really sad country song was playing on the car radio.

"The radio!" Angel exclaimed. If she was really almost an angel, then she ought to be able to sing. But could she sing like Johnny Mathis?

A moment later, after a commercial for the local feed and seed store, "I'll Be Seeing You" came crooning over the angelic airways to fill the old VW. Tory slowed the car, but didn't stop. She was still headed for New York—or anywhere away from Jim and love.

Angel was about to give up when the disk jockey said. "Why don't we turn this into a Johnny Mathis songfest. Here's another old favorite from the same album, *Open Fire, Two Guitars.* This one's for all you lonely lovers out there."

ALMOST HEAVEN 407

Angel gave a joyous whoop the moment she heard the first bars of "When I Fall in Love."

"You asked me for a sign, Tory, and I aimed a pine cone at you, but missed. Well, you can't miss this one. Now, dammit, turn this pile of junk around and go back to Jim. He loves you!"

Tears streaming down her cheeks, Tory pulled the car off the road. She leaned her head on the steering wheel and sobbed through the whole song. Then she turned around and headed back for Brunswick in the glowing light of dawn.

Angel was so exhausted by the time she got back to the garden, all she could do was fall into Alexander's arms. He held her close, whispering his congratulations.

"That's my *Angel!*" he said. Then, as a reward, he gave her one of his special, heavenly kisses.

Chapter Eighteen

Tory did go back to New York after all, but only for a long weekend to pack the rest of her things, and not before she'd returned to the house on Park Row. Not until she'd accepted Jim's proposal of marriage and set a date.

Numb with emotional exhaustion, Tory drove up to the house and saw Jim standing on the back steps in his bathrobe, staring off into the sunrise as if he were in a daze. His shoulders were slumped. His face looked haggard. He seemed lost and very alone.

She cut the engine and shoved the door open, then hit the ground running. In less than a heartbeat she was in his arms and he was hugging her, kissing her, moaning her name over and over again. Their kisses were as quick and frantic as their clipped words.

"Marry me, Victoria," he begged. "You have to!"

"Yes. Oh, yes, Jim! I will—I want to."

"When?"

"The first of September?"

He held her away for a moment and frowned. "That long?"

ALMOST HEAVEN   409

"The leaves will be turning then," Tory said between quick, hot kisses. "And I'll need a little time to
get ready. Let's have a garden wedding. Right here."
She swept her free arm toward the arbor.

Jim took careful aim with his lips again. "Yes. I like
that."

They moved inside. Tory clung to him, feeling as if
she might float up to the kitchen ceiling if she let go;
she was that happy.

"I shouldn't have run off last night. I'm sorry," she
said.

"No," he murmured against her parted lips. "I'm
the one who's sorry. I disappointed you, darling."

"Never!"

A long silence followed. They were too busy for
words, too caught up in the feel and the taste and the
sight of each other. It seemed they'd been separated
for months instead of hours. But those hours had been
agonizing, torturous, soul-wrenching. The night had
never seemed blacker to either of them. Nor had the
dawn ever brought more beautiful light and joy.

"We're all right with this now?" Tory ventured. "All
of us?"

By *all*, Jim was sure she included Angel as well as
the two of them. He nodded and smiled.

"How could Angel help but approve? She was as
close to you as if you were her sister. This is going to
sound crazy, I know, but I think she gave me a sign
last night. The wedding picture beside the bed," he
said cautiously, knowing that his words would remind
Tory of his sudden disability, "I looked at it after you
left, and it was the damnedest thing. It had changed.
The bride in my arms was *you*, Tory. We looked so

410   *Becky Lee Weyrich*

happy, so much in love. And in the background, I could see Angel among the wedding guests, smiling at the two of us like she was giving us her blessing."

Tory nodded her head and looked solemnly at Jim, the gold flecks in her hazel eyes glittering. "That doesn't sound crazy at all. It's just the sort of thing Angel would do. I'm convinced she's been here with us all the time, Jim. She probably even had a hand in getting us together."

"Could be," Jim mused.

"If so, she was a busy spirit last night. She caught up with me and turned me around."

"You actually saw her?" Jim's eyes grew wide and moist.

"No. But I felt her and heard her at work. You know that country music station, the only one my car radio will pick up?"

Jim laughed. "Sure! 'The Boxcar Willie Special.' "

"Right! Last night out of the blue they suddenly decided it was time to put away the country sound for a Johnny Mathis marathon. Your favorite songs played one after another. Those sad, sweet, wonderful ballads from the fifties. No Merle Haggard, no Dwight Yoakum, no Billy Ray Cyrus. Just Mathis and more Mathis. That's when I knew for certain my life was here with you and Hope." Tory sniffed back her tears and laughed gaily. "I'll bet that deejay is wondering this morning what got into him."

Jim grinned. "Angel, that's what!"

He hugged Tory tightly and murmured her name as if it were a prayer. "We almost blew it, didn't we?"

"I don't think we could have. I'm convinced this

ALMOST HEAVEN 411

was meant to be. I think ours is truly a match made in Heaven."

"Made by an angel," Jim murmured.

Hope came toddling in just then, followed by her towering shadow, The Monster. She glanced up, rubbing her eyes, and smiled at the two of them.

"Are you going to be my new mommy, Tory?"

Her question was blunt and to the point as only a child's query can be. Jim and Tory exchanged glances. He bent down and picked up his precious daughter.

"Would you like that, Hope?"

She reached out a chubby fist and touched Tory's cheek. "Uh-huh. My Angel-Mama promised that Tory'd make me blueberry pancakes and help me plant sweet peas and teach me how to make snow angels at Christmas."

Again, Jim and Tory's eyes met.

"When did she tell you all this, Hope?" asked Jim.

"Last night." Hope's smile grew wistful. "She came and sang to me with all the other angels. And she played a gold harp and she was dressed in a shiny rainbow. She was *so* pretty!"

Tears brimmed in Jim's eyes. "She was always beautiful," he whispered.

"Inside and out," Tory added, feeling a lump form in her throat as the silence grew heavy with emotion.

"How about it, Hope? Could you wolf down some of those blueberry pancakes right now?" Tory asked, bringing smiles back to all their faces.

Hope spread her arms to show how many. "A whole stack!" she cried excitedly.

"Then let's get the stove fired up and the griddle hot, you two."

412   *Becky Lee Weyrich*

Jim gave his two best girls a hug before they pitched into action. This was going to be a special breakfast—a celebration.

The garden looked different to Angel when she returned. Gone were the artifacts left over from her past lives with Alexander. No gladiator's mask, no wrecked ship on the river bank, no dungeon keys from the cells of Knossos. Even General Joshua's saber was gone. The garden looked clean and uncluttered, washed in a heavenly silver light and the shining mist of dawn.

"Alexander?" Angel called. "Where are you?"

"Here!" he answered.

She turned toward the deep, sweet sound of his voice, toward the beautiful bridge that spanned the mirror stream. She shielded her eyes against the brilliant light. She could barely see him. He stood in the very center of the radiant glow, an awesome figure, beckoning to her.

"What are you doing on the bridge?" she asked. "Come back down to the garden. I have so much to tell you."

"No, Angel. Your time of growth in the garden is done. You must come with me now."

"You called me *Angel!*"

"You've earned it. Look in the stream."

Angel found herself beside the mirror-surfaced water even though she didn't realize she'd moved. She looked down and gasped. Her lovely, rainbow gown glowed with a new intensity and sparkled all over with stardust. Beautiful, full wings shimmered with iridescence at her shoulders. Their tapering tips brushed the

ALMOST HEAVEN 413

ground. Above her halo of fiery hair glowed a second halo of shining gold and a crown tipped with many twinkling stars. Only when she saw her reflection did she realize she was clutching a golden harp in the crook of her right arm.

She turned back toward Alexander, her face glowing with happiness.

"We did it," she whispered.

"No," he answered. "*You* did it! You're a real angel now. Your work is done. You've passed all the tests." He held out his hand to her. "Come to me."

Again, without realizing she had moved, Angel found herself on the bridge. Alexander's warm hand clasped hers. His touch sent a rush of power and light and love blazing through her.

"What now?" she asked, staring up into his wonderful face, into eyes that spoke silent volumes of love.

"The Gates of Heaven await," he answered. "Are you ready, Angel?"

Behind him, she saw the tall, ornate gates of gold swing open. She hesitated and glanced back at the garden, back at the wishing well, her gateway to Earth.

"I'm not sure," she murmured. "What about Jim and Tory and Hope?"

"They'll be fine. You saw to that, Angel. You might not have brought them together, but you kept them together. That's the important part, the part that earned you your crown. Come now," he added gently. "Everyone's waiting for you."

Angel felt Alexander's strong arm slip about her waist. A moment later, they flew from the bridge toward the open gates. Music swelled in the heavens. The sweet, white light pulsed with love and welcome.

414   *Becky Lee Weyrich*

Bright shadows moved in the beam, other angels coming to greet her. Her grandparents and her Great-aunt Carrie, a friend who had drowned one summer during high school, teachers, pets she had loved and lost. They all moved about her—touching, welcoming, sharing their light with the new angel.

In Earth words, she could never have described it. But she knew what she felt. She felt everything *good.* Heaven was all that she had loved most on Earth, but without the evil, the sadness, the pain. It was all the answers without any of the bothersome questions. It was pure and total contentment. It was love on its highest plane.

In Earth terms, Heaven was like a holiday video tape, when you shoot the opening of presents but don't record the overdone turkey or the cranberry mold that didn't jell. Everything was there, everything Angel loved. The smell of honeysuckle on a warm day in spring. The feel of ocean waves lapping at her bare feet. The peal of church bells on a soft Sunday morning. The laughter of children. The mewing of baby kittens. The taste of gallberry honey fresh from the hive. Flowers blooming in her backyard garden. The first kiss she had given Hope. The first love she had felt for Jim. And over and above everything else was the knowledge of *all* the love she and Alexander had shared down through the ages, all the love they had yet to share.

She turned to him as if seeing him for the first time. He stood beside her, strong and tall, beaming down at her.

"It's wonderful," she whispered, struck with awe.

ALMOST HEAVEN 415

He smiled and touched her cheek. "It's Heaven, Angel."

"Will we be here long?"

"Only long enough."

"For what?"

"You'll see. Come now. The hosts are tuning up. Your harp will add new sweetness to our chorus. We'll be playing soon for a special event."

"Oh? What's that?"

"A wedding."

The hour before sunset was the appointed time of the wedding in the garden on Park Row. Cora Shute had spent the night before the wedding at the old Joshua place, as townsfolk still called Jim's house. She'd been bound and determined to keep the groom from seeing his bride all day. So Jim had been shooed out early that morning to spend most of the day at his office on campus. Meanwhile, back at the house, Cora and Tory along with Angel's mother and several neighbor ladies scurried about making final preparations. Tory's mom and dad were due in any moment.

Hope and The Monster, constantly underfoot, but never in the way, took everything in—all excitement and anticipation. Angel's dad offered to bathe the dog in a big tub out back. Several people had suggested that Monster be boarded during the ceremony, but neither Tory nor Jim would hear of such a thing.

Angel's dad beamed when he heard Tory say, "The Monster's part of the family. I certainly want him at the wedding. Angel loved that big mutt."

So Pete Gentry and his granddaughter Hope spent a

416   *Becky Lee Weyrich*

couple of quality hours together out by the garden, making sure Angel's mutt would look spiffy enough to come to the wedding.

"I'm going to be the flower girl," Hope proudly announced to anyone and everyone who came to the house. "And I have a long, pink dress and a white basket, and I get to throw rose petals at everybody."

Tory had given up trying to explain to Hope that she wasn't to throw the petals *at* the guests but simply to strew them along the ground. What the heck? Jim and Tory both wanted their wedding to be fun. If Hope wanted to throw petals, let her throw them.

As the afternoon shadows grew longer and longer, Tory headed upstairs to get dressed. All the other women were downstairs, busy in the kitchen, but she thought she could manage her simple wedding gown alone.

She was almost ready when she heard a knock at the door.

"Yes?" she called, trying to reach the last tiny satin buttons at the back of her dress.

"It's Aunt Shirley, Tory. May I come in?"

Tory smiled. How sweet of Angel's mother to arrive when she most needed help.

"The door's open," she called. "How are you at tiny buttons?"

Shirley, her hair done up in a modern imitation of a Gibson girl and her still-slender figure swathed in mauve lace, came in. She was carrying a small box in her hands.

A smile trembled on her lips as she handed the gift to Tory. "Jim wanted to give this to you himself, but he got hustled out of here so fast this morning he never

ALMOST HEAVEN 417

got a chance. He just called from his office and asked me to make sure you wore it today." She hesitated, and her smile seemed to falter a bit. "That is, if you'd like to, dear."

"What on earth?" Tory said, smiling with excitement. "Jim already gave me these beautiful pearl earrings. Why did he get me another gift?"

"It's sort of a tradition," Shirley explained. "Angel wore it on her wedding day. A couple of years ago, Jim sent it back to me, saying he thought it should stay in the family. Then when you said you'd marry him, he asked me to bring it for you."

"Angel wore it?" For a moment, Tory felt odd. Why would Jim want her to wear something of Angel's?

"Look in the box, dear. You'll understand."

When Tory opened the lid, her eyes went wide and her smile returned. "Why, it's Great-great-grandmother Rachel's cameo brooch! I'd forgotten all about it. Angel once tried to give it to me while we were in New York." Tears misted Tory's eyes at the memory. "I told her to keep it, that it would be a long, long time before I was a bride because I was going to wait for a special man—a man like Jim."

The two women went into each other's arms and hugged. It was special a moment—a moment for Angel.

When they were in control again, Shirley, all business, said, "Now, what about these pesky buttons? Let's see if my fingers are still nimble enough to deal with them."

Just then, Tory's mother popped in. Madge Cason looked as nervous as a hummingbird, but beautiful in her gown of turquoise satin.

418 *Becky Lee Weyrich*

"Shirley, how do you stay so calm?" Madge gasped, fidgeting with the perfectly styled wisps of fine brown hair about her face. "I'm a wreck!"

"Well, don't you bring your nerves up here and get Tory all bothered. She's the calmest bride I've ever seen."

Tory beamed at both women. "Because I know this is right, Aunt Shirley. I have no need to be nervous about anything. I love Jim. He loves me. And we both adore Hope."

Her mother eyed her sharply. "What about that dog? You aren't *still* set on letting him run loose in the yard during the ceremony?"

"Mom, we've been through all this. The Monster is *not* going to be shut up. He has perfect company manners." It was a rotten trick, she knew, but Tory couldn't resist the urge. With a pixielike smirk she said, "Hadn't you heard? Monster's in the wedding party. He's the ring bearer."

"Oh, Lord!" Madge collapsed in a chair and put her palm to her forehead. "I never heard of such a thing. First, you refuse to have the proper number of musicians and now this. The wedding's going to be ruined!"

But nothing could have ruined Tory and Jim's wedding. They had love on their side . . . and Angel.

A flautist from the college chamber ensemble provided the music for the ceremony, the delicate, birdlike notes floating up through the tall pines as sunset descended on the garden, and Hope, in her pink lace dress, tripped along spreading her rose petals, the great, black dog at her side. When they reached the arbor, Hope went to her father and slipped her tiny hand into his. He smiled down at her and winked.

ALMOST HEAVEN   419

A moment later, a murmur passed through the crowd as the bride appeared, escorted by her solemn-faced father. At the very moment they reached the arbor, the last of the sun seemed to light up the sky, casting a rosy, golden light over the gathering.

The ceremony was short and simple, the way Tory knew Jim wanted it. She was glad. She couldn't have concentrated on complicated words. Her whole being was caught up in Jim's nearness and the wonder of the moment. The touch of his hand. The loving look in his silvery eyes. The husky timbre of his voice. And the rightness of their being here together.

At the exact moment the minister pronounced them man and wife, the most extraordinary thing happened. For the rest of their long lives together, Tory and Jim would remember it and savor it. When Jim bent to kiss his bride, a glow of unearthly beauty lit the garden, and the sweet notes of the flute were joined by the music of heavenly harps.

At that same moment, Tory heard a voice—a familiar voice. "Take good care of Jim and Hope for me. They both need a lot of love. And you have that love to give them, Tory."

Next, the voice spoke to Jim. "I'm sorry I had to leave you so quickly. I never even said goodbye. I never even got to tell you how much I love you. But I do, Jim, and I always will. Now I'm passing on my love for you to Tory. Be happy, both of you. You have my blessing."

Hope's excited cry broke the spell. "Look, Daddy! An angel!"

Jim and Tory both stared into the sky where Hope was pointing. Among the glowing scarlet and gold

420 *Becky Lee Weyrich*

clouds, they saw a shimmering figure in a rainbow robe all frosted with stardust. She was smiling down on them. Smiling Angel's smile of love and joy.

Jim picked Hope up and held her close, slipping his arm around Tory. "Yes, honey," he whispered. "That's a very special angel. That's *our* Angel!"

Angel was warmed by her own glow of love and light and joy. She rose higher and higher until the scene below was only a blur of color. But the faces of the three people she had touched remained vivid in her heart—in a special spot to savor forever.

Alexander was waiting when she returned. On his handsome face, she saw the purest love she had ever imagined. He reached out to her and drew her close. For Earth-years, they embraced, filling their souls with each other.

When their heavenly kiss ended at last, Alexander smiled into Angel's eyes.

"We're going back," he whispered. "We've been granted another chance."

"So soon?" Angel asked.

"You aren't ready?"

Her whole spirit pulsed with love for Alexander. She clung to him, never wanting to let go, but eager to meet him in their new life.

She stared up into his brilliant eyes and smiled. "Oh, yes, Alexander! I'm more than ready!"

The music of Heaven swelled into a magnificent symphony. Shooting stars lit up the skies. And distant bells tolled joyously. A shimmering rainbow wrapped Angel and Alexander in its sheltering embrace.

ALMOST HEAVEN 421

Down on Earth, two mothers gave birth. In San Francisco, Mrs. Ander hugged her beautiful baby boy. In Paris, Madame DuBois cuddled her pretty, red-haired daughter. Both women smiled and kissed their tiny, innocent bundles from Heaven.

Far off in Maine, on the summer-green Bowdoin campus, Hope Rhodes was receiving her college diploma as her proud parents looked on.

Bells chimed joyously. Bowdoin's bells. Heaven's bells.

Epilogue

From New York to Paris to Beijing, every newsman who knew Angelique DuBois—and they all did, at least by reputation—considered her a "cold fish," to use an antiquated term from back in the twentieth century. She was a hard-nosed journalist of the first order. An earth-mover, a star-shaker, a female with only one objective: to report the story first and best, with her own special flair.

Today in the Manhattan penthouse of the Rhodes Pyramid, headquarters of the Angela Gentry Rhodes Center of Universal Infection and Disease Control, all eyes shifted when she walked in. Short black tunic, tall black boots that seemed to cover a yard of leg, and a sassy black vinyl helmet that showed only a hint of her close-cropped red hair. No one knew the color of her eyes. She always wore large, tinted glasses, her only touch of color. Today they were electric blue.

A few stifled groans and some murmurs of "The ice bitch cometh" went through the all-male ranks as she entered. The old boys were jealous as hell of this young female upstart from the number-one paper in Paris.

ALMOST HEAVEN 423

There'd even been some sick jokes circulating earlier about one of them planning to sabotage her spiffy little jet to keep her out of New York today. But nobody actually had the guts to mess with "The Black Angel" or her private rocket-jet.

Angelique knew they were staring. The moment she crossed the threshold, she felt conspicuous. She trembled inside. It was always like this. She paused a moment to compose herself. She couldn't let them know that behind her austere clothing and businesslike facade was a twenty-eight-year-old "kid" trying to claw her way through the pack.

She squared her shoulders and took a deep breath before she strode into their midst.

"Well, look who's here, boys," one of the old guard from the *Times* said with a smirk. "Now we can tell Dr. Rhodes she's allowed to begin."

One of the real old-timers, who'd been with the same Washington paper since the Bush administration blustered, "It's about time! If it'd been one of us who cut it this close, she'd have started the press conference early."

Standing slightly away from the others, a young science writer from the North Pole sized up the new arrival. He'd heard about her, but this was the first time their paths had crossed. She was a looker all right. That wasn't what impressed him, however. He got an odd feeling the minute she walked into the room. Sort of a weird sense of déjà vu. But how could that be? He'd spent the past eight years at the Global Survival Outpost at the top of the world. He and his folks had been early pioneers of the experimental pod community under the polar icecap. He wouldn't be here now

424 *Becky Lee Weyrich*

if Dr. Rhodes's press conference hadn't been billed as "of universal importance."

He moved through the crowd, trying to get closer to the DuBois woman. No telling when he'd get back to civilization. This might be his one and only chance to meet her.

She was right beside him and he was about to introduce himself when Dr. Hope Rhodes entered the room. Rhodes was an attractive woman in her late forties, the red of her hair softened by strands of gray. She looked as intelligent as she was, but the merry twinkle in her heaven-blue eyes belied her serious demeanor.

Silence fell over the crowd.

Dr. Marilyn Lambright, the President of Harvard, stepped to the podium. She cleared her throat and glanced about. "I know all of you are eager to hear this announcement, and there's certainly no need to introduce Dr. Rhodes to any of you. So we'll get on with it. Dr. Rhodes?"

She moved quickly to the podium, adjusted the lapel of her business suit, then smiled. "Thank you all for coming. As you know, we have been working for years here at the Pyramid, searching for answers to ancient medical questions. I am pleased to announce today that we've recently isolated a certain bacteria that we've proven to be the cause of all the most serious diseases that have plagued this planet for centuries. We have developed an inexpensive drug which will soon be distributed universally. We expect immediate and extremely rewarding results. Now, I'll be happy to take your questions."

The first question came from Angelique DuBois. She wanted to know exactly which diseases were in-

ALMOST HEAVEN 425

volved. But when Dr. Rhodes answered, Angelique found she could hardly concentrate on the woman's words for staring at her eyes.

"Then you're saying it won't cure the common cold?" the old fellow from the *Times* demanded.

Dr. Rhodes laughed and shook her head. "I'm afraid not. We're still working on that. But, thanks to this discovery, the head cold may soon be the most serious illness with which we're faced in the future."

There was relief in the laughter coming from around the room. The entire population of Earth had been in serious trouble for the past decades, overrun with curious, exotic diseases that started with AIDS and advanced from there. Until this discovery by Dr. Hope Rhodes, it had looked as if the days of Earth's people were numbered.

Angelique tried to concentrate on the questions and answers, but her thoughts remained focused on Dr. Rhodes herself. There was something so familiar about the woman.

The questions tapered off. Hope Rhodes motioned to two people standing nearby who had entered the room with her.

"I'd like to introduce my parents," she said. "Dr. and Mrs. James Randolph Rhodes."

Angelique watched the tall, bearded, silver-haired man step forward, his arm around the petite woman at his side. She noticed that when Dr. James Rhodes looked at his wife, his silvery eyes glowed with love, and when the couple looked at their daughter, they both beamed proudly.

"Thank you," James Rhodes said in response to the smattering of applause from the press. "I'd just like to

426   *Becky Lee Weyrich*

say that my wife and I share your excitement and relief
at this discovery. But no one could share our special
pride in and love for this brilliant woman—our daughter. Before she was born, I dreamed that her name
would be Hope. I believe that dream was prophetic.
No one in the history of this planet has offered us as
much hope as Dr. Rhodes. I always knew she was destined for great things.''

He hugged his daughter and then his wife before
stepping back from the podium.

For no reason she could think of Angelique realized
she had tears in her eyes. *Tears!* Real tears! She hadn't
cried since she was a child. Her whole life had been
spent unemotionally, in the serious pursuit of specific
goals. So why had this father's words touched her so?

Dr. Hope Rhodes stepped back to the podium.
"Thanks, Dad," she said, smiling at him. "I couldn't
have done any of this without the support you and
Mom have given me through the years.''

Hope Rhodes's smile faded. She stared down for a
moment. And Angelique realized she wasn't the only
professional in the room who had tears in her eyes.
Hope Rhodes was obviously fighting for control.

A moment later, Dr. Rhodes looked back at the audience. "There's someone else I'd like to thank today.
I never knew my real mother, Angela Rhodes. She
gave her life to save mine when I was a baby. But I've
felt her with me all my life. She's as much a part of all
this as anyone." A nervous smile twitched her lips. "In
fact, I feel her here with me now, more strongly than
I've felt her presence in a long, long time, and I'd like
to thank her. As my father has always said, she's our
special angel.''

ALMOST HEAVEN 427

As Dr. Rhodes spoke those words, she looked directly at Angelique, causing a kind of warmth to spread through the young woman from Paris. She felt stunned, mesmerized, and touched by some deep emotion she couldn't understand.

Then Dr. Rhodes thanked them all and left the room with her parents.

Angelique removed her solar glasses to wipe her eyes.

"She's really something, isn't she?" said the man who had been standing next to Angelique all this time.

She turned toward him, surprised by his voice. She was ready to agree with him, but the words caught in her throat when she looked at him. There was something in his gaze. Some secret she could almost . . . but not quite . . . grasp.

"Do I know you?" she asked, her voice barely a whisper as goose bumps crawled over her flesh.

He offered his hand and a warm smile. "You're about to," he said. "A. L. Ander. My friends call me Lex."

His voice was like a caress. And his eyes seemed so familiar. Angelique couldn't quite tell their color. They seemed to shift from silver to blue to almost black. Or was it only her imagination? The impact he had on her was otherworldly. It almost seemed to her that she remembered him from years past. No, she told herself, from *lifetimes past!*

"I know this is going to seem forward of me," he continued. "But I don't get down from the survival base often. Can I buy you a drink or something?"

Angelique finally took his outstretched hand. When their palms touched, a million fleeting moments from

428 *Becky Lee Weyrich*

the past flashed through her mind and soul. Cosmic memory.

"I'm happy you found me," she said in a breathless voice. "My friends call me Angie, Al."

He laughed, a good strong, male sound. "Nobody's called me Al since . . ." He paused and frowned. "Well, not since I can remember. I like that, Angie. How about that drink?"

Her blood sizzling with excitement, Angelique smiled and took his arm. "How about that *something?*" she countered, knowing somehow that she and A. Lex Ander had a long and wonderful life in store for them.

Just being with him was almost Heaven!

About the Author

ALMOST HEAVEN is Becky Lee Weyrich's nine-teenth novel. She is also the author of four novellas. Since she began publishing fiction in 1978, she has written for various publishers in a variety of genres, including historical romance, fantasy, saga, Gothic, horror/mystery, contemporary, and time-travel. Her first novel, *Through Caverns Infinite,* is now a collector's item among New Age aficionados.

In 1991, Weyrich won *Romantic Times* magazine's Lifetime Achievement Award for New Age Fiction, and in 1992 she was awarded the Certificate of Excellence in Career Achievement in Historical Fantasy and the Reviewers' Choice Certificate of Excellence for *Sweet Forever* (Pinnacle Books, May '92). Most recently, her time-travel novel, *Whispers in Time,* (Pinnacle Books, March '93) received the *Romantic Times* Reviewers' Choice Award as Best Time-Travel Historical, her third such award. Her time-travel novels have also made the "Best Reads of the Year" lists of both "The Talisman" and "Heartland Critiques."

Weyrich's novels have been translated into ten for-

430 *Becky Lee Weyrich*

eign languages and recorded as books for the blind. Her novel *Once Upon Forever* (Pinnacle, March '94) is now available in the gift shop at Cumberland Falls State Park in Kentucky because of its Cumberland Falls setting and the use of the moonbow in the story.

Beginning as a nonfiction writer in 1960, Becky Lee Weyrich did freelance work for several newspapers and magazines. She also wrote and illustrated two chapbooks of poetry before turning to a full-time career in fiction.

A member of Romance Writers of America, Novelists Inc., and a board member of Southeastern Writers' Association, Weyrich is the originator of the Becky Lee Weyrich Fiction Award presented annually at the Southeastern Writers' Workshop on St. Simons Island, Georgia. She established the cash award to aid and encourage new writers.

After roaming the world as a Navy wife, residing in such diverse locations as Maine, California, and Italy, the Georgia-born author now lives in a beach cottage on St. Simons Island with her husband of thirty-five years, six cats, a beagle named Barnacle, a pet possum, and assorted sea creatures. Her hobbies include golf, beachcombing, cruising to exotic shores, and collecting Victorian antiques. The Weyrichs have a daughter, a son, and four grandchildren.

If you would like to receive Becky Lee Weyrich's newsletter, please send a self-addressed, stamped envelope to P.O. Box 24374, St. Simons Island, GA 31522.

Here is an excerpt from
Becky Lee Weyrich's
next time-travel novel

THE SANDS OF DESTINY,

Coming from Zebra Books in 1996

Alexandria, Egypt—May 2, 1979

Olympia Byrd was born a dreamer. But until one sizzling-hot morning in her sixteenth year, she had always been able to distinguish fantasy from reality. The man she was about to meet and the events soon to unfold would change all that forever.

She spotted the golden Greek the minute she stepped off the tour bus in Alexandria. In a glance, the American teenager sized him up as a guy who could make a girl feel like his queen one minute, his slave the next. She wanted him!

She had spent the morning's rather dull sightseeing excursion pretending that she was Queen Cleopatra, touring her domain. After all, Pia mused, her own hair was as black as any Egyptian's and her eyes were the deep blue of the royal gemstone, lapis lazuli. If only her father would let her wear enough makeup, she was convinced she could look exactly like that exotic, old queen.

Everyone knew, of course, that the Queen of Egypt

434 *Becky Lee Weyrich*

required the services of a lover. All the books claimed she was an extremely passionate woman. That was why Pia had picked out her guy so quickly—the perfect man to aid her fantasies. Cleopatra's Mark Antony, she told herself. In reality, he was a Greek sailor, twentyish and golden from head to toe. He was so good-looking that every time Pia stole a glance at him, which was often, she felt a warm tingle right down to her strappy sandals.

"He's like a date cake dipped in beer," she murmured softly, remembering the words some long-ago Egyptian teenager had written about her sweetheart in one of the ancient tombs at Memphis. When their guide had translated the intricate hieroglyphics, Pia had thought that was a pretty funny way to describe anybody. But the words fit her handsome Greek to a tee. He had the sweet, golden look of a honey-drenched pastry that made Pia's mouth water for a taste. Yet there was a totally male ruggedness about him that hinted of late nights spent in seamy waterfront taverns over tankards of strong, Egyptian corn beer.

She'd shot him her special look at her first opportunity. Cool, but flirtatious. The same glance she used at high-school proms when she wanted to slow-dance with a certain football quarterback. The lazy flash of her blue eyes had worked like a charm. For the past half-hour, the sailor had been following along, close enough to keep his tiger-eyes on Pia, but not so close as to make himself obvious to her father.

Clearly, the Greek was flirting with Pia, as foreign men will. Naturally, she was flirting back, as teenage girls must.

THE SANDS OF DESTINY 435

"Pia! Don't lag," her father called from up ahead. "I don't want to lose you again like I did at Luxor."

She smiled. That day at the famous Temple of Karnak she had pretended to be Nefertari, the most beloved wife of Ramses II. Pia knew that for a fact because in Nefertari's tomb her husband had ordered the inscription: "Possessor of charm, sweetness, and love." She'd been a beauty, too. The perfect wife for the great Ramses, Pia figured.

Oh, the fantasies she had spun as she'd gazed up at the colossus of that strong, silent Pharaoh!

"What a hunk! No wonder he fathered ninety children. His wives probably couldn't keep their hands off him," Pia murmured to herself. "But Cleopatra's more fun. Poor Nefertari had to share Ramses. Ole Cleo took her pick. *All those lovers* and a golden barge to boot!"

Pia's mind wandered to romantic nights, cruising the Nile while some great, lusty Roman sat at her gold-sandaled feet, peeling grapes for a start, then later peeling—

"Olympia!"

She jumped, startled out of her lovely, wicked thoughts. When her father called her by her full name, Pia knew she'd better shape up. She quickened her pace in spite of the fact that she had little desire to stay close to their group of twenty or so sweaty American, European, and Oriental tourists.

"Do we have to go this fast? It's so hot, Dad," Pia complained. She caught up with her tall, husky, Navy-commander father, mopping her sweaty brow to make her point. "This is probably the sort of day when ancient Egyptians baked bricks."

436   *Becky Lee Weyrich*

"Exactly what they were doing back there at our last stop, Olympia." She was well aware of the reproof in his tone. "But you missed the demonstration because you're being such a slowpoke."

"Sorry, Daddy-o. I'll try to keep up."

Stephen Byrd gave his daughter *that look*—the brows pulled down and the mouth drawn to a hard, straight line. He hated being called "Daddy-o" and Pia knew it. It had just slipped out. By way of apology, she offered him her sunniest smile and linked her arm through his.

"What's next?" she asked brightly, trying to sound truly interested.

"If you really want to know, check the schedule our guide gave you."

Pia didn't bother. She simply followed along. To be honest, she found Alexandria a big disappointment. She hadn't read her tour handbook as her father had advised the night before. She'd been too busy writing a love sonnet to Ramses. Consequently, this morning she had expected to see the royal palace of the Ptolemies, the Pharos lighthouse, even the tomb of Alexander the Great. But, as the book clearly stated, those marvelous ancient wonders were long gone, struck down eons ago by earthquake, man, and time. Only a single column called Pompey's Pillar and the hilltop ruins of the Temple of Serapis remained from those distant centuries. The rest of Alexandria, though pretty enough with its modern buildings and some Victorian architecture, was not what she had hoped for. In fact, the delta city was nothing at all like the other parts of ancient Egypt they had toured in the past ten days. She might have been in a different coun-

THE SANDS OF DESTINY 437

try, any of a number of foreign places she had visited in the past with her dad.

This three-week vacation was a yearly treat for the two of them. His Navy career kept him on board ship most of the time. Since her mother's death eight years ago, their family life had consisted of summer jaunts to exotic places—Italy, France, Malta, Australia. This was her first trip to Egypt, although her father had been here many times. Most of the year Pia spent in an exclusive boarding school in Virginia. She would have only these three weeks with her dad before she was packed off to camp with her cousins in Maine. It was a strange life, but Pia had grown used to it over the years. And it almost seemed that she and her father were closer for having so little shared time.

"There's the agora, the old market place, just ahead," Stephen Byrd remarked, ending his brief, frosty silence. The return of his smile told Pia that her tacit apology had been accepted. Not a bad time to press her advantage, she decided.

"Can I buy a souvenir?"

Her father laughed and gave her ponytail a tug. "Sure, honey. But I don't know how we'll get the bags closed to fly home if you buy much more." He frowned down at her again, this time playfully. "Absolutely no more marble statues of naked men! Understood?"

"Dad-*dy!*" Pia groaned. "They aren't just naked men. They're gods."

"They still need some clothes on, if you ask me. Or at the very least, a well-placed fig leaf."

In spite of the fact that their guide, in her droning monotone, was still telling them about points of inter-

438   *Becky Lee Weyrich*

est, most of the group broke away to make a dash for the street vendors. The milling shoppers in the market suddenly swelled to mob proportions. There was nothing for Pia and her dad to do but wait for the crowd to thin.

Pia pulled off her wide-brimmed straw hat, hoping to catch a stray breeze off the Mediterranean. She shaded her eyes and glanced up at the unblemished sky. It was the most perfect pale turquoise, reminding her of the delicate color of the ancient Roman glass they had seen earlier in one of the museums. The tint of her sunglasses added the same iridescent sheen to the sky that so enhanced the beauty of that antique shard.

She peered over her shoulder. Her Greek, a few yards away, gave her a quick, golden wink. She smiled and fluttered her dark lashes alluringly. This game, she decided, was far more fun than sightseeing.

She was about to stray from the group when suddenly the tour guide's monotonous voice caught her attention.

"All of this area, right down to the water's edge at the Great Harbor on the east, was once the site of the marble palace of the Ptolemies. Cleopatra, as you will recall, was the final ruler of that line, which descended directly from Alexander the Great. She was the last Queen of Egypt."

Pia stared down at the cobbles beneath her dusty Jesus-sandals. *"She* might have stood on this very spot once!" she murmured, awestruck.

"Cleopatra's grave, next to Mark Antony's," the beak-nosed, spinster tour guide continued dramatically, "lies somewhere deep below where we now

THE SANDS OF DESTINY 439

stand. It was the queen's final request, before putting the asp to her breast, that she be laid to rest beside the man who was the greatest love of her life. And near where those two lovers are buried lies the alabaster sarcophagus of Alexander himself. Julius Caesar visited the conqueror's tomb as did many world leaders of ancient times. But the exact location of the royal mausoleum, the *soma,* has been lost to us for centuries."

Pia's heart gave a little bump of excitement. Lovers buried side by side, and so near Cleopatra's famous ancestor, Alexander! Her mind whirled suddenly with scenes and feelings conjured up by her fantastic imagination. If only she could visit Cleopatra's Alexandria for just one day . . . one hour. She closed her eyes, willing herself to see that fabulous ancient city. But when she opened them again everything was the same. Heat and dust and tourists.

"Come on, Pia," her father insisted. "We're going to the market now."

Pia's driving urge to buy something had deserted her. What was one more souvenir, after all? Another cheap piece of pottery made in an assembly-line factory especially for the purpose of conning rich American tourists. All at once, she felt disgust for all the junk she'd prized so highly and bought so impulsively, at inflated prices. She'd give it all—even her naked statuettes—for one brief glimpse of Cleopatra's Egypt.

As her father pushed through the crowd, tugging Pia along with him, she remembered her golden Greek. A quick glance told her that he was no longer trailing their group. She sighed with regret. He had been the most interesting sight in Alexandria all morn-

440   *Becky Lee Weyrich*

ing. Silly as it seemed, Pia experienced an enormous pang of disappointment. She actually felt rejected by the man, she realized with a start.

"Look, this is nice." Her father picked up a tooled-leather handbag stamped with gold hieroglyphics.

She barely gave the handsome purse a glance, busy as she was with scanning the crowd for her Greek sailor. But he seemed to have vanished entirely.

As they moved through the noisy throng, Pia passed up gold sandals inlaid with plastic turquoise, heavy brass necklaces in the shapes of ankhs and cartouches, scarabs that really did look old, even an alabaster statuette of Alexander in the buff.

"Shopped out, eh?" Her father laughed. "Well, you look around and I'll go buy us a Coke."

"Great, Dad," Pia answered without enthusiasm.

Her father had no more than left her side when she heard a man's heavily accented voice whispering to her. "Come, miss! Look! I got precious thing here."

Pia glanced at the old peddler. He was dressed in rags, filthy from the skin out. He reminded her of nothing so much as a grave robber.

"You look, miss. You buy."

Curious, Pia moved closer. The object he had for sale was wrapped in a piece of rusty black velvet. That seemed pretty strange when all the other vendors were waving their wares in the air, shouting for the tourists' attention.

"What do you have there?" she asked. Curious, tempted.

"Come close. I show you, miss."

Pia had no desire to get any closer. The stench of the

THE SANDS OF DESTINY

man took her breath away. But some invisible force seemed to draw her to the object he held in his hand.

"What's that you're selling?" she asked again.

The man hunched closer still. Pia noticed that his eyes had a strange, glazed look. She wondered if he was blind. But apparently not. He glanced furtively about, checking to make sure no one else was watching before he eased the tattered velvet from his prize.

Pia caught her breath when the cloth slipped away. A perfect pyramid of some opalescent crystal rested in his grimy palm. She reached out to touch it, but he quickly drew it away.

"You like? You buy!" he said emphatically. "You got thirty American dollar?"

Pia stared, transfixed, at the gleaming chunk of stone. It seemed to glow with an inner light, giving off a faint, greenish aura. The colors shifted, turning pink, then gold before her eyes.

"I'll give you twenty dollars," Pia—born to haggle—told the vendor.

He shook his turbanned head furiously, then covered the crystal pyramid once more. Quickly, he turned away from her.

"No!" he growled over his shoulder. "This very ancient, very sacred. Broke from tomb of Alexander by Queen Cleopatra herself. Talisman . . . has mysterious powers. You want, you pay *thirty dollar!*"

The tour guide's words came back to Pia suddenly—Alexander the Great, buried in an alabaster sarcophagus. In that instant, she knew she must have the thing. It was a genuine piece of Cleopatra's Alexandria. Pia dug into her purse, fishing for money.

"Oh!" she cried, coming up empty. "I don't have

442   *Becky Lee Weyrich*

thirty dollars!" Her father had all their American money. She had only a few Egyptian coins.

The dusky merchant shook his head at her and gave her an evil grimace. Convinced she was trying to trick him into selling his prize for less, he moved off, muttering to himself in some ancient tongue.

"Wait!" Pia called frantically. "I'll get the money from my father."

Her heart raced as she searched the crowd, trying to spot her dad. By the time Stephen Byrd came up behind her and touched her arm, Pia was almost in tears. Having the crystal pyramid suddenly seemed a matter of life and death.

"Oh, Daddy, thank goodness!" she cried. "I found exactly what I want. I have to have it! But I didn't have the money and now the man's disappeared and we *must* find him before he sells it to someone else. Hurry! Follow me!"

Pulling her father by the arm, Pia barged through the crowd, searching wildly for the dirty, little vendor. She almost laughed aloud when she spied her Greek sailor. Only a short time ago, she had been frantic to locate him. Now he seemed totally unimportant compared to the man with the crystal pyramid.

Suddenly, she gasped and stopped dead in her tracks. There, beside her golden Greek, stood the hunchbacked peddler. She watched, horrified, as the sailor counted out his money and took the glittering chunk of alabaster into his hand.

"Oh, no!" she wailed. "We're too late! He's sold it already."

The sight of tears streaming down his daughter's cheeks totally baffled Stephen Byrd. "Pia, what on

THE SANDS OF DESTINY 443

earth's gotten into you? Surely, he has another hunk of rock in his bag for sale. If not, you'll find something else you like."

She shook her head furiously. "I don't want anything else. I want that piece of alabaster!"

When she looked up again, she found herself staring right into the amber eyes of the Greek sailor. A shock went through her. He was even more handsome up close than he had seemed from afar. He didn't smile. He only gazed at her, his eyes smoldering like molten gold. His look was caressing, almost intimate. Pia opened her mouth to speak to him, but found herself unable to utter a sound.

As she stood frozen to the spot, the Greek raised his palm toward her. The sun struck the pyramid and the alabaster gave off a blinding, mesmerizing rainbow of color. Pia blinked her eyes shut against the brilliant glare.

In that instantaneous flash, the dusty market and its noisy tourists vanished. When she opened her eyes again, she had the strangest experience. It seemed she was inside cool marble walls. In the distance, she heard someone strumming a stringed instrument. Its soft music mingled with the faint murmur of a fountain.

She blinked again and the lovely scene faded. She was standing in the hot, dirty market. The Greek was still there, his tiger eyes fixed on her face.

"Will you sell that to me?" she pleaded.

The sailor said nothing. Perhaps he spoke no English. But as Pia waited for some reply, he reached down to the path and found a heavy stone. Pia cried out when she saw what he meant to do, but she was too late to stop him. With one sharp whack, he broke

444   *Becky Lee Weyrich*

the pyramid into two perfect halves. Still without a word, he handed one piece to her.

The alabaster felt warm in Pia's palm. She stared down at it, seeing its colorful aura intensify through the remnants of her tears. The hot wind swirling through the marketplace turned cool and refreshing. Again, she heard the music and the tinkling of the fountain. When she looked around, the agora had vanished. She found herself once again within the cool, quiet setting she had glimpsed moments before.

"Cleopatra? Cleopatra!" Someone was calling her name.

"Here, my darling." It seemed Pia uttered the words, but how could that be?

She looked down at herself. She was lying on a golden couch, cushioned in purple silk. Her diaphanous gown hid little of her shapely form. A wide gold collar set with gleaming gemstones and a matching girdle provided only token modesty to her exotic costume.

The sound of the man's voice, although she had yet to see him, sent a warm thrill through her blood. She let her fingers trail in the scented pool beside her couch as she gazed out over the silver-blue water beyond her marble terrace, savoring the moments of anticipation as her lover approached.

The soft slap of his sandals on the smooth, pebble mosaic of the palace floor made her smile. Her gaze drifted to his and held for long moments. She shifted slightly toward him and sighed, parting her full, carmine-tinted lips. She tried to act casual, but her heart was racing. It always did when he came to her. With

THE SANDS OF DESTINY 445

other men, she retained total control. But not with *this* man. Not *ever* with him!

He strode toward her, the muscles in his powerful thighs bulging. He devoured her with an arrogant, intimate gaze. Hungry for passion, he made love to her with his eyes before allowing her the pleasure of his long-awaited touch.

She drank in his presence as he drew nearer across the quiet court. He was tall, muscular, and so handsome that only to look at him made her ache and tremble with her need. His hair was a tumbled riot of sun-gold curls. His eyes, gone dark now with desire, were the warm, clear color of the finest amber. The wide, hammered-gold collar about his strong neck hid nothing of his powerful chest from her longing gaze. A golden girdle, from which fell his short, pleated kilt of snowy linen, hugged his trim waist. He had the face, the form, and, she knew, the passion of a god.

**PUT SOME PASSION INTO YOUR
LIFE . . . WITH THIS STEAMY SELECTION OF
ZEBRA *LOVEGRAMS!***

SEA FIRES (3899, $4.50/$5.50)
by Christine Dorsey
Spirited, impetuous Miranda Chadwick arrives in the untamed New World prepared for any peril. But when the notorious pirate Gentleman Jack Blackstone kidnaps her in order to fulfill his secret plans, she can't help but surrender — to the shameless desires and raging hunger that his bronzed, lean body and demanding caresses ignite within her!

TEXAS MAGIC (3898, $4.50/$5.50)
by Wanda Owen
After being ambushed by bandits and saved by a ranchhand, headstrong Texas belle Bianca Moreno hires her gorgeous rescuer as a protective escort. But Rick Larkin does more than guard her body — he kisses away her maidenly inhibitions, and teaches her the secrets of wild, reckless love!

SEDUCTIVE CARESS (3767, $4.50/$5.50)
by Carla Simpson
Determined to find her missing sister, brave beauty Jessamyn Forsythe disguises herself as a simple working girl and follows her only clues to Whitechapel's darkest alleys . . . and the disturbingly handsome Inspector Devlin Burke. Burke, on the trail of a killer, becomes intrigued with the ebon-haired lass and discovers the secrets of her silken lips and the hidden promise of her sweet flesh.

SILVER SURRENDER (3769, $4.50/$5.50)
by Vivian Vaughan
When Mexican beauty Aurelia Mazón saves a handsome stranger from death, she finds herself on the run from the Federales with the most dangerous man she's ever met. And when Texas Ranger Carson Jarrett steals her heart with his intimate kisses and seductive caresses, she yields to an all-consuming passion from which she hopes to never escape!

ENDLESS SEDUCTION (3793, $4.50/$5.50)
by Rosalyn Alsobrook
Caught in the middle of a dangerous shoot-out, lovely Leona Stegall falls unconscious and awakens to the gentle touch of a handsome doctor. When her rescuer's caresses turn passionate, Leona surrenders to his fiery embrace and savors a night of soaring ecstasy!

Available wherever paperbacks are sold, or order direct from the Publisher. Send cover price plus 50¢ per copy for mailing and handling to Penguin USA, P.O. Box 999, c/o Dept. 17109, Bergenfield, NJ 07621. Residents of New York and Tennessee must include sales tax. DO NOT SEND CASH.

Hot Hits by Martha Hix

MAIL-ORDER MAN (4622, $4.50/$5.50)
Skylla St. Clair needed a husband. Braxton Hale wanted to con her out of her ranch. A steamy story of deception and desire...as two lovers discover that an arranged marriage can sizzle with more heat than a Texas night!

WILD SIERRA ROGUE (4256, $4.50/$5.50)
Sparks flew when Rafe Delgado teamed with starchy and absolutely desperate Margaret McLoughlin on a rescue mission to save her mother. It irked Margaret, depending on the very rogue who'd wronged the family. And he figured to take the starch out of her drawers, then leave her stranded. They didn't count on falling in love . . .

LONE STAR LOVING (4029, $4.50/$5.50)
The law at her heels, smuggler Charity McLoughlin had enough trouble without getting abducted by a black-haired savage called Hawk. He would deliver her to a fate worse than death, yet for one night, she'd surrender to those dark eyes and his every desire . . .

CARESS OF FIRE (3718, $4.50/$5.50)
Lisette Keller wanted out of Texas. Why not hire on as trail cook with the McLoughlin outfit? To virile rancher Gil McLoughlin, a cattle drive was no place for a lady. Soon, he not only hired her, he also vowed to find out if her lips were as sweet as her cooking . . .

Available wherever paperbacks are sold, or order direct from the Publisher. Send cover price plus 50¢ per copy for mailing and handling to Penguin USA, P.O. Box 999, c/o Dept. 17109, Bergenfield, NJ 07621. Residents of New York and Tennessee must include sales tax. DO NOT SEND CASH.

TODAY'S HOTTEST READS
ARE TOMORROW'S SUPERSTARS

VICTORY'S WOMAN (4484, $4.50)
by Gretchen Genet
Andrew—the carefree soldier who sought glory on the battlefield, and returned a shattered man . . . Niall—the legandary frontiersman and a former Shawnee captive, tormented by his past . . . Roger—the troubled youth, who would rise up to claim a shocking legacy . . . and Clarice—the passionate beauty bound by one man, and hopelessly in love with another. Set against the backdrop of the American revolution, three men fight for their heritage—and one woman is destined to change all their lives forever!

FORBIDDEN (4488, $4.99)
by Jo Beverley
While fleeing from her brothers, who are attempting to sell her into a loveless marriage, Serena Riverton accepts a carriage ride from a stranger—who is the handsomest man she has ever seen. Lord Middlethorpe, himself, is actually contemplating marriage to a dull daughter of the aristocracy, when he encounters the breathtaking Serena. She arouses him as no woman ever has. And after a night of thrilling intimacy—a forbidden liaison—Serena must choose between a lady's place and a woman's passion!

WINDS OF DESTINY (4489, $4.99)
by Victoria Thompson
Becky Tate is a half-breed outcast—branded by her Comanche heritage. Then she meets a rugged stranger who awakens her heart to the magic and mystery of passion. Hiding a desperate past, Texas Ranger Clint Masterson has ridden into cattle country to bring peace to a divided land. But a greater battle rages inside him when he dares to desire the beautiful Becky!

WILDEST HEART (4456, $4.99)
by Virginia Brown
Maggie Malone had come to cattle country to forge her future as a healer. Now she was faced by Devon Conrad, an outlaw wounded body and soul by his shadowy past . . . whose eyes blazed with fury even as his burning caress sent her spiraling with desire. They came together in a Texas town about to explode in sin and scandal. Danger was their destiny—and there was nothing they wouldn't dare for love!

Available wherever paperbacks are sold, or order direct from the Publisher. Send cover price plus 50¢ per copy for mailing and handling to Penguin USA, P.O. Box 999, c/o Dept. 17109, Bergenfield, NJ 07621. Residents of New York and Tennessee must include sales tax. DO NOT SEND CASH.